AUSTRALIAN
SHORT STORIES

AUSTRALIAN SHORT STORIES

Edited by Carmel Bird

Houghton Mifflin Company
Boston 1991

Compilation and Introduction copyright © 1991 by Carmel Bird
All rights reserved.

For information about permission to reproduce selections from this
book, write to the individual copyright owners as identified herein.

Library of Congress Cataloging-in-Publication Data

Australian short stories / edited by Carmel Bird.
    p. cm.
  ISBN 0-395-58839-1—ISBN 0-395-58667-4 (pbk.)
  1. Short stories, Australian.   I. Bird, Carmel, 1940-
PR9617.32.A942   1991
832—dc20   91-294
                                  CIP

Printed in Australia

10 9 8 7 6 5 4 3 2 1

Contents

Contents

Contents

INTRODUCTION

I was a schoolgirl looking out the window of an upstairs classroom; it was 1955. I could see, as I looked down, the complicated foliage of a palm tree that grew on the front lawn of the school. I think it was raining. I lived in Tasmania; it was often raining. I used to look at the tree when the teacher was reading to the class. The teacher was reading aloud the first short story I had ever heard. The story was 'Mrs Packletide's Tiger' by Saki, and it was in a small book with a hard red cover. Every student had a copy of the book and we were meant to follow the text as the teacher read. I remember or imagine there was an image of a fountain embossed on the lower right-hand corner of the front cover of the book. I imagine running my finger over the image of the fountain. 'Mrs Packletide's Tiger' was my first short story; and it was in the first collection of short stories I had seen. I had read comics and novels, but on the day I was introduced to Saki's story I became conscious of a special form — the short story. Some other stories in the book were 'The Occurrence at Owl Creek Bridge' by Ambrose Bierce; 'The Fly' by Katherine Mansfield; 'The Journey of the Magi' by O. Henry; and a story about a kidnapped omnibus known as 'The General' by an author whose name I don't remember. I remember the whole book as being a thing to treasure, and as being important, even though it was only a school text book.

After I had read 'Mrs Packletide's Tiger', I looked for more stories by Saki, whose writing dazzled and fascinated me. I read about Saki's life. I tried to write like Ambrose Bierce. I read many of the stories of Katherine Mansfield, and I thought

O. Henry was old-fashioned. I know I didn't spare a thought for *why* these stories should have been brought together, but I remember the pleasure of the shock I got by going from the work of one writer to the work of another by turning the page. The stories in the red book continue to be linked in my mind. Readers are not necessarily as impressionable as I was, but even so I believe that stories can take on a new significance when they are juxtaposed with other stories.

I wonder whether my red book of stories had an Introduction. I know I did not imagine at all the presence of an editor who decided which stories to include, which to leave out. The book probably had twelve stories in it. Of all the stories written in the world before 1950 or thereabouts, somebody decided to put this tiny handful in a book. There would have been an editor. How did the editor decide on the stories? I believe none of the stories was written by an Australian writer; I think Katherine Mansfield was the only woman with a story in the collection. And I wonder who *does* read the introductions to collections of short stories and why. I wonder why the stories can not simply stand alone in their collected order without the preliminary comment and ornamentation of an editor.

As I write this introduction to a new collection of stories by Australian writers, I am working at a desk beside a window in the library of a college. I can look down into the garden. This garden has no palm tree, but beneath the window is a honeysuckle in bloom. The blossoms resemble white spiders and they are tangled among other bushes and vines which are nameless, dark and dense. The vines and flowers reach up into the branches of a Norfolk Island pine tree. This tree stretches out against the sky and stands taller than the library. It is raining. If I look closely through the raindrops on the window I can see that what I took for honeysuckle is really old man's beard.

All the stories in this collection were written by Australians, and I have chosen stories that will, when seen together, give readers a knowledge of the history of the short story in Australia. The earliest writer here was probably born in 1833, and the most recent writer was born in 1954. Halfway between these two dates, Henry Lawson, one of the finest writers of short fiction in the history of Australian writing, wrote a story called 'The Drover's Wife'.

From the past tense 'drove' of the verb 'to drive', the noun 'drove' came into existence. A drove is a herd or flock of animals being driven to market on foot over great distances. The man who drives the drove is 'the drover'. The word 'drover' is commonplace in Australia, although sheep and cattle are seldom driven on foot in the way that they were driven in earlier times. Henry Lawson's story 'The Drover's Wife' evokes the terrible loneliness and the remarkable courage of the woman who remains at home in the bush with the children while her husband, the drover, is absent. 'The Drover's Wife' is a powerful and haunting story, and has become one of the great icons of Australian writing. It inspired the Australian artist Russell Drysdale to paint a picture, and it also inspired two Australian writers, Murray Bail and Frank Moorhouse, both writing in the late twentieth century, to write stories using the title 'The Drover's Wife'. I took the three 'Drover's Wife' stories as the genesis for this collection, and requested that the painting of 'The Drover's Wife' by Russell Drysdale should go on the cover of the book. I am interested not only in the words that go into books, but in the physical nature of books and in the dynamics of the arrangement of their elements. I based my choice of stories for the collection on an idea and on a trio of stories related to each other by their common title, and by a kind of game which the recent authors are playing with the original story of 'The Drover's Wife' by Henry Lawson.

I reflected on the relationship between the three 'Drover's Wife' stories, between the characters, between the three methods of telling a story. The idea of 'relationship' gave the collection its direction. I read stories looking for many different kinds of relationships — between the characters in the story; between the people and the land; between the external and the internal world; fantasy and reality; action and reflection; between one story and another. I was on a trail (it was a kind of game too) where I could link stories by certain relationships I found between them. Some links were large and obvious; some were fine and subtle.

The relationship between parents and children is painfully enacted in Thea Astley's story 'Write Me, Son, Write Me'. I went from the parents in that story to the parents in 'The Empty Lunch-tin' by David Malouf. In 'The Empty Lunch-tin' the parents' sense of loss takes the story into a dimension that is surreal. And, following that eerie thread, I went to 'The Lost Wedding' by David Brooks.

The things I remember best about the stories I read are the images, the feelings and the structures, and, often some phrases or a sentence — the last words in 'Mother' by Judah Waten, for instance: 'her shoes equally down at heel on each side'. In going from one story to another in the process of choosing stories, I often followed images. I went from the image of the church in 'The Lost Wedding' to an imagine in 'On the Train' by Olga Masters. This last was the image of 'the roof of the station jutting above the street'. The story explores a relationship between a mother and her children. It is very different from the story by Thea Astley, but it is still about children and parents. If I followed the idea of relationship, would I get too many stories about mothers and babies? I thought of essays I have read, essays in which the writers suggest that anthologies of stories have too little of one thing, not enough of another. It is as if there exists a Recipe for the Perfect Anthology. The critics hold this secret recipe; the editors of anthologies have to guess at the ingredients. I have read of anthologies that are 'too uneven'. Is smooth good? I remember a critic who complained that a collection had too many *aunts* in it. Was I getting too many aunts? Was I getting enough? Australian writers have often written about aunts — Patrick White's novel *The Aunt's Story* is a glorious example. To omit aunts as subject matter in this collection would be to misrepresent Australian writing. But is it possible, with twenty-six stories, to *represent* Australian writing?

I read 'The Last Days of a Famous Mime' by Peter Carey and the image of the woman with the handbag in 'On the Train' came back to me: 'The Mime arrived on Alitalia with very little luggage: a brown paper parcel and what looked like a woman's handbag'. This is a story of the relationship between the Mime and his audience. The image of the Mime's head 'visible above water for a second or two. And then he is gone', recalled the beginning of 'Proem' by Henry Handel Richardson: 'In a shaft in the Gravel Pits, a man had been buried alive'. My focus shifted from the writers of the present to a writer from the past. The themes of misery and death began to dominate. Looking for something lighter I read the stories of Peter Goldsworthy. Although the recent collection by this writer is called *Bleak Rooms* the writer is often very funny. The story I have chosen because it is a story about relationships is 'Frock, Wireless, Gorgeous, Slacks'. It doesn't lighten the gloom very much, but I find its tone and structure irresistible.

I read articles about Australian writing and two from the forties I found particularly instructive. In 1943 A.R. Chisholm wrote: 'In literature: to be a good Australian you must assume that letters began in 1788, that the scene of all novels has to be laid in Australia, that only gums and wattles grow in heaven, that people like reading about sun-drenched plains'. In spite of the tone and intention of A.R. Chisholm's words, I know that any collection of Australian short stories that aims to select work from the history of the genre must contain a certain amount of material about gum trees and wattle trees and the sun. I looked, then, for stories where the sun is important. 'The Late Sunlight' by Jessica Anderson is a favourite story of mine, and it is certainly a story about relationship. The sun is crucial to Ethel Anderson's story 'Donalblain McCree and the Sin of Anger'. I don't think Jessica and Ethel are related: it would have been elegant for the purposes of the book if they had been.

Gum trees and wattle trees, but not heaven, came to the collection with a story by Mary Fortune, 'The Dead Man in the Scrub'. Published in *The Australian Journal* of 1867, this is the oldest story in the collection; with it came more death and misery. In John Morrison's story there is a dead man under a train. I was particularly pleased to include a story by Mary Fortune because, although she wrote long ago, readers are not familiar with her work. Until 1989 when Lucy Sussex edited a collection of work by Mary Fortune, this writer's stories were unknown to readers of today.

Another essay I found instructive was Vance Palmer's introduction (!) to the 1945 edition of *Coast to Coast*: 'Nowadays a short story may be a dream, a dialogue, a study of character, a poetic reverie; anything that has a certain unity and movement of life'. The words have a modern ring to them, and they give comfort to a reader and writer of short stories in Australia in the nineties. Today we would add more and more licence, saying with Frank Moorhouse in *his* introduction to *The State of the Art* in 1983: 'The great need in Australian story writing is still that it should "go too far" and resist blandness'. I hope some of these stories go too far.

I am addicted to reading short stories, and so the task of finding twenty-six stories that would be linked to each other in some ways and that would cover a range of styles and themes was a very pleasurable task. I often hear the complaint that there are too many short stories written in Australia, and that there are too many short story collections. Because I am an addict I don't really follow the argument. I love short stories. And just as the prescription for the ideal collection remains mysterious, so the correct number of stories, writers and collections in the country remains hidden knowledge.

The balance between the number of stories by men and women in a collection is sometimes called into question. As I compiled this book I paid no conscious attention to the gender of the writers until I had decided on the selection. There are fourteen women and twelve men, as it happens. In the past twenty years the number of women publishing fiction in Australia has risen. Fourteen women out of twenty-six authors, then, seems about right for now.

Beginning with the idea of relationship I allowed the stories, often the images in the stories, to take me from one place, one writer, to the next. In the end I did not know whether there were enough aunts or too many wattle trees, or whether I had omitted a writer or a story that no collection of Australian short stories could be without. But I knew I had brought together stories that would, seen together, take the reader through some of the rich realms of the short story in Australia. And in order to draw attention to the relationship between the past and the present, I placed the story by George Papaellinas, the most recent story, first, and moved the reader back in time to the oldest story which is 'The Dead Man in the Scrub' by Mary Fortune.

Carmel Bird

AUSTRALIAN SHORT STORIES

CHRISTOS MAVROMATIS IS A WELDER

George Papaellinas

Christos Mavromatis is a welder.

I'll tell you because he mightn't.

Try him.

Whaddayado, mate? Simple question. Ask him. You want to know, don't you?

And if *you* can get it out of him then you're doing better than the old bloke did. His overalls don't tell you much, dirt's dirt and dirty overalls could mean any one of a million jobs, couldn't they? So ... whaddayado, mate? Sit down next to him. Take it easy, you only want half the seat. That's how the old bloke on the bus home got started the other day.

'Are you doin' well for yourself?' Voice like a South's supporter.

There's Chris sitting on the bus home, hard up against the window, pretending Cleveland Street's something new to him. A face on him that'd frighten kids at a bus stop. Chris as sour as the hops on the old bloke's breath. Nothing is what the old bloke got from Christos.

But you'd be polite, wouldn't you? Suit creased. Smile like a dentist.

Good luck.

My guess is Chris would keep to his window, scaring kiddies. You'd be left rattling your *Herald* and baking in the couple of whiskies that got you asking in the first place. Forget Christos. No speaka da English. Turn to page five, past what Fraser isn't doing and what Hawke's going to, to the bit on who's having to leave what country. Try and guess where Chris is from.

Shift over. You'd make room for him, wouldn't you?

But this old bloke just undid the top button of his King

1

Gees. He arranged himself. He squeezed Christos against the window.

'Whadda *you* do, mate?'

Dopey wog, he thinks.

'What ... you ... do? Mate?' Voice like a magistrate. Old bloke with a circle of hair sitting up on his head as stiff as a grey hedge, wet blue eyes.

No wife, thinks Chris, who else would be drunk before he's even home, before he's even eaten?

Or knowing Chris ... how can you tell with an Australian?

Christos does not have much choice.

'Job mate ... like you, mate.'

The bus is filling by now, almost full, people standing and they're all trying to keep their eyes from wandering away from the windows, but if this old bloke doesn't keep his voice down, if he has to ask again and he *has* been drinking, then all those eyes ...

Chris's mouth starts to work so much it should be on overtime rates. Somewhere between a stranger's smile and something a little bit too eager. Chris's English isn't too bad and he doesn't want to seem unfriendly.

'Work.'

Old fool, he thinks, these old ones especially. They are quick with their abuse and this one's been drinking ...

Better whaddayado then whereayafrom.

'Job ...' and Chris nods his head again, tries another smile, this one as hard as the old bloke's stare.

Again.

'Job, mate ... like you.'

Again?

The old bloke's eyes swing away only they're slow eyes, impatient with a bad joke.

'Yeah, know that ... but whaddaya*do*, mate?' and the old bloke takes a breath that swells his belly. For a good laugh? I mean it's not a bad joke ... well, he's had a few and you like a laugh after a few, don't you? I mean, it's a pretty simple question and Chris ...

'Sorry, mate, sorry ... I ... sorry.'

Chris is going to trust to silence. Time for a bit of shush. Time to shut up, he shrugs his shoulders, points to his mouth. He's a dumbie. No speaka da English.

Chris reckons it's easier.

Look. The old bloke's going to cop this, no speaka da English, he assumed as much anyway, before he started with his questions.

That's right. No speaka da English.

The old bloke's going to maintain a silence too but a jolly sort of silence his, a private one, like a giggle, unless, of course, he happens to catch the eye of, say, another old bloke standing in the aisle when he might just choose to translate it into a joke, matey sort of joke, you know the type, the sort that'll cause a little bit of rocking in the seat or on the feet, the sort that you get to hear again, louder and funnier the longer Chris nods and smiles and shrugs and says nothing. Old blokes swaying and bumping into people, making a fuss over Chris. Can you see it? Chris grinning, no speaka da English, and the old blokes laughing like old mates . . .

Chris interrupts.

He can see it.

'Builder, mate . . .' and Chris who can't *really* see a joke sits up, tense, the way a tightrope walker looks, smiling like he's going to cry and never still. Well, Chris has been swaying ever since the old bloke sat down as easy as a loose punch. Chris sits up now, balancing, and sure on his feet now that he's started. Have you ever seen a pub fight starting?

Who does the old bloke think he is?

'I'm builder, mate . . . workin' out Werrington . . . houses . . . lotsa houses, lotsa work, mate . . .' And he sits back too.

'Yeah?' and the old bloke's blinking, he smooths his soft face with a wipe of a hand, he's been woken up, he was just getting settled, 'yeah?'

Chris's talking is an elbow in his ribs.

'Yeah . . . good, mate,' and he throws another look over Chris. Beer is waking him up as quickly as it almost put him to sleep.

Who's this wog?

'Whaddayado? . . . Brickie's labourer?'

He hasn't been listening.

Look at him, thinks our Chris.

Old fool. Five o'clock and already drunk. Who is he? What does *he* do? Is he a property owner, is he, out collecting his rents in clothes that have never seen soap? No wife even? Whose boss does he think he is? Is he a judge? Is he?

Chris might as well be as drunk as the old bloke now. He's forgotten where he is, he's forgotten he's on the bus. He doesn't even know what country he's in.

'Boss mate . . . I'm boss!' It's a game of darts, one after the other and Chris wants to take the chook and the half dozen bottles too.

'Twenty men, mate ... boss for twenty men!'

Have you ever seen a drunk who's been punched in the head? The way they stand there saying nothing and shaking their faces? That's what Chris wants. He wants a silent old bloke. He combs his wavy hair with fingers.

'Boss, eh?' and the old bloke believes him, you can see that. All he wanted was Christos's silence and now Chris has got the old bloke looking like he believes him.

Chris can see this.

The old bloke rubs his nose. He swings his arm in a long arc. Stares at his watch. Lost for words, eh?

'Long way from Werrington,' he pauses, 'still early,' and he smiles at Chris, he congratulates him.

'Make your own hours, do ya?'

'Yes, yes ...' and Chris sees himself in his own story, 'yes, mate ... boss.'

'Where's ya Rolls, then?'

And Chris looks like he's going to stand up and shake a hand now (twenty men!).

And the old bloke's chuckling. 'Rolls in the garage?' and Chris chuckles, doing well in his story, he's smiling and grinning, the old bloke's grinning and smiling. Old mates!

Chris is just about on his feet, taking bows. But it's the others on the bus. Chris checks them. That one, a secretary, she's staring at her feet, and that other one whose eyes keep dropping on Christos, he looks away, he's back to counting cars in lines outside the window. An accountant. In case they're listening, Chris keeps his voice low. This story is for this old bloke who thinks he's better than Christos, but isn't.

Who does he think he is?

'Done well in this country, 'ave ya mate?' and the old bloke's not keeping his voice down. A voice like he's calling the winner at a pub raffle, he's checking for an audience in the aisle too.

'Yes, mate,' nods Christos who fidgets.

'Yeah, I bet you done well ... yeah ...' and the old bloke shifts large-bellied in his seat, too large a belly to squeeze by easily. The old bloke can pick Chris.

He scans a tweed skirt, looks up for a face to nod with and questions Chris who's doing well out Werrington way.

'Done well enough for yaself?' and Chris watches the old bloke watching the accountant, watches him poke him in the leg, friendly.

'They do well outta this country, don't they ... these blokes do *bloody* well,' and the secretary is staring at Christos, he catches her doing it and the old bloke's cackling and she looks away, back out the window, everyone does, but they *are* listening, of course they are, and as soon as Christos looks away, she'll be looking at him again, or the accountant will or they'll be looking at each other and they'll be smiling, like you do at strangers when somebody's kid is being smacked.

'Well you'll be goin' back 'ome, won't ya? ... Won't ya?' and Christos sits silenced in the old bloke's trap, caught by the old bloke's leg, swinging and playing as the old bloke faces Christos.

And the old bloke crosses his arms, showing interest.

'Whereareyafrom?'

'My stop ... please ... my stop ...' and Chris is pushing past the old bloke's legs, slow as the arms of a turnstile, 'my stop, here, please ...' and he almost drops his bag, it's slippery, vinyl, one of those Qantas ones, he catches it, pushes the accountant out of the way, a receptionist almost goes over, he pulls himself along the handrail.

''Scuse me ... 'scuse me ...'

'Well, go back there, you smart bastard!'

''Scuse me ... 'scuse me!'

Ever seen a crab? Always in a panic. Avoiding things sideways.

So, there you go. He's off the bus. He has to walk the rest of the way home. And the old bloke isn't even looking out the window. You are.

But Christos wouldn't know that. He isn't looking up at it.

Christos just off the bus.

Christos holding his bag.

Christos. Back the other way, mate.

Go home, Christos.

THE LOST WEDDING

David Brooks

Miss Jennifer Cooley lives amidst tall trees on the edge of town with a dog that hoards things under the house and a cat that stays mainly on the roof, where it stalks sparrows. In her rather sequestered existence in between, Miss Cooley is hardly ever seen but for the one morning a fortnight when she does her shopping, and for one week each year when she does a kind of spring cleaning, during which time she sometimes hangs upon the line out back a faded wedding dress in the style of twenty years ago.

They say that every town and village has its crazy person. I wouldn't know, and I'm sure Miss Cooley isn't, but certainly she is different. I think people call her crazy because they need someone like that, and since she keeps to her house so much, and when she does come out has such a lost look about her, she fits most readily into the role, whatever better candidates there are. It's mainly the young, anyway, who call her mad; older people have a sort of respect for her.

You couldn't say her behaviour is all that strange. You don't see enough of it. And her circumstances aren't really all that different from others in the town. It's her story that singles her out — so strange and so well known that it's become something of a local myth.

The church she claimed it was all going to happen in is a little convict-built chapel half-way between Albatross and Vincentia. On the day it's supposed to have taken place she had got almost there — close enough to see, from the top of the hill, people milling around the door, just beginning to file in, someone who looked like her uncle standing in the lychgate, and the sounds of the old, windy organ cranking up to play 'O Perfect Love' — when she had to turn back, having forgotten something which is now forgotten, or at least uncertain, but which must have been somehow vital at the time, a piece of old jewellery, or the bridal bouquet, or something else that you get superstitious about on occasions like that. And when she got back there was nobody there. She went right to the door, thinking that they would be waiting inside, but the place was locked, and there was nothing, only the dusty road, and the hot sun beating down, the cicadas, the long grass stirring faintly over the graves.

When at last she dared to mention it — she was too embarrassed, of course, at first — nobody knew anything about it. They were rather surprised to hear that she'd been thinking of getting married at all. Indeed, some — even some she thought she'd seen at the church — were perturbed that they'd not got an invitation. It was as if the whole thing had been an illusion, a mirage, a figment of her own imagination. And yet she distinctly remembered it all — the groom (though he hotly denied it), the proposal (beside the hibiscus outside the Albatross Town Hall, on a hot night near Christmas), the preparations, the congregation around the church door.

It might, people said, have been that she dreamt it. The world of dreams and the waking world are often so similar that, moving from one to the other, we can be quite unaware that we've crossed a border, and everyone has a story about one time or another when they had thought they had done something they'd only dreamed they'd done, or that they knew someone they'd only dreamed they knew. But it's hard to dream something that takes a month or so, proposal to almost-happening, let alone to remember it all in such detail, and for a long while Jennifer Cooley thought instead that she'd been the victim of a conspiracy, a cruel practical joke. At last, however, she conceded that too many were involved for that, and everyone remained so adamant that nothing of the kind had ever happened that she decided, eventually, that she must simply have lost it, in the same, exasperating, incomprehensible way that one can lose other, more tangible things — a gold watch, say, or a pair of spectacles, or the clipping from *The South Coast Record*, that shows one with the biggest silver bream ever caught in Mooney Creek.

A few years ago, my father mentioned one night that, when he was much younger and she more beautiful, he used to dream about Jennifer Cooley. And on the wharf once, shortly before he died, I got Old Man Cooley to propose the astonishing hypothesis that something very like what had happened to his daughter must have happened to his father's sister. Generally, however, when I mention the lost wedding I get the feeling from the older people that it's not a thing to talk about. Nobody, anyway, seems to have much to add, though sometimes they look as if they might. It might be that this business has been around so long that some are not as positive as they used to be, and begin to suspect that somehow, somewhere, they too might have lost it. After all, a wedding must have a congregation, even a lost wedding. It seems to me that there must be a whole lot of lost things around, just under the surface, if only you knew what they were, or where to look for them.

When she talks about her wedding, as she sometimes still does, Jennifer Cooley keeps changing things — one time, say, it'll be a brooch she goes back for, another time a ribbon — as if fitting the wedding into the real history of things were a bit like a jigsaw puzzle, or like one of those shapes that in the children's game you have to get into the right-shaped holes. Maybe she just doesn't have the right shape yet. Maybe there's just one little, niggly thing that stops it all from slipping neatly into place: perhaps it was grevillea, not hibiscus, outside the Albatross Town Hall; perhaps it had not been 'O Perfect Love', but 'Love Divine, All Loves Excelling'; perhaps, if she had spoken up earlier, if she hadn't been so nervous, someone might have remembered, and this silence, this blankness, this awful process of forgetting might not have set in.

FROCK, WIRELESS, GORGEOUS, SLACKS

Peter Goldsworthy

1

I walked out of the front gate and crossed the road. As usual she was waiting on the verandah. A thick schoolbook lay open on her lap: she was reading Chaucer. We were sixteen. School exams were just days away.

'Have you heard?' she said. 'Isn't it terrible!'

'What?'

'You haven't heard?'

A farmer's daughter, and a teacher's son — but we were neighbours. Her parents' land began at the edge of town, abruptly. The farmhouse even had a town address: 32 West St, a row of sheds and stone buildings behind which there was nothing but wheat, like a movie set.

'Heard what?' I said.

'President Kennedy. He's been shot.'

What Were You Doing That Day, people still ask from time to time — more as an amusement, an idle memory game. But it's true: even now, years later, the details remain vivid. I remember each word, each gesture. Odd things, also, ridiculous trivia: the itch of a shaving-nick, the sudden screech of a peacock in the back-garden.

And especially the frock she was wearing: floral-print, best Swiss cotton.

Frock. How quaint the word sounds. How ... far distant. Like something out of that poetry book in her hands, perhaps. Pothecary, sweete, thine ... frock.

'What do you mean ... shot?'

'He's been shot. It was on the wireless.'
'Is he alright?'
'He's dead.'

We stood on the verandah steps, holding hands, thinking it through: a pair of sixteen-year-olds, in a bush town, in another country, the whole thickness of a planet away.

'Poor Jackie,' she said. 'She's so gorgeous.'

Tears seeped from her eyes. Gorgeous herself — that Saturday night, in her white frock — she knew that tragedy was far worse for Gorgeous People.

2

Until that year she had always been a jeans person — a slacks person, to retrieve another word from somewhere. Slacks, and jodhpurs — she kept a pony in the home paddock.

I often wondered what her parents made of it: the tomboy who had never worn a frock in her life, suddenly wearing a frock, every Saturday night, to the movies. No, to the *pictures*.

'I'm wearing nothing underneath,' she would breathe in my ear.

They trusted us, of course. Or rather: me. My first visit to the farmhouse was still fresh in everyone's mind. The horizontal dive into the hall after tripping over the front doorstep. The broken Willow dinner plates — two — as I helped wash up, desperate to impress.

I think they were somehow reassured by those feats of clumsiness. If I couldn't eat peas with a fork how could I possibly manage to impregnate their daughter?

Also they were grateful: relieved to see the end of the tomboy, the end of that . . . phase.

Her mother saw us off that night. I can see her still, smiling from the verandah as her sixteen year old Quite The Grown Up Young Lady walked down the path with her Young Man.

'Have a nice time, children. And try not to worry about the news.'

3

If I open my snapshot album I can find none of her.

There are many of the baby: our baby. And many of *parts* of her. A single finger emerging, corner-frame top-right, to tickle a chubby chin. Two legs, amputated at the thigh, the child crawling between. A back view of her head, a cascade of dark hair, a peep of baby-face over one shoulder.

'No,' she would insist, turning abruptly from the camera. 'I look terrible. Take another of the baby.'

I sometimes spread these snaps — these severed parts, anatomical odds and ends — across the desk-top, as if it were possible to fit them together, jigsaw-fashion, into some sort of complete portrait.

But there are always pieces missing.

If I try to recall our marriage much of it also seems lost, severed, disconnected, purged of unrequired memories. And I don't mean the unpleasant memories. *Those* I remember. It's the pleasant that apparently no longer meet current requirements.

Perhaps I deserve it: the piecemeal death of amnesia.

I am permitted — well, I am permitted to recall the bad times. I am permitted to remember . . . the night I threw up on the ceiling. Not on the walls, or the floor, or the furniture — but the ceiling. We had been to a university Ball, but of that I remember nothing. I remember nothing also of the impossible feat of ballistics which followed.

But I remember clearly the morning-after.

'I'm beginning to wonder,' she told me as she squeezed out the mop, 'If you belong to the race of men whose wives outgrow them.'

4

Lying here, unable to sleep, trying to form some image of her, to touch her again, I am reduced to tricks, to the handful of Good Times I can still lure into the open. To the odd glimpse of her I can find in other backgrounds — even in the backgrounds of Famous Events.

'Do you think the Russians did it?' I asked, as we walked.

'Maybe,' she said.

I held her closely. This, certainly, is clear. She was wearing her perfume. Her dress — her Swiss cotton frock — crushed against me. My veins fizzed, my head felt . . . weightless, aerated. It was a long walk, and already the crotch of my trousers was tight. I loved every cramped, painful, wonderful step.

There was less urgency in our touchings that night, however. Less lust, and more . . . tenderness. There was something solemn, almost ceremonious about it. This one is dedicated to the memory of . . .

We sat there in the back-row of the Majestic, in a double Lovers' Seat, filled with exquisite movie feelings: joy, sadness, the ephemerality of material things.

'I love you very much,' she whispered. 'I'll never want anyone else.'

5

I *do* still have her letters. Her endless messages, notes, postcards, internal household memoranda, billet-doux...

Even at school, she was a great one for Passing Notes. I kept them carefully: and all the communiques which followed, messages scribbled on scraps of paper that she would leave stuck all over the house, even after we married.

But I open the scrapbook and receive no pleasure. Now I can see only this: the way she always signed 'Luv from ...'

I thought it fun at first: those irreverent fun-spellings. Strange Chaucer-spellings: Luv, nite, thru.

But now it seems merely false. I seem to hear that same inflexion in her voice:

'Of course I still luv you.'

It seems a kind of evasion. As though she were embarrassed by any correctly spelt show of emotion.

6

'Turn on the TV,' she told me. 'While you're up.'

'You want to watch TV on your honeymoon?'

'It's nearly three. They must be almost down.'

'I would have thought you had other things on your mind.'

'I've made love to you hundreds of times before,' she said. 'Including several times already today. But I've never seen a man walk on the moon.'

'It's a waste of money.'

'So you've said. Often. Do something with the aerial, will you. The picture's fuzzy.'

'It's the transmission, not the set.'

'SSh ... Look, that white blur there — is that the lunar module?'

'It's moving,' I said. 'It looks like a man.'

'The first man on the moon!'

'If that's the first man on the moon, who's holding the camera?'

'Okay — the second man on the moon.'

That day she was wearing... nothing. Or nothing apart from a thin film of sweat. We lay amid the wreckage of bedclothes in a rented beach-shack, drinking cold beer and eating cheese-

and-pickled-onion sandwiches. It was hot: the curtains — grimy, pale blue — hanging limp in the open windows. The hot air rubbed like liniment against our skins whenever we moved. Again, the fine details are still there: I could paint a picture of that room and leave nothing out. Each brittle fly-husk in each window-groove. Each red-rimmed oval label on each empty bottle scattered about the bed: *Cooper's Sparkling Ale.*

As human beings waded for the first time through the dust of the moon I pressed my ear against her belly.

'Do you think it's a boy or a girl?'

'I hope it's a boy or a girl,' she said.

I had never been happier.

7

'I'll always remember the good times,' she told me the last time. 'I'll always be grateful to you.'

This I remember perfectly. These strange words. I remember how she was able to pack her things, and the baby's things, and smile, simultaneously. I remember how she was even able to kiss me goodbye: on the mouth, warmly, lovingly, no hard feelings.

I take down our old school poetry anthology from the shelves — her copy, her name on the flyleaf, perhaps she took mine by mistake — and opening at random, find this:

His nosethirles blake were and wyde.
A swerd and bokeler bar he by his side.

Or this:

Hire gretteste ooth was but by Seinte Loy:
And she was cleped madame Eglentyne.

8

'They've sacked Gough,' she told me.

She was wearing . . .

Angels

Joan London

1

I slept, I woke, I slept again. In one of my waking times I thought that yes, I had caught the Russian virus. I thought that I had never been to Russia and was therefore extremely vulnerable to a Russian virus. When I woke up again I saw the snow.

I sat up. The roof garden glowed like a Mediterranean beach. Seagulls arrived and scrabbled outside my window. Although they had been coming for weeks now — Maida and Faye threw them bread — I saw them differently. They seemed like a new species come to a new world. Snowbirds. I fell back on my pillow and slept.

The flat was small but the women's voices echoed at me as if they were calling from the end of a long hall. Back from the cold streets their laughter was vast and relieved. I could hear in their voices the breath of snow.

I hoped they wouldn't come in to see me yet. I thought I couldn't stand the onslaught of such energy. But there was more laughter in the kitchen and the crackle of paper — they'd been shopping. Pop! The plug jumped out of the electric jug. A spoon dropped. Then the living-room window scraped open. Silence.

I looked out my window. Sure enough Faye came squeaking across the snow of the roof garden. She sat down on one of the benches and lit a cigarette. I had often watched her scramble over the sill in the living room: now I was witnessing the private end of the ritual. The light fell on her from the flat above, outlining her cap of grey hair. A mug of coffee steamed beside her. She looked like a larger species of snowbird, crouched forward in her puffy silver parka.

Then suddenly she turned towards my window and smiled straight at me. She lifted one hand and wriggled her gloved fingers. I lay still, shocked. How visible was I? Was there enough reflected light from her to see my face against the pillow, watching her? Or was she smiling on trust, that I was there, awake, and likely to be watching somewhere in the darkness?

Maida was on the phone, talking to our daughters. I knew it was them by the way she projected her voice, as if to help it across twelve thousand miles. And because she sounded apologetic.

'Oh, what time is it there then? I'm sorry, love, I'd have thought you'd both be up by now.' She gave a little defiant laugh.

I could picture Rachel or Jane, yawning by the phone, examining her feet, wondering whether she should wash her hair. The truth was, no time was the right time to ring the girls. Our calls, like those of outgrown lovers, could only be a disappointment, our concern a bore.

'Did you get our photos?' I asked Rachel the last time I phoned.

'Yes,' she said. 'You both look so *white*. And kind of tense. What are you worried about? I hope you're not worrying about Michael. He's *fine*.'

This time none of the children had wanted to come with us. Michael wanted to stay with his teacher, Mrs Everett. He was very decided about this. Mrs Everett's son, Chris, is eighteen, four years older than Michael. He is white-blond, with freckled lips, endlessly good-natured, a Christian. He plays cricket with Michael every day. He's a credit to Mrs Everett, who is also a Christian. They stood together on Mrs Everett's front steps as we got back into our taxi. They waved, Mrs Everett and Chris, and Michael watched them waving, his suitcase and cricket bat at his feet. Maida and I turned to the rear window as we drove off, but he was still watching them.

'How's Michael?' I heard Maida saying now. 'Have you seen him?'

Maida had tiptoed in to see me. I felt, rather than heard her, as an interruption in the teeming molecules of the air around me. The engine in my head wouldn't allow me to open so much as one eye. This jealous Russian virus!

The night she hit me we had eaten in a restaurant near Trafalgar. It was no more than a tizzied-up hamburger joint, but it was raining, and the process of getting ourselves back to the flat, on one of those shiplike red buses that swished past us, seemed too much to tackle straight away.

But it was not a place to linger. There was a queue. The light, in mock lantern clusters, seemed to shrink back from us, made us feel the hour was late, our table needed. Before we were disposed of, Faye picked up her coffee and, waving her little golden box at us, threaded her way to the lower part of the restaurant. This was fenced off with a tasseled rail and a gate marked SMOKING PERMITTED. Maida and I sipped our tea with that seeping of energy we allowed each other. This was when I started to feel it, the tingling all through my limbs as if I was being reminded of something. All my edges started to draw in, and the rhythm of everything beyond me fell slowly out of time.

My eye traveled the room. I saw on the stand by the door our three coats hanging one on top of the other, Faye's parka which kept its human shape, arms sticking out stiffly like a child's drawing, on top of Maida's Burberry, my tweed. Faye had struck up conversation with a fellow smoker, a young man with a shaven head and a shawl around his shoulders. They nodded and laughed, brandishing their forked fingers at one another, and butted out in a shared ashtray.

I studied Maida's gloves lying by her cup, small soft brown leather gloves like paws, bearing the creases of her knuckles, the teardrop of each fingertip. Again and again I measured the distance between the two tables. It seemed to me that behind the tasseled rail, Faye had returned to her own unknowable element: when she joined us at the door she smiled in the kindly, absent way our daughters might when returning home from somebody's arms.

Out on the street again, it had stopped raining and the city's wet glitter made everything tremble with clarity. A middle-aged woman in a raincoat came walking towards us at the bus stop. Swinging her bag, shaking her head, her walk was purposeful as if she was rehearsing something she was going to say. I stepped back for her as she passed.

Thwack! Her handbag struck me square in the stomach.

'That was for *you*!' she shouted, thrusting her face at me, and for a moment I accepted the pure, insistent logic of that glare. Then I clutched my stomach, and it did not seem strange that the street tilted and swung its length of lights above me.

'So sudden,' I heard Maida say to the taxi driver. The city tacked with wild accuracy in and out the window beside her.

'That's how she goes,' the taxi driver called out over his shoulder. 'Laid up thousands — just knocks them down out of the blue.'

I didn't try to tell them. It wasn't a sudden arrival, more a recognition, of a presence that had been there all the time. For weeks now, or was it years, I had felt it coursing through my blood, like a drug, something fretful and chill, and now it had started to speak.

London stayed quiet outside my window. There were reports — Maida gave me details from the bedroom door — of burst pipes, derailed trains, roads buried under drifts that were *the deepest, the furthest south* ... statistics thrived. The snow had taken the country's breath away. And the Russian flu now claimed twelve lives.

Maida and Faye were not daunted. Each morning Maida tiptoed into our bedroom — since my fever she had slept in Faye's room — and dressed in the milky light. I woke to a thief-like rustle, the tiny whirr of a zip. Whispering, they let themselves out the hall door.

Once or twice I got up and walked around the flat. I didn't recognize it. Maps and guides were piled up by the unmade beds in Faye's room. Newspapers were spread around the living-room floor. On the table was a mound of airletters, friendly blue Australian airletters, opened greedily, in the middle, in the wrong way. I stood shivering by the window and watched the birds fight over crusts left for them in the snow.

This was not the first holiday we had spent with Faye. Once when the girls were very small, before Michael, Faye invited us to share a rented beach house with her and Henry Schmitt and their four children. It wasn't a real beach house, it was an abandoned suburban bungalow, with Venetian blinds that no longer opened and an autumn-leaf carpet that smelt sour and dusty like the coat of an old dog. Its front porch faced scrubby sandhills that blocked off the view of the sea. Here Henry sat all day, smoking and reading, sometimes absently pushing the baby's pram back and forth with his big toe. Here, I said, light-hearted, just unpacked, a daughter on my shoulder, we will drink gin and tonic at sunset. This was the first time I had met Henry and Faye.

I came to think of the Schmitt children as a tribe. Their fringes hung in their eyes, they had all inherited Henry's pinched nostrils. They never slept. They rode their battered bikes through the house on long hot afternoons when everyone was supposed to rest. When I held up my hand to stop Luther, the eldest, he stared at me and rode across my foot. Our own little girls became alarming tell-tales.

Even the sea seemed given over to the children. It stretched for miles, warm, knee-deep: no hint of a wave entered that flat bay. I did not know what to do with myself. Each morning I shared the newspaper with Henry across the gritty table. He was a slow reader. While he muttered over the headlines, I started to look through Positions Vacant and Office Space To Let. Later he puddled dishes in grey water in the sink. I dried. There was no question of conversation with Henry unless you felt strong enough for political debate. I paced the house and plotted my future. I stood on the porch and watched Faye and Maida and the children.

All day long they stood by a swing under tuart trees, super-vising turns. Faye wore a shirt of Henry's over sagging bathers and a peaked cap pulled low, like a camp leader. Her short legs were snaked with veins. She and Maida slapped sunburn cream on writhing backs, and talked. They talked as they piggy-backed children in convoy across hot sand and prickles. In the kitchen they talked and laughed and waved their knives around while the lino beneath them crunched with sand and spilt cordial.

'What do you two find to talk about?' I knew I sounded disagreeable. I had lain all afternoon in this airless bedroom with a transistor on my stomach, listening to the cricket. Maida was sitting on the end of the bed, quiet again, rubbing cream into her sunburned arms. I thought of how I saw her with Faye, hooting, bent double, as if something had been released in her.

'As a matter of fact, we made a pact today. We promised to take each other's children if anything happened to us.'

'Christ! . . . Don't Henry and I have a say in this?'

'The trouble is, Roy, you never think that anything could happen to us.'

Someone was wailing in the hall. Maida turned on her way to the door. 'I feel relieved,' she said.

'A test run,' Maida said. She wedged her cap onto my head and wrapped my neck in a red scarf. I had forgotten about the cold in the streets. I had forgotten how to look after myself. I looked in the hall mirror. I saw that my hair, pushed down by the cap, now covered my ears. My square face had become rectangular, my stubbled cheeks now fell into my scarf. I saw a man in an outsize coat, stooping to look at himself with dark, diffident eyes.

'Ready?' Maida said. She and Faye kept saying how glad they were that I was better. Yesterday I had sat in the living room and drunk chicken noodle soup and read the paper. Now the fever's gone you won't look back, they said.

It was true that the pounding had gone quiet. But I couldn't believe that this was for long. All the time I was listening out for its return. But we were booked into a guesthouse in Scotland, a famous guesthouse in the North, with open fires and grouse and deer. We had only got the booking through a cancellation. A little walk in the Square, they said. Try your legs. See the snow. I followed them out of the flat, down the stairs.

The roof garden had not prepared me for it, the vast even-handed whiteness laid across the grubby street, the meticulous quiet. A square black taxi cruised gently by. The whole city had been brought to order.

'Gorgeous, isn't it?' they said. We crossed the road into the Square. Here they stooped and plastered snowballs together in their gloved hands, grinning at each other. They ran, ducking and squealing, and their breath held its shape as it rose towards the great black trees.

I walked a little. The crunch of my footsteps made me shiver: I could scarcely bear the clarity of the air.

It was back. I was not surprised. It seemed natural that it would start up again here, in the snow, as if the same witch had set us sparkling ... The glare enclosed me. All around the Square the houses reared up with grinning windows. I heard the women hailing me from a long way off. My eyes sought out the darkness in the bare thickets by the fence, but I could not see the gate.

2

I put myself in their hands. Our departure was swift, in a freezing dawn: they helped me down the stairs of the flat whispering, as if they were spiriting me away. They stowed me with pillows and blankets into the back seat of the car they had hired. I sat stiffly, like a packed-up corpse in my cap and red scarf, while they ran back to get our bags.

Faye drove, Maida read the map. They seemed very pleased with the car. 'If you want to stretch out we can let down the back seat,' they said. They said how I would be tucked into my bed in Scotland that night. With feather pillows most likely. And a hot toddy. They laughed.

They found their way to the M1. An uneasy silver light was rising over the rooftops of the suburbs. 'Oh, isn't that nice,' Maida said. They found the nice in everything, the courteous drivers, the clear signposting, some horses galloping behind a low stone wall ... I sank lower and lower into my pillows. My head rolled and jolted on my chest. The car was a capsule of throbbing warmth. I thought suddenly of Henry Schmitt, the last time I had seen him, after years. A glimpse, under a banner, passing me in the lunchtime crowd. I saw his round-shouldered lope, his tight fanatic jaw, as he marched, alone, towards the other banners.

I wondered if I would ever return to the world of men again.

We stopped once, at a roadside café, somewhere far to the north. There were already stars in the afternoon sky. Snow lay piled like surf against the steaming windows. It was a place of clatter and scraping chairs, lone men in suits bent over newspapers, families chewing together in numbed, stricken silence. We might have dreamt it as we entered, out of the arctic air.

We were served by a waitress with skin as fine as powder and an accent we could hardly understand. We sat amongst the hiss of fat and steam, under the neon glare. I watched Faye pace like a sentry with her cigarette outside the door. I could have laid my swirling head down on the plastic cloth, and stayed.

Then I saw a boy at the pinball game in the corner. One pointy shoe rocked over the other as his wrists shook it to life. I must note down the game, I thought, and its highest recorded score, and send a postcard to Michael. Michael likes facts. Before the snow came I had sent him a postcard nearly every day. No answer, of course, no knowing their effect: I sent them off the way I played these games with Michael, without much skill or hope. Then there is room for something else, that sudden lift or flare. He always recognizes it. I look around for him and see it, on his face.

When Michael was nearly three, Maida could take no more. She took the girls out of school and they went on a holiday together. Although there was more work than we could handle in the agency by then, I took a month off to look after Michael. Maida wouldn't leave him with a stranger: she was afraid that would break whatever fragile links he had with us, he would never trust us again.

I told myself it was a holding operation. We had our routines. We steered a careful course around the house, the suburb. There was a playground near us where in summer the slide winks, red hot, and the swing hangs empty in an acre of dead grass. Even now I choose not to drive home that way. Once, in an endless afternoon, I took him to the beach, and while he howled, I gave myself for five minutes to the sea. Sometimes at night, when even the reruns of the *Twilight Zone* had finished, I carried him around the dripping garden, both of us in pajamas. Twisting away from me in his big nappy, he looked over my shoulder at the shadows, his eyes as dark and ringed as a possum's.

I had to leave him, once a week, to go to the office for a couple of hours. Maida said that Faye would mind him for me. He was used to Faye, she said, he would stay with her. He did. She clasped him to her hip and as I drove away I saw that she was picking something off a leaf and he was stretching over her to look.

The same old Faye, I thought. Her own house was like a beach house, a real one, weatherboard with a verandah, lost among peppermint trees. It was no good going to the front door, Maida warned me, it was blocked off, one of the children slept in the hall. I found Faye each time in the back yard, reading. They had made a whole room out there. At the bottom of the back steps, straight onto the grass, they had set chairs and a table and an old velour couch. And all around in the trees, slung over branches, were bathers and towels, a school shirt, pajama pants, a bathmat, flapping peacefully among the leaves.

The last time, just before Maida came back, I was late picking him up. I had a drink with a client and then another with my partner and staff. I found I couldn't always follow what they were saying. My laughter seemed a beat behind the rest. Another drink might help me to catch up, I thought. Faye won't mind. I was careful not to think of Michael. Then I realized I was three hours late. That drive, too fast, to make amends, it was like all the past weeks, years, swerving along the edge, *something was wrong*, Maida said, and then everything was out of line, everything had to be negotiated. To think of Michael was like sending off a silent prayer.

He was asleep on the leaf-shadowed couch. He slept like that, suddenly, deeply, after one of his fits of rage.

'About half an hour after you usually come he started to wail to the skies.'

'I'm sorry. I was held up.'

'It doesn't matter. He survived. It doesn't matter at all.'

She must have smelt the alcohol, and the sweat that slashed my shirt. She must have seen it all. I closed my eyes.

She put her arms around me.

It was so quiet there, the way a noisy place is quiet when it has been deserted by its usual voices. I saw above her head the strange cloths nesting in the trees. And higher still a fierce whiteness blazed around the edges of the leaves. Everything was strange and yet piercingly familiar, and the stillness held us as we waited there.

Michael stirred. I gathered him up, and kissed her like a wife, and went away.

3

The North. It was a moving darkness as if the sky kept pace with us. Lights swung in strings and disappeared and sometimes a denser darkness, a huge curved flank, traveled alongside us and then dropped behind. Sometimes trees were revealed, black bare fists held up to us in the headlights. The car warbled and sighed and the rhythm played through my blood until it seemed the whole journey was fired by the energy of fever.

And then silence.

The car was tentlike in weak orange light.

'Where are we?'

'Three or four miles from the guesthouse, we think. But it's snowing so hard Faye can't see the road.'

Then later: 'It isn't going to stop. We'll have to stay here for the night.'

Their voices were calm and soft.

'Lie between us, Roy, for the warmth.'

Feeble and clumsy in my thick coat, I eased myself into the bed they had made in the back for the three of us. Side by side we stared at the ceiling.

'Abraham and his Two Wives,' Faye said into the darkness.

'If I remember rightly,' I said, 'wasn't one of Abraham's wives *young?*'

They thought this was very funny.

They seemed cheerful and matter-of-fact. The guesthouse was expecting us. Tomorrow there would be a search party. Or in the light we would see how ridiculously close we were, and would set off walking, lugging our bags across the snowy fields. Thank goodness there are no children with us, they said, hooting a little in the darkness. They would never let us forget this ... They yawned and snuggled down. It was almost as if this was part of the plan. And all at once I thought of their maps and whispers, their haste, their insistence, dragging me and my Russian flu on and on, right into the arms of the snow ... they had all conspired against me ... they had got me where they wanted me ...

A sound broke out of me that I didn't recognize, the deep rasp of a stranger, talking through me. I felt it scrape against my ribs and throat. My limbs trailed and twitched behind it. Tears ran from my eyes.

They went quiet then. Maida found my cap and settled it on my head. From time to time one of them would wriggle free of our cocoon and switch on the car engine. The heater roared and snow slithered from the gently vibrating roof. Mist ran in rivulets down the windows, like curtains parting, and we could see the dim broken whiteness flocking past.

Something gripped my chest and tightened. I had to reach further for every breath. And as my eyes closed and my fists clenched, I saw it. I saw her face.

Out of this whiteness crawls the Humber, with my mother and father peering out on their separate sides for street numbers, and the boy in the back, bent over something, something new, a pocket knife. It's a Christmas present. It is Christmas Day, circa 1950.

This is a new suburb, War Service, and we have never been here before. The scrubby grey bush is being pushed back block by block into a valley. The houses are all the same, grey-white asbestos, on stilts at the back for the slope. Nothing is growing here yet, and there are drifts of grey-white sand.

'We need your eyes, Roy,' my mother says. She is rather anxious about finding the house, rather annoyed. Christmas Day is a family day, she says. There is something about Harry Crewe and Natasha — never 'the Crewes' — whose house we are looking for, that has singled them out, left them adrift, free for drinks on Christmas Day.

Then my father spots Harry on his porch, the Humber wheels down a steep driveway and lurches to a stop with the handbrake. My father, responsible for this outing, gets out first. Squinting, clearing our throats, tucking and patting, my family descends on the porch.

There is a lot of hand-shaking. Harry Crewe is the same as ever, when he comes to pick up my father for golf on Saturday afternoons, except he isn't wearing his tartan cap. He's a solid man with a broad forehead and gold-rimmed glasses. Natasha is handing round a bowl of cherries. Not just a little damp bagful, a token quarter pound to be scattered in amongst the Christmas nuts and raisins, but a great wooden bowl filled to the top. She shakes it and smiles in front of each one of us. 'Take, take,' she says.

And when I take a little dangling bunch, it is forked over another, so that a whole linked branchful falls into my lap. My mother looks alarmed, but Natasha laughs and leaves the whole bowl beside me. Then she sits down, not next to my mother, but back next to Harry.

And though my knife is beautifully heavy in my pocket, and I am free to wander off now, I opt for the cherries, which, I can see, are going to be unrationed. And for Natasha. One after another I put the cherries in my mouth, and every word that I have heard, but never listened to, about Natasha, comes flying back to me. She is a White Russian. She has had what they call a Terrible War. Harry Crewe met her in Singapore. She is a woman with no children, but there are other husbands, other wives somewhere. Harry Crewe has given up everything. There are two sides to a story. He doesn't come in for a drink after golf any more because Natasha gets lonely. When my father says the name 'Natasha', there's a smile in his voice. He says it quickly and easily to include it in his vocabulary, like the brand name of a new, promising car. He is smiling now, receiving a drink from Natasha, and Harry Crewe is smiling, and my mother, they're all smiling because of Natasha.

Natasha isn't young, she isn't as young as her name sounds. She's as old, maybe even older than my mother. She isn't pretty, but in another way she is like the source of everything pretty in the world. She seems uncluttered, as if, wherever she came from, she could not bring much with her, not even a surname. There are no folds or drapes to her outline. Her hair is coarse and dark, parted, close to her head. She has a long olive-skinned face and her long eyes have a bruised darkness about them. When she smiles, looking into your face, her eyes have a secret life to them, close to something extreme, which might be tears.

My mother talks to her slowly and clearly like she does to our ironing lady, who is a New Australian. But Natasha talks back quickly and laughs, and her laugh breaks ragged and violent across the porch.

Like the men I sit there with my hands on my knees and I look out across the sand to the Humber, held back, mid-turn, down the driveway, and far away down the street I hear kids' voices, rising thin as smoke, arguing over their new toys.

They had turned off the car engine. With every cough I sank back further. I saw our car, a tiny speck amongst the whiteness, and the whiteness spread and became a map of a tiny country, and the map spread and became the globe in Michael's room, set to spin so all the countries blurred together, and the tiny speck, of course, had disappeared.

'I'd give anything for a smoke,' Faye said.

I couldn't speak. But in between my gasps, I listened to their steadfast breathing. I am glad you are with me, I wanted to say. But as if they had heard me, they pressed closer to me, their heads beside my shoulders, their hands in mine. An arm pillowed my heavy neck, and I felt a wing of precious breath catch across my cheek.

'Isn't this what you've always wanted?' someone whispered. 'To die in a woman's arms?'

The Last Days of a Famous Mime

Peter Carey

1

The Mime arrived on Alitalia with very little luggage: a brown paper parcel and what looked like a woman's handbag.

Asked the contents of the brown paper parcel he said, 'String'.

Asked what the string was for he replied: 'Tying up bigger parcels.'

It had not been intended as a joke, but the Mime was pleased when the reporters laughed. Inducing laughter was not his forte. He was famous for terror.

Although his state of despair was famous throughout Europe, few guessed at his hope for the future. 'The string,' he explained, 'is a prayer that I am always praying.'

Reluctantly he untied his parcel and showed them the string. It was blue and when extended measured exactly fifty-three metres.

The Mime and the string appeared on the front pages of the evening papers.

2

The first audiences panicked easily. They had not been prepared for his ability to mime terror. They fled their seats continually. Only to return again.

Like snorkel divers they appeared at the doors outside the concert hall with red faces and were puzzled to find the world as they had left it.

3

Books had been written about him. He was the subject of an award-winning film. But in his first morning in a provincial town he was distressed to find that his performance had not been liked by the one newspaper's one critic.

'I cannot see,' the critic wrote, 'the use of invoking terror in an audience.'

The Mime sat on his bed, pondering ways to make his performance more light-hearted.

4

As usual he attracted women who wished to still the raging storms of his heart.

They attended his bed like highly paid surgeons operating on a difficult case. They were both passionate and intelligent. They did not suffer defeat lightly.

5

Wrongly accused of merely miming love in his private life he was somewhat surprised to be confronted with hatred.

'Surely,' he said, 'if you now hate me, it was you who were imitating love, not I.'

'You always were a slimy bastard,' she said. 'What's in that parcel?'

'I told you before,' he said helplessly, 'string.'

'You're a liar,' she said.

But later when he untied the parcel he found that she had opened it to check on his story. Her understanding of the string had been perfect. She had cut it into small pieces like spaghetti in a lousy restaurant.

6

Against the advice of the tour organizers he devoted two concerts entirely to love and laughter. They were disasters. It was felt that love and laughter were not, in his case, as instructive as terror.

The next performance was quickly announced.

TWO HOURS OF REGRET.

Tickets sold quickly. He began with a brief interpretation of love using it merely as a prelude to regret which he elaborated on in a complex and moving performance which left the audience pale and shaken. In a final flourish he passed from regret to loneliness to terror. The audience devoured the terror like brave tourists eating the hottest curry in an Indian restaurant.

7

'What you are doing,' she said, 'is capitalizing on your neuroses. Personally I find it disgusting, like someone exhibiting their club foot, or Turkish beggars with strange deformities.'

He said nothing. He was mildly annoyed at her presumption: that he had not thought this many, many times before.

With perfect misunderstanding she interpreted his passivity as disdain.

Wishing to hurt him, she slapped his face.

Wishing to hurt her, he smiled brilliantly.

8

The story of the blue string touched the public imagination. Small brown paper packages were sold at the doors of his concerts.

Standing on stage he could hear the packages being noisily unwrapped. He thought of American matrons buying Muslim prayer rugs.

9

Exhausted and weakened by the heavy schedule he fell prey to the doubts that had pricked at him insistently for years. He lost all sense of direction and spent many listless hours by himself, sitting in a motel room listening to the air-conditioner.

He had lost confidence in the social uses of controlled terror. He no longer understood the audience's need to experience the very things he so desperately wished to escape from.

He emptied the ashtrays fastidiously.

He opened his brown paper parcel and threw the small pieces of string down the cistern. When the torrent of white water subsided they remained floating there like flotsam from a disaster at sea.

10

The Mime called a press conference to announce that there would be no more concerts. He seemed small and foreign and smelt of garlic. The press regarded him without enthusiasm. He watched their hovering pens anxiously, unsuccessfully willing them to write down his words.

Briefly he announced that he wished to throw his talent open to broader influences. His skills would be at the disposal of the people, who would be free to request his services for any purpose at any time.

His skin seemed sallow but his eyes seemed as bright as those on a nodding fur mascot on the back window ledge of an American car.

11

Asked to describe death he busied himself taking Polaroid photographs of his questioners.

12

Asked to describe marriage he handed out small cheap mirrors with MADE IN TUNISIA written on the back.

13

His popularity declined. It was felt that he had become obscure and beyond the understanding of ordinary people. In response he requested easier questions. He held back nothing of himself in his effort to please his audience.

14

Asked to describe an aeroplane he flew three times around the city, only injuring himself slightly on landing.

15

Asked to describe a river, he drowned himself.

16

It is unfortunate that this, his last and least typical performance, is the only one which has been recorded on film.

There is a small crowd by the river bank, no more than thirty people. A small, neat man dressed in a grey suit picks his way through some children who seem more interested in the large plastic toy dog they are playing with.

He steps into the river, which, at the bank, is already quite deep. His head is only visible above the water for a second or two. And then he is gone.

A policeman looks expectantly over the edge, as if waiting for him to reappear. Then the film stops.

Watching this last performance it is difficult to imagine how this man stirred such emotions in the hearts of those who saw him.

LITTLE HELEN'S SUNDAY AFTERNOON

Helen Garner

Late on a winter Sunday afternoon, Little Helen stood behind her mother on the verandah of Noah's house. Her mother raised her finger to the buzzer but the door opened from the inside and Noah's father came hurrying out.

'Bad luck, girls,' he said. He was pulling on his jacket. 'Just got a call from Northern General. Some kid's cut his finger off.'

'His whole finger?' said Little Helen. 'Right off?'

'I hope someone slung it in the icebox,' said Little Helen's mother. 'What a time to make you work.'

'*Unpaid* work,' said Noah's mother. 'Will I save you some soup, Jim?'

'Let's see,' said Noah's father. 'Four-thirty. I'll have to do a graft. Five thirty, six, six-thirty. Yeah. Save me some.'

As he talked he walked, and was already in the car. The drive was full of coloured leaves.

Little Helen's mother and Noah's were sisters and liked to shriek a lot when visiting.

'Little Helen!' said Noah's mother. 'Jump up! Let me have a hold of you!'

Little Helen stepped out from behind her mother, bent her knees, raised her arms and sprang. Noah's mother caught her, but staggered and gave a cry. 'Ark! You used to be such a fairy little thing. Last time you were here you sat on my knee and do you know what you said? You said, "I *love* being small!".'

Little Helen went red and dropped her eyes. She saw her own foot, in its large, strapped blue shoe, swinging awkwardly near her aunt's hip.

'Come on, Meg,' said Little Helen's mother. 'Let's pop

into the bedroom. I've got some business to conduct. It's in this bag.'

Noah's mother unclasped her hands under Little Helen's bottom and let her slide to the ground.

'Another hair shirt, is it?' she said to Little Helen's mother. 'I suppose I'll be left holding the baby.'

'What are you going to call it if it's a boy?' said Little Helen.

The women looked at each other. Their cheeks puffed out and their lips went tight. They went into the bedroom and closed the door without answering her question. Little Helen could hear them screeching and crashing round in front of the mirror. She knew that it was not a hair shirt at all, but a pair of shoes her mother had paid a lot of money for and worn once then discovered they were too big, and which she hoped that Noah's mother would buy from her. Little Helen brushed the back of her tartan skirt down flat and stood in the hallway. She saw her own feet parallel. She thought of a waitress. It was a long time ago, in the dining room of the Bull and Mouth Hotel in Stawell. The waitress was quite old and she stood patiently, holding her order pad and pencil, while Little Helen's father took a long time to make up his mind what to have. Little Helen, who always had roast lamb, tried to stop looking at the waitress's feet, but could not. There was nothing special about the feet. But the neatness of their position, two inches apart and perfectly parallel on the carpet's green and orange flowers, caused Little Helen to experience a painful sadness. She decided to have chicken instead.

'Chicken's pretty risky,' said her father.

'I want chicken, though,' said Little Helen.

She got chicken. It was all right but rather dry. She ate more of it than she wanted.

'How's the chicken?' said her father.

'A bit risky,' said Little Helen.

Her father laughed so much that everyone at the other tables turned to stare.

Little Helen knew she was clever but she noticed that words did not always bear the same simple, serious meaning that they had at school when she copied them into her exercise book. On her spelling list she had the word 'capacious' to put into a sentence. 'The elephant is a capacious beast,' she wrote. Her mother's mouth trembled when Little Helen showed her the twenty finished sentences, in best writing and ruled off. She explained why 'capacious' was not quite right. Her polite kindness and her trembling mouth made Little Helen blush until tears filled her eyes.

Little Helen stood outside her aunt's bedroom and waited for something to happen. Time became elastic, and sagged. She hated visiting. She had to be dragged away from her wooden table, her full set of Derwents, her different inks and textas, her special paper-cutting scissors, her rulers and sharpeners and rubbers. The teacher never gave her enough homework. She could have worked all weekend.

She did not like the feeling of other people's houses. There was nothing to do. Pieces of furniture stood sparsely in chilly rooms. The long stretches of skirting board were empty of meaning, and the kitchen smells were mournful, as if the saucepans on the stove contained nothing but grey bones boiling for a stew.

The bedroom door opened and Little Helen's mother poked her head out. She had been laughing. Her face was pink and she was wearing nothing but a bra and pants and a black hat like a box with a bit of net hanging over her eyes.

'We're having dress-ups,' she said. 'Want to come in and play?'

Little Helen was embarrassed and shook her head. They didn't know how to play properly. They were much too tall and had real bosoms, and they talked all the time about how much they had paid for the clothes and where they would go to wear them, instead of being serious and thoughtful about what the clothes meant in the game.

'Oh, don't be so unsociable!' said her mother. 'Go and see Noah.'

'He won't want to see me,' said Little Helen. 'Anyway I don't know where he is.'

'He's out the back,' shouted his mother from inside the bedroom. 'Probably making something. Some white elephant or other.'

They started to laugh again, and Little Helen's mother went back into the bedroom and slammed the door.

Little Helen plodded down the hall and entered the kitchen. The lunch dishes were all over the sink. Between the stacked plates she found quite a lot of tinned sweet corn, crusted with cold butter. She put her mouth down to the china and sucked up the scrapings. Her palate took on a coating of grease. She moved over to the pantry cupboard and helped herself to five Marie biscuits, some peeled almonds, four squares of cooking chocolate and a handful of crystallised ginger. Eating fast and furtively, bolting the food inside the big dark cupboard, she started to get that rude and secret feeling of wanting to do a shit. She crossed her legs and squeezed her bum shut, and went on guzzling. A little salvo of farts escaped into her pants and if something funny had occurred to her at that moment she would not have been able to hang on; but she kept her mind on that poor boy who had cut his finger off, and gradually she felt the lump go back up inside her for later.

If she ate any more she would spoil her tea. She hitched up her skirt, wiped her palms on her pants, and set out across the kitchen towards the wide glass door.

Noah's yard was long and sloped steeply down to the back fence. The trees had no leaves, and from the porch steps Little Helen could see for miles and miles, as far as the centre of the city. She paused to stare at the tiny bunch of skyscrapers, like a city in a film, and at the long curved bridge beyond them with its chain of lights already flicking on. The afternoon was nearly over. It was not raining now. Water lay in puddles on the sky-blue plastic cover of the swimming pool. The branches of bare bushes were a glossy black, like a licked pencil lead.

Little Helen's feet sank into the spongy grass. Her shoes looked very large and blue on the greenness. The grass was so green that it made her feel sick. The sky was low. An unnatural light leaked out of the clouds, and the chords the light played were in the same dull, complicated key as the grass-sickness. The air did not move. It was cold. Her legs felt white and thin under the pleated skirt.

Grass grew right up to the shed door, which was shut. Noah must be in there. She stood outside it and paid attention. There was a noise like somebody using sandpaper on a piece of wood, but softer; like two people using sandpaper, two rhythms not quite hitting the same beat. Someone laughed.

Little Helen saw a red plastic bucket half under the shed. She pulled it out and turned it upside down. Its bottom was cracked and it was almost too weak to hold her, but by keeping her shoes on the very outside of its rim she could balance on it and get her head up to the window. Rags had been hooked across it on the inside, and only one small corner was uncovered. She put her eye to it. It was even darker inside. In there the night had already begun. How could he see what he was doing?

She shifted her left foot on the bucket and missed the rim. The toe of her shoe pierced the split base. Her fingers lost their hold on the windowsill. A fierce sharpness scraped through her sock and raked its claws up her shin. She swivelled sideways with a grunt, lurched against the shed wall, and stumbled out onto the lawn. Shocked and gasping, she found herself still upright, but with the red bucket clamped around her left leg just below the knee.

In the upper part of the sky, above the bunch of skyscrapers, the clouds split like rotten cloth and let a flat blade of light through. It leaned between sky and earth, a crooked pillar. Little Helen took a breath. She clenched her fists. She opened her mouth and bellowed.

'Noah!'

There was a silence, then a harsh scrabbling inside the shed.

'Come out!' bawled Little Helen. 'Come out and see me! It's not fair! I'm tired of waiting!'

Her shin was stinging very hard, as if her mother had already pressed onto the broken skin the Listerine-soaked cottonwool. Her invisible left sock felt wet. Little Helen thought, 'I could easily be crying.' The shed door was wrenched open and a huge boy with red hair and skin like boiled custard burst through. He was croaking.

'You were spying! Who said you could spy on me?'

Something strange had happened to Noah, and not only to his voice. The whole shape of his head had changed. He didn't look like a boy any more. He looked like a dog, or a fish. His eyes were like slits, and had moved higher up his face and outwards into his temples.

'Look, Noah,' whispered Little Helen. She was not sure whether she meant the drunken pillar of light or the bucket on her leg. He took three steps towards her and grabbed her by the arm. She jerked her face away from the smell of him: not just sweaty but raw, like steak.

'If you tell what you saw,' he choked. Red patches flared low on his speckled cheeks.

'It was dark,' said Little Helen. She could feel blood running down into her cotton sock. 'I couldn't even see in. I couldn't see anything. I only heard the noise. I promise.'

He dragged her towards the shed door. The grass squelched under his thick-soled jogging shoes. She had to stagger with her legs apart because of the bucket, but he did not notice it, and pushed her up the step. Another boy was standing just inside. Their great bodies, panting and stinking, filled the shed.

'Don't bring her in here, you fuckwit!' said the other boy. His shoelaces were undone and he was doing up his trousers. 'I'm going home.'

The shed smelt of cigarettes. They must have smoked a whole packet. They would get lung cancer. They would get into really bad trouble. The other boy bent to tie his lace and Little Helen saw that there was a third person in the shed. A girl was sitting on a sleeping bag that was spread out on the floor. She was pulling on her boots. As she scrambled to her feet she spotted Little Helen's bucket. She stopped on all fours in dog position and looked up into Little Helen's face. Her eyes were caked with black stuff and her hair was stiff, like burnt grass. She laughed; Little Helen could see all her back teeth.

'Ha!' said the girl. 'Now you know what happens to people who snoop. Come on, Justin. Let's go.'

She stood up and buckled her belt. The two of them barged out the door. Little Helen heard their feet thumping on the grass and then crunching on the gravel drive.

'I know what *you've* been doing,' said Little Helen. The butts were everywhere. Some had lipstick on the yellow end.

'Shut your face,' said Noah. In the grey light from the open door his head with its short orange hair and flat temples was as smooth and savage as a bull terrier's. He gave a high snigger. 'You look stupid with that bucket on your leg.'

The moment for crying was long gone. She would have had to fake it, though she knew she had the right. 'It hurts,' said Little Helen. 'I can feel blood still coming out. It hurts quite a lot, actually. It might be serious.'

'You want to know about blood?' said Noah. His small, high, dog's eyes began to glow, as if a weak torch battery had flicked on inside his head. 'I'll show you want can happen to people.'

'I think I'd better speak to my mother,' said Little Helen. 'I need to ask her about something very important.'

'First I'll show you something,' said Noah.

'I can't walk,' said Little Helen. She folded her arms and stood square, with her knees apart to accommodate the bucket, but he scooped her off the ground in one round movement and ran out of the shed and across the garden.

From her sideways and horizontal position Little Helen saw the grassy world bounce and swing. She kept her left leg stuck out straight so the bucket would not be interfered with. His big hip and thigh worked under her waist like a horse's. He took the back steps in a couple of bounds. At the top he swung her across his front while he fumbled with the glass door, and in its broad pane she saw reflected her own white underpants, twisted half off her bottom, and down in its lower corner, half obscured by the image of her faithful bucket, the bunch of sky-scrapers flaming with light. She writhed to cover her pants and his hard fingers gripped her tighter. He forged through the kitchen, along the passage and into a small dim room that smelt of leather and Finepoint pens with their caps off.

Dumped, she staggered for the door, but he got past her and kicked it shut.

'Mum!' said Little Helen, without conviction.

'Look,' said Noah. He kept one foot against the door and reached behind her to a large, low, wooden cupboard that stood on legs against one wall. He slid open its front panel and switched on a light inside it.

It was not a cupboard. It was a box. It was deep, and it was full of pictures, tiny square ones, suspended in space, arranged in neat horizontal rows and lit gently from behind so that they glowed in many colours, jewel-like, but mostly yellow, brown and red. The magical idea, the bright orderliness of it, took Little Helen's breath away. She limped forward, smiling, favouring her bucketed leg. Noah left the door and crouched beside her. He must have forgiven her: he was panting from his run, from his haste to bring her to this wonder.

The pictures were slides. They seemed to be of children's faces. But there was something unusual about them. Were they children in face paint? Were they dressed in Costumes of Other Lands, or at a Hat Competition? Were they disguised as angels, or fairies? Little Helen tried to kneel, but her bucket bothered her. She spread her legs wide and bent them, and opened her arms to keep her balance. In this Balinese posture she lowered herself to contemplate the mystery.

The children were horrible. Their heads were bloodied. Their hair had been torn out by the roots, their scalps were raw and crisscrossed with black railway lines. Their lips were blue and swollen and bulged outwards, barely contained by stitches. Their eyes had burst like pickled onions, their foreheads were stove in, their chins were crushed to pink pulp. One baby, too new to sit up, had a huge purple furry thing growing from its temple to its chin. Another had two dark holes instead of a nose and its top lip was not there at all.

But the worst thing was that not a single one of them was crying. The ones whose eyes still worked looked straight at Little Helen with a patient, sober gaze. They were not surprised that these terrible things had happened to them, that there mothers had turned away at the wrong moment, that the war had come, that men with guns and knives had got into the house and found them. Little Helen's hackles went lumpy and her stomach rose into her throat. She shut her eyes and tried to straighten up, but Noah put his hand down hard on her shoulder and croaked.

'See that kid there? A power line fell on him. His brain woulda blown right out of his skull.'

Little Helen squirmed out from under his hand and crawled away. He did not follow her, but watched her drag her bucket to the door and stand up and reach the high handle. She got her good foot out into the hall and looked back. He was crouching before the picture box. The soft white light from inside it polished his furry hair. Little Helen saw that he could not stop looking at the pictures. He turned to her.

'See?' he said. 'See what can happen to little kids?'

She nodded.

'Don't you like it?' The dim torch battery went on behind his eyes. He was smiling. 'You don't, do you. Piss weak. Look at this equipment. Best that money can buy.'

'What — ' She cleared her throat. 'Did they all die?'

'Die? Course they didn't die. My dad sewed 'em up. But they were very sick. And afterwards they were always ugly. For the rest of their lives.'

Little Helen let go the door handle and slid out into the hallway. Her palms were sticky and the backs of her hands had shrunk and gone hard, but she was not going to be sick. She stumped away down the passage towards the front of the house. The bucket made a soft clunk with every second step.

Her mother and Noah's were sitting quietly on the edge of the big double bed. They were dressed in their ordinary clothes and sat with their hands folded in their laps as if waiting for something. Little Helen clumped into the doorway and stopped. They looked up. She saw their two white faces, round and flat as dinner plates, shinning above their dark dresses in what remained of the light.

Vase with Red Fishes

Beverley Farmer

At the beginning of summer she invites him down to stay at
the Point in the house in the tea-trees in the lee of the dunes
which she is minding for a friend. 'No strings,' she says. 'Come
and paint,' and he accepts. He arrives late one night bringing
wine and a framed print as a present.

'Oh, thank you!' She props it up. 'Oh, I love this.'

'I thought you would.'

' "Henri Matisse. *Vase with Red Fishes* (1914). Centre G.
Pompidou" — I wonder where he painted it.'

They lie in bed together sipping the wine. 'They're moving,'
she says. 'Look. The fish.'

'Fish-es.'

'They're negative of us. White inside, red out.'

'Mmm.' He wants to sleep now, not talk.

'If we immersed it in water they could swim off.'

'You dare!'

'Fresh water, of course. Salt water'd be fatal. They'd float
away with their bellies up. Over the balcony and off into the
flooded square where gulls would swoop and snatch them away.'

On a stand with long grey wooden legs is a jar of thick glass
more than half-full of water in which are circling two goldfish,
poissons rouges, red-gold fishes nosing at the fragmenting
shrunken and swollen shadows they inhabit. They are in the
window of a dark blue room, seen by someone inside leaning
back to take in the wooden chair-back, the divan with square
cushions, the pot or jar of pale green water in the foreground.
A pillar stands behind the vase. Black iron is curled round the
blue of the balcony. The sun strikes one side of the tall building

across the square, its tower hooded with black tiles, slate tiles like the scales of the giant fish; its other side, four storeys of wall with narrow windows, is in shade. Next to it is a sunny façade with black loops for windows. The sky is thick blue. Carts crawl over the square. A terracotta flowerpot by the vase holds two long black stems out over the balcony, which has a top rail of darker red. There is an archway below. Serrations, a staircase. The perspective is fractured, refracted.

It is hot, a hot summer evening in the south of France. Out of sight beyond the frame two people are sitting in the dark interior, which, like the painting, is touched here and there with red and gold — the bright edge of a cushion, the strip of rosy light at the floor of the balcony. A man, a woman. They are translucent. They have just woken up from the siesta. Colours flow from and over them listening to watery piano pieces: Debussy, *Reflets dans l'eau, Poissons d'or, La cathédrale engloutie.* Or the record has stopped and sound — a bird, a shouted exchange of words, a cat's yowl — floats in on a silence.

He has been painting what he sees out the window. He sits watching the fishes. They are two ripples of blood that dissolve and twine, red whips in the light of the water. In the glass with them are fragments of the hot blue and wheat-brown square with its turret and loophole windows sunk in a slab of shade. Their eyes, hollow black, look out at her. As if in a concave mirror they see hollow towering walls and encased in them a red bubble, which is the woman. She had put on a long red robe today and the folds and shadows of its silk lap her whiteness, trailing loose from her arms and on the floor at her feet. The silk feels like cool water.

They have been lent this room by a friend. They will feed the goldfish and water the overgrown potplant; walk about on the green floor of the square under the stone walls in the cool of the evening. She knows a beach that disappears and reappears with the tides. The tide will be low, she says, at sunset, if he wants a swim. There is a long metal staircase down from the clifftop. When you walk on it in wooden-soled shoes each step chimes; when you run, the small sounds shimmer together like gamelan music. The whole staircase thrums. At its foot lie two flat round rocks with a fan of flutings on their backs like giant scallops. Black straps of kelp twist on the sand and in pools. The waves in the shallows turn cloudy gold as they rise, full of sand they have scooped up. He can watch the moon rise, she says, the lighthouses flicker under their green helmets, ships

edge by into the open sea. And the other bay at low tide is
all sweeps of pale water and sand, she says, tangles of kelp and
red weed, and birds gathering, rowing boats tilted to one side
half a mile out, lying on broken mirrors.

"Low tide. I love low tide,' he says.

'Yes, it's best at low tide,' she says, 'here at least.'

'How come?'

'When the tide's in, the water comes right up to the foot
of the cliff and the sea wall. But there's sand at low tide.'

' "As I Ebbed with the Ocean of Life." '

'Yes. Fancy you remembering that. Well, I ebb and flow. I
still love Walt Whitman. Remember you said we all do at one
stage and then we grow out of him? "Your summer wind was
warm enough, yet the air I breathed froze me..." I'm less
depressive than I once was.'

'Good,' And he squeezes her arm. 'That's good.'

'Why do you love low tide?'

'Seeing what's hidden at other times. I think that must be
why. Revelations. It's like love, don't you think? Like revisiting
a past love. Each time the sheets are pulled down and then
up again. The water sheets.'

He goes out on the dunes to paint. Sandstone is honeycomb
in the late summer sun, pitted with swallows' nests. All this
beach is the same colour — sand, rock and rock pool. The small
mouse-shrieks of swallows skim and soar. The wave-shaped,
whale-shaped headland is dark in the spray of the western sky
and into the eastern sky a ship surges from behind the lighthouse.
Its surfaces flash. A point like a star pierces the masthead. Its
smoke is a rope pulling it away. His footprints flatten the crisp
arrowheads left by gulls. At the high tide mark, along the hairline
of the marram grass, he sees a soaked spaniel head, but it's
a drowned penguin, its dense wings folded under and hanging
out like earlobes. Here and there are splashes of jellyfish. Long
pink and white eggs are cuttlefish bones, in nests of seaweed.

He sees her down on the beach lying in a dark gold rock pool
and paints the small sandy prongs of her stretched out, weedy
head back, hands open on the edge out of the water. He shows
her that night. 'Want to have a look at this, Narcissus?' he says.

'Me, Narcissus? Oh, this is lovely! Monochrome, is it? Yes,
it's tawny all over. Were you up on the cliff this afternoon?
Why didn't you come in for a swim?'

Later, looking at the painting again, she says: '*You* were looking
in the pool, I was what you saw. That makes *you* Narcissus.'

'And you, now that *you're* looking in the pool.'

She smiles. 'Okay. But Narcissus can only be a man. Only a man can be Narcissus.'

'He was human, ultimately. Both male and female.'

'No, women don't see themselves in him. He doesn't reflect — echo! — anything in women.'

'Echo! He's the Self, it seems to me, in search of the Other, brought up against the impossibility of finding an Other. The boundary of the Self as a mirror. It's not a matter of male or female.'

'Men made Narcissus. In their own image, or so it seems to me. He's a male myth.'

'All right. But one that transcends gender.'

'I think it's an illusion,' she says, 'that human beings can transcend gender.'

He sighs.

A wooden table stands against one wall, with a second chair. In the next room is an iron bed under a window with shutters; the window faces the back and fills up with hot strips of light every day. So they lie back against the blue wall in the front room, sipping wine or tea and watching the coolly spiralling fiery fishes.

'The heart of the painting,' she says one day, 'is the red fishes.'

'*And* the vase. You could take out the fishes and still the vase would be the heart.'

'Not if the fishes weren't there it wouldn't.'

'You're wrong. The vase is enough. By itself.'

'I don't think so. I think that sunlit building would dominate. I wonder what it is? A town hall? A convent? Of course, we're used to it as it is. If we'd seen it first without the fishes or the vase . . .'

One afternoon she comes in from the water, drives over to the fish-shop boat moored at the pier and buys two red fish for dinner. While he is still out sketching she uses his paints, on the glass not on the print, to hide the fishes; she fills the vase with the colours of the water. He sees as soon as he walks back in that they are missing and his face smiles, dark with annoyance at the mutilation of his gift.

'A glass of wine?'

'Thanks. And thanks for proving my point. I suppose next thing you'll go off and paint the vase out.'

'Your point or mine? Look at that bright building. Anyway I have other things to do just now. Such as dinner. What if I bake the fishes?'

'Oh, right? Bake the fishes, eh?'

'They'd taste quite good baked. With herbs in their bellies, stuffed inside the slit, and a little garlic. Lemon juice. Or I could slash and oil them and grill them whole, if you like.'

'Oh, yes. Grill them whole. Great idea.'

'You don't believe me.'

'Have you got loaves as well?'

'See,' And she opens out the wet newspaper.

'Red fishes!'

They are not red-skinned; they have silvery white skin tightly covered in a mesh, a red net with a sheen, densest at the peak at the back. They have a rack of spines and their long-lipped jaws sag. Blood has leaked in and tarnished their ringed eyes; though the pupils you can see into the dim caves of their skulls. At the base of the great wound behind the head and in the skin along the edges of the slit belly is a bluish pearly gleam. Their fins are braided bright vermilion.

Grilled, they are toast-brown with black bubbles and their eyes are white as the flakes of flesh and the skeleton.

Early next morning she has wiped her paint off the glass and the fishes are back. 'Look,' he says, ignoring that, pointing at his mug of tea. '*Poissons bleus.*' The white mugs have a blue fish painted on the outside.

'That room, that window, must be in France. The Côte d'Azur.'

'*Poissons d'azur,*' He turns the print over. 'We could probably find out. Let's see: 1914.'

'Fancy you remembering my birthday.'

'1914?'

'No! The Matisse. Wasn't it for my birthday?'

'Was it your birthday?' He raises his glass. 'I didn't remember. I just thought I'd give it to you. Happy birthday, eh? What does that make you?'

'Older.'

'Indeed. I meant your star sign.'

'You don't know?'

'Don't go in for star signs myself.'

'Pisces!'

'No!'

'You knew.'

'It was pure coincidence.'

'It was fate. Or maybe you were remembering my ring.'

Her ring has a stone, a clear bright bubble of amber with dark flecks, some close to the surface, some resting on the silver bottom. In the silver on each side of the stone a fish is embossed. The two full-lipped identical fishes face opposite ways, so that their movement is a clockwise circling of the stone. She slips her finger in.

'*Poissons d'argent*. Remember it now?'

'Never set eyes on it. Never seen you in a ring.'

'In a ring! No, well, I don't wear it all that often, it's too heavy.'

'Honey turned to stone.'

'I love amber as clear as this. Sometimes it's opaque like butterscotch. Like bottle glass from the sea. They harvest amber on seashores, don't they? On the Baltic, I think I've read. Imagine fossicking for shells and starfish and bottle glass, and suddenly — this! What's your star sign, anyway?'

'Gemini.'

'No!'

'Don't say they're compatible?'

'No idea. They ought to be, though, don't you think? They're both mirror images, twin fish and twin boys. Swan-begotten, water-born. They match.'

They ought to be. Are they? They have moments of felt intimacy, but different ones, that quickly seem to have been illusions. Their conversations leave them stranded in silence. Each is a past love of the other's. Each moves through the house, night and day. They sleep in the one bed. Alone and together they go to the beach, to the dunes. He is a painter. Of interiors? Exteriors? Where to draw the line? She serves as his model. The images of her in his mind are flat, all shape, so much like a sole or a flounder, those moon fish, that it would hardly surprise him if she had a dark underside to match the pearly belly he is labouring on. The shadow where the flesh sags down from the hipbone ... He peers, brush high. His astonishment on first entering her is repeated, though more mildly, every time. Suddenly she is three-dimensional, four, yes; suddenly he finds himself engulfed, embedded in a warm and clinging soft mass moving over and under. His eyes had given him no foreknowledge of this. He is as astonished as if he had fallen into the canvas into this embrace. He could go on pushing more and more of himself in with every thrust, all of himself until he is wholly contained in her. But as if in his thrusting he has touched some giant sting in the deepest part of her, he convulses. And burns, and is paralysed. Later, chilled, he opens his eyes to detach himself carefully. She is glistening and limp in her sleep, glazed, translucent, yes, a stranded jellyfish.

The hair under her arms and between her legs has a damp, mossy savour which stays on his fingers long after she goes back to her pose and he to his easel. Soon he has forgotten what it is that his fingers smell of. The sea comes into his mind. Seaweed on the sand.

The dunes are growing fine long green hairs all over. Their skin shows through.

The waves are the loudest sound in the room at night. Twice she slides out from under the sheet in the dark, pulls a tracksuit on over the damp mass of her body and walks to the lighthouse. Both times the tide is out and so is the moon. Restless, she walks on the sand, peering in pools in the light of the tide-lanterns (green one time, red the other) and of the turning lantern in the great helmet, Orion at its ear. The first time the water is rough, a turbulence of green froth; the next time she slips off the tracksuit and lies in one of her pools, in red-glinting water in which she can only just see herself. Silently she comes back to the room, to the bed with the man in its centre, who sighs in his sleep and turns to lie along her back with a hand on her cold thigh.

One day while she is posing for him she says with a laugh, out of the blue, that when she is ready to go she will end her life here by wading out to sea with the tide. 'Better to end up as sweet strong meat for fishes,' she says. 'Not liquefy in a grave or be dry ashes.'

'Or food for seagulls. Dogs loose on the beach. Feral cats. Rats.'

'Not if you study the tides.'

'What's the difference, if it comes to that?'

'Fish are clean. Clean beasts.'

'Hmm,' he says. And later, staring into space: 'Well, I can't help you with this one, love. Whatever it is. Sorry.'

She sits and watches the fishes. They are two ripples of blood that dissolve and twine, two red whips. In the glass with them are fragments of the hot blue and wheat-brown square with its turret and loophole windows sunk in a slab of shade. The fish gasp; their films of fin flutter in hot mid-air. Their bubbles mirror that other bubble, the vase. They see hollow walls towering and encased in them a red bubble, the woman. She has a long red silk robe on; cool folds and shadows lap her whiteness, trailing loose from her arms down over her feet. She is a shape, a pearl, a vase with handles. Shutting her eyes she sees red silk.

She reaches for a white mug of water on the table inside the room, outside the frame, but the water has gone, the darkness inside is only shadow, hot shadow. He has no recollection of drinking the water. Perhaps it evaporated in the intense heat over the space of the afternoon, or is such a thing not possible? She is not at the moment able to coerce her brain into remembering whether or not it is possible. If it is, though, wouldn't the water in the vase also have to be more than shadow? With the fish lying in draggled lumps on the thick glass of the bottom like the hanks of red seaweed the high tide leaves on the sand?

A blue fish latticed with scales is curled high and dry on the outside of the mug. It has a barbed back and a twin-barbed fan-tail. A shadow of it shows on the inside, inscribed in the white porcelain.

So as not to have to get up for a drink of water, she tells herself she is lying in sea water, in a deep pool of blue rock. Tails of red weed drift rocking around her wrists and ankles. The undersurface of the water is a mirror in which the pool is held and in it she sees that the two red fishes are fluttering at the weedy edges, each following the other and each a mirror of the other. So without turning her head she knows that the vase on the sill is empty for the time being. Empty, that is, of fishes: almost full of empty water.

'Thirsty?' He stretches, finished for now. 'I'll make the tea.'

Sometimes he comes to the beach with her and they swim around each other among the honey-coloured rocks in shallow water flecked with weed on the surface or on the bottom. Wherever he has gone to paint he swims as well, diving in, pounding through the waves until he has cooled off. She lies in pools and dries off in the sun, moving up and down the beach with the tide.

'There was a Matisse book in the local library,' he says one evening at a restaurant with a mirror wall facing east over the sea. 'I had a look. It's got your picture in it, but called *Interior with Goldfish.*'

'Not, "Vase"? Oh well, yes. Different translators. And the vase being *their* interior as well makes it a double interior. That's nice.'

'He did a whole series of goldfish paintings. There was a Moroccan one with *three* fishes, and a *Woman and Goldfish* with four, yellow ones. He *was* in Nice in 1914 but he came back for the winter to 19 Quai St-Michel and there he painted ...'

'He painted it in winter! Then he had summer in mind. *Quai*

St-Michel, did you say? On the Seine? The arch is a bridge, then! No, it can't be, it's not wide enough. But then — '

'That would be the span that crosses to the Ile de la Cité.'

'Oh, then the arch is the Pont Neuf? No. It can't be.'

'Pont St-Michel?'

'If you could see that smirk! Okay, then, what's the building?'

'With the morning sun on it?'

'Afternoon — '

'Whatever. I don't know for sure. I wish I could remember. The Palais de Justice is over there, and Notre-Dame, but facing the other way. So it has to be the Louvre. Over on the Right Bank.'

'I see. You wish you could remember!'

'I can't, sad to say. I consulted the *Blue Guide.*'

'The *Blue Guide!*' She stares. 'You went to all that trouble!'

'No, no trouble, it was a pleasure. It brought Paris back.'

'I see. So, now we know. This was a certain room, in Paris, in the winter of 1914.'

'It was that roof, that steep slate roof that — '

'Oh, stop it, will you.'

'Sorry?'

'You and your *Blue Guide!*'

'*Guide bleu. Guide d'azur.* What's got into you?'

'Nothing. Nothing. Now if I ever go to Paris again I can make my little pilgrimage to the Quai St-Michel, can't I? Armed with my *Guide bleu.* And go and see the original at the Pompidou Centre — right? Though the original, don't forget, is much larger and for all we know its colours are different. So often with prints... *My* print is still a window in summer on the Côte d'Azur. It's an interior of the *mind* —'

'Complete with goldfish — '

'Where it's as hot as here. And close to the sea. That blue in the air: clearly it comes from water — '

'The Seine — '

'And its light is the same as in the vase. It's a submerged room.'

The window and the mirror brim over with water. There is a haze of pink over the town on the hill, its black roofs and trees and lighthouse, and over the water. From behind it rises a faint pink balloon turning small, cold and sharp in mid-air.

The tide is going out when they walk round under the cliff to the lighthouse on the point. Its red glass panels and the dark clear ones that face out to sea enclose a lantern like a gold beehive, a Chinese paper lantern staining the ceiling with a light no brighter than the lamps in houses. Dark shapes wander on the walls inside. The sky is red-gold. Beyond the last rim of the rock pools a ship low in the water carries its girdle of lights away, its red smokestack like a candle burning.

In the morning she wakes knowing before she sees that all his things are gone. She thinks there is no message left for her this time, no small painting to keep. But there is one of each. One on the table he has scribbled on the back of an envelope:

> *A thick gloom fell through the sunshine and*
> *darken'd me,*
> *Must I change my triumphant songs? said I to myself,*
> *Must I indeed learn to chant the cold dirges of the*
> *baffled?*
> *And sullen hymns of defeat?*

> Walt Whitman

And on the Matisse, one of the red fishes has been perfectly painted out. She peers: yes, perfectly. Not on the glass, on the print. The other fish hangs ringed in its glass and reflected there it glimpses fragments of red-gold, an apparition, a sufficient self.

THE DROVER'S WIFE

Murray Bail

The Drover's Wife (1945)

There has perhaps been a mistake — but of no great importance — made in the denomination of this picture. The woman depicted is not 'The Drover's Wife'. She is my wife. We have not seen each other now... it must be getting on thirty years. This portrait was painted shortly after she left — and had joined him. Notice she has very conveniently hidden her wedding hand. It is a canvas 20 × 24 inches, signed l/r 'Russell Drysdale'.

I say 'shortly after' because she has our small suitcase — Drysdale has made it look like a shopping bag — and she is wearing the sandshoes she normally wore to the beach. Besides, it is dated 1945.

It is Hazel all right.

How much can you tell by a face? That a woman has left a husband and two children? Here, I think the artist has fallen down (though how was he to know?). He has Hazel with a resigned helpless expression — as if it was all my fault. Or, as if she had been a country woman all her ruddy life.

Otherwise the likeness is fair enough.

Hazel was large-boned. Our last argument I remember concerned her weight. She weighed — I have the figures — 12 st. 4 ozs. And she wasn't exactly tall. I see that she put it back on almost immediately. It doesn't take long. See her legs.

She had a small, pretty face, I'll give her that. I was always surprised by her eyes. How solemn they were. The painting shows that. Overall, a gentle face, one that other women liked. How long it must have lasted up in the drought conditions is anybody's guess.

A drover! Why a drover? It has come as a shock to me.

'I am just going round the corner,' she wrote characteristically. It was a piece of butcher's paper left on the table.

Then, and this sounded odd at the time: 'Your tea's in the oven. Don't give Trev any carrots.'

Now that sounded as if she wouldn't be back, but after puzzling over it, I dismissed it.

And I think that is what hurt me most. No. 'Dear' at the top, not even 'Gordon'. No 'love' at the bottom. Hazel left without so much as a goodbye. We could have talked it over.

Adelaide is a small town. People soon got to know. They ... shied away. I was left alone to bring up Trevor and Kay. It took a long time — years — before, if asked, I could say: 'She vamoosed. I haven't got a clue to where.'

Fancy coming across her in a painting, one reproduced in colour at that. I suppose in a way that makes Hazel famous.

The pictures gives little away though. It is the outback — but where exactly? South Australia? It could easily be Queensland, Western Australia, the Northern Territory. We don't know. You could never find that spot.

He is bending over (feeding?) the horse, so it is around dusk. This is borne out by the length of Hazel's shadow. It is probably in the region of 5 p.m. Probably still over the hundred mark. What a place to spend the night. The silence would have already begun.

Hazel looks unhappy. I can see she is having second thoughts. All right, it was soon after she had left me; but she is standing away, in the foreground, as though they're not speaking. See that? Distance = doubts. They've had an argument.

Of course, I want to know all about him. I don't even know his name. In Drysdale's picture he is a silhouette. A completely black figure. He could have been an Aboriginal; by the late forties I understand some were employed as drovers.

But I rejected that.

I took a magnifying glass. I wanted to see the expression on his face. What colour is his hair? Magnified, he is nothing but brush strokes. A real mystery man.

It is my opinion, however, that he is a small character. See his size in relation to the horse, to the wheels of the cart. Either that, or it is a ruddy big horse.

It begins to fall into place.

I had an argument with our youngest, Kay, the other day. Both she and Trevor sometimes visit me. I might add, she hasn't married and has her mother's general build. She was blaming me, said people said mum was a good sort.

Right. I nodded.

'Then why did she scoot?'

'Your mother,' I said thinking quickly, 'had a silly streak.'

If looks could kill!

I searched around — 'She liked to paddle in water!'

Kay gave a nasty laugh. 'What? You're the limit. You really are.'

Of course, I hadn't explained properly. And I didn't even know then she had gone off with a drover.

Hazel was basically shy, even with me: quiet, generally non-committal. At the same time, I can imagine her allowing herself to be painted so soon after running off without leaving even a phone number or forwarding address. It fits. It sounds funny, but it does.

This silly streak. Heavy snow covered Mt Barker for the first time and we took the Austin up on the Sunday. From a visual point of view it was certainly remarkable. Our gum trees and stringy barks somehow do not go with the white stuff, not even the old Ghost Gum. I mentioned this to Hazel but she just ran into it and began chucking snowballs at me. People were laughing. Then she fell in up to her knees, squawking like a schoolgirl. I didn't mean to speak harshly, but I went up to her, 'Come on, don't be stupid. Get up.' She went very quiet. She didn't speak for hours.

Kay of course wouldn't remember that.

With the benefit of hindsight, and looking at this portrait by Drysdale, I can see Hazel had a soft side. I think I let her clumsiness get me down. The sight of sweat patches under her arms, for example, somehow put me in a bad mood. It irritated me the way she chopped wood. I think she enjoyed chopping wood. There was the time I caught her lugging into the house the ice for the ice chest — this is just after the war. The ice man didn't seem to notice; he was following, working out his change. It somehow made her less attractive in my eyes, I don't know why. And then of course she killed that snake down at the beach shack we took one Christmas. I happened to lift the lid of the incinerator — a black brute, its head bashed in. 'It was under the house,' she explained.

It was a two-roomed shack, bare floorboards. It had a primus stove, and an asbestos toilet down the back. Hazel didn't mind. Quite the contrary; when it came time to leave she was downcast. I had to be at town for work.

The picture reminds me. It was around then Hazel took to wearing just a slip around the house. And bare feet. The dress in the picture looks like a slip. She even used to burn rubbish in it down the back.

I don't know.

'Hello, missus!' I used to say, entering the kitchen. Not perfect perhaps, especially by today's standards, but that is my way of showing affection. I think Hazel understood. Sometimes I could see she was touched.

I mention that to illustrate our marriage was not all nitpicking and argument. When I realized she had gone I sat for nights in the lounge with the lights out. I am a dentist. You can't have shaking hands and be a dentist. The word passes around. Only now, touch wood, has the practice picked up to any extent.

Does this explain at all why she left?

Not really.

To return to the picture. Drysdale has left out the flies. No doubt he didn't want Hazel waving her hand, or them crawling over her face. Nevertheless, this is a serious omission. It is altering the truth for the sake of a pretty picture, or 'composition'. I've been up around there — and there are hundreds of flies. Not necessarily germ carriers, 'bush flies' I think these are called; and they drive you mad. Hazel of course accepted everything without a song and dance. She didn't mind the heat, or the flies.

It was a camping holiday. We had one of those striped beach tents shaped like a bell. I thought at the time it would prove handy — visible from the air — if we got lost. Now that is a point. Although I will never forget the colours and the assortment of rocks I saw up there I have no desire to return, none, I realized one night. Standing a few yards from the tent, the cavernous sky and the silence all round suddenly made me shudder. I felt lost. It defied logic. And during the day the bush, which is small and prickly, offered no help (I was going to say 'sympathy'). It was stinking hot.

Yet Hazel was in her element, so much so she seemed to take no interest in the surroundings. She acted as if she were part of it. I felt ourselves moving apart, as if I didn't belong there, especially with her. I felt left out. My mistake was to believe it was a passing phase, almost a form of indolence on her part.

An unfortunate incident didn't help. We were looking for a camp site. 'Not yet. No, not there,' I kept saying — mainly to myself, for Hazel let me go on, barely saying a word. At last I found a spot. A tree showing in the dark. We bedded down. Past midnight we were woken by a terrifying noise and lights. The children all began to cry. I had pitched camp alongside the Adelaide-Port Augusta railway line.

Twenty or thirty miles north of Port Augusta I turned back. I had to. We seemed to be losing our senses. We actually met a drover somewhere around there. He was off on the side making tea. When I asked where were his sheep, or the cattle, he gave a wave of his hand. For some reason this amused Hazel. She squatted down. I can still see her expression, silly girl.

The man didn't say much. He did offer tea though. 'Come on,' said Hazel, smiling up at me.

Hazel and her silly streak — she knew I wanted to get back. The drover, a diplomat, poked at the fire with a stick.

I said:

'You can if you want. I'll be in the car.'

That is all.

I recall the drover as a thin head in a khaki hat, not talkative, with dusty boots. He is indistinct. Is it him? I don't know. Hazel — it is Hazel and the rotten landscape that dominate everything.

THE DROVER'S WIFE

Frank Moorhouse

Memo Editor:

Chief, I picked this paper up while hanging out at the Conference on Commonwealth Writing in Milan. This Italian student, Franco Casamaggiore, seems to be onto something. As far as I know it's a scoop, me being the only press around. I'd go with it as the cover story if I were you. This study of Australian culture is a big deal here in Europe — twenty-six universities have courses on Australian writing. I'm hanging out angling for a professorship or something like that. This Casamaggiore has got a few of his facts wrong, but the subs can pick those up. Great stuff, eh! He could do for the Merino what Blainey did for Asians. (The inspired Suzanne Kiernan helped me with the translation.)

CONFERENCE PAPER BY FRANCO CASAMAGGIORE

The writing of a story called *The Drover's Wife* by Henry Lawson in 1893, the painting of a picture called *The Drover's Wife* by Russell Drysdale in 1945, and the writing of another story by the same name in 1975, by Murray Bail, draws our attention to what I will argue in this paper, is an elaborate example of a national culture joke, an 'insider joke' for those who live in that country — in this example, the country of Australia. Each of these works has the status of an Australian classic and each of these works, I will show, contains a joking wink in the direction of the Australian people which they understand but which non-Australians do not. The joke draws on the colloquial Australian humour surrounding the idea of a drover's 'wife'.

First, a few notations of background for those who are un-
familiar with Australian folklore and the occupation of a drover,
which is corruption of the word 'driver'. The drover or driver
of sheep literally drove the sheep to market. The sheep, because
of health regulations governing strictly the towns and cities
of Australia, were kept many kilometres inland from the sea-
market towns. The sheep had then to be 'driven' by the driver
or drover from inland to the towns, often many thousands of
kilometres, taking many months. I am told that this practice
has ceased and the sheep are now housed in the cities in high-
rise pens.

The method of driving the sheep was that each sheep individ-
ually was placed in a wicker basket on the backs of bullock-drawn
wagons known as the woollen wagons. This preserved the sheep
in good condition for the market. These bullocks, it is said, could
pull the sheep to the coast without human guidance, if needed,
being able, of course, to smell the sea. But the sheep had to be
fed and the drover or driver would give water and seed to the
sheep during the journey. The wagon in the Drysdale painting
is horse-drawn, denoting a poorer peasant-class of drover. The
wagon in the painting would probably hold a thousand sheep in
wicker baskets.

Now the length of the journey and the harshness of conditions
precluded the presence of women and the historical fact is that
for a century or more there were no women in this pioneering
country. This, understandably, led men to seek other solace in
this strange new country. Australian historians acknowledge the
closeness of men under this conditions of pioneering and have
described it as mateship, or a pledging of unspoken alliance
between two men, a marriage with vows unspoken.

Quite naturally too, with the drover or driver, a close and
special relationship grew between him and his charges who
became an object for emotional and physical drives, but this
remains unacknowledged by historians for reasons of national
shame, but is widely acknowledged by the folk culture of Australia. And now acknowledged by art. Interspecies reciprocity.
Hence the joke implicit in the use of two writers and a painter
of the title *The Drover's Wife* and the entry of this unacceptable
historical truth from the oral culture to high culture via coded
humour and until this paper (which I modestly consider a
breakthrough study) absent from academic purview.

I elicited the first inkling of this from answers received to
questions asked of Australian visitors to Italia about the sheep

droving. First, I should explain. Unfortunately, I am a poor student living in a humble two-room tugurio. It is a necessity for me to work in the bar of the Hotel Principe e Savoia in Milano and for a time before that, in the Gritti Palace Hotel Venezia. If the authorities would provide more funds for education in this country maybe Italia would regain its rightful place at the forefront of world culture. But I wander from my point. This experience in the bar work gave me the opportunity on many occasions to talk and question visiting Australians, although almost always men.

There is an Australian humour of the coarse peasant type not unknown in Italia. Without becoming involved in these details it is necessary for me to document some of the information harvested from contact with the Australian, not having been to the country at first hand — thanks to the insufficiency of funds from the educational authorities in Italia — however, my brother Giovanni is living there in Adelaide, but is not any help in such matters, knowing nothing of the droving or culture and knowing only of the price of things and the Holden automobile. Knowing nothing of things of the spirit. You are wrong, Giovanni.

Yes, but to continue. A rubber shoe or boot used when hunting in wet weather called the gun boot was used by the drovers or drivers and found to be a natural love aid while at the same time a symbol used in a gesture of voluntary submission by the drover before his charge.

The boots were placed on the hind legs of the favoured sheep. The drover would be shoeless like the sheep and the sheep would 'wear the boots' (cf. 'wearing pants' in marriage). The toe of the boots would be turned towards the drover who would stand on the toes of the boot thus holding the loved sheep close to him in embrace. These details suffice.

According to my Australian informants the sheep often formed an emotional attachment to the drover who reciprocated. But the journey to the coast had its inherent romantic tragedy. The long journey and shared hardship, shared shelter, and kilometres of companionship, daily took them closer to the tragic conclusion with the inevitable death of the loved one through the workings of capitalist market forces. But also the return of the drover's natural drives to his own species as he re-entered the world of people. And the limited vision of the anti-life Church.

'Why not dogs?' comes the question. Close questioning of my Australian sources suggests that dogs as bed companions was characteristic of the Aboriginal and thus for reasons of racial prejudice considered beneath the Australian white man. The sheep from Europe was a link with the homelands from whence he had migrated and further, I speculate, that the maternal bulk of the merino sheep, with its woolly coat and large soft eyes, its comforting bleat, offered more feminine solace than the lean dog with fleas. Again, on this and other matters, Giovanni is of no assistance being concerned only with his Holden automobile and the soccer football. The unimaginative reaction of the educational authorities for research funding for this project indicts our whole system of education in this country.

Returning now to the art works under study. In Henry Lawson's story the woman character lives out her life *as if she were a sheep*. She is not given a name — in English animal husbandry it is customary to give cows names (from botany) and domestic pets are named, but not sheep. The scholar Keith Thomas says that a shepherd however, could recognise his sheep by their faces. She is penned up in her outback fold, unable to go anywhere. Her routines of the day resemble closely the life of a sheep and it can be taken that this is a literary transformation for the sake of propriety. She tells in the story how she was taken to the city a few times in a 'compartment', as is the sheep. In the absence of her drover husband she is looked after by a dog, as is a sheep. The climax of the Henry Lawson story is the 'killing of the snake' which needs no Doctor Freud, being the expression of a savage and guilt-ridden male detumescence (in Australia the male genitalia is referred to in folklore, as the 'one-eyed trouser snake'. The Australian folk language is much richer than its European counterpart, which is in state of decay). I am told that to this day, Australian men are forever killing the snake. The drover is absent from the story, a point to be taken up later.

In the Drysdale painting (1945) oddly and fascinatingly, there are no sheep. Then we realise uneasily that it is as if they have been swept up into a single image overwhelming the foreground — the second drover's 'wife'. This unusually shaped woman is, on second glance, in the form of a sheep, a merino sheep, the painter having given her the same maternal physical bulk as the merino. Her shadow forms the shape of a sheep. Again, the drover is all but absent. He is a background smudge. The snake, you ask? In the trees we find the serpents. They writhe before our eyes.

Murray Bail is a modern Australian long removed from the days of pioneering and droving. However, his biography reveals

his father was a drover, but our discipline requires us to
ard this fact when considering his work of art. In his
contemporary story he pays homage both to the Drysdale
painting and the Lawson story. In the Bail story the woman
is referred to as having one defining characteristic, what author
Bail calls a 'silly streak'. This is a characteristic traditionally
ascribed to sheep (cf. 'woolly minded'). The woman figure in
this Bail story, or precisely the 'sheep figure', wanders in a
motiveless way; strays, as it were; away from the city and her
dentist husband. Curious it is to note that she flees the man
whose work it is to care for the teeth which are the instruments
used to eat the sheep, and for the sheep, symbol of death. Recall:
the journey from the inland paradise in the protection of a loving
drover to the destination of death: the city and the slaughterhouse
and finally the teeth of the hungry city. In the Bail story the
woman goes from the arms of her natural predator, the one
who cares for the predator's teeth — the dentist — into the
arms of the natural protector, the drover or driver. The Bail
story reverses the tragedy and turns it to romantic comedy.
Again, the drover himself is absent from the story. The Bail
story also has a 'killing of the snake'.

So, in all three works of High Art under discussion we have
three women clearly substituting (for reasons of propriety) for
sheep, but coded in such a way as to lead us, through the term
'drover's wife' back into the folk culture and its joke. And we
note that in the three works there is *no drover*. This is a reversal
of situation, an inside-out-truth, for we know historically that
there was a drover but there was historically *no wife*, not in
any acceptable conventional sense.

The question comes, given that the drover has a thousand
sheep in his care, how did the drover choose, from that thousand,
just one mate? This question, intriguing and bizarre at the same
time, was put to my Australian sources. Repeatedly I also ask
Giovanni to ask the other men at GMH factory, but he has
a head that is too full of materialism to concern himself with
exploration of the mythology of this new culture.

How was the sheep chosen? But as in all matters of the human
emotion the answer comes blindingly plain. It was explained
to me that it is very much like being in a crowded lift, or in
a prison, or on board a ship. In a situation of confinement it
is instinctive for people to single out one another from the herd.
There is communication by eye, an eye-mating, the search for
firstly, mate, and then community. The same it is with sheep,

my Australian sources tell me (thanks to educational authorities in Italia I have no chance to research this first hand). In the absence of human contact the eyes wander across species, the eyes meet, the eyes and ewes (that is English language pun).

Yes, and the question comes, was I being fooled about by these Australian visitors and their peasant humour after they had drunk perhaps too much? Was I being 'taken in' as they, the Australians, say. I ask in return — were the Australian visitors telling more than they knew or wanted to tell? The joking is a form of truth telling, a way of confession. They were also, by joking with my questions, trying to make me look away from my enquiry. To joke away something that was too painfully serious. But they were also telling me what they did not wish me to know as outsider, for the confession is precisely this, and brings relief. They experience an undefined relief from their joking about such matters — that is, the relief of confession. I let them joke at me for it was a joke to which I listened not them. This is the manoeuvre of the national joke, the telling and the not telling at the same time. So yes, I was being 'taken in' by my Australian sources — 'taken in' to the secret. Taken in to their confidence.

We are told that humour has within it the three dialogues. The dialogue between the teller and the listener, where the teller is seeking approval and giving a gift at the same time. The dialogue between the teller's unconscious mind and his voice, to which the teller cannot always listen. The dialogue between the joker, teller, and the racial memory which is embodied in the language and the type of joke the teller chooses to tell, the well of humour from which the joker must draw his bucket of laughter. Humour is the underground route that taboo material — or material of national shame — must travel, and it is the costume it must wear.

Today such relations between sheep and men are, of course, rare in Australia. However, the racial memory of those stranger and more primitive days — days closer, can we say, to nature and a state of grace — still lingers. It is present in a number of ways. As illustrated, it is present in the elaborate cultural joke of High Art. The art which winks. It is there in the peasant humour of the male Australian, the joke which confesses. It is present, I would argue (here I work from photographs and cinema) in the weekly ritual called 'mowing the lawn'. On one afternoon of the weekend the Australian male takes off grass from his suburban garden which in earlier times would have been fodder for the sheep — this is an urban 'hay-making ritual', Australian city man's last connection with agriculture. But, alas, his sheep is gone, and the grass, the hay, is burned, to a memory of an association all but forgotten. Finally, I am told that there is an Australian national artefact — the sheepskin with wool attached. It is used often as a seat cover in the automobile. That today the driver or drover of a car sits (or lies) with sheep, as it were, under him while driving not a flock of sheep but a family in a modern auto. It gives comfort through racial memory far exceeding the need for warmth in that temperate land. The car sheepskin covering is an emotional trophy from the sexual underworld of the Australian past. The artefact which remembers.

Naturally, all this is still not an open subject for academic explicitness in Australia and it is only here in Italia where such candour can be enjoyed with our perspective of centuries — and our knowledge of such things. But I say, Australia — be not ashamed of that which is bizarre, seek not always the genteel. Remember that we, the older cultures, have myths which also acknowledge such happenings of interspecies reciprocity (cf Jason and Search for Golden Fleece). See in these happenings the beginnings of your own mythology. See it as an affirmation of the beautiful truth — that we share the planet with animals and we are partners, therefore in its destiny.

So, in Lawson, Drysdale and Bail, we see how High Art in this new culture, admits a message of unspeakable truth (albeit, in a coded and guilty way), this being the ploy of all great national cultures.

Thus is the magic of the imagination.

At the Picasso Exhibition

Brian Matthews

EARLY WORK 1895-1900, BLUE AND ROSE PERIODS 1900-1906

— Jesus, Irma, you could have warned me!

He said it loudly enough to make three people ahead of them turn around.

— I told you it would be fairly expensive. I told you that. But anyway, it's not as if we often —

— Fairly! Twelve dollars for two of us to see a few paintings? *Fairly!* Jesus.

She stared without seeing at *Peasant Woman/Paysanne*, as if by looking away, by withdrawing her attention from him, she could somehow stop the words. In this way she found herself shuffling past *The Two Men/Les Deux Hommes* and the bearded man and the peasant woman with her child caught in one curved arm (but did notice with a second glance as the queue's ponderous momentum drifted her irresistibly past, the weight of the pitcher straightening the woman's left arm and fowls pecking about at her feet; and, noticing, experienced an intensely poignant memory of holidays with her parents in the country all those years ago, when a trip to the Dandenongs was like an outback expedition). Feeling rushed, wanting to go back and check *The Artist's Sister/La Soeur de l'artiste* because of the red light at the window-pane and the pointiness of the girl's nose, she stood, free of crowd at last because once clear of the entrance people were fanning out, in front of a nude woman. A yellowish, square-faced nude woman.

Harry came up alongside her.

— Look, I was only pointing out that —

— I know what you were pointing out, Harry. We shouldn't have come. I'm sorry. It *is* expensive and it's probably a mistake anyway. It's my fault. I'm sorry. I just thought it might be nice to see something a bit different. And together. See something — something *new* together, and — sort of — learn it together. I'm sorry.

— Well, this'd take a bit of learning, Irm. I mean, look at her...

He pointed towards the *Reclining Nude/Nue couchée*.

— ...she'd kill a man. The thighs!

My thighs, she thought, are heavy too, now. And my bust isn't nearly as high and as rounded as hers. And sometimes, she added to herself, I feel yellowish all over — like her. He must mean the colour to show...

But she couldn't put into words what he meant the colour to show.

Harry's tolerance as he walked from picture to picture beside her was almost touchable. And whenever she looked across at him, he would be grinning; it might be because of what he saw — like the pubic bulge and hair smudge of one of the women in the circus performer sketches, or the pendulous balls of the circus clown; but mostly, it was to show that he *didn't mind*, that not even a peak of lunacy like this visit to the Picasso Exhibition would diminish his devotion to her. And he *was* devoted. She knew that.

All in the one instant she felt for him love, guilty sadness, and a depth of anger whose fleeting violence astounded her.

CUBISM 1907-22

— Not like any woman I've ever come across, joked Harry in front of *Head of a woman/Tête de femme*, or want to for that matter. I mean. No, seriously, love, what's he on about? No one looks like that. Y'know?

Behind her silence and shrug of agreement to assure Harry of fellow-feeling, she mused: that's the way she feels, perhaps, her face all blocks and sections, the way you think you must look when you're — telling a lie, or hiding grief. Blocky. Lumpy. And green; with blotches of dark red.

— It's the way *I* feel, she said. At those times.

— What? asked Harry, half-hearing her and wondering if it mattered.

— No, it's all right, she said. Nothing.

As they both stopped in front of a tapering series of angles and quadrilaterals — *Half-length female nude/femme nue*, read the French with catastrophic simplicity. Harry's grinning, knowing look was eloquent. This was beyond description, did not require insult. Irma sensed that the lines of her face were turning to edges, becoming squared; her shoulder blades were slopes ending in points and angles, her breasts and the smooth downward outlines of her waist and hips had turned jagged, were squares, leaning rectangles, shape-assortments. She was all edges, points, hard lines tilting, a geometry of frustration. Graduations of green against a background of green, she waited. A just-warm light, three removes from the sun yet of the sun, played about her angularity: at, perhaps, groin level.

— Harry, you go on, she said, returning to herself. You go ahead and I'll catch you up. I'm all at sea too, but I'll just look about a bit more — you know. But you go ahead.

— No worries, he said, grinning. We'll battle it out together, then have a counter lunch. I promised you.

Irma sighed, took his arm and they moved on.

She was pleased and excited to identify the voluptuous feminine curves within the austere planes of *Woman in a corset reading a book* and she pointed them out to Harry. But Harry's grin was now, had he but known it, as ghastly as the rictus sported by each of the *Three Skulls/Trois crânes* which lay in wait for them further on (the 1930s and the War Years); and so, he was incapable of response.

REALISM, NEO-CLASSICISM AND THE 1920s

Olga Koklova's black, problematical eyes held Irma stunned and motionless while the crowd parted to pass her and joined up again beyond her like the sea surging round a rock. *Portrait of Olga Koklova/Portrait d'Olga Koklova.* Irma consumed the picture: the tilt of the woman's head, the strong muscular arms, the fall of the dress in creases from her shoulders and hips. She thought: if you look only at the mouth, if you cut out the rest of her face for a minute, then the mouth is — sad. Perhaps sour. Bitter? Who was Olga Koklova? She wished, again, that they had bought a catalogue; but ten dollars on top of the entrance fee had been unthinkable as far as Harry was concerned and she hadn't pressed the point. But someone passing by her just at that moment said: One of his wives. Irma wanted to put a hand out and cover the face so that everyone could see the line of the mouth.

Harry was nowhere to be seen. A sudden glut of people near the end of Cubism 1907-22 had separated them because he had been a little way ahead of her, impatient she knew to be through with the multiplying and mystifying succession of shapes. Irma was quite mystified too, as she said to him several times; yet he seemed unwilling to share, seemed almost angry with the paintings. His developing mood puzzled her quite as much as any of the paintings, in whose presence (the mellow, earthy tones of *Landscape at Ceret/Paysage de Céret*, the oval, peculiar 'Guitar' pictures) she felt a curious peacefulness, as if Picasso, by looking at the world in such an odd and unexpected way, had released her from the necessity to worry about it.

— Olga Koklova, she said aloud. And a woman passing nearby looked across at her, sharply.

Reclining Bather/Baigneuse Étendue. No one else seemed embarrassed, yet Irma felt sure she was seeing what she thought she was seeing. It was not just the two sparkly protuberant, pointy, red-nippled breasts; it was the rest . . . she felt certain it must mean . . . between her legs; between the sunbather's legs. Suddenly Irma knew — knew with an excitement that made her feel strange and certainly caused a *feeling* not describable between her *own* legs — that the bather had such a small head, a ridiculous blob of a head, because sunbathers stretched out on the sand were all about breasts and . . . and:

Cunt, she said inside her head. *Cunt.*

Not about faces, but about breasts and nipples and . . . cunt.

She was blushing, she knew, in front of the angular bather. A rush of desire ran through her whole body. Welled up in her. Not for anyone in particular. Not for Harry. But just for physical contact, for guiltless abandonment. In imagination she saw herself arching up at someone, thrusting in return . . .

Irma turned and walked on, threading the crowd; feeling hot: and damp in various places. *Woman, full length/Femme en pied; Head of a Woman/Tête de Femme.* And so to

THE 1930s AND THE WAR YEARS

and Harry appearing all at once in front of her, wanting to know where she had been and then, as he looked at her, what was the matter and why wouldn't she answer and what was the matter?

— I'm sorry, she said.

Side by side they went, Harry worrying and wanting to check with her, into a world of sensuously sleeping women — and Irma knew now why you could see *all* of their bodies; breasts and bottoms and underarms and cunts all at once, even though really you wouldn't have been able to — and a world of writhing horses and angry bull's heads and horned, animal-headed men towering over waiting women. She lost Harry again briefly when she walked back against the gallery tide for a last look at the sad, vulnerable monstrousness of *Woman weeping/La Pleureuse*, but caught up with him in

LATE PICASSO

where he stood looking at a stick-like bronze figure with its penis pointing stiffly out, long and blunt. .

— *Young man*, read Harry, then, leaning closer to her ear: y'd have to be young to get it up like that.

Then there were nudes, seated, reclining, holding a bird or flower; all shamelessly revealing. So moved that tears prickled at her eyes, Irma felt at the same time passionate, intensely sexual. Walking along prim at Harry's side, going too fast now to see the pictures properly because she knew they would really *have* to leave, she ran phantom-imaged hands over her body which seemed to ripple with exquisite tremors that surely anyone with half an eye would notice.

— What's the matter? asked Harry. As he walked, he leaned towards her, anxious. What's up, Irm?

EXIT

Out on the footpath among the noise of trams and the chatter of a school party milling round two harassed teachers, a cold wind gusted at their clothes and wintry sunlight made them squint after the calculated gloom of the gallery.

— We're pretty well on time, Harry said, starting to walk towards Princes Bridge and stretching out one arm to usher Irma along with him.

— Harry, I think I'll give the lunch a miss. Do you mind? It's just that I . . .

Someone brushed past them and a snippet of conversation hung a moment: Fum noo, said the person.

Irma realised that that must be the way you said *Femme*

nue and remembered the thick thighs, the high round breasts, the yellowish skin.

— Fum noo, she said, just above a whisper. Fum noo.

— What the hell's the matter with you this morning? Harry's patience had cracked.

— What d'you mean y'not coming to lunch? What're y'mutterin' about? C'mon, let's get going. Irma! For Chris' sake.

— Harry, I really don't feel very well. I'd rather go home. I'm sorry. You go on though. Snowy and Dell will be there. You know they will — that's why you arranged for the Commercial Club for lunch. So you'll have company. I'll be OK. I'll pop home.

They argued a little till Harry, quite hurt, puzzled because he didn't believe she felt ill, and angry without understanding why, finally gave up and strode off towards the city. He always looked back and waved to her at such partings, or blew the car horn if he was driving off; but this time he walked a long way and was almost indistinguishable in the lunchtime crowd before, as if finding it impossible not to relent, he raised his arm to her in the distance.

As soon as he was out of sight, she asked the door attendant if she could go back into the gallery foyer for a minute. He watched her with great suspicion as she strode to the counter and handed over ten dollars for a catalogue.

Back outside, she flicked through the thick, glossy book, recognizing barest glimpses of lineaments and figures and faces. The pages jumped too quickly past her thumb and she found herself looking at the last one. There was rough, hasty-looking printing on it, like chalk on a blackboard:

ACTUALLY, EVERYTHING DEPENDS ON ONESELF. IT'S THE SUN IN THE BELLY WITH A MILLION RAYS. THE REST IS NOTHING...

Irma felt such a lovely sob in her chest that it was almost painful to hold it back. She thought she would have to sing or shout out.

— Fum noo, she said; and several people glanced up with surprised amusement at the flourishing swing of her small, dowdily-dressed figure as she tucked the catalogue under her arm and set off against the plucking of the wind.

THE EMPTY LUNCH-TIN

David Malouf

He had been there for a long time. She could not remember when she had last looked across the lawn and he was not standing in the wide, well-clipped expanse between the buddleia and the flowering quince, his shoulders sagging a little, his hands hanging limply at his side. He stood very still with his face lifted towards the house, as a tradesman waits who has rung the doorbell, received no answer, and hopes that someone will appear at last at an upper window. He did not seem in a hurry. Heavy bodies barged through the air, breaking the stillness with their angular cries. Currawongs. Others hopped about on the grass, their tails switching from side to side. Black metronomes. He seemed unaware of them. Originally the shadow of the house had been at his feet, but it had drawn back before him as the morning advanced, and he stood now in a wide sunlit space casting his own shadow. Behind him cars rushed over the warm bitumen, station-wagons in which children were being ferried to school or kindergarten, coloured delivery vans, utilities — there were no fences here; the garden was open to the street. He stood. And the only object between him and the buddleia was an iron pipe that rose two feet out of the lawn like a periscope.

At first, catching sight of him as she passed the glass wall of the dining-room, the slight figure with its foreshortened shadow, she had given a sharp little cry. Greg! And it might have been Greg standing there with only the street behind him. He would have been just that age. Doubting her own perceptions, she had gone right up to the glass and stared. But Greg had been dead for seven years; she knew that with the part of her mind that observed this stranger, though she had never accepted it in that other half where the boy was still going on into the fullness of his life, still growing, so that she knew just how he had looked at fifteen, seventeen, and how he would look now at twenty.

This young man was quite unlike him. Stoop-shouldered, intense, with clothes that didn't quite fit, he was shabby, and it was the shabbiness of poverty not fashion. In his loose flannel trousers with turnups, collarless shirt and wide-brimmed felt hat, he might have been from the country or from another era. Country people dressed like that. He looked, she thought, the way young men had looked in her childhood, men who were out of work.

Thin, pale, with the sleeves half-rolled on his wiry forearms, he must have seen her come up to the glass and note his presence, but he wasn't at all intimidated.

Yes, that's what he reminded her of: the Depression years, and those men, one-armed or one-legged some of them, others dispiritingly whole, who had haunted the street corners of her childhood, wearing odd bits of uniform with their civilian castoffs and offering bootlaces or pencils for sale. Sometimes when you answered the back doorbell, one of them would be standing there on the step. A job was what he was after: mowing or cleaning out drains, or scooping the leaves from the blocked downpipe, or mending shoes — anything to save him from mere charity. When there was, after all, no job to be done, they simply stood, those men, as this man stood, waiting for the offer to be made of a cup of tea with a slice of bread and jam, or the scrapings from a bowl of dripping, or if you could spare it, the odd sixpence — it didn't matter what or how much, since the offering was less important in itself than the unstinting recognition of their presence, and beyond that, a commonness between you. As a child she had stood behind lattice doors in the country town she came from and watched transactions between her mother and those men, and had thought to herself: *This is one of the rituals. There is a way of doing this so that a man's pride can be saved, but also your own.* But when she grew up the Depression was over. Instead, there was the war. She had never had to use any of that half-learned wisdom.

She walked out now onto the patio and looked at the young man, with just air rather than plate glass between them.

He still wasn't anyone she recognised, but he had moved slightly, and as she stood there silently observing — it must have been for a good while — she saw that he continued to move. He was turning his face to the sun. He was turning with the sun, as a plant does, and she thought that if he decided to stay and put down roots she might get used to him. After all, why a buddleia or a flowering quince and not a perfectly ordinary young man?

She went back into the house and decided to go on with her housework. The house didn't need doing, since there were just two of them, but each day she did it just the same. She began with the furniture in the lounge, dusting and polishing, taking care not to touch the electronic chess-set that was her husband's favourite toy and which she was afraid of disturbing — no, she was actually afraid of *it*. Occupying a low table of its own, and surrounded by lamps, it was a piece of equipment that she had thought of at first as an intruder and regarded now as a difficult but permanent guest. It announced the moves it wanted made in a dry dead voice, like a man speaking with a peg on his nose or through a thin coffin-lid; and once, in the days when she still resented it, she had accidentally touched it off. She had already turned away to the sideboard when the voice came, flat and dull, dropping into the room one of its obscure directives: *Queen to King's Rook five;* as if something in the room, some object she had always thought of as tangible but without life, had suddenly decided to make contact with her and were announcing a cryptic need. Well, she had got over that.

She finished the lounge, and without going to the window again went right on to the bathroom, got down on her knees, and cleaned all round the bath, the shower recess, the basin and lavatory; then walked straight through to the lounge-room and looked.

He was still there and had turned a whole quarter-circle. She saw his slight figure with the slumped shoulders in profile. But what was happening?

He cast no shadow. His shadow had disappeared. The iron tap cast a shadow and the young man didn't. It took her a good minute, in which she was genuinely alarmed, to see that what she had taken for the shadow of the tap was a dark patch of lawn where the water dripped. So that was all right. It was midday.

She did a strange thing then. Without having made any decision about it, she went into the kitchen, gathered the ingredients, and made up a batch of spiced biscuits with whole peanuts in them; working fast with the flour, the butter, the spice, and forgetting herself in the pleasure of getting the measurements right by the feel of the thing, the habit.

They were biscuits that had no special name. She had learned to make them when she was just a child, from a girl they had had in the country. The routine of mixing and spooning the mixture on to greaseproof paper let her back into a former self whose motions were lighter, springier, more sure of ends and means. She hadn't made these biscuits — hadn't been able to bring herself to make them — since Greg died. They were his favourites. Now, while they were cooking and filling the house with their spicy sweetness, she did another thing she hadn't intended to do. She went to Greg's bedroom at the end of the hall, across from where she and Jack slept, and began to take down from the wall the pennants he had won for swimming, the green one with gold lettering, the purple one, the blue, and his lifesaving certificates, and laid them carefully on the bed. She brought a carton from under the stairs and packed them in the bottom. Then she cleared the bookshelf and took down the model planes, and put them in the carton as well. Then she removed from a drawer of the desk a whole mess of things: propelling pencils and pencil-stubs, rubber-bands, tubes of glue, a pair of manacles, a pack of playing cards that if you were foolish enough to take one gave you an electric shock. She put all these things into the carton, along with a second drawerful of magazines and loose-leaf notebooks, and carried the carton out. Then she took clean sheets and made the bed.

By now the biscuits were ready to be taken from the oven. She counted them, there were twenty-three. Without looking up to where the young man was standing, she opened the kitchen window and set them, sweetly smelling of spice, on the window ledge. Then she went back and sat on Greg's bed while they cooled.

She looked round the blank walls, wondering, now that she had stripped them, what a young man of twenty-eight might have filled them with, and discovered with a pang that she could not guess.

It was then that another figure slipped into her head.

In her middle years at school there had been a boy who sat two desks in front of her called Stevie Caine. She had always felt sorry for him because he lived alone with an aunt and was poor. The father had worked for the railways but lost his job after a crossing accident and killed himself. It was Stevie Caine this young man reminded her of. His shoulders too had been narrow and stooped, his face unnaturally pallid, his wrists bony and raw. Stevie's hair was mouse-coloured and had stuck out in wisps behind his ears; his auntie cut it, they said, with a pudding-basin. He smelled of scrubbing-soap. Too poor to go to the pictures on Saturday afternoons, or to have a radio and hear the serials, he could take no part in the excited chatter and argument through which they were making a world for themselves. When they ate their lunch he sat by himself on the far side of the yard, and she alone had guessed the reason: it was because the metal lunch-tin that his father had carried to the railway had nothing in it, or at best a slice of bread and dripping. But poor as he was, Stevie had not been resentful — that was the thing that had most struck her. She felt he ought to have been. And his face sometimes, when he was excited and his Adam's apple worked up and down, was touched at the cheekbones with such a glow of youthfulness and joy that she had wanted to reach out and lay her fingers very gently to his skin and feel the warmth, but thought he might misread the tenderness that filled her (which certainly included him but was for much more beside) as girlish infatuation or, worse still, pity. So she did nothing.

Stevie Caine had left school when he was just fourteen and went like his father to work at the railway. She had seen him sometimes in a railway worker's uniform, black serge, wearing a black felt hat that made him look bonier than ever about the cheekbones and chin and carrying the same battered lunch-tin. Something in his youthful refusal to be bitter or subdued had continued to move her. Even now, years later, she could see the back of his thin neck, and might have leaned out, no longer caring if she was misunderstood, and laid her hand to the chapped flesh.

When he was eighteen he had immediately joined up and was immediately killed; she had seen it in the papers — just the name.

It was Stevie Caine this young man resembled, as she had last seen him in the soft hat and railway worker's serge waistcoat, with the sleeves rolled on his stringy arms. There had been nothing between them, but she had never forgotten. It had to do, as she saw it, with the two forms of injustice: the one that is cruel but can be changed, and the other kind — the tipping of a thirteen-year-old boy off the saddle of his bike into a bottomless pit — that cannot; with that and the empty lunch-tin that she would like to have filled with biscuits with whole peanuts in them that have no special name.

She went out quickly now (the young man was still there on the lawn beyond the window) and counted the biscuits, which were cool enough to be put into a barrel. There were twenty-three, just as before.

He stayed there all afternoon and was still there among the deepening shadows when Jack came in. She was pretty certain now of what he was but didn't want it confirmed — and how awful if you walked up to someone, put your hand out to see if it would go through him, and it didn't.

They had tea, and Jack, after a shy worried look in her direction, which she affected not to see, took one of the biscuits and slowly ate it. She watched. He was trying not to show how broken up he was. Poor Jack!

Twenty-two.

Later, while he sat over his chess set and the mechanical voice told him what moves he should make on its behalf, she ventured to the window and peered through. It was, very gently, raining, and the streetlights were blurred and softened. Slow cars passed, their tyres swishing in the wet. They pushed soft beams before them.

The young man stood there in the same spot. His shabby clothes were drenched and stuck to him. The felt hat was also drenched, and droplets of water had formed at the brim, on one side filled with light, a half-circle of brilliant dots.

'Mustn't it be awful,' she said, 'to be out there on a night like this and have nowhere to go? There must be so many of them. Just standing about in the rain, or sleeping in it.'

Something in her tone, which was also flat, but filled with an emotion that deeply touched and disturbed him, made the man leave his game and come to her side. They stood together a moment facing the dark wall of glass, then she turned, looked him full in the face and did something odd: She reached out towards him and her hand bumped against his ribs — that is how he thought of it: a bump. It was the oddest thing! Then impulsively, as if with sudden relief, she kissed him.

I have so much is what she thought to herself.

Next morning, alone again, she cleared away the breakfast things, washed and dried up, made a grocery list. Only then did she go to the window.

It was a fine clear day and there were two of them, alike but different; both pale and hopeless looking, thin-shouldered, unshaven, wearing shabby garments, but not at all similar in features. They did not appear to be together. That is, they did not stand close, and there was nothing to suggest that they were in league or that the first had brought the other along or summoned him up. But there were two of them just the same, as if some *process* were involved. Tomorrow; she guessed, there would be four, and the next day sixteen; and at last — for there must be millions to be drawn on — so many that there would be no place on the lawn for them to stand, not even the smallest blade of grass. They would spill out into the street, and from there to the next street as well — there would be no room for cars to get through or park — and so it would go on till the suburb, and the city and a large part of the earth was covered. This was just the start.

She didn't feel at all threatened. There was nothing in either of these figures that suggested menace. They simply stood. But she thought she would refrain from telling Jack till he noticed it himself. Then they would do together what was required of them.

WRITE ME, SON, WRITE ME

Thea Astley

Moth tells me this. And what she doesn't tell Bo does. And what he doesn't tell I see.

She says: Dad was given to such phrases as 'a woman should fruit her loins', a rich unctuous statement of such masculine simplicity his wife had believed him. They had produced an elfin, buck-toothed girl who had entered her teen years on ballet points and had proceeded to give them all the versions of a middle-class hell. They wanted security for her, a go-ahead husband with an expense account and a house that could possibly be marked in the real estate guides with an asterisk — their version of the Trinity. She wanted success without effort (which the education system would surely have provided for her had she stayed with it), scruffy boys with bulging jeans, the pillion seats of motor-bikes, and pot.

At fifteen she was expelled from her convent school for scrawling 'Mother Philomène has it off with the bishop' on the wash-room walls. She vanished overnight with boys.

'Love,' her poor mother told her, 'isn't something you toss around like garbage. Love,' — holding her right hand somewhere on her chest — 'love hurts.'

'Not if you do it right,' her daughter said.

At eighteen she was removed from the back row of a Brisbane ballet company when, convinced by hallucinogenic drugs, she insisted she was the soloist in the only performance of the *Nutcracker* ballet that ever had two sugarplum fairies. She bought herself some cheap Indian frockery, lengths of clacking wooden beads, began to call herself Moth, and vanished into the hills.

When her parents discovered her address they wrote despairing little notes and sometimes she answered. She answered with demands for money. They sent clothes she never wore, and plastic-protected food parcels and once, after a couple of years, she came to visit them with three remarkable others and a tiny boy called Wait-a-while whose parenthood she seemed vague about.

At twenty she was still loosely connected with a large and shambling young man who, like Moth, appeared to have no regular employment though his desperate search for work had taken him to every surf-spot on the eastern seaboard. It would have been difficult to imagine such splendid physique going unwanted by those who needed to employ brawn; but apart from brief periods when a degrading love of survival forced him into well-paid terms as a strike-breaker, he took the dole. He was gentle, had a candid smile and a kind of flecked innocence.

'I can watch,' Bo explained to Moth's parents, allowing Wait-a-while to gnaw on his big harmless thumb, 'the sun come up in the morning. And I can track its progress all day across the sky.'

They were too stunned to discuss the work ethic.

'But how do you eat?'

'We manage.' His paws moved gently across Wait-a-while's fragile shoulders. 'People are kind. You wouldn't believe. And we've given up meat altogether. That's a gas saving, man. We're into fruit. We've rejected all animal products.'

'Has Wait-a-while rejected meat?'

They ignored this. 'We won't be sending him to school,' someone else said. 'We're not going to give him the hang-ups we had, man.'

'Good God!' cried Moth's father. 'Good God! Do you always travel in threes?'

They moved on and north.

There was a hypothetical quality about the aimless mists of early morning rain-forest, a demi-postulation that appealed to the very indeterminateness of their life-style. (I felt it, feel it, but then I belong to an older breed; and despite all that joy, that juice, mister poet man, I'm able to withstand those sensual assaults and stand back a bit, eh? I've always found the trappings of nature to be very soft porn, the landscape's centre-page spread.)

They found others like themselves. They skulked in lean-tos made from iron and timber off-cuts. They twanged out-of-tune guitars, sang their particular rain-forest dirges, got stoned on grass, and each fortnight, responding like children trained

by the Jesuits to the vestiges of ritual, hiked in to Mango to
pick up their dole cheques.

Dust. Shag-wagons. Blue Kombis.

One of them played flute, I might have told you. Its mournful
embroideries would flutter in rags past my office windows and
Willy Fourcorners, who now does a little odd-jobbing for me,
would look up from his spading to wave, to grin. It looked
like a rag-tail of Hamelin as they headed for the road-house,
startling the travellers who'd paused for a bottle of soft. Some
of the girls made dancing movements, doing their own eyes-
down thing, absorbed by the fretwork of their feet on the smudged
grass-strip. Moth, who had the edge on them, would dash off
a series of *entrechats* between the beat-up tables or hold a
tremulous arabesque in the bright sun long enough to catch
applause. 'Hey, hey, Moth!' her buddies uttered listlessly. 'Hey!
Way out!'

Some months before she had registered with the Reeftown
employment office as a teacher of ballet. Reeftown, she felt,
was sufficiently remote for work demands never to be made.

The official was fascinated by the small gold ring that decorated
Moth's left nostril.

'Can you,' he asked, 'dance?'

'Of course.' She whipped into immediate gambades. The lethar-
gic applicants lining the wall stirred for the first time in days.

'Certificates?' the official asked, ignoring a *grand jeté* that
brought her panting slightly to the edge of the counter.

'Not with me.' Moth smiled engagingly and the little ring
sparkled. 'I can send for them.'

'Do that,' the official said, checking his tea-break watch.

She returned to the rain-forest.

After a month Moth went back down to the coast and returned
to the employment office. The loungers were where she had
left them. They seemed to have grown a little older.

'I'm not getting any money,' she said. 'I'm starving.'

'You have to wait six weeks.'

'Six weeks?'

'Six.'

'A person could starve!'

'A person could.' He smiled at her quite nicely.

'Any jobs then?'

He hunted out her card and read it slowly. 'Could be.' He
looked up at her. 'Could well be.'

'In ballet? I mean ballet? That's all I can do.'

'It so happens,' the employment clerk said deliberately, 'that we have a request for just that. For just very that. Down town here. Three afternoons a week at a private dancing school. Payment by the hour.'

He watched interestedly as she went pale.

She told him she lived out of town. She told him she had no transport.

'But you managed to get here.' He was very gentle.

'Get stuffed!' she said.

There were delays of chequeless bravado during which her friends consoled, nourished, advised.

'Longest time I've been employed was a month last year. Actually I've only had to do three months' work in the last eighteen. Not bad, eh?' one said. He was plumply in the pink and given to bib-front overalls above which his seraph smile challenged the world. 'No hassle. No sweat. Look at it this way: We're eating, aren't we? We got no problems, have we? As long as we purchase we're keeping the economy fluid. Someone pays, hey hey hey!'

But after another six weeks the rest of the commune became a little weary of her having no money to contribute. It cut right across community spirit. And at times Wait-a-while's yowling seemed excessive. Dimly, vaguely, like an afterthought, she recalled her parents.

Dear folks, went her letter home after memory had dredged up her address, *I've got it all together up here. The climate most of the time means relax relax, the family's working pretty hard at self-sufficiency (guess you city-slickers don't know what that means, huh?) and we're growing lots of our own stuff.* She chewed on her pen end and inspected the wilting banana-tree that cringed away from the door. *But it's tough going sometimes and most of us are trying for jobs in town but it's like everywhere I guess there's simply nothing going. Sometimes I feel I should have done a typing course like you suggested but who wants that sort of coop-up? Not me. Sun light trees air — we've got it all.*

Well almost all. It's like this Mum and Dad if you can see your way to sending me a little something, the clinking kind I mean to tide me over for a couple of weeks I'd be ever so. We're flat out of fertiliser and stuff and the old agro-eco system (sorry to get so tech!) needs a jolt.
Take care.
    Your Moth child.

It was three weeks of shag-wagon Kombis and talcum dust before their reply came.

Darling, they wrote, *we were so happy to hear from you and know you are all right. It's a very long time since we've heard and we weren't even sure of your address. Dad and I would have answered sooner but we've been ever so busy these last weeks painting the old place up (you wouldn't know it! — bamboo beige with chocolate trim) and then the roof developed this terrible leak. I suppose you read about the floods we had last month. Anyway, everything was chaos. So we've had all this enormous expense, what with getting the mud out and the paint and the roof and everything.*

We're so glad to know you've been thinking about suitable employment. Dad says he'd be only too happy to pay for you to go to business college, but he would like you to do it down here where it would be more practical. Please think about —

Moth dropped the letter like an unclean tissue onto the foor.

'Oh, shit!' she cried. 'Those mean bastards. Those stinking shit-mean bastards!'

Wait-a-while hooked onto the dangling skirts and worked away with a banana.

'Don't worry,' Bo advised tenderly. 'Don't worry, Moth. No hassles, eh? I'll try my olds.'

He wrote them a postcard because there was less space to fill. He asked for fifty dollars.

It was a long time since he had written and even longer since he had seen them. They still had other children to worry about and wisely assumed their son's sheer largeness was his best protection. Yet now and then, moved by some memento of her eldest in the quirks of her youngest — a puckered grin, the vulnerability of large scabby knees — his mother had sent him soft concerned notes that said, 'Write me, son. Let me know if I can help.' Peering through the brightly lit picture-windows of love, she observed her own unquenchable devotion but believed it to be his.

She wrote at once, a long paragraph of tenderness. She told him about his brothers; she uttered oblique and timid pleas for his return; she worried about his health; she hoped he was able to find a job; she wondered humbly would they see him for Christmas. Also she included a large cheque — and as she gummed down the envelope her youngest child dropped from the tree where he had been terrifying some currawongs and broke his shoulder.

She forgot to post the letter.

It was a month before she remembered, for during that time as well she had discovered a lump in her breast and there had been all the bother of an operation. Her penitence expanded like some monster balloon gassed up with affection as she tore the unposted letter open, added a postscript of contrition and an even larger cheque. She didn't tell him about the lump. 'Write me,' she wrote. 'Tell us how you're getting on.' And she explained about his brother's nasty accident.

Each day for that month Bo, who was worrying himself out of the boyish freshness that marked him, foot-padded the four miles into Mango, sometimes with Moth and Wait-a-while, sometimes with a very plump girl who had just joined the family after finding Jesus, sometimes on his own.

Blue Kombis, dust, shag-wagons.

In what passed for winter in the distant north, the landscape became clear, definite, and the canopy of the rainforest, he observed, trudging along his high ridge, looked like astrakhan across which the shadows lay in wispy layers of blue. He remained care-free; but in the third week Moth ran away to Brisbane with a passing folk-singer who was forming a skiffle band. Absent-mindedly she forgot to take Wait-a-while, who failed to miss her; but unexpectedly Bo pined as he munched on his pumpkin seeds and finally he scrounged a few sheets of paper and wrote.

Dear remembered friend,

I welcome this opportunity to dispense with bullshit say what fond memories I have of you. I can't say that the thought of you being so far away hurts, time was always the best remedy for hurt but I would really dig to hear from you, the cherished memories mean less when I realise how much you'd changed you must have. I still read the old letters you sent me a year ago when you went away P.S. with no returning address, remember those days? which stir a fondness which never seem there in old situation. I'm glad you make me realise the affinity I had for you listen kid I want to see your ass back this summer. Funny how a hick town like Mango becomes the other half just because I'm here and converse. So package yourself away from Mister Acne and other city shrinking pains and preserve thyself my child. The best package I seem to find is happy friends that's one thing I wish on you — so if you ever run short remember your own puss is magnificent. Other choice newsy items follow: — Over the last two weeks everyone has grown two weeks. Everybody is a far more interesting thing I'm starting to get a head together making more different friends in what we need most (eh? as someone once wrote me) it's easier now all is less tense pretty big 'adolescent' type problem to conquer!! Pause for a think mind is blank Wait-a-while pretty cool but pining, have been reading Nabokov man just like the old 'tin drum' beat away while I read it does me good also scrape the copper together and get along to see the first Fellini Film you come across man we miss out on so much colour speaking Englisk (said he spelling it with ISK) How go narcotics down there, not as good as food — I had such a WOW time over the last few weeks — dope mescaline music leading into a pill pop party which cooled me off for the present while Heavy Heavy Scene kid it's like whiskey payout or keep dry no inbetween Why do I tell you this What am I doing I hope Brisbane mail has more respect than fucking Mango customs Ho hum long arm of the Queensland law. Well kid? get the picture — saying may head is coming together is sure sign that it aint Bliss to be insane and irrelevant. Give us all the dope, huh, joke!

There was further silence while Moth in the dry south became the slightest of wing flickers around the twenty-watt bulb.

Bo kept walking the road to town with the dust, the shag-wagons, the blue Kombis. One of the farmers along the river offered him a job, but he only stayed two days, blushed, and told the bloke he had a crook back.

The weather changed. Clouds marshalled their slow moving ranks up from the coast, nudged the hills and burst into an apocalypse of water. After, there was calm and penitence, a smidgin of penance during the steady wash-away round the piles of the damp humpy where five of them now stared miserably out through the sticky air at Wait-a-while slushing round in the mud beneath the banana suckers. He fell and was covered in slime and came back inside to complain.

'Cool it, man,' they told him. 'Don't make a heavy scene.'

Bo kept promising the others that the olds had to write. The spirit of the commune was becoming impatient and Bo felt he was a terrible burden.

When the Wet had got into rhythm, when Moth had failed to answer, he trailed one day during a sun-burst, lugging Wait-a-while along the highway slush into town. The corner pub had sculptured arrangements of darkies and despair. There was a further grouping beneath the awning of the old picture hall. It was three days to Christmas and Mango was sweating its expectation. An old Aboriginal woman was squatting on the steps of the hall mulling over her shopping-list aloud with a bent old black man. 'I'll git a poun' a' sausage mince,' she was saying. 'An' tripe. Maybe bitta tripe.'

Bo's rush of pity changed to pain for himself. He wanted to howl. Jesus, he thought, back home they'd be doing the tree and all, and mum cooking herself stupid and chicken and the lot: pudding with sauce and the kids crackling round on wrappings all colours, blowing the squeakers: even the old man mellowed out after a couple of jugs. He gave Wait-a-while a hug that made the kid bellow with surprise, hollering with his mouth stretched wide and a nose that needed wiping. Write to me, mum, Bo was pleading inside. Write. And hugging away at the stringy kid.

Charlie Hanush, the postmaster, was watching through the door; he was an acid cove, filled with the wonder of near-retirement. He moved dedicated and deadly through the paper-work of his days in which each memo was planted square and each day rectangular; and he couldn't stand these bums always coming in bugging him for mail and cheques. His face didn't alter as he watched Wait-a-while yelp for a pee, saw Bo take off the kid's pants and steer the little trickle onto the grass patch.

Bo hauled the kid up the post-office steps, still holding Wait-a-while's pants, and dumped him on the office counter. Bo's candid grin was beginning to be muddled by hopelessness.

'Hi, Mr Hanush!'

'Son,' Mr Hanush said, 'get that kid of yours off the counter.'

'Any mail for me?'

'Look, I said to get that kid off, eh? You deaf or something? Don't want any bare bottoms there, see? Not where the public has to use it.'

Bo lifted Wait-a-while from another small frightened puddle.

'Oh, God!' Mr Hanush said. His wife fussed over with a rag.

'Geez,' Bo said. 'Geez, I'm sorry, man. That's a lousy scene.'

'It's a wet scene, son.'

There was a smell of Dettol. A couple of Bo's buddies lounged in the door behind him and started fidgeting near the telegram forms. Bo grinned uneasily.

'I thought this was the high-smile area.'

'What,' Mr Hanush asked, leaning his bitter bones forward in threat, 'can I do for you?'

'Any mail then? I asked. Kimball.'

'Say please.'

Bo sniggered with embarrassment. 'Please,' he said.

Elaborately avoiding the damp patch, Mr Hanush stretched over to the pigeon-holes and took down a wad of mail. Slowly, extra slowly, he began sorting it over, not looking up at Bo's strained face. 'Here,' he grunted after a bit. 'There's one for you.' And he held out a letter to one of Bo's buddies who cackled pleasantly and went down the steps. Bo shuffled his thongs about on the floor. He felt like a dog waiting for — Jesus! even a pat!

Mr Hanush went right down to the bottom of the bundle and then started again from the top. 'Might have missed it.' He gave Bo an ironic smile. 'We can't be too careful, can we?'

Finally he looked up as he extracted a bulky letter from the pile and stared hard into Bo's face.

'Here. One for you.' And he placed it carefully in the circle of wet. 'I was beginning to think you didn't have a pal in the world.'

Bo giggled, wide-eyed. 'Who, me? Me?'

He grabbed the letter.

'And listen, Bo,' Mr Hanush said, 'just get that kid out. We can do without the Wet indoors.'

'Like funny, man!' Bo said, cheeky again. He didn't care. He could recognise his mum's hand. 'Hey hey hey! They've written!'

Dumping Wait-a-while on the top step he ripped open the envelope and opened up the letter. There it was. The cheque. Jee — *sus*! Carelessly he crumpled the letter into a ball, shot it light-heartedly across the footpath into the gaping trash bin and raced down the steps flapping the cheque at his waiting buddies.

'Geez, man!' he cried. 'Geez!' And his eyes filled with tears. 'They've written!'

Woman in a Lampshade

Elizabeth Jolley

One cold wet night in July Jasmine Tredwell took several sheets of paper and her typewriter together with a quantity of simple food and some respectable wine and, saying goodnight fondly to her dozing husband, she set off in search of solitude.

'I'm going up to the farm,' she said, 'I'll be home first thing on Monday morning,' she promised. But her husband, Emeritus Professor of Neo Byzantine Art, was encased in head-phones listening to Mahler and paid no attention to the departure.

It was not her custom to give lifts to strangers. Indeed, because of reported bashings and murders in lonely suburbs, she had, in an impulsively tender moment, promised the elderly Professor that she would never pick up from the roadside any stranger however pathetic or harmless his appearance.

She saw the young man standing in the dark. He seemed to be leaning rather than standing, the storm holding him up in its force. He was an indistinct outline, blurred because of the rain. It was as if he had come into existence simply because someone, hopelessly lost among words, had created him in thoughtful ink on the blotting paper. Immediately, forgetting her promise, she stopped the car and, leaning over, opened the door with some difficulty.

'Hop in quick young man, you're getting drowned!'

The grateful youth slipped quickly into the warm and secure fragrance. He tried, without success, not to mark the clean upholstery with the water as it ran off him in dirty little streams. Jasmine took the hills noisily, the windscreen wipers flying to and fro flinging off the splashings as if the car boasted small fountains on either side.

'Thanks,' he said, 'thanks a lot.'

'Such a terrible night,' she said, 'are you going far?'

'As far as I can get.'

'Where shall I drop you?'

'Oh, anywhere. It'll do if you drop me off when you've gone as far as you're going.' He gave a nervous little laugh. 'Tah very much,' he said. 'Thank you very much, tah!'

That the young man had no definite destination did not cause Jasmine to wish that she had not stopped to offer him a ride. They hardly spoke. Almost at once Jasmine was touched to notice that her youthful travelling companion had fallen asleep.

'He must have been exhausted,' she thought and she wondered about his ragged soaked clothes. 'He's probably hungry too,' she said to herself.

Jasmine felt safe in the lamplight. And she felt safe in the lampshade, pretty too. She was not a pretty woman, she never pretended to be. But the lampshade, when she put it on, made her feel pretty, softly so and feminine. It was the colour of ripe peaches and made of soft pleats of silk. It was light and it fitted her perfectly. It was like a garden-party hat only more foolish because it was, after all, a lampshade. To wear the lampshade suggested the dangerous and the exotic while still sheltered under a cosy domesticity.

She never guessed the first time she placed it on her head how she would feel. She had never experienced such a feeling before. It had taken her by surprise. After that first time she had looked with shy curiosity at other women in shops and at parties, at the hairdresser's and even while passing them in the street, quietly noticing the private things about them, the delicate shaping of the back of the neck or the imaginative tilt of the ears. She wondered too about all the tiny lines and folds and creases, all the secret things. So recently having discovered something about herself, she wondered what secret pleasures they had and whether they had known them long before she had discovered hers.

She sang softly,

> *I love my little lampshade*
> *So frilly and warm*
> *If I wear my silky lampshade*
> *I'll come to no harm.*

'Are you awake?' she asked the young man later that night. He was buried under a heap of old fur coats and several spoiled pages.

'Are you awake? Hey! Are you awake? God? how soundly you sleep! It's being young, I suppose, hey! wake up!'

'What's that? What the . . . ?' he hardly moved.

'Young man, could you move over a bit, my typewriter's falling off my knee, it's giving me the most awful cramp. Also I'm getting a pain in my back. Ah! that's better. No, no further or you'll fall out. That'll do beautifully. Hey!' she laughed, pleased with the music of her own voice, 'don't roll back! You know, if you lie on the edge of the bed, you'll soon drop off!'

He drew the coats closer and made no sound.

'That was supposed to be a joke,' she said noisily rearranging the papers. 'But seriously,' she said, 'it's like this, I've got a young man, he's a bit of a nuisance really. First he's in a suburban post office in Australia. Can you imagine him behind the counter with his pale offended eyes about to burst into tears and all the little veins and capillaries flushed on his crooked boyish face, or something like that?

'Then he turns up again in a depressing hotel in Calais where two lesbians have gone to have a bit of privacy. The younger one wants to get away from her husband and the older one is the husband's secretary, a really boring stuffy old maid. She's quite empty headed and very irritating to be with for more than a few minutes as the younger one discovers quite quickly. In addition, the secretary, the boring one, drinks heavily and is not really very clean. An unfortunate situation altogether. Anyway, my young man's there at the hotel reception desk, in the night, being absolutely useless.'

'Who?' the voice muffled in furs could hardly be heard.

'My young man of course,' Jasmine, preening, fingered her peach-ripe silk pleats lovingly. 'He's left the P.O. to be a hotel receptionist in Calais,' she continued, 'And then, to my surprise, he moves to a cheap hotel in India, Madras to be exact, and I've got him there exactly the same, the pale offended eyes filled with tears, the same blushing capillaries, perhaps he's a bit thinner, more haunted looking and, as usual, he's no earthly use,' Jasmine sighed sadly. 'He's absolutely unable to help the guests when they arrive exhausted in the night. It's two more lesbians, younger than the others and one is very uncomfortable with an unmentionable infection. Not a very nice subject really but, as a writer, I have to look closely at *Life* and every aspect of it.' Jasmine sighed again thoughtfully, her long fingers reaching up restlessly plucked the folds of unexpected foolishness.

'*C'est un triste métier,*' she knew her pronunciation was flawless. 'In all the stories,' she said, 'one of the women is horrible to my young man. Absolutely horrible! I mean one in all three. So that's three times he has a really bad time, in all, he's despised, rejected and betrayed. But I'm glad to say that on all occasions the awful unkind behaviour is deeply regretted as soon as the resulting wretchedness is evident.'

'What's the trouble?' the young man sat up and yawned almost dislocating his lower jaw.

Jasmine banged her typewriter.

'Can't you understand, I'm stuck! I'm stuck, stuck, stuck.' She shuffled the papers across the bed. 'Oh by the way,' she said as calmly as she could, 'would you mind not smoking in bed. My husband can't stand it.'

'He's not here is he?' the young man began uneasily, 'you said, I thought . . . '

'No of course not,' Jasmine said, 'but the smoke hangs around and he's very sensitive, his nose I mean.' She laughed. 'But,' she said, 'whatever shall I do with them?'

'Who?'

'My characters of course. I suppose,' she paused, 'I suppose they could carry on in bed.' She began to type rapidly.

'Eh? Yeah!' He turned over.

'Mind the typewriter! Oops! I thought it was gone that time. That's better. You know I must tell you I've got a friend, Moira, well she's not a friend really, more of an enemy. Writers don't have any friends.' She settled comfortably against her mountain of pillows. 'Well Moira's trying to get a psychiatric musical off the ground. God! That woman's a Bore when she talks about her work. She never stops talking! All last week she was on about an official speech she'd been asked to write for the ceremonial opening of a deep sewerage system, I mean what is there in deep sewerage?'

'Quite a lot I should think,' he yawned again. 'Have you got going now?'

'No, not at all, it's awful!' she pulled another spoiled page from her typewriter. 'I'm afraid,' she said, watching the paper as it floated to the floor, 'I'm afraid, well, you must feel so trapped and cheated. I mean, being here with me in this lonely place. Just think! I brought you all this way and then everything happening like that!'

'What d'you mean, happening,' he said patiently, 'I mean nothing has yet, has it?'

'I didn't expect my young man and the lesbians . . . '

'I thought they was in Madras,' he interrupted.

'Yes, yes that's right, so they should be, but my young man . . . '

'Well, where is he then? I thought the idea was we'd be having the place to ourselves and I'd work the farm and — ' a note of disappointment replaced the impatience in his voice.

'It's such a nuisance,' Jasmine replied. 'Really I'm sorry. I was so looking forward, you know, to our getting to know each other and,' she paused, 'and there he is, stupid and useless!'

'Who? Where is he?' he sat up.

'In my brief-case. Would you mind awfully? I left it just outside in the porch, I'd be so grateful if you would.'

Reluctantly he looked at the cold floor.

'No stop!' Jasmine cried. 'Stay where you are in the warm. I must be mad! I'm the one who should go. It's my fault he's out there. I should go. I'm going out to get him. You stay in bed. I'm going!'

Jasmine slipped from the bed and pattered with quick bare feet over the boards. He heard the outside door open and slam shut. He heard the noise of plates and cups and cutlery, a plate dropped somewhere crashing and breaking.

'What's that? Who's there?' he called.

'It's nothing,' she replied through a mouthful of food, 'nothing at all to worry about. I'm just having a cheese sandwich.' She came to the bedside. 'Would you like some or are you the kind of person who doesn't like eating in bed? I've sliced up an onion and a hard-boiled egg. Do have some!'

'No thank you,' he said. 'I'm not hungry really no; no thank you, really not hungry thanks all the same.'

Jasmine ate ravenously.

'Have some Burgundy,' she said, 'or would you prefer a beer?' She poured a generous glass of wine for herself and opened a can for her guest.

'Just move over a bit,' she said with her mouth full, 'thanks.' She chewed and swallowed, 'I'm sorry, really I am,' she said, 'about these papers all over the bed. I'd like to be able to make it up to you in some way. You see I should never have picked you up. When I saw you at the side of the road absolutely drenched I simply couldn't help offering you a lift.' She studied the remains of the egg apparently lost in thoughts for which there were no words. 'Ever since I decided to become a writer,' she announced. 'I've been an absolute Pain! You hardly know me really. I mean, take tonight, I've been perfectly terrible. Please, please don't try to contradict me.'

In the silence of his obedience he hiccupped.

'Manners!' he apologised.

'Oh dear!' Jasmine was dismayed. 'Perhaps you shouldn't drink beer in bed. My husband always get hiccups if he drinks lying down. Try walking about.'

He was not inclined to leave the bed.

'Well,' Jasmine said, 'if you're shy put this old nighty on. You walk about and I'll think up a fright for you.'

Self-conscious and solemn in brushed nylon the young man paced to and fro on the creaking floor boards. He hiccupped at regular intervals. Every minute his thin body jerked.

'Manners!' he muttered, and one minute later, 'Manners!'

Suddenly she screamed, 'Help! Help!'

'What the, who's there? Where the hell are you?' he hiccupped. 'Manners!'

'Help! Hellup!'

He hiccupped, 'Manners! Where the hell are you?'

'Under the bed silly! Help me out there's not much space.' She was out of breath. 'Such a pity it didn't work.' In the brief silence he hiccupped again.

'Look out!' she whispered. 'Look out! There's a spider behind you. A great black spider. S.P.I.D.E.R. Look behind you!'

'Manners! What? I can't hear you. Manners!'

'Oh, it's no good. You'll simply have to wait till they wear off.' She was just the tiniest bit sulky. 'I really can't help it,' she said, adjusting the lampshade with one delicate finger, 'if He visits me in the middle of the night.'

'Who? Here? Who visits you?' He began to search through the heap of furs. 'Where's my clothes? I'd better be off. Look, I shouldn't be here.'

Jasmine laughed. 'Oh relax! The Muse of course,' she said, 'perhaps I should say My Muse.' She paused. 'It's very amusing really Oh!' Her laughter was like a shower of broken glass. 'Oh!' she said. 'I made a pun there. I wonder if I could use it somewhere in here, let me see.' She rearranged several of the papers. She laughed again. 'You look so serious walking up and down in that tatty old gown.' He turned to look at her seriously and steadily.

'I've been wondering what's that, I mean, what's that on your head?'

'It's a lampshade,' she replied.

'If you don't mind me arskin', why do you?'

'Always when I'm writing,' her voice was deep with reverence.

'But I thought we was going to have it away together.'

'Yes,' Jasmine said, 'I thought so too but it's my young man —'

'The one who was in all those places?'

'Yes.'

'Oh, I see,' he paused and said in a flat voice, 'praps I'd better go then.'

'Oh no,' Jasmine said, 'there's absolutely no need. I know,' she said, 'let's dance! My little transistor's here somewhere. I know it's here, somewhere here.' She rummaged among the bear skins and the ancient silver fox. 'Ah! here we are. If we danced, you never know, it might be better. I'll just see if I can get some music. Ah good! here's music. Listen there's a dancing teacher too. What a scream!'

The pulse of the music noticeably caused life to return and the dancing instructor's voice flowed quietly bringing shape and order into the disordered room.

'Now for the stylised step. Starting position,' the Irish voice was kind, 'beat one step up beat two step together beat three step back beat four step together up together back together and up together and back together arms loose relax and smile.'

'Come on!' Jasmine was laughing.

'I don't dance. Really, I don't dance.'

'Oh come on!'

'Not on beds. I don't dance on beds. It's too dangerous and, besides, it's rude.'

Jasmine laughing and breathless reached out and turned the volume on more.

There was a change in the music.

'Now the basic camel walk and step and kick and camel walk,' the instructor's patient voice continued. 'Beat one stub left beat two stub right beat three stub left beat four stub right beat five stub left beat six kick left beat seven stub right beat eight and kick and kick that's just fine you'll make it in time beat one stub left beat two stub right think happy and relax beat three stub left beat four stub right that's great you're great the greatest!'

Jasmine fell off the bed with a crash.

'And now the Latin Hustle,' the dancing instructor's persistent voice changed rhythm as the music changed. 'Touch and one and two and step back three and four forward five and six repeat touch and one and two and step and one and two and one.'

'Now you've properly done it!' The young man fell over the furniture. 'You've knocked over the light. Have you broke it? It's pitch dark!' He stumbled again, knocking over a chair. 'Where are you?' he shouted. 'It's pitch black dark. Yo' must 'ave broke the lamp.'

'Over here!' Jasmine sang, teasing through the music and the darkness.

'Where's the matches?' Panic made him angry.

'Yoo hoo! Here I am,' Jasmine was beside him, and then she was far away. 'I'm over here,' she called, and suddenly she was close again. Both were breathing heavily, gasping even, furniture fell and crockery crashed as if something was rocking the cottage. Jasmine was laughing and laughing, pleased and excited.

'Oh go on,' she cried. 'Don't stop!' she pleaded.

'Repeat those movements till you feel comfortable and confident in your performance,' the dancing instructor's voice, keeping time perfectly, penetrated above and below the sound of the music. 'Follow the beat sequence and turn and turn repeat and turn and repeat,' his patience was endless.

'I'm going outside,' the young man was polite and strained. 'If you'll excuse me,' he said, 'I'll 'ave to go outside.'

'Yes, yes of course,' Jasmine said. 'Just through the yard and up the back you can't miss.'

'Thanks,' he let the door slam. 'Sorry!' he called.

'You'll make it in time,' the dancing master's voice consoled. 'Try once more beat one stub left beat two stub right.'

Jasmine switched off her tiny radio. She was laughing softly, breathlessly. 'Now where's the other lamp and the matches? Ah! here they are.'

In the soft light she made herself comfortable with three pillows at her back. She began to type rapidly.

'My story just needs a bit of action,' she said.

A gun shot sounded close by, it was followed by a second shot.

'Splendid!' Jasmine said. 'That's just what I needed. Now I know what happens next.' She continued to type. 'He'd better do it at once. But not in Madras. He'd better get on a 'plane quickly.' Her typewriter rattled on. 'Oh well to save time he can do it at the airport.' She read aloud what she had written in the mincing tones reserved for her work. '*Quietly he took the jewelled pistol from its silky case and held it to his pale crooked forehead. His eyes were full of tears . . .* ' She changed her voice. 'That's a nice touch, the crooked forehead, what exquisite writing. I've never written so well before.' She read again in the special voice, as she typed, *'Closing his eyes, he pulled the trigger . . .'*

The young man came in. He hiccupped.

'Oh my God!' said Jasmine. 'What happened?'

'I missed both times,' his voice was flat.

'Oh what a nuisance. So you're still here.' She pulled the page from her typewriter and crumpled it in her hand.

'Of course I'm still here. Where should I be?'

'But the shots,' Jasmine interrupted, 'I thought — '

'Oh that! I tried to get a rabbit but it was too quick,' he gave a shy laugh. 'I've never pointed a gun at anything before.'

'Useless, absolutely useless,' Jasmine was exasperated, 'you've muffed the whole thing. You muffed it. Can't you do anything properly.'

'I don't know,' he was almost tearful. 'I've never had the chance.'

'I suppose you've never tried for long enough,' she said.

'I would be able to if I stayed here. I — ' he was eager. 'I've had a look out there. I like your place. It's just beginning to get light out there, I could see all the things that need doing. I'll fix the fence posts and paint the sheds. I think I know what's up with the tractor, I'll be able to get it going. There's all the things I'd like to do out there.' He paused and then rushed on, 'on the way up here in the car you said I could stay and work the farm, you said you needed someone like me.'

'You never stay anywhere long enough, you said so yourself.' She put a fresh sheet in the typewriter.

'Well it's not my fault. Like I said, "I've had no chance." '

'What do you do?' Jasmine asked.

'What d'you mean?'

Outside a rooster crowed.

'Oh never mind!' Jasmine yawned. 'I suppose you're, how do they describe it,' she paused, 'discovering yourself.'

'I'm between jobs,' he shouted. 'That's where I've always been, between jobs. Between jobs. Between nothing!' he paused.

'But out there,' he was breathless and excited, 'I saw it all out there waiting to be done, there's everything to do out there. I'll fix everything, you'll see.'

'We like it as it is,' Jasmine said. 'My husband and I like it as it is, we don't want any change.'

'There's even a turkey yard,' he interrupted her, 'you'd like some turkeys wouldn't you, the yard only needs a bit of new wire netting. I'd have some fowls too.'

'But don't you understand,' Jasmine said, 'we only come here to get away from it all. We like the place as it is. It's only a weekender you know, we like it like this.'

'I'll measure up how much wire,' he ignored her, 'I'll need a bit of paper and a pencil. I'll work out how much paint.'

'Australia, Calais, Madras,' Jasmine said softly, 'what does it matter where I set him, London, New York, Bombay, Paris, Rome, it's all the same wherever he is. What does it matter where he pulls the trigger. First, I'll get him somewhere alone and then I'll kill him off.'

'What's that,' he said quickly, 'what did you say?'

Outside another rooster answered the first one.

'Oh, nothing,' she fussed through her papers. 'I think it's really quite light outside now. There's a bus down at the crossroads about five fifty. It should get you back to town around eight o'clock.' She paused and then said, 'I want you to know I feel really bad about the whole thing. I mean about bringing you all the way to the cottage like this, and I do feel bad about it, I'm going to give you this poem I've written. You can keep it. I have other copies.'

'Thank you,' he was only just polite, 'thank you very much.'

'Fourteen stanzas,' Jasmine crooned, 'fourteen stanzas all with fourteen lines and every one all about my adorable little black poodles.'

'What'll I do,' the young man said, 'when I get to the empty town at eight?'

'There's a little refrain,' Jasmine murmured, 'in the middle of every stanza.'

'What'll I do,' he said, 'when I get to the empty town at eight? I mean where will I go? What can I do there?'

'All the stanzas,' she continued, 'have this little refrain to include every one of my little black dogs.'

'I mean,' he said, 'where will I go when I get there? I'd rather stay here and fix the fences. Where will I go? What's there to do in the empty town at eight?' He smiled a moment at his own thoughts. 'You know,' he said, 'there's something good about putting new paint on with a new brush. Dark glossy green, I can just see it out there,' he smiled in the direction of the yard.

'When I wrote the poem,' Jasmine said, 'I knew it was good. I was really pleased with it. It's a good poem. I love my poem.'

'Where will I go in the empty town?' he whined. 'I'll have nothing to eat and nowhere to sleep. Can't I stay and paint the shed? Please?'

'I want everyone to be pleased with the poem,' she said.

'Eight's early to reach town if you've no reason,' he shouted.

'There!' Jasmine smiled, 'I've just thought of a wonderful line for a new poem. I must get it down because I forget everything I think up if I don't get it down.' She began to type, made a mistake, and pulling the spoiled page out, started a fresh page.

'I mean,' the young man cried, 'where will I go when I get there? What's there in town for me to do?'

'I never realised before,' Jasmine yawned, 'that my young man in Madras is an absolute Bore!'

He went to the door and opened it. 'Well, I'd better be on my way then,' he said in a quiet flat voice. He went out carefully closing the door behind him.

Jasmine sat in bed writing her autobiography. *My father,* she typed, *was the distinguished scientist who discovered heat and light.* She stopped typing to sing to herself,

> *I love my little lampshade*
> *So frilly and warm*
> *If I wear my silky lampshade*
> *I'll come to no harm.*

He wrote, she typed, *in his lifetime, two text books, the one on light was blue and for heat, he chose red.*

ON THE TRAIN

Olga Masters

The young woman not more than twenty-seven slammed the gate on herself and the two children both girls.

She did not move off at once but looked up and down the street as if deciding which way to go.

The older girl looked up at her through her hair which was whipped by the wind to read the decision the moment she made it.

Finally the woman took a hand of each child and turned in the direction of the railway station.

'Oh goody!' cried Sara who was nearly five.

'The sun's out,' the woman murmured lifting her face up for a second towards it.

Sara looked again into her mother's face noticing two or three of her teeth pinning down her bottom lip and the glint in her eyes perhaps from the sun? She felt inadequate that she seldom noticed such things as sun and wind, barely bothering about the rain as well, being quite content to stay out and play in it. The weather appeared to figure largely in the lives of adults. Sara hoped this would work out for her when she was older.

The mother bent forward as she hurried the younger child Lisa having difficulty keeping up. Her face Sara saw looked strained like the mother's. Sara hoped she wouldn't complain. The glint in the mother's eyes was like a spark that could ignite and involve them all.

She saw with relief the roof of the station jutting above the street but flashed her eyes away from the buildings still to be passed before they reached it.

The ticket office was protected by the jutting roof.

Sara was glad of the rest while her mother had her head inside the window and laid her cheek lightly against her rump clad in a blue denim skirt.

The business of buying tickets went on for a long time. Sara's eyes conveyed to Lisa her fear that the mother's top half had disappeared forever inside the window. She clutched her skirt to drag her out and opened her mouth to scream. Lisa saw and screamed for her.

The mother flung both arms down brushing a child off with each. They dared not touch her when she turned around and separated the tickets from change in her purse.

She snapped it shut and looked up and around in a distracted way as if to establish where she was.

It was Sara who went in front taking the narrow path squeezed between a high fence on one side and the station wall on the other. She swung her head around to see that her mother and Lisa were following her bouncy confident step.

On the platform waiting for the train the few other passengers looked at them.

Sara's dress was long and her hair was long and she was not dressed warmly enough.

The people especially a couple of elderly women noted Sara's light cotton dress with a deep flounce at the hem and Lisa's skimpy skirt and fawn tights. They looked at the mother's hands to see if there was a bag hanging from them with cardigans or jumpers in. But the mother carried nothing but a leather shoulder bag about as large as a large envelope and quite flat.

'She's warm enough herself,' one of the women murmured to her companion with a sniff.

They watched them board the train noticing the mother did not turn her head when she stepped onto the platform. It was Sara who grasped the hand of Lisa and saw her safely on.

'Tsk, tisk,' said the watching woman wishing she could meet the mother's eyes and glare her disapproval.

The mother took a single seat near the aisle and let Sara and Lisa find one together across from her.

Dear little soul, thought the passenger on the seat facing them seeing Sara's face suffused with pleasure at her small victory. Lisa had to wriggle her bony little rump with legs stuck out stiffly to get onto the seat.

Sara read the passenger's thoughts.

'She doesn't like you helping,' she said.

This was almost too much for the passenger whose glance

leapt towards the mother to share with her this piece of childish wisdom.

But the mother had her profile raised and her eyes slanted away towards the window. The skin spread over her cheek-bones made the passenger think of pale honey spread on a slice of bread.

She's beautiful. The woman was surprised at herself for not having noticed it at once.

She returned her attention rather reluctantly to Sara and Lisa. She searched their faces for some resemblance to the mother. Sara's was round with blue worried eyes under faint eyebrows. Lisa's was pale with a pinched look and blue veins at the edges of her eyebrows disappearing under a woollen cap with a ragged tassel that looked as if a kitten had wrestled with it.

The passenger thought they might look like their father putting him into a category unworthy of the handsome mother.

For the next twenty minutes the train alternated between a rocking tearing speed and dawdling within sight of one of the half dozen stations on the way to the city and the passenger alternated her attention between the girls and the mother although at times she indulged in a fancy that she was not their mother but someone minding them.

'I can move and your mummy sit here,' she said to Sara with sudden inspiration.

I'll find out for sure.

Sara put her head against the seat back, tipping her face and closing her eyes with pink coming into her cheeks.

The passenger looked to Lisa for an answer and Lisa turned her eyes towards her mother seeing only her profile and the long peaked collar of her blouse lying on her honey coloured sweater.

Lisa looked into the passenger's face and gave her head the smallest shake.

Poor little soul.

The passenger stared at the mother knowing in the end she would look back.

The mother did her eyes widening for a second under bluish lids with only a little of her brow visible under a thick bank of fair hair. There was nothing friendly in her face.

The passenger reddened and looked at the girls.

'Your mummy's so pretty,' she said.

Sara swung her head around to look at the mother and Lisa allowed herself a tiny smile as if it didn't need verification.

'Do you like having a pretty mummy?' the passenger asked.

The mother had turned her attention to the window again and her eyes had narrowed.

The passenger felt as if a door had been shut in her face.

'Are you going into the city for the day?' she said to the girls.

Sara pressed her lips together as if she shouldn't answer if she wanted to. Lisa's mouth opened losing its prettiness and turning into an uneven hole.

There's nothing attractive about either of them, thought the passenger deciding that Lisa might be slightly cross-eyed.

She sat with her handbag gripped on her knees and her red face flushed a deeper red and her brown eyes with flecks of red in the whites were flint-hard when they darted between the mother and the girls and vacant when they looked away.

After a moment the mother turned her head and stared into the passenger's face. The girls raised their eyes and looked too. The train swayed and rushed and all the eyes locked together. The mother's eyes although large and blue and without light were the snake's eyes mesmerising those of the passenger. Sara swung her eyes from the passenger to the mother as if trying to protect one from the other. Lisa's face grew tight and white and she opened her small hole of a mouth but no sound came out.

The mother keeping her eyes on the passenger got up suddenly and checked the location through the window. Sara and Lisa stumbled into the aisle holding out frantic fingers but afraid to touch her. Sara stood under her mother's rump as close as she dared her eyes turned back to see Lisa holding the seat end. The train swayed and clanged the last hundred yards slowing and sliding like a skier at the bottom of a snow peak stopping with a suddenness that flung Sara and Lisa together across the seat end.

This was fortunate.

The mother level with the passenger now leaned down and sparks from her eyes flew off the hard flat stones of the passenger's eyes.

'I'm going to kill them,' the mother said.

THE LATE SUNLIGHT

Jessica Anderson

As Gordon crossed the park on the way back to his chilly rented flat, and felt the stored warmth of the day's sun rising from the terra cotta paving, he was tempted into turning aside and sitting next to an old woman on a sheltered bench. He put his folder and notebooks beside him, let the sunlight settle on him, and felt his body sigh. The old woman said, 'You are taking the sun?'

He did not try to define her European accent, knowing only that it was not French or Italian. Nowadays he tried to provide against his tendency to be too friendly too soon; in his youth it had led him into so many long useless conversations, had wasted so much of his time; warring couples whose only aim was to condemn each other had made him their confidant, and evangelists for the more unusual religions had scarcely been able to believe their luck. Without looking at the woman he murmured an assent.

'The sun in winter is like the medicine.'

Gordon gave the slightest of nods.

'You need the medicine of the sun?'

Gordon had had such a disappointing day at the library that he could not help saying that at the moment, he certainly felt he did.

'You have been sick?'

This was how it had always started. He tried to retreat by shutting his eyes, as if his eyelids especially needed the sun.

'You look as if you have been sick.'

Such a voice, so loud and acid, gave him a choice. He could get up and go, or he could turn and talk to her. His old tendency

98

was always inclined to revive when he was away from his wife and family.

Her eyes were a faded black, lustreless yet intense, perhaps hostile. But to their stare she added the smile of long painted lips, the vivacity of eyebrows drawn far above her natural browline, and a sociable inclination towards him of her thick body. 'You are too pale,' she said. 'You have none of the pink.'

Neither had she. Her skin was olive with undertones of lead. He saw now that she was dressed in what his two elder children called 'money-money clothes'. Richness glistened in her fur collar, in the velvety pile of her elaborate asymmetrical hat, in her narrow finely-crafted shoes, and in the handbag, made of the skin of some reptile, which lay rigid and sharp-angled in her lap. 'A young man,' she said, 'should have a little of the pink.'

The inclination of her body seemed ingratiating, but her tone was still acid. Forty may really seem young to her; Gordon absolved her of flattery. 'I suppose I'm so thick-skinned,' he said lazily, 'that no pink can get through.'

'Thick-skinned? No.' She shook her head in absolute negation. No, no, no, no, no.' She leaned back on the bench. 'You are refined,' she said, and gave a single sharp nod.

Scottish ancestors had given him a lean gingery ascetic look, and he supposed it was this she called refinement. But from her generation to his, it could be a dubious compliment. He made an ironical mouth and said, *'Am I?'*

Below the thin black arcs, the two lumps of her hairless brows drew together in a scowl. 'You think I don't know?' she said. 'You think I can't tell? When I see these others, all around me?'

Her little gloved hand, curved downward, stabbed towards the other occupied benches, towards the sunburst fountain, where people were taking photographs, towards the paths on which they were daring to pass up and down.

'They are so common.'

The last word was delivered on a guttural of hatred and contempt. Gordon's recoil was swift and instinctive. His parents had put an absolute embargo on this epithet, assuring him that his own inferiority, and possibly wickedness, was all its use would prove. Nor had the sympathies of his maturity tempted him far in a contrary direction. Indeed, if blasphemy existed for Gordon, this painted old woman had just committed it. He folded his arms and raised his face again to the sun. There was no point in anything but politeness. 'Excuse me,' he said. 'I'll take a bit more of this curative sun.'

He knew she would speak again. But now the sun was holding him, as was a reluctance to face the depressing flat. When she asked if he was a writer, he prepared to pay for a few more minutes of the sun, and replied that he was a teacher.

'Those papers,' he said patiently, guessing what had prompted her question, 'are notes I've been taking in the library. I've got time off to do some research.'

'You teach in a school?'

'I teach in a university.'

'You are a professor?'

The word was pronounced with respect. 'I am a tutor,' said Gordon. 'I teach history in Canberra.'

'Ah. Can-*bair*-ah.'

The respect this time sounded false. She asked him what history he taught, and when he said Australian, she asked with dangerous playfulness whether there was such a thing. But the sun was her enemy; it was easy not to reply. Behind his closed lids, light motes sweetly floated. Her voice, like the footsteps on the path, changed timbre, became muffled, retreated. And sweet as a light mote, there drifted into his brain the knowledge that his thesis should not be on the colonial institution he had chosen, but on one man, the one whose character had permeated that institution. There that man stood. Details, so carefully gathered by Gordon, worried over, mauled, but stubbornly disparate, flew to assemble round him. The voice at Gordon's side, continuing to speak of Can-*bair*-ah, still sounded distant, but he knew it was not. Begging his man to stay, not to fade, he jumped to his feet and picked up his papers. 'But what does Can-*bair*-ah matter,' cried the woman, giving her little gloved stabs, 'when there are no real cities in Australia anyway?'

Gordon wished he had a hat to raise, something to placate her for his abrupt departure. But he could only apologise for leaving so suddenly, and hurried away. 'You are a gentleman,' she called after him, loud enough for half the park to hear.

In the depressing flat, which he had taken unseen, Gordon sat down immediately to his books and notes. He worked, with a short break for dinner at the Indian restaurant three doors down, until midnight. By that time his excitement was tamped to a sober hopefulness. More information was needed to confirm that vision. But Gordon thought he knew where to find it.

The next day in the library, he crashed. The information in which he had trusted diminished the man's importance. Yet his vision had made it impossible to return to his old institutional subject, which now spread itself out like so many lumber rooms. He dropped again into the dullness and perplexity that had brought him to search in Sydney. The library, because in his boyhood and youth it had often been a refuge from the enthusiasms of his family, had always rested in his mind like a point of peace. But now even the library was uncongenial to him. He left early, crossing Macquarie Street with the hunched gait by which his wife Marion said she could detect his low moods.

In the park the old woman sat in the same seat. Seeing her before she saw him, Gordon recalled the words she had called after him yesterday — 'You are a gentleman' — and speculated on their meaning: they were a sarcastic reproach for his abrupt departure; they were flattery to make him come back; they were simply wild and heedless. He intended to pass her by, but she saw him, and gave him her slow red foxy smile, and for some reason — perhaps because disappointment had made him apathetic — he went and sat at her side. 'Today I will tell you of my son,' she instantly announced. But then she turned the red smile downwards, brooded, and said, 'No, I will not.' She eyed his notebooks, became sociable. 'You have been at your library.'

He nodded. He kept the notebooks in his hand, and did not relax into this seat. Today she was dressed with a richness that at four thirty in this scrap of a park amounted to grotesquerie. Her jacket and cap were mink, he was sure. Only diamonds could have the flashing power of the stones in her dangling ear rings, and in that case, the stones surrounding them must be — yes — rubies. That was to say nothing of the rings on her fingers, perhaps six. She wore no gloves today. The handbag was the same one. She opened it, shook a pill from a tiny round silver box, and shut the bag with a satisfied snap of its double clasp. In some recess of his mind he had already decided she was middle European, and now, from those turbulent countries crushed together on the map, Hungary stood out. She rolled the pill in her mouth and eyed him sideways. Both her painted and real brows were at rest, but the smile of her sucking mouth was anticipatory. She was waiting to finish the pill before speaking. Her legs were shapely; she crossed them and kicked out the upper one. Had she been a performer of some sort? An actress? Perhaps she had even ridden a white horse round a circus ring. He could see it. And then had married a rich man, and puffed herself up with jewels and furs, and begun to call people common. He wondered why he rather liked her. She finished her pill.

'You are married?'

'Yes.'

She was at her most ingratiating. 'You have the look of a man nicely married.'

'Well, I am.'

'Your wife's name?'

'Marion. And,' he said, before she could ask, 'we have three children. Peter, Tess, and Joel. Twelve, eleven, and seven.'

'I once knew a Marion.' She deepened her voice and drew a hand downward from her chin. *'Such a chin!* That was when I was first in Australia. Has your Marion — *such a chin?'*

He foresaw an analysis of Marion's appearance; he would not encourage it. 'Have you been long in Australia?' he asked.

She subsided into disgust. 'One hundred years.'

'But actually?'

'But actually, since during the War.' She was watching him keenly. 'No, I am not Jewish, in case you will now want to forgive me everything. Yes, that is what some people do. My husband, who was also not Jewish, acted in a political way, so we had to leave.'

He knew from experience that if he replied to this, the conversation would certainly be long, and if not useless, infinitely knotted. He put down his notes and leaned forward with his elbows on his knees. 'What part of Europe do you come from?'

She spread a hand on her breast. The stubby little ringed fingers sank in fur. 'I am Viennese.'

He made a swift mental appraisal of his inaccurate guess, and another of his passing thought that it had been near enough. But now she said, with sudden prim finality, 'And you, sir? You are Australian?'

He said he was.

'Of Australian parentage also?'

'On both sides.'

'From one of the big country estates perhaps?'

He could not help laughing. He thought of the little bungalow, so flimsy that in memory it shook with the thump of argument and exhortation, and threatened to burst with the people who had nowhere else to go. Worthy causes had slept on the verandah or on a mattress in Gordon's room, and a victim of society had stolen his Cambridge histories. Leaning back on the bench, he gave a long soft laugh not only at the contrast of the suggestion with the reality, but in tribute to his dead parents, so good, tireless, and indignant. But she was looking at him with her long mouth shut as tight as the clasp on her handbag. He stopped laughing and said, 'Sorry. In fact I was born right here in Sydney. My father was a teacher too. Only he taught little kids, in primary school.'

Her hard angry calculating look did not waver. She said, 'You should not tell anyone. No one would ever know.'

He could have laughed again, but did not want to anger her further. Nothing she said could matter. He half-shut his eyes against the sun, and at that moment knew at what point in the day's research he had taken the wrong direction. He saw his own hand as it wrote the request for the misleading material. She was speaking, but he shut his mind to her words, while quickly he allowed to enter the knowledge of the path he should have taken. But he could not help hearing that he was the very model of an Englishman she had once known, who was a very great aristocrat, and a model of refinement, so that when he rose quickly to his feet, and picked up his notes, he gave her a little bow of farewell. He had never bowed in his life before, but he wanted to please her. Today's insight, like yesterday's was without doubt the result of relaxation after hard mental work, but she had been present on both occasions, and though he knew he was not superstitious, he could not afford to take risks. Bowing, he explained that he must hurry back to the library. She gave her consent with a nod, but did not let him go until he had told him his name, and she, again with that precise gesture of hand on breast, had given him hers. It was long, and he was too distracted to listen with his usual care, and all he retained was her Christian name, Vera.

On his way back to the library he bought a pack of chicken and gobbled it up behind one of the advertising fixtures on the railway platform. He was glad Vera could not see him. He did not have much time in the library before it shut, but enough to assure himself that this time he was not mistaken, and to reserve his material for tomorrow. When he got back to the flat he rang Marion. While he waited for an answer he envisioned he walking through their pleasant haphazard rooms, wearing the padded black Indian dress and the boots she had hardly changed out of lately. Her fair hair would be loose on her shoulders, and as she walked she would slip a hand beneath it and massage the back of her head, where the knot had been pinned all day. When she answered she sounded tired.

'Darling,' he said with a rush. 'I'm sorry I didn't ring before. Is everything okay? Kids okay? You?'

'Everything's fine. How's your work?'

'Oh — all right.' He knew she would understand, from his guarded yet airy tone, that at this stage he wanted to keep it to himself. She would recognize it as a good sign. 'What about yours?' he asked.

'Guido is sick, and I'm taking one of his tutorials. But don't worry. Don't hurry home. Peter and Tess cooked dinner tonight, and Joel set the table. How is the grisly flat?'

He had not even noticed it tonight. 'I guess it serves its purpose.'

'I long to see you, Gordon.'

'I long to see you, my love.'

'How much longer?'

'Two more days.'

'That's not bad.'

'At the most. Has Joel got his glasses yet?'

'No. Tomorrow.'

'Home on Friday, then. I'm fairly sure.'

'Try hard. Goodnight, darling.'

'Goodnight, sweet.'

He felt deeply contented as he undressed. He sometimes felt more genuinely a part of his family when away from them than when at home. There, he occasionally had the curious feeling that he had had no part in their making, but that he had come gambolling to their door one day, and they, calmly, smilingly, kindly, had taken him in and given him a good home. Marion was a mathematician, and so, potentially, were all three children. All passionately loved music, though never to dance to, as he had once done, and none read fiction for pleasure. They disregarded their own beauty, and in their cupboards hung few more than the essential garments. Interchangeable hats hanging on pegs in the hall guarded their fair skins. The oddest thing of all about them was that on Sundays all went to the Anglican church, Marion simply insisting when he teased her about it that that was how she had been brought up.

But when Gordon was away, none of these differences caused him the alienation (which sometimes became resentment) that they caused him at home. The contentment with which he went to sleep continued into the next day. In the library he proceeded with absolute certainty to find his material. It was one of those rare days when nearly everything he turned up was useful, and could be accepted without surprise. The congeniality of the room — the peace of its polished timber and high pale panes of glass — was restored to him. Flickering only on the margin of his consciousness were the morbid shadows on Vera's skin, her disquieting eyes and the long red lips sucking at her pill. As he walked to his train in Martin Place, these settled into a conclusion that she was very sick.

The first sight of her seemed to contradict it. She sat in the same place, and when she saw him, she kicked up a leg and patted the seat at her side. She had no pill in her mouth, and again her smile was mocking, deliberate, and foxy. She was dressed entirely in black, on her coat an astrakhan collar, on her head an astrakhan toque incredibly twisted to one side in a kind of cockade. 'So today you carry the brief case,' she said as he sat down.

She took no notice of his explanation that he had had some documents copied. She seemed excited, bursting with talk. 'My son also carries the brief case. He is like a good little doggie, carrying the brief case. I do not mean you are like a doggie. You are so tall. But he is little and neat, and should not carry the brief case.'

'Is your son here in Sydney?' asked Gordon.

'Of course he is here in Sydney. He is Australian. His wife is Australian. His children are Australian. He is a little Australian doggie. And now my neighbour tells me how I must see him, this doggie, how I must ring him and tell him to come.'

It disturbed Gordon that she had only a neighbour to tell her this. 'You have no other children?'

'I have no children at all. I do not count doggies. He will get everything. That is the law. That is enough. I will not see him also.'

Her handbag was again the same one. She shook out a pill from the little silver box. 'Last time I see him was two years ago. He comes to me and he says, "Mutti, you must do this thing for your health, you must do that thing." I say yes, yes, and now go home, good doggie, to your *Sand*-ra.'

She pronounced the name with even more hatred and contempt than she had used for the word common, but because this time it was merely personal, it did not shock Gordon so much. The late sunlight was having its usual benign effect. His thoughts settled contentedly on his work. His colonial man stood before him in promise of full life. He estimated that tomorrow about three hours of work would give him enough to go on with for months.

Vera finished her pill. 'Now I wish to speak of your wife.'

He was good-humoured but wary. 'What about her?'

'You have her photograph?'

'Not here.'

'Please to describe her.'

Gordon laughed. 'She is slim and fair. You want to know if she is beautiful, don't you?'

She gave one of her consciously dignified nods. He had changed his mind about her having been a circus performer, but the suggestion of theatre lingered. He said, 'Yes, she is beautiful.'

'And — excuse me — is she common?'

'I'm amazed that you excuse yourself. I don't quite know how to answer you, but if in your opinion I am not common, then neither is Marion.'

'That is good then. I would like her to have the dark beauty, but the fair is also good. Though not so good for the men to have.'

Her son, she went on to say, was of that fairness they called washed-out. Gordon was not attending. He was thinking of the tick Marion had found that summer before last in her pubic hair. They had been bush walking, and that night she had found it, and had lain on the bed while Gordon anaesthetized it and plucked it out. Now he could never hear darkness and fairness contrasted without seeing again, in the light of the halogen lamp drawn down to the bed, the black tick in the curling shining flaxen hair, its head already embedded in her white skin. Nor could he ever think of it without feelings of tenderness, lust, and romance. The prospect of an early start at the library tomorrow, his certain return home in the afternoon, made him tolerant of Vera's vehement wanderings about Sandra and the doggie, for both of whom he felt a humorous sympathy.

'Before that last time he came to see me, he would come every Friday. Alone, of course, without his *Sand*-ra. He would make the conversation. First he would want to speak of the old days, as he would call them. But I do not speak of the old days to doggies. And then there is the weather. Or the news. He would make the long face. "The news is bad, Mutti." And I would say, "If it is Australian news, do not tell me. Here is no news." My husband used to get the European papers, you understand. And when they would come, he would put away your *Heralds* and *Telegraphs*, and he would say, "Now we will have some real news." '

Gordon wondered how often she must have been asked why, since she hated Australia so bitterly, she didn't go back where she came from. So many times, he guessed, and with such hostility, that she now scornfully invited the question. He said, 'Have you never been back?'

'We went back, but it is here my husband makes the money, so it is here we must stay. Then my husband dies,' she said, with one of her angry looks, 'and it is too late to go back.' With one gloved hand she stabbed the air. 'And of Vienna what is left anyway?'

'I have never been to Vienna.'

She said with calm contempt, 'Of course you have never been to Vienna, my dear. In your lifetime is no real Vienna left.'

He was about to reply that he knew people who said there was no real Sydney left, when a voice above them said, 'Well, Vera, you look happy enough today.'

A tightly stout and smiling woman stood behind the bench. She was perhaps not much younger than Vera. 'All the same, Vera,' she said gently, 'I wish you would come home with me.'

Gordon got to his feet and picked up his briefcase.

'This is my neighbour,' said Vera, beginning to kick up her leg again, to smile and to mock.

'Mildred Reed,' said the woman. 'Vera and I have lived next door in Charton Towers for ten years.'

'Gordon Harbage,' said Gordon.

'Well, Mr Harbage,' said Mildred Reed, 'I suppose it's no good asking if you have any influence with Vera, but I wish someone had. I wish someone could persuade her to see Arthur.'

'Arthur is the name of the little doggie,' said Vera complacently.

'I understand your concern, Mrs Reed,' said Gordon, 'but as for influence, I've none. We've simply met a few times here in the park.'

'He is the very image of that Englishman I was once talking you about.'

'Talking me? Vera, you're tired. And it's getting cold out here.'

'Yes, I will come,' said Vera calmly.

'I think we'll get a taxi.'

'Wait,' said Vera. 'First I will give my new friend this. I will not see him again.' She opened her bag. 'I wish for him to take this little gift to his beautiful wife.'

The little parcel she offered was wrapped in a twist of red paper, tied with a crumpled red ribbon. 'It is one of my pill boxes.'

'Those pill boxes are solid silver,' said Mildred Reed with respect.

'Well, thank you,' said Gordon, taking the little parcel, trying to imagine Marion using a pill box.

He got the two women a taxi. He was surprised that Vera did not look at him after he had helped her into it. It was Mildred Reed who smiled and raised a hand, while Vera sat hunched, her face turned away, as if offended. He had, he supposed, omitted some ceremony natural to a great gentleman.

At the flat he rang Marion. 'Three hours is all I'll need tomorrow. I'll go straight from the library to the airport.'

'The two o'clock plane?'

'For sure. I'll be home before you. Has Joel got his glasses?'

'Yes. He keep screwing up his face. He says he can't forget those things are on it.'

'Poor old boy.' Gordon suddenly clapped a hand to his pocket. 'I've got a present for you.'

'What?'

'No. Wait.'

'All right. A surprise.'

'It certainly surprised me.'

The next morning, when Gordon was getting ready to go to the library, he saw the little red parcel among his papers, and impulsively opened it. He knew by the worn embossing that the box was very old, and he smiled to see that, small as it was, room had been made for minute cherubs to loll about it here and there, linked by garlands. Marion would probably become fond of it, and keep it on the shelf with the sea shells, pieces of blue glass, and the Chinese figurine with the missing hand. He opened it and took out a piece of stiff paper which he thought may be a note, but from which fell into his hand the diamond and ruby earrings Vera had worn in the park on the second day.

He felt himself flush hot with anger. Now he must get them back to her; now he could miss the two o'clock plane. And now, above all, the precious steadiness of his investigation would be disrupted. He stamped about dressing, he cursed, scowled, chucked papers into his case. Then he abruptly checked himself. Like this, he was compounding the danger. Instead, he could congratulate himself on remembering the name of Vera's building. It would not take long to go there and return them — nothing, nothing, would induce him to argue or talk — and if he maintained his steadiness, kept his goal immovably in sight, neither his research nor his return to his family need suffer.

A taxi took him to Charton Towers in five minutes. The directory in the foyer showed M. Reed in 99, but both 98 and 100 were shown only as occupied.

Without more than a few seconds of grinding his teeth, he took the lift to the ninth floor. As he walked down the corridor he saw Mildred Reed coming out of a door. She saw him, and stood with the knob in her hand for a moment before shutting it. She waited until he was within close speaking range. 'Vera is dead,' she said then. 'I found her two hours ago.'

He breathed out an automatic 'Good heavens'. The door behind her was marked 98. When she moved towards her door, 99, he followed her, not wanting to, yet not knowing what else to do. 'Will you come in?' she said.

'For a few minutes.' As she opened the door he looked quickly at his watch.

They sat on opposite chairs in her hall. 'It could have happened any old time,' she said. 'It was just good luck it didn't happen in that park.'

'Her heart?'

'Yes, Hopeless. Hopeless. But when it came to the last, she wouldn't take advice. The moment they told her she would have to go to hospital, she went straight to the bank and got all her jewellery out, and every day after that she had to get dressed up and go wandering about talking to people in shops, and sitting in that park.' Mildred Reed grimaced, close to tears. 'I'm going to miss her. I'll tell you that.'

Though still uncertain what to do, Gordon had drawn his case on to his knees. He took out the pill box. 'There's this,' he said.

'It's valuable, do you mean? That's right. But Vera wanted your wife to have it. I heard her myself. But if it puts your mind at ease, ask Arthur.'

'Her son's here?'

'Of course. I got in touch with him at once.'

'Good. Splendid. Because there are these, too.'

He tipped the earrings into the palm of his hand. She plucked one of them out, held it dangling, and smiled while she shook her head.

'They're not genuine?' he asked.

'Oh, they're genuine. I was just thinking of the time Sandra had the cheek to try them on. Which, I might mention, was the absolute end.' She smiled again, dropping the earring back into his hand, closed the fingers of both her hands around his, and put her face near his like a plotting schoolgirl. 'That's what Vera was doing. Making damn sure Sandra wouldn't get them. If I were you, I wouldn't ask Arthur anything. He never stood up to her, that was his trouble. If I were you, I would do just as she wanted.'

Gordon disengaged his hand. 'No chance.'

'It was her last wish.'

But now Gordon was standing, looking openly at his watch. 'I want to see Arthur, Mrs Reed.'

'Well, all right.' She sighed and laughed as she hoisted herself out of her chair. 'But I only wish you could see Sandra too.'

Vera's furnishings were as rich and weighty and tortuous as her clothes had been. They dominated the man who stood among them. Gordon found in him no resemblance to the little doggie projected by his mother. He was of medium height, slender, with grey among his fair hair, and a finely moulded and thoughtful face. In other circumstances, Gordon would have liked him on sight, but at present he knew what he had to hold on to; he knew what was threatened; he would not divert himself by taking one of his sudden likings. He noticed that the man had been crying; the flesh about his eyes was puffed, the eyeballs were inflamed. He did not offer his hand, but stood straight, his arms hanging.

'Of course you must keep them.' He spoke coldly, or perhaps only distractedly; Gordon could not tell. Gordon's explanation had been too much interrupted, too much vouched for, by Mildred Reed, and to his great irritation, he saw that she was now about to burst out again.

'Mrs Reed,' he said, 'please let me speak for myself.' He turned to the grieved man. 'The point is, I simply don't want these. I'll give the pill box to my wife. That's okay. I consented to that. But I won't keep these.'

'I understand,' said Vera's son. But he did not extend his hand to take the earrings, and Gordon was forced to lay them on the nearest surface, which was a small inlaid table. He did this gently and with great relief. 'I wouldn't have chosen to come now,' he said, 'only I leave Sydney early this afternoon. I'm sorry about your mother's sudden death.'

Tears filled the eyes of Vera's son, and he turned away. 'I am sorry about her whole life,' he said. He opened the door of the inner room. 'Goodbye. And thank you.'

In the corridor again with Mildred Reed, Gordon saw by his watch that he had lost less than half an hour. He had remained steady; the day was fine, and taxis would be easy to get. He said, 'I liked her son.'

'Arthur's all right.' She lowered her voice. 'She did have a cruel streak.'

'Still, I can quite see how you will miss her. She had such a strong presence. Was she an actress of some sort?'

Mildred Reed drew in a breath of half-pretended shock. 'Lucky you didn't ask her that. She was a countess. That's why she used to go about saying everyone was so terribly common.'

'I thought they didn't,' said Gordon.

'What, countesses? Titled people? Well, she's the only one I've ever known, and she did, no doubt about that. And no doubt about the title either. It was in her own right. I saw the documentation. I suppose there are lots of them in those countries. Her father was Hungarian. But still.'

'Well,' said Gordon. 'I see I've been badly educated.'

He was alone in the sealed lift on the way down. At the rim of his steadiness he knew there was some disturbance, some little clamour. He said aloud, 'May God rest her soul.' The words dying away left him surprised. She had made him bow, she had made him pray, and each time for the same purpose.

In the two o'clock plane, with the morning's solid work behind him, Gordon allowed himself to wonder what would have happened if he had agreed to keep the earrings. He imagined Marion, in front of the mirror, laughing as she held them up to her ears. He imagined one of the children — it would be Joel — saying with anxiety, 'But they're worth a lot of money.' He imagined Marion saying, 'Then we can sell them, and buy Tess her violin.' Beyond that, he would not allow himself to imagine. He knew he would never regret having refused them.

Willy-Wagtails by Moonlight

Patrick White

The Wheelers drove up to the Mackenzies' punctually at six-thirty. It was the hour for which they had been asked. My God, though Jum Wheeler. It had been raining a little, and the tyres sounded blander on the wet gravel.

In front of the Mackenzies', which was what is known as a Lovely Old Home — colonial style — amongst some carefully natural-looking gums, there stood a taxi.

'Never knew Arch and Nora ask us with anyone else,' Eileen Wheeler said.

'Maybe they didn't. Even now. Maybe it's someone they couldn't get rid of.'

'Or an urgent prescription from the chemist's.'

Eileen Wheeler yawned. She must remember to show sympathy, because Nora Mackenzie was going through a particularly difficult one.

Anyway, they were there, and the door stood open on the lights inside. Even the lives of the people you know, even the lives of Nora and Arch look interesting for a split second, when you drive up and glimpse them through the lit doorway.

'It's that Miss Cullen,' Eileen said.

For there was Miss Cullen, doing something with a brief-case in the hall.

'Ugly bitch,' Jum said.

'Plain is the word,' corrected Eileen.

'Arch couldn't do without her. Practically runs the business.'

Certainly that Miss Cullen looked most methodical, shuffling the immaculate papers, and slipping them into a new pigskin brief-case in Arch and Nora's hall.

'Got a figure,' Eileen conceded.

'But not a chin.'

'Oh, hello, Miss Cullen. It's stopped raining.'

It was too bright stepping suddenly into the hall. The Wheelers brightly blinked. They looked newly made.

'Keeping well, Miss Cullen, I hope?'

'I have nothing to complain about, Mr Wheeler,' Miss Cullen replied.

She snapped the catch. Small, rather pointed breasts under the rain-coat. But, definitely, no chin.

Eileen Wheeler was fixing her hair in the reproduction Sheraton mirror.

She had been to the hairdresser's recently, and the do was still set too tight.

'Well, good-bye now,' Miss Cullen said.

When she smiled there was a hint of gold, but discreet, no more than a bridge. Then she would draw her lips together, and lick them ever so sweetly, as if she had been sucking a not unpleasantly acid sweetie.

Miss Cullen went out the door, closing it firmly but quietly behind her.

'That was Miss Cullen,' said Nora Mackenzie coming down. 'She's Arch's secretary.'

'He couldn't do without her,' she added, as though they did not know.

Nora was like that. Eileen wondered how she and Nora had tagged along together, ever since Goulburn, all those years.

'God, she's plain!' Jum said.

Nora did not exactly frown, but pleated her forehead the way she did when other people's virtues were assailed. Such attacks seemed to affect her personally, causing her almost physical pain.

'But Mildred is so kind,' she insisted.

Nora Mackenzie made a point of calling her husband's employees by first names, trying to make them part of a family which she alone, perhaps, would have liked to exist.

'She brought me some giblet soup, all the way from Balgowlah, that time I had virus 'flu.'

'Was it good, darling?' Eileen asked.

She was going through the routine, rubbing Nora's cheek with her own. Nora was pale. She must remember to be kind.

Nora did not answer, but led the way into the lounge-room.

Nora said:

'I don't think I'll turn on the lights for the present. They hurt my eyes, and it's so restful sitting in the dusk.'

Nora *was* pale. She had, in fact, just taken a couple of Disprin.

'Out of sorts, dear?' Eileen asked.

Nora did not answer, but offered some dry martinis.

Very watery, Jum knew from experience, but drink of a kind.

'Arch will be down presently,' Nora said. 'He had to attend to some business, some letters Miss Cullen brought. Then he went in to have a shower.'

Nora's hands were trembling as she offered the dry martinis, but Eileen remembered they always had.

The Wheelers sat down. It was all so familiar, they did not have to be asked, which was fortunate, as Nora Mackenzie always experienced difficulty in settling guests into chairs. Now she sat down herself, far more diffidently than her friends. The cushions were standing on their points.

Eileen sighed. Old friendships and the first scent of gin always made her nostalgic.

'It's stopped raining,' she said, and sighed.

'Arch well?' Jum asked.

As if he cared. She had let the ice get into the cocktail, turning it almost to pure water.

'He has his trouble,' Nora said. 'You know, his back.'

Daring them to have forgotten.

Nora loved Arch. It made Eileen feel ashamed.

So fortunate for them to have discovered each other. Nora Leadbeatter and Arch Mackenzie. Two such bores. And with bird-watching in common. Though Eileen Wheeler had never believed Nora did not make herself learn to like watching birds.

At Goulburn, in the early days, Nora would come out to Glen Davie sometimes to be with Eileen at week-ends. Mr Leadbeatter had been manager at the Wales for a while. He always saw that his daughter had the cleanest notes. Nora was shy, but better than nothing, and the two girls would sit about on the verandah those summer evenings, buffing their nails, and listening to the sheep cough in the home paddock. Eileen gave Nora lessons in making-up. Nora had protested, but was pleased.

'Mother well, darling?' Eileen asked, sipping that sad, watery gin.

'Not exactly *well*,' Nora replied, painfully.

Because she had been to Orange, to visit her widowed mother, who suffered from Parkinson's disease.

'You know what I mean, dear,' said Eileen.

Jum was dropping his ash on the carpet. It might be better when poor bloody Arch came down.

'I have an idea that woman, that Mrs Galloway, is unkind to her,' Nora said.

'Get another,' Eileen advised. 'It isn't like after the War.'

'One can never be sure,' Nora debated. 'One would hate to hurt the woman's feelings.'

Seated in the dusk Nora Mackenzie was of a moth colour. Her face looked as though she had been rubbing it with chalk. Might have, too, in spite of those lessons in make-up. She sat and twisted her hands together.

How very red Nora's hands had been, at Goulburn, at the convent, to which the two girls had gone. Not that they belonged to *those*. It was only convenient. Nora's hands had been red and trembly after practising a tarantella, early, in the frost. So very early all of that. Eileen had learnt about life shortly after puberty. She had tried to tell Nora one or two things, but Nora did not want to hear. Oh, no, no, *please*, Eileen, Nora cried. As though a boy had been twisting her arm. She had those long, entreating, sensitive hands.

And there they were still. Twisting together, making their excuses. For what they had never done.

Arch came in then. He turned on the lights, which made Nora wince, even those lights which barely existed in all the neutrality of Nora's room. Nora did not comment, but smiled, because it was Arch who had committed the crime.

Arch said:

'You two toping hard as usual.'

He poured himself the rest of the cocktail.

Eileen laughed her laugh which people found amusing at parties.

Jum said, and bent his leg, if it hadn't been for Arch and the shower, they wouldn't have had the one too many.

'A little alcohol releases the vitality,' Nora remarked ever so gently.

She always grew anxious at the point where jokes became personal.

Arch composed his mouth under the handle-bars moustache, and Jum knew what they were in for.

'Miss Cullen came out with one or two letters,' Arch was taking pains to explain. 'Something she thought should go off tonight. I take a shower most evenings. Summer, at least.'

'Such humidity,' Nora helped.

Arch looked down into his glass. He might have been composing further remarks, but did not come out with them.

That silly, bloody English-air-force-officer's moustache. It was the only thing Arch had ever dared. War had given him the courage to pinch a detail which did not belong to him.

'That Miss Cullen, useful girl,' Jum suggested.

'Runs the office.'

'Forty, if a day,' Eileen said, whose figure was beginning to slacken off.

Arch said he would not know, and Jum made a joke about Miss Cullen's *cul-de-sac*.

The little pleats had appeared again in Nora Mackenzie's chalky brow. 'Well,' jumping up, quite girlish, she cried, 'I do hope the dinner will be a success.'

And laughed.

Nora was half-way through her second course with that woman at the Chanticleer. Eileen suspected there would be avocadoes stuffed with prawns, chicken *Mornay*, and *crêpes Suzette*.

Eileen was right.

Arch seemed to gain in authority sitting at the head of his table.

'I'd like you to taste this wine,' he said. 'It's very light.'

'Oh, yes?' said Jum.

The wine was corked, but nobody remarked. The second bottle, later on, was somewhat better. The Mackenzies were spreading themselves tonight.

Arch flipped his napkin once or twice, emphasizing a point. He smoothed the handle-bars moustache, which should have concealed a harelip, only there wasn't one. Jum dated from before the moustache, long, long, very long.

Arch said:

'There was a story Armitage told me at lunch. There was a man who bought a mower. Who suffered from indigestion. Now, how exactly, did it . . . go?

Jum had begun to make those little pellets out of bread. It always fascinated him how grubby the little pellets turned out. And himself not by any means dirty.

Arch failed to remember the point of the story Armitage had told.

It was difficult to understand how Arch had made a success of his business. Perhaps it was that Miss Cullen, breasts and all, under the rain-coat. For a long time Arch had messed around.

Travelled in something. Separator parts. Got the agency for some sort of phoney machine for supplying *ozone* to public buildings. The Mackenzies lived at Burwood then. Arch continued to mess around. The War was quite a godsend. Arch was a real adje type. Did a conscientious job. Careful with his allowances, too.

Then, suddenly, after the War, Arch Mackenzie had launched out, starting the import-export business. Funny the way a man will suddenly hit on the idea to which his particular brand of stupidity can respond.

The Mackenzies had moved to the North Shore, to the house which still occasionally embarrassed Nora. She felt as though she ought to apologize for success. But there was the bird-watching. Most week-ends they went off to the bush, to the Mountains or somewhere. She felt happier in humbler circumstances. In time she had got used to the tape recorder which they took along. She made herself look upon it as a necessity rather than ostentation.

Eileen was dying for a cigarette.

'May I smoke, Arch?'

'We're amongst friends, aren't we?'

Eileen did not answer that. And Arch fetched the ash-tray they kept handy for those who needed it.

Nora in the kitchen dropped the beans. Everybody heard, but Arch asked Jum for a few tips on investments, as he always did when Nora happened to be out of the room. Nora had some idea that the Stock Exchange was immoral.

Then Nora brought the dish of little, pale tinned peas.

'Ah! *Pet-ty pwah!*' said Jum.

He formed his full, and rather greasy lips into a funnel through which the little rounded syllables poured most impressively.

Nora forgot her embarrassment. She envied Jum his courage in foreign languages. Although there were her lessons in Italian, she would never have dared utter in public.

'Can you bear *crêpes Suzette?*' Nora had to apologize.

'Lovely, darling.' Eileen smiled.

She would have swallowed a tiger. But was, *au fond*, at her gloomiest.

What was the betting Nora would drop the *crêpes Suzette?* It was those long, trembly hands, on which the turquoise ring looked too small and innocent. The Mackenzies were still in the semi-precious bracket in the days when they became engaged.

'How's the old bird-watching?'

Jum had to force himself, but after all he had drunk their wine.

Arch Mackenzie sat deeper in his chair, almost completely at his ease.

'Got some new tapes,' he said. 'We'll play them later. Went up to Jurrajong on Sunday, and got the bell-birds. I'll play you the lyre-bird, too. That was Mount Wilson.'

'Didn't we hear the lyre-bird last time?' Eileen asked.

Arch said:

'Yes.'

Deliberately.

'But wouldn't you like to hear it again? It's something of a collector's piece.'

Nora said they'd be more comfortable drinking their coffee in the lounge.

Then Arch fetched the tape recorder. He set it up on the Queen Anne walnut piecrust. It certainly was an impressive machine.

'I'll play you the lyre-bird.'

'The *pièce de résistance*? Don't you think we should keep it?'

'He can never wait for the lyre-bird.'

Nora had grown almost complacent. She sat holding her coffee, smiling faintly through the steam. The children she had never had with Arch were about to enter.

'Delicious coffee,' Eileen said.

She had finished her filter-tips. She had never felt drearier.

The tape machine had begun to snuffle. There was quite an unusual amount of crackle. Perhaps it was the bush. Yes, that was it. The bush!

'Well, it's really quite remarkable how you people have the patience,' Eileen Wheeler had to say.

'Ssh!'

Arch Mackenzie was frowning. He had sat forward in the period chair.

'This is where it comes in.'

His face was tragic in the shaded light.

'Get it?' he whispered.

His hand was helping. Or commanding.

'Quite remarkable,' Eileen repeated.

Jum was shocked to realize he had only two days left in which to take up the ICI rights for old Thingummy.

Nora sat looking at her empty cup. But lovingly.

Nora could have been beautiful, Eileen saw. And suddenly felt old, she who had stripped once or twice at amusing parties. Nora Mackenzie did not know about that.

Somewhere in the depths of the bush Nora was calling that it had just turned four o'clock, but she had forgotten to pack the thermos.

The machine snuffled.

Arch Mackenzie was listening. He was biting his moustache.

'There's another passage soon.' He frowned.

'Darling,' Nora whispered, 'after the lyre-bird you might slip into the kitchen and change the bulb. It went while I was making the coffee.'

Arch Mackenzie's frown deepened. Even Nora was letting him down.

But she did not see. She was so in love.

It might have been funny if it was not also pathetic. People were horribly pathetic, Eileen Wheeler decided, who had her intellectual moments. She was also feeling sick. It was Nora's *crêpes Suzette*, lying like blankets.

'You'll realize there are one or two rough passages,' Arch said, coming forward when the tape had ended. 'I might cut it.'

'It could do with a little trimming,' Eileen agreed. 'But perhaps it's more natural without.'

Am I a what's-this, a masochist, she asked.

'Don't forget the kitchen bulb,' Nora prompted.

Very gently. Very dreamy.

Her hair had strayed, in full dowdiness, down along her white cheek.

'I'll give you the bell-birds for while I'm gone.'

Jum's throat had begun to rattle. He sat up in time, though, and saved his cup in the same movement.

'I remember the bell-birds,' he said.

'Not these ones, you don't. These are new. These are the very latest. The best bell-birds.'

Arch had started the tape, and stalked out of the room, as if to let the bell-birds themselves prove his point.

'It is one of our loveliest recordings,' Nora promised.

They all listened or appeared to.

When Nora said:

'Oh, dear' — getting up — 'I do believe' — panting almost — 'the bell-bird tape' — trembling — 'is damaged.'

Certainly the crackle was more intense.

'Arch will be so terribly upset.'

She had switched off the horrifying machine. With surprising skill for one so helpless. For a moment it seemed to Eileen Wheeler that Nora Mackenzie was going to hide the offending tape somewhere in her bosom. But she thought better of it, and put it aside on one of those little superfluous tables.

'Perhaps it's the machine that's broken,' suggested Jum.

'Oh, no,' said Nora, 'it's the tape. I know. We'll have to give you something else.'

'I can't understand,' — Eileen grinned — 'how you ever got around, Nora, to being mechanical.'

'If you're determined,' Nora said.

Her head was lowered in concentration.

'If you want a thing enough.'

She was fixing a fresh tape.

'And we do love our birds. Our Sundays together in the bush.'

The machine had begun its snuffling and shuffling again. Nora Mackenzie raised her head, as if launched on an invocation.

Two or three notes of bird-song fell surprisingly pure and clear, out of the crackle, into the beige and string-coloured room.

'This is one,' Nora said, 'I don't think I've ever heard before.'

She smiled, however, and listened to identify.

'Willy-Wagtails,' Nora said.

Willy-Wagtails were suited to tape. The song tumbled and exulted.

'It must be something,' Nora said, 'that Arch made while I was with Mother. There were a couple of Sundays when he did a little field-work on his own.'

Nora might have given way to a gentle melancholy for all she had foregone if circumstances had not heightened the pitch. There was Arch standing in the doorway. Blood streaming.

'Blasted bulb collapsed in my hand!'

'Oh, darling! Oh *dear*!' Nora cried.

The Wheelers were both fascinated. There was the blood dripping on the beige wall-to-wall.

How the willy-wagtails chortled.

Nora Mackenzie literally staggered to her husband, to take upon herself, if possible, the whole ghastly business.

'Come along, Arch,' she moaned. 'We'll fix. In just a minute,' Nora panted.

And simply by closing the door, she succeeded in blotting the situation, all but the drops of blood that were left behind on the carpet.

'Poor old Arch! Bleeding like a pig!' Jum Wheeler said, and laughed.

Eileen added:

'We shall suffer the willy-wags alone.'

Perhaps it was better like that. You could relax. Eileen began to pull. Her step-ins had eaten into her.

The willy-wagtails were at it again.

'Am I going crackers?' asked Jum. 'Listening to those bloody birds!'

When somebody laughed. Out of the tape. The Wheelers sat. Still.

Three-quarters of the bottle! Snuffle crackle. *Arch Mackenzie, you're a fair trimmer!* Again that rather brassy laughter.

'Well, I'll be blowed!' said Jum Wheeler.

'But it's that Miss Cullen,' Eileen said.

The Wheeler spirits soared as surely as plummets dragged the notes of the wagtail down.

But it's far too rocky, and far too late. Besides, it's willy-wagtails we're after. How Miss Cullen laughed. *Willy-wagtails by moonlight!* Arch was less intelligible, as if he had listened to too many birds, and caught the habit. Snuffle crackle went the machine . . . *the buttons are not made to undo* . . . Miss Cullen informed. *Oh, stop it. Arch!* ARCH! *You're* TEARING *me!*

So that the merciless machine took possession of the room. There in the crackle of twigs, the stench of ants, the two Wheelers sat. There was that long, thin Harry Edwards, Eileen remembered, with bony wrists, had got her down behind the barn. She had hated it at first. All mirth had been exorcized from Miss Cullen's recorded laughter. Grinding out. Grinding out. So much of life was recorded by now. Returning late from a country dance, the Wheelers had fallen down amongst the sticks and stones, and made what is called love, and risen in the grey hours, to find themselves numb and bulging.

If only the tape, if you knew the trick with the wretched switch.

Jum Wheeler decided not to look at his wife. Little guilty pockets were turning themselves out in his mind. That woman at the Locomotive Hotel. Pockets and pockets of putrefying trash. Down along the creek, amongst the tussocks and the sheep pellets, the sun burning his boy's skin, he played his overture to sex. Alone.

This sort of thing's all very well, Miss Cullen decided. *It's time we turned practical. Are you sure we can find our way back to the car?*

Always trundling. Crackling. But there were the blessed wagtails again.

'Wonder if they forgot the machine?'

'Oh, God! Hasn't the tape bobbed up in Pymble?'

A single willy-wagtail sprinkled its grace-notes through the stuffy room.

'Everything's all right,' Nora announced. 'He's calmer now. I persuaded him to take a drop of brandy.'

'That should fix him,' Jum said.

But Nora was listening to the lone wagtail. She was standing in the bush. Listening. The notes of bird-song falling like mountain water, when they were not chiselled in moonlight.

'There is nothing purer,' Nora said, 'than the song of the wagtail. Excepting Schubert,' she added, 'some of Schubert.'

She was so shyly glad it had occurred to her.

But the Wheelers just sat.

And again Nora Mackenzie was standing alone amongst the inexorable moonlit gums. She thought perhaps she had always felt alone, even with Arch, while grateful even for her loneliness.

'Ah, there you are!' Nora said.

It was Arch. He stood holding out his bandaged wound. Rather rigid. He could have been up for court martial.

'I've missed the willy-wagtails,' Nora said, raising her face to him, exposing her distress, like a girl. 'Some day you'll have to play it to me. When you've the time. And we can concentrate.'

The Wheelers might not have existed.

As for the tape it had discovered silence.

Arch mumbled they'd all better have something to drink.

Jum agreed it was a good idea.

'Positively brilliant,' Eileen said.

AUCTION SALE IN STANLEY STREET

Kylie Tennant

The auction was being held in the yard behind the auction rooms.
The only patch of shade, cast by a big pepper tree, was jammed
with people. A group of stout old women had established
themselves there in armchairs and on a sofa, where they sat
stolidly fanning. There were orange trees by the empty broken-
down fowl run and against the tank, but their shade was an
illusion. The beds and dressing tables had been placed where
it should have fallen, but they were so hot in the blaze of the
sun that the varnish had almost a quiver of heat haze over
it. Chairs baked until the leather seats were too hot to touch;
and the wardrobes, palm-stands, pot-racks, all the poor litter
of wood cheaply nailed together, looked as though they would
crack and snap apart at any moment.

Dogs circled about yelping when they were trodden on; bicycles
leant against the entry-gate; a row of shining cars were drawn
up along the footpath outside the auction rooms; a horse tethered
to the fence beat its front hoof impatiently. The babies in their
perambulators, the small children wandering about grizzling,
the auctioneer with a knotted handkerchief over his head —
all felt the heat.

Along a row of tables laden with the dead woman's china
and glass, with pepper castors and teapots and sugar-bowls,
spoons, forks and kitchenware, the women bobbed their black
umbrellas, pushing, murmuring, nudging each other with
shopping baskets and hand bags. They stood chatting in groups,
linen dresses, floral dresses and stripes making a pattern of pink
and green, of mauve and grey and yellow. Mostly they wore
white hats and shoes because it was such hot weather. Older

women, wrinkled and shapeless, in black that shone white with the heat, crawled about like cockroaches upset by the disturbance. The few men lounging about were creatures of a different species from the coloured throng of women. 'I never seen such a big crowd at an auction since I been living here,' one old lady with whiskers like a tomcat remarked to another stout old lady who was sitting on a box to rest her swollen feet.

'Well I don't suppose now it would make any difference to a wardrobe ... what happened to her.'

The noise and the heat, the shifts and changes of the crowd, beat down the shouting of the auctioneer. 'Ten, ten-a-half! Over there Joe. Gone at ten-a-half. Mrs Armstrong. No, not you, Mrs Clancy. Pass them over there. Now next lot. Two ...'

The noise rose up round him, making an undercurrent to his rapid babble, as the pebbles in a stream have each a separate ripple under the roar. They were selling off the woman's iron roasting dishes.

'I remember the time mother cooked a sucking pig in the big one,' her daughter Julie said. 'You remember, Maisie, when mother cooked that sucking pig and two roast fowls?' They stood together in the shade of the auction-room doorway.

'I can't see for them black umbrellas bobbing up and down,' Maisie said fretfully. 'You look a sight, Jule. You got a big smear of dirt by your nose.'

'Well I had to unpack all them things, didn't I? Doing all the dirty work. I hadn't time to clean up.'

'Oh look at that chap with the horse! It nearly stepped on that little child. They got no right to bring horses in a crowd.'

'Did you see all the cars outside?'

'It was a good thing she lived next-door and we could just lift all the furniture over the fence.'

They were stout women with glasses, with pearl necklaces, with big bosoms and tight corsets and grey bobbed hair. Their aprons and bare arms cut them off from the crowd.

The auctioneer was holding up a handful of knives. 'Come on.' He cast a glance round the crowd. 'Why don't you bid? They haven't ever been used.'

There was a deadly silence and then smothered laughter that was half-shocked.

'It was with the bread-knife he did it,' someone murmured.

The bidding began again rapidly. 'Three. Three-a-half. Four. Four ... Gorn to Mrs Sorby. Pass 'em across, Joe, over there ...'

The sisters exchanged glances. 'He hadn't ought to have said that,' Julie said. She looked with a vague hostility at the milling black umbrellas, the green and flowery frocks, the white hats and shoes in the shade of the pepper tree.

'They all come to get things cheap because they knew she kept the linen and towels from the time we had the hotel in Stanton.'

They could think of their mother as she had been, stout and jolly and coarse. It wouldn't do to think of what had happened to her since she bought the business in Stanley Street. Just a small shop with a residential attached. They had talked it over a hundred times, but they still couldn't realise that their mother had been murdered. It had been in all the papers, 'Woman found Murdered in Residential'. Just another sordid crime, a drunken man who had been on good terms with mother. It didn't do to think of it. Now there was nothing of her except the chairs cracking with the heat; the rugs tossed down in a heap in the dust; the wardrobes and dressing tables and beds. There would be no bids for one of those beds. You could see by the way the people huddled away from those iron bedsteads that they knew. They joked and laughed more than usual at sales. It was as though in the strong sunlight they had to keep their courage up.

The old men and women gossiped as they sat in the shade on the dead woman's chairs and sofas; old wrinkled men leaning on their sticks; stout matrons who had come from curiosity just to stare; they sat and fanned themselves and did not think. Sometimes one woman would say to another in the crowd with a half-joking, half-nervous laugh, 'Why, Millie, what are you doing here?'

'I came to see if I could get some glasses, May. You know Alf's always bringing home fellows and I'm real ashamed of those old chipped cups.' But there was an edge of defence on her voice.

Only the auctioneer's eyes moved in his face, a yellow face cracked and seamed. His mouth was just another crack bellowing. His eyes were screwed up against the glare. 'Nine, nine-a-half.' The two women stood immobile in the doorway.

'It's the dinner service I'm worried about. If they put it up in separate lots, it'll never fetch what it's worth. They don't know what she paid for it. It's real good china.'

They had been two little girls when mother bought that dinner service. It had cost twenty pounds. A dozen of everything. Nothing had ever been broken. It had been treasured, scarcely ever brought out.

'Run down and tell George to put it up in one lot. Don't let them have it' — Maisie's voice was fierce — 'just in half-dozens.'

Her sister nodded and waddled off very fast to look for her husband somewhere down in the throng. 'I'd sooner we kept it for the children,' Maisie confided to one of the stout old women who sat on a box. 'We could divide it among us.' There was a greed in her eyes. 'It's too good to sell, but Julie *would* have it put up. That's just like her.'

The auctioneer had bent down and was talking earnestly to the dead woman's elder daughter. 'All right, all right,' he said rapidly. 'Just as you like.'

Presently the stout woman came back panting, her arms full of plates, her husband following behind with the rest of the dinner service. 'I wasn't going to let them have it,' she said grimly, 'not for that price.'

The old woman who had been sitting on a box, began fingering the linen which overflowed from another box beside her. 'A pity it's stained,' she grunted. 'It'll go cheap.'

'It's only water-stain,' the daughter said quickly. 'It 'ull bleach out.' The terrible, terrible stain, it had run through the sheets, it was all over the floor. In the strong sunlight, with the stout women crowding to finger the things mother had touched, it did not do to remember. 'It's only water-stain,' she said again anxiously.

The auctioneer, standing on his box, was holding high above the black umbrellas and white hats a china ornament. At first they thought it was a jug, a shiny black china jug. Then as he turned it around, it was a cat, hideous, elongated grotesque. He waved the black china cat carelessly above his head.

'Here you are.' His carven face jutted expressionless over the moving and shuffling, fidgeting mob. 'Here you are. A black cat! A black cat for luck! Who wants a black cat? A lucky black cat?'

There was silence and then suddenly the crowd burst into a roar of laughter. They laughed and laughed, under the green shade of the pepper tree, in the baking sunlight. The stir and rush of their laughter went through the thin orange tree boughs where the green oranges hung tarnished with scale. The horse tied to the fence turned its head and twitched its ears, then dropped its head again. They were laughing out in the strong sunlight, roaring the defence of life against the terrible shadow that was there among the kitchen pots, the linen, and the smell of sweat, laughing high and nervously to banish the thought that the murdered woman had touched that cat, that she had thought black cats lucky.

'Two, two-a-half, three,' the auctioneer chanted. He waved the cat with a triumphant leer at his own success. 'Four, five, seven, eight, -a-half. Here you are, Mrs Garetty.'

The elder sister had returned from bestowing the treasured dinner service.

'How they going?' she asked.

The other nodded, satisfied. 'Seem to be getting good prices.'

MOTHER

Judah Waten

When I was a small boy I was often morbidly conscious of Mother's intent, searching eyes fixed on me. She would gaze for minutes on end without speaking one word. I was always disconcerted and would guiltily look down at the ground, anxiously turning over in my mind my day's activities.

But very early I knew her thoughts were far away from my petty doings; she was concerned with them only in so far as they gave her further reason to justify her hostility to the life around us. She was preoccupied with my sister and me; she was for ever concerned with our future in this new land in which she would always feel a stranger.

I gave her little comfort, for though we had been in the country for only a short while I had assumed many of the ways of those around me. I had become estranged from her. Or so it seemed to Mother, and it grieved her.

When I first knew her she had no intimate friends, nor do I think she felt the need of one with whom she could discuss her innermost thoughts and hopes. With me, though I knew she loved me very deeply, she was never on such near terms of friendship as sometimes exist between a mother and son. She emanated a kind of certainty in herself, in her view of life, that no opposition or human difficulty could shrivel or destroy. 'Be strong before people, only weep before God,' she would say and she lived up to that precept even with Father.

In our little community in the city, acquaintances spoke derisively of Mother's refusal to settle down as others had done, of what they called her propensity for highfalutin day-dreams and of the severity and unreasonableness of her opinions.

Yet her manner with people was always gentle. She spoke softly, she was measured in gesture, and frequently it seemed she was functioning automatically, her mind far away from her body. There was a grave beauty in her still, sad face, her searching, dark-brown eyes and black hair. She was thin and stooped in carriage as though a weight always lay on her shoulders.

From my earliest memory of Mother it somehow seemed quite natural to think of her as apart and other-worldly and different, not of everyday things as Father was. In those days he was a young-looking man who did not hesitate to make friends with children as soon as they were able to talk to him and laugh at his stories. Mother was older than he was. She must have been a woman of nearly forty, but she seemed even older. She changed little for a long time, showing no traces of growing older at all until, towards the end of her life, she suddenly became an old lady.

I was always curious about Mother's age. She never had birthdays like other people, nor did anyone else in our family. No candles were ever lit or cakes baked or presents given in our house. To my friends in the street who boasted of their birthday parties I self-consciously repeated my Mother's words, that such celebrations were only a foolish and eccentric form of self-worship.

'Nothing but deception,' she would say. 'As though life can be chopped into neat twelve-month parcels! It's deeds, not years, that matter.'

Although I often repeated her words and even prided myself on not having birthdays I could not restrain myself from once asking Mother when she was born.

'I was born. I'm alive as you can see, so what more do you want to know?' she replied, so sharply that I never asked her about her age again.

In so many other ways Mother was different. Whereas all the rest of the women I knew in the neighbouring houses and in other parts of the city took pride in their housewifely abilities, their odds and ends of new furniture, the neat appearance of their homes, Mother regarded all those things as of little importance. Our house always looked as if we had just moved in or were about to move out. An impermanent and impatient spirit dwelt within our walls; Father called it living on one leg like a bird.

Wherever we lived there were some cases partly unpacked, rolls of linoleum stood in a corner, only some of the windows had curtains. There were never sufficient wardrobes, so that clothes hung on hooks behind doors. And all the time Mother's things accumulated. She never parted with anything, no matter how old it was. A shabby green plush coat bequeathed to her by her own mother hung on a nail in her bedroom. Untidy heaps of tattered books, newspapers, and journals from the old country mouldered in corners of the house, while under her bed in tin trunks she kept her dearest possessions. In those trunks there were bundles of old letters, two heavily underlined books on nursing, an old Hebrew Bible, three silver spoons given her by an aunt with whom she had once lived, a diploma on yellow parchment, and her collection of favourite books.

From one or other of her trunks she would frequently pick a book and read to my sister and me. She would read in a wistful voice poems and stories of Jewish liberators from Moses until the present day, of the heroes of the 1905 Revolution and pieces by Tolstoy and Gorky and Sholom Aleichem. Never did she stop to inquire whether we understood what she was reading; she said we should understand later if not now.

I liked to hear Mother read, but always she seemed to choose a time for reading that clashed with something or other I was doing in the street or in a nearby paddock. I would be playing with the boys in the street, kicking a football or spinning a top or flying a kite, when Mother would unexpectedly appear and without even casting a glance at my companions she would ask me to come into the house, saying she wanted to read to me and my sister. Sometimes I was overcome with humiliation and I would stand listlessly with burning cheeks until she repeated her words. She never reproached me for my disobedience nor did she ever utter a reproof to the boys who taunted me as, crestfallen, I followed her into the house.

Why Mother was as she was only came to me many years later. Then I was even able to guess when she was born.

She was the last child of a frail and overworked mother and a bleakly pious father who hawked reels of cotton and other odds and ends in the villages surrounding a town in Russia. My grandfather looked with great disapproval on his offspring, who were all girls, and he was hardly aware of my mother at all. She was left well alone by her older sisters, who with feverish impatience were waiting for their parents to make the required arrangements for their marriages.

During those early days Mother rarely looked out into the streets, for since the great pogroms few Jewish children were ever to be seen abroad. From the iron grille of the basement she saw the soles of the shoes of the passers-by and not very much more. She had never seen a tree, a flower, or a bird.

But when Mother was about fifteen her parents died and she went to live with a widowed aunt and her large family in a far-away village. Her aunt kept an inn and Mother was tucked away with her cousins in a remote part of the building, away from the prying eyes of the customers in the tap-rooms. Every evening her aunt would gaze at her with startled eyes as if surprised to find her among the family.

'What am I going to do with you?' she would say. 'I've got daughters of my own. If only your dear father of blessed name had left you just a tiny dowry it would have been such a help. Ah well! If you have no hand you can't make a fist.'

At that time Mother could neither read nor write. And as she had never had any childhood playmates or friends of any kind she hardly knew what to talk about with her cousins. She spent the days cheerlessly pottering about the kitchen or sitting for hours, her eyes fixed on the dark wall in front of her.

Some visitor to the house, observing the small, lonely girl, took pity on her and decided to give her an education. Mother was given lessons every few days and after a while she acquired a smattering of Yiddish and Russian, a little arithmetic and a great fund of Russian and Jewish stories.

New worlds gradually opened before Mother. She was seized with a passion of primers, grammars, arithmetic and story books, and soon the idea entered her head that the way out of her present dreary life lay through these books. There was another world, full of warmth and interesting things, and in it there was surely a place for her. She became obsessed with the thought that it wanted only some decisive step on her part to go beyond her aunt's house into the life she dreamed about.

Somewhere she read of a Jewish hospital which had just opened in a distant city and one winter's night she told her aunt she wanted to go to relatives who lived there. They would help her to find work in the hospital.

'You are mad!' exclaimed her aunt. 'Forsake a home for a wild fancy! Who could have put such a notion into your head? Besides, a girl of eighteen can't travel alone at this time of the year.'

It was from that moment that Mother's age became something to be manipulated as it suited her. She said to her aunt that she was not eighteen, but twenty-two. She was getting up in years and she could not continue to impose on her aunt's kindness.

'How can you be twenty-two?' her aunt replied greatly puzzled.

A long pause ensued while she tried to reckon up Mother's years. She was born in the month Tammuz according to the Jewish calendar, which corresponded to the old-style Russian calendar month of June, but in what year? She could remember being told of Mother's birth, but nothing outstanding had happened then to enable her to place the year. With all her nieces and nephews, some dead and many alive, scattered all over the vastness of the country only a genius could keep track of all their birthdays. Perhaps the girl was twenty-two, and if that were so her chance of getting a husband in the village was pretty remote; twenty-two was far too old. The thought entered her head that if she allowed Mother to go to their kinsmen in the city she would be relieved of the responsibility of finding a dowry for her, and so reluctantly she agreed.

But it was not until the spring that she finally consented to let her niece go. As the railway station was several miles from the village Mother was escorted there on foot by her aunt and cousins. With all her possessions, including photographs of her parents and a tattered Russian primer tied in a great bundle, Mother went forth into the vast world.

In the hospital she didn't find that for which she hungered; it seemed still as far away as in the village. She had dreamed of the new life where all would be noble, where men and women would dedicate their lives to bringing about a richer and happier life, just as she had read.

But she was put to scrubbing floors and washing linen every day from morning till night until she dropped exhausted into her bed in the attic. No one looked at her, no one spoke to her but to give her orders. Her one day off in the month she spent with her relatives who gave her some cast-off clothes and shoes and provided her with the books on nursing she so urgently needed. She was more than ever convinced that her deliverance would come through these books and she set about swallowing their contents with renewed zest.

As soon as she had passed all the examinations and acquired the treasured diploma she joined a medical mission that was about to proceed without a moment's delay to a distant region where a cholera epidemic raged. And then for several years she remained with the same group, moving from district to district, wherever disease flourished.

Whenever Mother looked back over her life it was those years that shone out. Then she was with people who were filled with an ardour for mankind and it seemed to her they lived happily and freely, giving and taking friendship in an atmosphere pulsating with warmth and hope.

All this had come to an end in 1905 when the medical mission was dissolved and several of Mother's colleagues were killed in the uprising. Then with a heavy heart and little choice she had returned to nursing in the city, but this time in private houses attending on well-to-do-ladies.

It was at the home of one of her patients that she met Father. What an odd couple they must have been! She was taciturn, choosing her words carefully, talking mainly of her ideas and little about herself. Father bared his heart with guileless abandon. He rarely had secrets and there was no division in his mind between intimate and general matters. He could talk as freely of his feelings for Mother or of a quarrel with his father as he could of a vaudeville show or the superiority of one game of cards as against another.

Father said of himself he was like an open hand of solo and all men were his brothers. For a story, a joke, or an apt remark he would forsake his father and mother, as the saying goes. Old tales, new ones invented for the occasion, jokes rolled off his tongue in a never-ending procession. Every trifle, every incident was material for a story and he haunted music-halls and circuses, for he liked nothing better than comedians and clowns, actors and buskers.

He brought something bubbly and frivolous into Mother's life and for a while she forgot her stern precepts. In those days Father's clothes were smart and gay; he wore bright straw hats and loud socks and fancy, buttoned-up boots. Although she had always regarded any interest in clothes as foolish and a sign of an empty and frivolous nature Mother then felt proud of his fashionable appearance. He took her to his favourite resorts, to music-halls and to tea-houses where he and his cronies idled away hours, boastfully recounting stories of successes in business or merely swapping jokes. They danced nights away, though Mother was almost stupefied by the band and the bright lights and looked with distaste on the extravagant clothes of the dancers who bobbed and cavorted.

All this was in the early days of their marriage. But soon Mother was filled with misgivings. Father's world, the world of commerce and speculation, of the buying and selling of goods neither seen nor touched, was repugnant and frightening to her.

It lacked stability, it was devoid of ideals, it was fraught with ruin. Father was a trader in air, as the saying went.

Mother's anxiety grew as she observed more closely his mode of life. He worked in fits and starts. If he made enough in one hour to last him a week or a month his business was at an end and he went off in search of friends and pleasure. He would return to business only when his money had just about run out. He was concerned only with one day at a time; about tomorrow he would say, clicking his fingers, his blue eyes focused mellowly on space, 'We'll see'.

But always he had plans for making great fortunes. They never came to anything but frequently they produced unexpected results. It so happened that on a number of occasions someone Father trusted acted on the plans he had talked about so freely before he even had time to leave the tea-house. Then there were fiery scenes with his faithless friends. But Father's rage passed away quickly and he would often laugh and make jokes over the table about it the very same day. He imagined everyone else forgot as quickly as he did and he was always astonished to discover that his words uttered hastily in anger had made him enemies.

'How should I know that people have such long memories for hate? I've only a cat's memory,' he would explain innocently.

'If you spit upwards, you're bound to get it back in the face,' Mother irritably upbraided him.

Gradually Mother reached the conclusion that only migration to another country would bring about any real change to their life, and with all her persistence she began to urge him to take the decisive step. She considered America, France, Palestine, and finally decided on Australia. One reason for the choice was the presence there of distant relatives who would undoubtedly help them to find their feet in that far away continent. Besides, she was sure that Australia was so different from any other country that Father was bound to acquire a new and more solid way of earning a living there.

For a long time Father paid no heed to her agitation and refused to make any move.

'Why have you picked on Australia and not Tibet, for example?' he asked ironically. 'There isn't much difference between the two lands. Both are on the other side of the moon.'

The idea of leaving his native land seemed so fantastic to him that he refused to regard it seriously. He answered Mother with jokes and tales of travellers who disappeared in balloons.

He had no curiosity to explore distant countries, he hardly ever ventured beyond the three or four familiar streets of his city. And why should his wife be so anxious for him to find a new way of earning a living? Didn't he provide her with food and a roof over her head? He had never given one moment's thought to his mode of life and he could not imagine any reason for doing so. It suited him like his gay straw hats and smart suits.

Yet in the end he did what Mother wanted him to do, though even on the journey he was tortured by doubts and he positively shouted words of indecision. But he was no sooner in Australia than he put away all thoughts of his homeland and he began to regard the new country as his permanent home. It was not so different from what he had known before. Within a few days he had met some fellow merchants and, retiring to a café, they talked about business in the new land. There were fortunes to be made here, Father very quickly concluded. There was, of course, the question of a new language but that was no great obstacle to business. You could buy and sell — it was a good land, Father said.

It was different with Mother. Before she was one day off the ship she wanted to go back.

The impressions she gained on that first day remained with her all her life. It seemed to her there was an irritatingly superior air about the people she met, the customs officials, the cab men, the agent of the new house. Their faces expressed something ironical and sympathetic, something friendly and at the same time condescending. She imagined everyone on the wharf, in the street, looked at her in the same way and she never forgave them for treating her as if she were in need of their good-natured tolerance.

Nor was she any better disposed to her relatives and the small delegation of Jews who met her at the ship. They had all been in Australia for many years and they were anxious to impress new-comers with their knowledge of the country and its customs. They spoke in a hectoring manner. This was a free country, they said, it was cultured, one used a knife and fork and not one's hands. Everyone could read and write and no one shouted at you. There were no oppressors here as in the old country.

Mother thought she understood their talk; she was quick and observant where Father was sometimes extremely guileless. While they talked Father listened with a good-natured smile and it is to be supposed he was thinking of a good story he could tell his new acquaintances. But Mother fixed them with a firm, relentless gaze and, suddenly interrupting their injunctions, said in the softest of voices, 'If there are no oppressors here, as you say, why do you frisk about like house dogs? Whom do you have to please?'

Mother never lost this hostile and ironical attitude to the new land. She would have nothing of the country; she would not even attempt to learn the language. And she only began to look with a kind of interest at the world round her when my sister and I were old enough to go to school. Then all her old feeling for books and learning was re-awakened. She handled our primers and readers as if they were sacred texts.

She set great aims for us. We were to shine in medicine, in literature, in music; our special sphere depending on her fancy at a particular time. In one of these ways we could serve humanity best, and whenever she read to us the stories of Tolstoy and Gorky she would tell us again and again of her days with the medical mission. No matter how much schooling we should get we needed ideals, and what better ideals were there than those that had guided her in the days of the medical mission? They would save us from the soulless influences of this barren land.

Father wondered why she spent so much time reading and telling us stories of her best years and occasionally he would take my side when I protested against Mother taking us away from our games.

'They're only children,' he said. 'Have pity on them. If you stuff their little heads, God alone knows how they will finish up.' Then, pointing to us, he added, 'I'll be satisfied if he is a good carpenter; and if she's a good dressmaker that will do, too.'

'At least,' Mother replied, 'you have the good sense not to suggest they go in for business. Life has taught you something at last.'

'Can I help it that I am in business?' he suddenly shouted angrily. 'I know it's a pity my father didn't teach me to be a professor.'

But he calmed down quickly, unable to stand for long Mother's steady gaze and compressed lips.

It exasperated us that Father should give in so easily so that we could never rely on him to take our side for long. Although he argued with Mother about us he secretly agreed with her. And outside the house he boasted about her, taking a peculiar pride in her culture and attainments, and repeating her words just as my sister and I did.

Mother was very concerned about how she could give us a

musical education. It was out of the question that we both be
taught an instrument, since Father's business was at a low ebb
and he hardly knew where he would find enough money to pay
the rent, so she took us to a friend's house to listen to gramophone
records. They were of the old-fashioned, cylindrical kind made
by Edison and they sounded far away and thin like the voice
of a ventriloquist mimicking far off musical instruments. But
my sister and I marvelled at them. We should have been willing
to sit over the long, narrow horn for days, but Mother decided
that it would only do us harm to listen to military marches
and the stupid songs of the music hall.

It was then that we began to pay visits to musical emporiums.
We went after school and during the holidays in the mornings.
There were times when Father waited long for his lunch or
evening meal, but he made no protest. He supposed Mother
knew what she was doing in those shops and he told his friends
of the effort Mother was making to acquaint us with music.

Our first visits to the shops were in the nature of reconnoitring
sorties. In each emporium Mother looked the attendants up
and down while we thumbed the books on the counters, stared
at the enlarged photographs of illustrious composers, and studied
the various catalogues of gramophone records. We went from
shop to shop until we just about knew all there was to know
about the records and sheet music and books in stock.

Then we started all over again from the first shop and this
time we came to hear the records.

I was Mother's interpreter and I would ask one of the salesmen
to play us a record she had chosen from one of the catalogues.
Then I would ask him to play another. It might have been
a piece for violin by Tchaikovsky or Beethoven or an aria sung
by Caruso or Chaliapin. This would continue until Mother
observed the gentleman in charge of the gramophone losing his
patience and we would take our leave.

With each visit Mother became bolder and several times she
asked to have whole symphonies and concertos played to us.
We sat for nearly an hour cooped up in a tiny room with the
salesman restlessly shuffling his feet, yawning and not knowing
what to expect next. Mother pretended he hardly existed and,
making herself comfortable in the cane chair, with a determined,
intent expression she gazed straight ahead at the whirling disc.

We were soon known to everyone at the shops. Eyes lit up
as we walked in, Mother looking neither this way nor that with
two children walking in file through the passageway towards the

record department. I was very conscious of the humorous glances and the discreet sniggers that followed us and I would sometimes catch hold of Mother's hand and plead with her to leave the shop. But she paid no heed and we continued to our destination. The more often we came the more uncomfortably self-conscious I became and I dreaded the laughing faces round me.

Soon we became something more than a joke. The smiles turned to scowls and the shop attendants refused to play us any more records. The first time this happened the salesman mumbled something and left us standing outside the door of the music-room.

Mother was not easily thwarted and without a trace of a smile she said we should talk to the manager. I was filled with a sense of shame and humiliation and with downcast eyes I sidled towards the entrance of the shop.

Mother caught up with me and, laying her hand upon my arm, she said, 'What are you afraid of? Your mother won't disgrace you, believe me.' Looking at me in her searching way she went on, 'Think carefully. Who is right — are they or are we? Why shouldn't they play for us? Does it cost them anything? By which other way can we ever hope to hear something good? Just because we are poor must we cease our striving?'

She continued to talk in this way until I went back with her. The three of us walked into the manager's office and I translated Mother's words.

The manager was stern, though I imagine he must have had some difficulty in keeping his serious demeanour.

'But do you ever intend to buy any records?' he said after I had spoken.

'If I were a rich woman would you ask me that question?' Mother replied and I repeated her words in a halting voice.

'Speak up to him,' she nudged me while I could feel my face fill with hot blood.

The manager repeated his first question and Mother, impatient at my hesitant tone, plunged into a long speech on our right to music and culture and in fact the rights of all men, speaking in her own tongue as though the manager understood every word. It was in vain; he merely shook his head.

We were barred from shop after shop, and in each case Mother made a stand, arguing at length until the man in charge flatly told us not to come back until we could afford to buy records.

We met with rebuffs in other places as well.

Once as we wandered through the university, my sister and I sauntering behind while Mother opened doors, listening to lectures for brief moments, we unexpectedly found ourselves in a large room where white-coated young men and women sat on high stools in front of arrays of tubes, beakers and jars.

Mother's eyes lit up brightly and she murmured something about knowledge and science. We stood close to her and gazed round in astonishment; neither her words nor what we saw conveyed anything to us. She wanted to go round the room but a gentleman wearing a black gown came up and asked us if we were looking for someone. He was a distinguished looking person with a florid face and a fine grey mane.

Repeating Mother's words I said, 'We are not looking for anyone; we are simply admiring this room of knowledge.'

The gentleman's face wrinkled pleasantly. With a tiny smile playing over his lips he said regretfully that we could not stay, since only students were permitted in the room.

As I interpreted his words Mother's expression changed. Her sallow face was almost red. For ten full seconds she looked the gentleman in the eyes. Then she said rapidly to me, 'Ask him why he speaks with such a condescending smile on his face.'

I said, 'My mother asks why you talk with such a superior smile on your face?'

He coughed, shifted his feet restlessly and his face set severely. Then he glared at his watch and without another word walked away with dignified steps.

When we came out into the street a spring day was in its full beauty. Mother sighed to herself and after a moment's silence said, 'That fine professor thinks he is a liberal-minded man, but behind his smile he despises people such as us. You will have to struggle here just as hard as I had to back home. For all the fine talk it is like all other countries. But where are the people with ideals like those back home, who aspire to something better?'

She repeated those words frequently, even when I was a boy of thirteen and I knew so much more about the new country that was my home. Then I could argue with her.

I said to her that Benny who lived in our street was always reading books and papers and hurrying to meetings. Benny was not much older than I was and he had many friends whom he met in the park on Sunday. They all belonged to this country and they were interested in all the things Mother talked about.

'Benny is an exception,' she said with an impatient shrug of her shoulders, 'and his friends are only a tiny handful.' Then she added, 'And what about you? You and your companions only worship bats and balls as heathens do stone idols. Why, in the old country boys of your age took part in the fight to deliver mankind from oppression! They gave everything, their strength and health, even their lives, for that glorious ideal.'

'That's what Benny wants to do,' I said, pleased to be able to answer Mother.

'But it's so different here. Even your Benny will be swallowed up in the smug, smooth atmosphere. You wait and see.'

She spoke obstinately. It seemed impossible to change her. Her vision was too much obscured by passionate dreams of the past for her to see any hope in the present, in the new land.

But as an afterthought she added, 'Perhaps it is different for those like you and Benny. But for me I can never find my way into this life here.'

She turned away, her narrow back stooped, her gleaming black hair curled into a bun on her short, thin neck, her shoes equally down at heel on each side.

THE HOLD UP

John Morrison

We'd got as far as Mont Albert, and the compartment was still full. I'd travelled on that line for over five years and knew every train in the peak-hour, so there was nobody to blame but myself. Joan, my wife, had been at me since early in the afternoon to dodge the crowds by making an early start home, but I'd taken the view that as long as we got seats we could put up with a little discomfort. I thought it was worth it, because I was on holidays, we were in the middle of a January heat-wave, and the children very rarely got to the beach. What I hadn't sufficiently allowed for was getting into a coach where everybody was bound for Box Hill and points beyond, having to nurse two thoroughly exhausted children, and — the hold-up.

The hold-up.

Joan, sitting opposite me in the other corner seat where she would get the breeze when the train was moving, held eighteen-months-old Bobby, his hot little body pressed against hers. He was sleeping, but not soundly. He'd grasped a handful of the neck of Joan's dress, dragging it towards him so that he could get his thumb into his mouth the way he did in his cot every night. She kept dabbing his face with a handkerchief already moist. Her own face was red with sun and salt water, and I knew by the way she kept closing her eyes that she still had the headache in spite of the aspirins she'd taken just before we left the beach.

I myself was just thoroughly uncomfortable. Betty, nearly five, was old enough to have a seat to herself — if grown-ups hadn't been standing. She's a fair lump of a girl, and I was getting the good of every ounce of her, like a big warm poultice.

My thighs, where she was sitting, felt ready to burst into flames, and every time she moved the wet shirt came away from my chest like sticking plaster, letting little trickles of perspiration run down to my trousers band. She was only lightly dozing, and when the train came to a stop just after leaving Mont Albert she lifted her head and looked out, as she'd done at every station since leaving Flinders Street.

'Where are we now, Daddy?'

'Nearly at Box Hill, Bette. We won't be long now.'

She saw the back fences of houses near the line. 'What have we stopped for, Daddy?'

'To let another train get out of the way, I suppose.'

'Will it be long?'

'No, not long.'

She gave a little sigh of resignation and settled down again.

Joan also had sighed, not so resignedly. She was staring out through the doorway with an expression of complete disgust.

In the whole compartment nobody spoke, but it wasn't a peaceful silence. Here and there a head came up from a newspaper or forty winks. Passengers glanced out to see where we were, or across at those sitting opposite, or up at the dingy ceiling. That was all. The alert silence of suspicion. You could almost hear them thinking: Now what the hell . . .

Five-fifteen. With the cessation of movement the heated air closed in around the standing train like a blanket. Alongside the line were a few sapling gum trees with the full sun still on them. The thought came to me that if I were to throw a stone into them their hard, pendant, glistening leaves would shatter like glass. Between them and the paling fences of the houses there ran a dusty track fringed with dry yellow grass. A girl, wearing what looked like a two-piece swimming-suit, cruised slowly down it on a motor-cycle, leaving behind her a plume of fine dust that kept going upwards like smoke. A man's head appeared over the fence, staring first one way, then another. Nothing arrested his attention, and he bobbed down again. Further along, where the ground fell away and we could see into the back gardens, a woman was hosing her lawn. The sparkling jet of water set me thinking of all the joys waiting at home: a cold bottle of beer in the fridge, a shower, fresh clothing, a salad, cool grass under bare feet.

Bobby woke up, began to whimper, and had to be soothed. Joan gave me an appealing look.

'Two more stations, kid,' I said, 'not long now.'

The minutes passed, and there was no movement. Except among the passengers. I heard a man's voice say with infinite contempt: 'Good old Victorian Railways!'

One of the standing passengers edged into the open doorway and looked forward along the line.

'What d'you know?' I asked him.

'Nothing,' he replied grumpily. 'The signal's against us, that's all I can see.'

It was a Tate carriage, and a murmur of talk was beginning to go up further back. Trying not to disturb Betty, I took out my tobacco to roll a smoke, found that perspiration had soaked through into my pocket, and had to throw away a dozen papers before I came to a dry one.

Two women sitting opposite me, next to Joan, looked more than merely annoyed. They looked anxious. One of them, an attractive young Miss with beautifully-tanned arms and legs and wearing a delightfully summery frock, sat with hands clasped over a white leather handbag in her lap. She had a tiny jewelled wrist-watch and couldn't keep her eyes off it for ten seconds on end. I thought: she's got a date. He's meeting the train. He's just a new one, and she feels she can't depend on him yet.

The one next to her was older, matronly. Through white mesh gloves I could make out a wedding ring. A trifle plump, but charming also, and very smartly turned-out. She looked even cooler than the girl, but was every bit as worried. She, too, kept consulting her watch, turning back the frilled cuff of a glove to do so, and invariably casting a stealthy glance at those of us sitting opposite to see if we were observing her anxiety. I thought: She's been gadding about in town, and has a husband who likes to find his tea ready when he comes home.

Ten minutes passed. Sounds of impatience were going up all along the train. I looked out. Teenagers were crowding the open doorways, whistling and chiaking each other. From the next carriage to ours a man jumped down to the line, stepped over the signal wires, and made off through the grass towards the dusty track.

My movement woke Betty up, and she asked peevishly when we were going to start again.

'In a minute, Bette. As soon as the man in the station gives the signal.'

'What station, Daddy?'

'Box Hill. We only have two more to go.'

It was a relief when she didn't lie back against me again.

Instead, she became absorbed in studying the woman in the white gloves, staring at her with a frank, unblinking innocence of childhood.

'Harold Clapp would turn in his grave if he could see what the Victorian Railways have come to,' said the man on my left.

I agreed with him, rather disinterestedly, not because I had any doubts, but because he spoke with what I thought was unnecessary bitterness.

I didn't like him anyway. He was a pale, podgy little fellow wearing a pork-pie hat and a well-rubbed blue serge suit. There was an alert, birdlike watchfulness about him that went oddly with his mature years. I hadn't liked him since he got in at Flinders Street. All seats were taken when he arrived, but we'd squeezed up and made room enough at least for him to get the weight off his feet. But by the time we'd reached Glenferrie he was adequately snugged back against the cushions, with elbows well out to make sure he kept what he'd won. He had a technique, familiar to all peak-hour travellers, of sitting pat while the train was in motion, and allowing himself to be jerked an inch or two further in every time we stopped at a station. This one wasn't hard to read. He'd been buying himself a shrub, and had the pot resting on the floor with the slender stem growing up between his protecting knees. Every now and then he subjected it to a careful examination, turning back the funnelled brown-paper wrapping and fingering the leaves as if to see if it was shrivelling — or as if doubtful of his bargain. I'm a keen gardener myself, but his solicitude for that little tree seemed to go all too well with the seat-cribbing. The delay was obviously working him up into a vile temper. He kept darting angry little glances around the compartment, ready to take issue with anybody prepared to defend the railways.

He picked on me. 'They wouldn't know how to run a raffle. We got Buckley's chance of getting to Croydon by six.'

I smiled patiently. 'Got a date?'

'I *had* a date!' He repeated that, as if he were hinting at a profound secret. Then, just as I thought that was the end of it, he swivelled his head and looked me full in the face. 'I had a date with two beautiful big cold pots!'

That at least I could understand. He went on to tell me about it.

'I'm not a boozer, mind you. I'm just one of those blokes that likes a taste every night. Two pots, never more, never less. Gives me an appetite. Haven't missed once in fifteen years.'

'That's a fair effort,' I said. 'Travelling all the time?'

He missed the point. 'Travelling all the time. I go to South Melbourne. Been with the one firm all me working life. They think the world of me.'

I nodded coldly.

'I won't be worth much to them tomorrow. This'll upset me for the rest of the week. Won't be able to eat a bite when I get home. Finish up with a splitting headache too.'

'Think of the four pots you'll have tomorrow night!'

I think he realised then that he'd got himself an unsympathetic audience, for he shrugged his shoulders and let the subject drop.

Two men came across from the far side of the compartment, looked out, held a muttered conversation, and jumped down to the permanent way.

It was going on all along the train now, with an explosive crunch of metal ballast. There was a lot of good-natured shouting from the younger element. One particularly gleeful outcry made me put my head out of the window just in time to be in the fun — a tallish girl being lowered out by two youths, her skirts caught up, two magnificent legs reaching for the ground.

The track along the backs of the houses became hazy with the dust of those who, presumably, lived no further away than Box Hill. The fence was dotted with curious faces.

Twenty minutes. I was beginning to get uneasy myself, thinking of derailment and electrical breakdowns. Betty, still wide awake, had transferred her attention from the woman with the white gloves to the girl with the white handbag. But she'd gradually relaxed, and was once more subjecting me to all the torments of a Turkish bath. I had a raging thirst, and hated to think of what was in store if we didn't move soon and the children began asking for drinks. An elderly woman, sitting on the other side of the gangway from White Gloves, gave me a sympathetic smile and gently nodded her head. She knew all about it.

There were no standing passengers left, so that we could all see each other.

The Two-Pot man had got into conversation with his other neighbour. He was doing most of the listening, and, judging from the tone of the voice that came over to me, was getting a tale of woe more touching than his own.

Joan was sitting bolt upright, brows puckered, eyes and lips tightly closed. There was nothing I could do for her. Over her head, on the luggage-rack, the big basket full of wet towels and swimming-togs was having the same effect on me as the sight of empty bottles on a morning after.

White Gloves was getting desperate. She'd been taking a lot of interest in the men jumping off, and had twice leaned over in an effort to gauge the depth of the drop to the tracks. She fidgeted ceaselessly, smoothed her frock, stuck out one of her little white shoes where she could see it, clasped and unclasped her hands, fingered the gold pendant at her throat, then one of the pale amber drops at her ears. Her finery was manifestly on her mind. I felt sorry for her. Perhaps she had more to worry about than a husband who liked to find his tea ready.

White Handbag was also in increasing distress, but it was the distress not of panic but of sulks. For her too I felt sorry. The disappointments of youth are painful. Zero hour must have passed, for she looked at her watch less often. I decided that she had trouble enough, told Betty to stop staring, and was rewarded with a dazzling, though fleeting, smile. So fleeting that it was a matter of question whether her gratitude for being rescued from Betty was greater than her embarrassment over being noticed. She was sitting now with her head well up, staring out at the offside landscape and trying bravely to appear as if nothing at all was the matter. She had a lovely neck, and knew it.

Utter peace reigned in the far window seats. In one a man in overalls, head lolling backwards and mouth wide open, was softly snoring. In the other a teenage youth probably didn't care if the train never started. He had his arm around a sleeping girl whose head rested on his chest. He also had his eyes on the landscape, but was seeing nothing of it. Dreams. Their hands were clasped over his knees. They looked as hot as the rest of us, but, as the fishwife said, circumstances alters cases ...

Two-Pots' neighbour droned on: 'Fair dinkum — thirty quid, if it costs me a cracker!'

A train suddenly clattered past on the up line, sending in a swirl of warm dust-laden air, and disposing of any question of a general power breakdown. Only when the noise of it died away did I realise how quiet our own train had become. Most of the restless and rebellious ones had gone. The murmur of voices was low and conspiratorial. Railways organisation was getting a thorough going-over: 'Could have sent word down the line, anyhow ... could do something about it ... emergency buses ... used to be the best suburban railways in the world ... never be good till they wipe off the capital debt ...'

A sense of imprisonment was taking possession of me. The carriage was like an oven. On my own I'd have got out, if only to lie down on the tracks until there was some sign of movement. It would have been necessary to get under the train fo find shelter. The white ballast was probably hot enough to fry eggs on, and the grass outside it thickly-coated with fine dust.

Bobby woke up and began to cry. The sudden cry of a child frightened by the discomfort it finds itself to be in.

The elderly woman leaned out past the other two women and said to Joan: 'Would the baby like a drink?'

Wold the baby like a drink! Joan's weary face lit up. The woman picked up a vacuum flask I'd noticed peeping out of a basket at her feet.

'It's milk, nice and cold. I took it with me in case it was wanted, but it wasn't. Would he drink out of the cap?'

Would he drink out of the cap! We all watched him, enviously. Even Two-Pots, who'd been getting some of his own back by telling the other fellow about the lost beer.

Betty had been in another half-doze, but something of what was going on must have penetrated her dreams, because she too suddenly came to life. It helped a lot, particularly when Joan was urged to finish what was left. She passed the cap of the flask back gratefully, and the woman re-stowed her basket and sat fanning herself with a paper she'd been reading, and smiling across at Betty like a benign female Santa Claus.

Soon afterwards the man next to Two-Pots got out. He was a fellow in the prime of life, nicely-weighted, and made light of squatting in the doorway and from that position dropping down to the line. It fell to me to pass him his brief-case. His upturned face, at the level of the floor, was full of anger. He thanked me curtly, muttering something about being 'stuck here all night like a shag on a rock'. I watched him step firmly over the signal wires after a hateful stare that took in the whole length of the standing train.

Two-Pots confided to me that the man was anything up to thirty pounds out of pocket over the delay.

'He's a salesman. His car's in dock for the day. You can be stiff, can't you?'

'What does he sell?' I wasn't really interested, but there was no point in snubbing him.

'Cash registers. He had an appointment with a bloke for a quarter to six. He says the other bloke had practically decided on another buy, but he talked him out of it till he'd had a look at his own line. He won't be in the hunt now.'

All these unhappy people . . .

White Gloves turned unexpectedly to Joan and asked her something in a low voice. Joan shook her head and referred her to me.

'Do you know, Jim? How far behind us is the next Ringwood?'

'Mont Albert Station!' I replied spontaneously. 'There'll be one in every section by now!'

Next instant I was sorry for it. White Gloves had evidently been too worried to do any constructive thinking. She clapped a hand to her lips, drew in a short breath, and turned a shade paler.

'What's the matter?' I asked her. 'Is there anything we can do for you?'

'No. No, thank you. You can't do anything.' She cast a glance around the compartment like a trapped animal. 'I've got to get off!'

'Well, perhaps I can help you.'

She stood up, stepped over to the doorway, and seemed appalled by the distance between ground and carriage floor. I joined her, putting Betty into my empty seat, and wondering why I hadn't thought of it before. It was good to move freely.

'Do you really have to go?' I asked White Gloves.

'Oh, I must . . . I must!' She was almost crying.

'All right. I'll get you down if you're game.'

She nodded urgently and I dropped out to the line. I was surprised myself how far it was.

'You'll have to sit on the floor,' I said. 'You'll muss your frock, but it's only dust.'

She sat down with her legs dangling, and I cupped my hands under the white shoes.

'Put your hands on my shoulders and stand up. Right — push off!'

It was quite easy, pleasant in fact. For an instant she was over the top of me, my chin in the neck of her dress. Then she was on the ground, red as a beetroot, and thanking me in a strained little voice shaking with excitement.

A few minutes previously I'd caught her in the act of checking the contents of a purse in her handbag.

'You're a long way from a taxi,' I said.

'I'll ask someone to let me use a phone.'

Trust a woman in an emergency like that. Because I believed it was an emergency like that. The French have a word for it — *assignation.* Perhaps she guessed that I guessed, because there was guilt in her pretty face as she turned away. Full of pity I watched the immaculate little figure hurrying away through the grass. She'd get covered with dust. She made two pots of beer look very trivial.

When, sweating afresh, I got back into the train I found that there had been a slight redistribution of seats. Two-Pots, for some reason I couldn't perceive, had moved along towards the courting couple, Betty was in the seat vacated by White Gloves, and the elderly woman and White Handbag had exchanged places. This put Betty between her mother and the elderly woman, who was trying to pacify her — she thought something terrible had happened to Daddy.

The bit of commotion had awakened the workman in the corner, and after trying in vain to get his bearings he asked White Handbag where we were. She told him, and he heaved a sigh of relief.

'I thought we might have gone past Blackburn.'

But his relief vanished when he took a look at is watch. He stared incredulously. 'Struth! What time is it?'

'Ten to six.'

'What!' He looked at the rest of us for confirmation. 'Is that fair dinkum?'

'We've been stuck here for over half an hour,' I informed him. 'We don't know what's wrong.'

He pushed back his hat and scratched his head. 'Well, this is lovely, this is!'

'You won't get a drink now, mate!' said Two-Pots maliciously.

The man gave him an offended stare. 'I'm not interested in a drink, mister,' he said shortly. 'If it's of any interest to you, I'm not going home — I'm going to work. This is liable to cost a man his job.' After which he took out his pipe, lit up, and showed no further interest in any of us. Every time I looked at him afterwards he was quietly smoking, and thinking, his brows knitted, an expression of deep concentration on his healthy face.

Two-Pots accepted the snub meekly, rather to my surprise. I had a view of the back of his fat neck as he bent over his precious shrub. His fingers, hooked around it, twitched now and then either from nerves or irritation. The toe of one of his carefully polished boots drummed on the floor. Miss White Handbag was on to him too, getting — yes, like me! — a catty satisfaction out of his misery. Her pretty lips wore a vindictive little smile: You think you've got troubles!

Little talking was going on anywhere. Two-Pots wasn't the only one who was sulking. With the departure of so many fellow-passengers we felt abandoned, forgotten. Most of the people looking over the fence had got bored and gone back to their affairs. The dusty track was deserted, the gum trees still stood in full blazing sunlight. A cicada started up somewhere, others joined in, and in an instant the whole air was uncomfortably vibrating. Within the carriage the silence, and the knowledge of the fact that we were all privately obsessed with the same thought, made us self-conscious. Like people in a dentist's waiting-room. Only the workman in the corner remained completely withdrawn, wrestling with his problem of how to save a mate who, I guessed, had shot through before his relief came. There might be machinery running unattended.

I think we were all relieved when Two-Pots broke into speech, although it was to make the kind of remark we might have expected of him.

'I was going to plant this tonight,' he complained. 'Had a place picked out for it and everything.'

'It'll keep,' I said with a dry smile.

'It'll keep?' He had a good look at me. 'Of course it'll keep. I just happen to be one of them blokes that likes to get things done, that's all. And I don't like to be put out of me stride by mugs.'

My expression must have reacted to that rather sharply, because he went on without drawing breath:

'I'm talking about railway mugs. When I left work this afternoon I had everything nicely worked out. Me two drinks, a nice cold tea, and an hour in the garden before I hit the cot. Now, just because some other Alec can't do *his* job . . .'

He grappled for words, but before he could find them the train started.

A prolonged blast on the whistle, a series of half-hearted cheers all along the carriages, and we jerked at last into blessed movement. Joan, who certainly had not been sleeping, opened her eyes and gave me a joyous smile. It was exciting to see the gum trees begin to slide away from us, and to have the song of the cicadas drowned in the clatter of wheels.

As if the train itself had been eager to go, we accelerated quickly, roared and swayed over the short mile or two to Box Hill, and ran into the station with a screeching of brakes.

Inevitably a lot of people were waiting, crowding towards the doorways as we came to a standstill.

I was surprised to see White Handbag get off. She was young enough to have made the jump away back along the line, but must have been too much concerned about her dress. I watched her push through the crowd and run through the barrier gates just as a station assistant advanced to close them. Perhaps she made it after all.

Several people were getting in, including an elderly man with a woman, presumably his wife, who was holding a handkerchief over her face. We were almost opposite the gates. Walking out to the edge of the platform to give the all-clear, the assistant stood right alongside my window.

'What was the hold-up, mate?' I asked him.

'Accident.' He was standing with one arm uplifted, looking back at the guard's end. 'Bloke fell off the platform.'

'Badly hurt?'

'Killed.' A whistle blew, he dropped his arm, and as we moved off again he began to worm his way through the people around the barrier. He seemed upset.

Man and wife had taken the seats next to me. The woman held herself rigidly upright, her splayed fingers holding the handkerchief, obviously her husband's, over the whole of her face. She seemed to be holding her breath. He had one arm around her and kept patting her on the knees.

'I told you not to look! I told you not to look!' he kept on repeating.

I asked him if he would like to put her in the window seat.

He shook his head. 'No, thank you just the same. She'll be all right in a minute. She shouldn't have looked. That's what did it.'

'What happened?'

'A man fell off the platform. Right under a train. Bent down to pick up his bag and over he went. Blackout — I get them myself.'

'You know he's dead, don't you?'

'Yes, I know. They wouldn't move the train until a doctor came. He was right in under the bogie.'

Joan's arm had tightened convulsively around Bobby.

Two-Pots was staring with morbid interest.

My Friend, Lafe Tilly

Christina Stead

Lafe Tilly wore his hat brim down, and his coat collar up; there were round spectacles over his hollow eyes. A little of the yellow face could be seen. He stood by the lamp, looking down. He did not take off his gloves.

'I was at a funeral last week. There was the widow and another woman, the man's brother and I myself, his only mourners. Once he had hundreds of friends, thousands perhaps. Hundreds of women loved him.'

Lafe Tilly smiled.

'He was cremated; and before that they had to embalm him and make him a new face. His was gone.'

'Gone?'

'Eva and I knew them years ago, years before any of us were married. I was a stunt pilot then: I lived in Brooklyn like everyone in our crowd; and Joe Cornaco stood out in the crowd, very political, a big talkative man, dark, thin-faced, greedy for women, spending a lot on dress, always clean shaved. He treated all the women badly. We believed in sex equality and did not think any woman had the right to complain. I married Eva, the first to marry; and soon after that Joe married Donna, a woman in our set who had been with us for years.

'She was a few months older than Joe and he talked about it. He made her a partner in his real estate business. She became his office manager. She worked hard, stayed back every night to clean up business; she looked after the staff and did his work when he was out with girls. He was out nearly every evening.

'She had been working since she was fifteen. She had never been to college. Joe had a younger brother Victor who was sent to college and became a lawyer. Donna turned out to have a good business head, better than Joe had; and she put her savings into his business, about five thousand dollars.

'Although Joe was never sentimental, always calling a spade a spade, he got into trouble several times with women. A young woman who was always dressed in black, a thin thing, committed suicide. She tried several times; no one believed her and in the end she managed it in the bath.'

He smiled most curiously. It was like a waxen face reflected in moving water, not a smiling man.

'It was after that that Donna asked him to marry her, for his own sake. He knew she was in love with him and he liked that, the quiet, loyal, patient woman to whom he complained and who understood him. They had a talk; he put his views to her: she agreed with everything he said.

'He said, "You are getting the best of the bargain, since you will be both my wife and my partner; and you are getting the man you love, whereas I do not love you." "Yes," she said. "Therefore," Joe said, "we had better have an agreement to safeguard me. You agree to look after my business and my home; you study at night to get a degree so that you will be my equal. No children. I am to have my entire liberty, as I have now, as an unmarried man." Donna agreed to everything. Between them they drew up the marriage contract and they made his brother, Victor, a lawyer by then, go over the clauses. Victor told Donna that it had no validity being contrary to public policy. She said, "If I keep to it and he keeps to it, it will be binding. We both know what we are doing." "But if he divorces you?" "He will not divorce me. He will have no reason to." "But what about you, Donna?" "I love Joe and I never expected to marry him. I know I'm not good looking. I consider I'm lucky." "Why get married?" people said to them both. But they were satisfied. A friend called Cowan and I signed the contract as witnesses. Cowan died years ago.'

He looked straight ahead, continued, 'Now Donna took into her office young girls who attracted Joe and she made friends of any other women he wanted. It was strange how they all trusted her. When, at home, he went into the backroom with a girl, she sat chatting with the others, or read a book, or did the housework till the couple came out. If they stayed there for long, she went to bed. She always said that jealousy had been left out of her nature. She didn't know how it was. All women are jealous, aren't they?' said Lafe Tilly smiling.

'Joe's brother Victor was tall, dark, fleshy, with red damp lips. He was very fond of women, too; but he went after them differently, explaining his troubles, abusing Joe, using the word love. When Joe was away for the weekend with some girl, Victor would be at the house, eating and drinking with Donna. If ever Donna complained, it was to Victor. Victor had always been jealous of Joe and he would go round spreading gossip; Donna told me this. Joe had illegitimate children, all being supported by the mothers. Donna had no children. Victor sometimes stayed the night at Donna's apartment. It was a long way to his mother's home in Queen's. "I want children," he said to Donna; "when my mother dies, I will marry. I am sorry you have no children; you would make a good mother." But Donna did not sleep with him and never had a sweetheart. She was respected and had a following among Joe's male friends.'

After a pause, Lafe said harshly, 'She was a bawd for Joe, she played on the trust the girls had in her. She was good to them as long as he wanted them and afterwards she might dry their tears for them. It depended on how they stood with Joe.'

Lafe Tilly laughed suddenly; and then became serious and reasonable as before.

'I used to see Joe on the street. He was always the same, smart, spending money on himself; and they were making money between them, a lot of money. He nicked himself once when shaving and the nick didn't heal. He went about with bits of sticking plaster on his cheek. The scratch grew and he would go about without dressing it saying the air would heal it. Later he had an operation and he kept going to the hospital for skin graftings. He went about as jaunty as ever. People began to avoid him. I did. But he didn't understand it. I know Donna tried to persuade him to stay at home; and when he insisted on going to work, she wanted him to go in the car and come straight home afterwards. They had some rows over it. He thought she was trying to keep him away from girls. He said, "Remember you signed a contract with me; keep your word." The worse his looks, the more frantic he was about girls and he thought everyone was standing in his way.'

Tilly glimmered a smile.

'Naturally, I guessed. I told him to go home and stay home. He got very angry and I didn't see him again.

'About four months ago, I had a note at the office from Donna, which said, "Joe says please come to see him and bring Eva with you. Come Thursday afternoon." Underneath this was written, "I have written what Joe asked me to, but do not bring your wife. If you want to see him you had better come now."

'It was a new address, away out, a wooden house, on an earth bank in a long dusty street of such houses, all three-storey, with steps in front, downhill off a four-lane highway. There was a funeral home a few doors down.'

Lafe showed the sharp point of his tongue as he drew in his breath.

'I found the number which was one that Joe had always thought a lucky number. The windows were shut, with drapes on all the windows; it looked well cared for. The door was opened by a good looking young girl, serious, fair type, in a house dress. She showed me into the front room and went away. There was complete silence for a while, then Donna came in. She had changed very little. She had healthy looks; her cheeks were fat and red, her black hair was braided over her broad head and she had on some sort of aesthetic smock, brown, with hand embroidery and unusual buttons. She collected buttons. It was the same sort of squaw outfit she had always worn and which she liked better than shop clothes. It was part of their revolt against machine-made things. She had fine eyes, but solid as stones, denser than dogs' eyes. Otherwise, she is short, thickset and has a slow flat voice.

'When I started to get up, she said, "Sit down, Lafe."

'She spoke in low tones, like a girl, and said Joe was asleep. He needed all the sleep he could get; he would be in a bad temper if not rested. She said she'd get me a drink. I said, "Not yet, wait for Joe." She said, "You'll need it." She went out and came back with a full bottle of Scotch whisky, which she opened and put in front of me on the table, with one glass. She didn't want any. She asked me if I wanted some water and went away for it; but did not return.

'No one came. I thought I heard a whisper once; apart from that, the house was quiet. I poured myself a drink and had it. After a long time, the young girl came in with a jug of water and some ice. She seemed to be a servant, so I didn't offer her any; and Donna stayed away. I just sat there and drank by myself. It was hot and still. Sometimes I thought I heard a soft noise somewhere in the house or a car on the dirt road; that was all. There was nothing to do, so I just sat there on the sofa and got quite comfortable.

'The curtains were partly drawn. The sun fell on blue patches of carpet and various yellows. The place was kept very clean.

On the wall were crude paintings, the sort we used to collect when naïve art was the fad. Besides these and the furniture, there were two mirrors, a long one between two windows and a big square one standing on the floor, very large, with a lacy acanthus-leaf gilding. It was out of place. There was a woman's handglass on the mantelpiece, some bookshelves with old intellectual bestsellers, nothing for me to read. I could see the door of the room across the hall; that was all.

'I had drunk at least half the bottle when I heard footsteps and something being dragged. There was a slow shuffle coming nearer. A door opened, there was a whisper and in answer to it, I heard a strange voice, a cawing. People were coming along the hall together. Then three people stood in the doorway. There were women behind and in front, in a dressing-gown, and slippers, wearing an eyeshade was a man. He had an immense lipless mouth, the cheeks were blown out and he wore an eyeshade. There was a paisley scarf round his neck up to the chin. They must have just fixed the scarf around his neck, because he was impatiently pulling it off as he shuffled into the room. He took no notice of me, but he approached the glass on the floor, which was at an angle so that he could see himself walking. He signalled, and they put the handglass into his hand. He dropped the scarf on the floor and took off the eyeshade. Then he began taking a careful look at himself, turning his face this way and that. He made a sound of irritation and gestured. The girl switched on the top light. The man continued to observe himself in detail. While this was going on, the girl went away and returned with a tray of coffee and other things, which she placed on the table near me. Donna stood there calmly, looking from one to the other. Presently, she said, "Lafe Tilly is here, Joe."

'The man made an irritable sound which they seemed to understand.

'The wife said in her flat commanding voice, "He's at the table by the window, if you'll look, Joe. He's been waiting."

'The man turned. I started to get up. I was drunk perhaps. I looked at him and fell back again into the soft old couch. Joe seemed to laugh. He touched his cheek, shook his head, uttered sounds and looked at me, nodding his head slowly. Donna said, "Joe says he thinks he has improved this week. It is the hot weather which does him good." The man said something. The wife said, with calm shining eyes, "Joe thinks you can understand him and that I am insulting him by interpreting. Tell him you can't, Lafe."

'I said, "Are you feeling better, Joe?"

'At further sounds from him, the girl left the room; but the wife said, "Joe, I must stay if you are going to talk to Lafe. Lafe doesn't understand a word you say." She continued to me, 'Lisbeth has gone to make more coffee. Joe's is cold. Joe always drank very hot coffee, you remember; but now he never gets it. It takes so long to drink. Well, it is not our fault, Joe." There seemed to be mirth underlying her stubborn words. She continued, "Joe is not allowed to drink whisky. It would choke him. He would choke to death."

'Joe made conversation. He drew me out about politics, contradicting everything I said. He talked a lot about his health, with which he was fairly satisfied. He had improved considerably, he said, since his teeth had come out. It was a good idea of his doctor's; and it should have been done years before. He ate better and felt better. If the teeth had been taken out years before he would not have had the skin trouble. He had always had excellent teeth, always sound and white; so he had not thought of it. "Joe always had a bad skin," said the wife.

'She interpreted everything he said, being constantly interrupted by Joe. She laughed once, saying, "Joe says I am treating him like a child; he just has a speech impediment for a short time, but his speech is coming back."

'Lisbeth came with fresh coffee and poured a cup for Joe. He took a drop on his tongue from time to time and complained. Donna said. "It is no use getting mad at us, Joe. You drink so slowly that it can't help getting cold. You take a whole hour to drink a single cup of coffee."

'Joe was sitting at the table facing the long mirror between the windows. He held out his hand and Lisbeth brought him the handglass. He continued to study his appearance with care, while he drank.

' "Ah-ah-ah," said Joe.

' "Joe wants to know why you supplied such bad paper for those new books. The ink shows through."

'I said, "We were told not to waste paper; but to use paper that the men could tear out and use in the latrines."

'Evidently Joe was laughing.

' "Ah-ah-ah."

'Joe says "Are you still with Tacker and Taylor?"

' "Yes."

'Joe says, "Is Ben Taylor still a melancholic?"

' "Just the same."

'Joe says, "He never did appeal to women. He couldn't get them."

'Joe was trying to shout with rage. In an undertone, Lisbeth said to Donna, "Let him talk."

'He wrangled with the women, equally furious if they translated or if they neglected his remarks; and at times, he rolled a drop of cold coffee round his tongue. He made enquiries after people and asked why Eva had not come.

' "She used to be one of my girls in the old days. She had a crush on me. She always had her blue eyes fixed on me." Joe laughed.

' "Donna had the crazy idea of moving out here where no one can reach me and where I can't get into town. She made a promise to me. You know that. She is not keeping that promise. I'm a prisoner here. These women keep me in jail. Afraid of competition, they're not getting any younger."

'He kept insulting Donna and Lisbeth. Donna translated the insults without emotion.

' "I'll soon be back in circulation and I'll make up for lost time. You won't cheat me!"

'He showed temper, shouted, caught sight of himself and once more began his careful inspection.

'Presently, they helped him to get out of his chair. He wanted to lie down; he was tired.

' "Rest is everything. Sleep rests the skin. I look much better in the morning when I get up," he said to me.

'Donna went out to the front gate with me and I said, "How long will it be?"

' "The doctor said it might be two months; he's starving."

' "He doesn't seem to suffer much."

' "He's drugged all the time. He's full of aspirin. And they did some slight operation. Joe's last message to you was to bring Eva. Don't bring her and don't tell anyone. I can't have people."

' "Who's the girl?"

' "A girl he wanted me to engage about eighteen months ago. I don't know whether she fell for him or she was sorry for him. I don't know if they had an affair. What does it matter now? It's six months since that. But he wouldn't understand it if I sent her away. It's all he's got. It was always the greatest thing in his life, his way with women. He would never have gone in for politics; he didn't care for the business. This was the greatest thing. It's not his fault, is it? It's a fault of nature."

' "And he doesn't know it's over?"

'She laughed shortly. "It's hard to believe; but he has just bought two tickets for himself and Lisbeth to go to Lourdes. It's only a lupus he has, he says. It's nerves. He'll be cured there. He read about a thing like that in Zola. The girl in the book washed her face in the fountain and the lupus at once began to heal."

' "And you, Donna?"

' "I'll keep on looking after the business. We've done very well. There'll be big changes round here. Victor helps me. We got the land and houses cheap years ago. I'll be all right."

'A couple of days ago,' said Lafe Tilly, 'I got the funeral notice at the office. Eva knows nothing about it, so don't mention it to her.'

'No.'

'She used to admire Joe in the old days; he dazzled her. Eva never understood him. She's naïve. Joe took her sister and left her; that is why she married me. Eva and her sister were always rivals. I thought of marrying her sister, too.'

After a pause, he continued quietly, 'Lisbeth was at the funeral. Joe's brother Victor was there, assisting Donna. I think Donna expected to marry him. I went back with them to the gate. Donna said, "You'll come in, won't you, Victor?" But he jammed on his hat, said he had an appointment and hurried up the street, his big legs going fast.

'Donna did not seem to notice anything. She told Lisbeth to wait at the gate and asked me to go in. I went. She gave me a valise and a box tied with string and asked me to carry them to the girl at the gate. Donna stood on the porch and called out to the girl, "You must go away now. You can't stay here." The girl took the bag and box, said goodbye and turned away.

' "Come in, Lafe and have a drink," said Donna. "In a minute," I said. I said to the girl, "Where are you going? Home?"

' "No, they threw me out. I'll find a place."

' "Can I get you a taxi?"

' "No. I have no money. I'll find a place."

'I went in just to see what Donna would say. "You don't mind letting the girl go like that."

' "What has she to do with me?"

' "But you lived together for eight months."

' "I don't know her name or her address; she is nothing to me. She took my husband from me. I don't care what happens to her."

' "But Donna she has nowhere to go."

' "He never cared for her. She threw herself at him. The women are shameless these days. You can't blame Joe. I was not like the others. He married me."

' "Would you like to see Eva?"

' "No. No women any more. I don't have to now."

' "Donna, why did you go through with it?"

' "You know I signed a contract with him. You were there: you witnessed it."

' "And you stood it for that reason?"

' "Joe and I had a contract. We agreed on everything. We understood each other."

'I passed Donna today,' Lafe said. 'She looked just the same, leathery skin, and a slight moustache, a dark felt hat, a black-belted dress, her satchel. Her eyes were on the sidewalk and her brown lips muttered occasionally. I was going to meet a blonde, so I avoided her.'

He glanced sideways. 'Donna's a virgin. Imagine it.' He grinned.

'Why do you tell these stories, Lafe?'

He said nothing.

'Because you feel the pain?'

'Yes, people live in pain.'

'Would you like a drink?'

'No. Goodbye. Don't tell Eva.'

'No.'

HABIT

Marjorie Barnard

Miss Jessie Biden was singing in a high plangent voice as she made the beds. It was a form of self-expression she allowed herself only when there were no guests in the house, and she mingled the hymns and sentimental songs of her girlhood with a fine impartiality. She made the beds with precision, drawing the much-washed marcella quilts, with spiky fringes, up over the pillows so that the black-iron bedstead had an air of humility and self-respect. The sheets, though not fine, smelt amiably of grass, and the blankets where honest, if a little hard with much laundering. With the mosquito nets hanging from a hoop, which in its turn was suspended from a cup hook screwed into the wooden ceiling, the beds looked like virtuous but homely brides.

Jessie stopped singing for a minute as she pulled the green holland blind to the exact middle of the window, and surveyed the room to see if all were in order. She had very strict notions about the exact degree of circumspection to which paying guests were entitled. Yesterday everything washable in the rooms had been washed, the floor, the woodwork, the heavy florid china on the rather frail, varnished wooden washstands. The rooms smelled of soap, linoleum polish and wood. The lace curtains were stiff with starch. Indeed, there was more starch than curtain, and without it they would have been draggled and pitiful wisps.

As every door in the house was open and it was a light wooden shell of a place, old as Australian houses go, and dried by many summers, Jessie could quite comfortably talk to Catherine, who was cooking in the kitchen, from wherever she happened to be working. But presently, the rooms finished, she came to stand in the kitchen doorway with a list of the guests they were expecting for Easter, in her hand.

The kitchen was a pleasant room looking on to the old orchard, a row of persimmon trees heavy with pointed fruit turning golden in the early autumn, squat, round, guava bushes, their plump, red-coroneted fruit hidden in their glossy dark leaves, several plum and peach trees, one old wide-spreading apple tree and a breakwind of loquats and quinces. Beyond again was the bush, blue-green, shimmering a little in the morning sunshine.

Catherine Biden, too, was pleasant, and in keeping with the warm autumn landscape. Her red-gold hair, fine, heavy and straight, made a big bun on her plump white neck, her milky skin was impervious to the sun and her arms, on which her blue print sleeves were rolled up, were really beautiful. In the parlance of the neighbours, neither of the sisters would see forty again, which somehow sounded duller and more depressing than to say that Catherine was forty-two and Jessie forty-six.

'I'm putting the Adamses in the best room,' Jessie was saying, 'because they don't mind sharing a bed. And Miss Dickens and her friend in the room with the chest of drawers. Mrs Holles says she must have a room to herself, so it will have to be the little one. The Thompsons and Miss George'll sleep on the verandah and dress together in the other room. The old lady and her niece next to the dining room. That leaves only the verandah room this side, for Mr Campbell.'

'It's quite all right while the weather is cool,' said Catherine, in her placid way, rolling dough.

Jessie looked at her list with disfavour. 'We know everyone but Mr Campbell. It's rather awkward having just one man and so many women.'

'Perhaps he'll like it,' Catherine suggested.

'I don't think so. His name's Angus. He's probably a man's man.'

'Oh, if he's as Scotch as all that he won't mind. He'll fish all the time.'

'Well, all I hope is he doesn't take fright and leave us with an empty room.' The Easter season was so short, they couldn't afford an empty room.

'I hope,' said Catherine, 'we don't get a name for having only women. We do get more teachers every year and fewer men, don't we?'

'Yes, we do. I think we'd better word the advertisement differently.'

She sighed. Jessie, growing stout, with high cheek bones and a red skin, was the romantic one. She had always taken more kindly to this boarding house business than Catherine, because of its infinite possibilities — new people, new chances of excitement and romance. Although perhaps she no longer thought of romance, the habit of expecting something to happen remained with her.

Their father had married late. This house beside the lagoon had come to him with his wife and he had spent his long retirement in it, ministered to by his daughters. When he and his pension had died together, he had not, somehow, been able to leave them anything but the house, the small orchard and the lovely raggedy slope of wild garden running down to the water. Jessie, in a mood of tragic daring, advertised accommodation for holiday guests, carefully copying other advertisements she found in the paper. This expedient would, they hoped, tide them over. That was twelve years ago. A makeshift had become a permanency. In time, with the instrumentality of the local carpenter, they had added a couple of rooms and put up some almost paper-thin partitions. It looked as if they had developed the thing as far as they could.

They both still looked on their home as something different from their guest house. It was vested in that company of lares and penates now in bondage to mammon, but some day to be released. 'Our good things,' the sisters called them, the original furniture of the house, the bits and pieces that their mother had cherished. The big brass bed that had been their parents' was still in the best room, though the cedar chest of drawers with pearl buttons stuck in its knobs and the marble topped washstand had gone to raise the tone of other rooms. The dining room was very much as it had always been. The sideboard with the mirrors and carved doors took up the best part of one wall, and set out on it was the old lady's brightly polished but now unused silver coffee service. The harmonium, with its faded puce silk, filled an inconvenient amount of room by the window. The old people's enlarged portraits, an ancient, elaborate work table with dozens of little compartments, and other intimate treasures not meant for paying guests, but impossible to move out of their way, gave the room a genteel but overcrowded appearance. In the dining room in the off season it was almost as if nothing had ever happened.

In twelve years Jessie's hopefulness had worn a little thin and Catherine's gentle placid nature had become streaked with discontent, as marble is veined with black. Sometimes she asked herself where it was all leading, what would happen to them by and by and if this was all life had in store? She began in a slow blind way to feel cheated, and to realise how meaningless was the pattern of the years with their alternations of rush and stagnation, of too much work and too little money. Of their darker preoccupations the sisters did not speak to one another. In self defence they looked back rather than forward.

The guests began to arrive at lunchtime. Angus Campbell was the last to come, by the late train, long after dark. Catherine went up to the bus stop with a lantern to meet him. He saw her for the first time with the light thrown upwards on her broad fair face, and he thought how kind and simple and good she looked. His tired heart lifted, and he felt reassured.

Undressing in the small stuffy room they shared, next to the kitchen, Jessie asked her sister, 'Do you think he'll fit in all right?'

'I think so,' Catherine answered. 'He seems a nice, quiet man.'

'Young?' asked Jessie with the last flicker of interest in her tired body.

'About our age.'

'Oh well ...'

They kissed one another goodnight as they had every night since they were children, and lay down side by side to sleep.

The shell of a house was packed with sleeping people, all known and all strangers.

Angus Campbell evidently did not find his position of solitary man very trying, for on Easter Monday he asked, rather diffidently, if he might stay another week. He was taking his annual holidays. When the other guests departed, he remained. One week grew into two, then he had to return to Sydney.

He was a tall, gaunt, slightly stooped man with a weather-beaten complexion — the kind of Scots complexion that managed to look weather-beaten even in a city office — and a pair of clear, understanding, friendly, hazel eyes. His manner was very quiet and at first he seemed rather a negligible and uninteresting man. But presently you discovered in him a steadfast quality that was very likeable. You missed him when he went away.

When he was alone with the sisters, life settled inevitably into a more intimate rhythm. They ate their meals together on a rickety table on the verandah, where they could look over the garden to the lagoon. He would not let the sisters chop wood or do the heavy outdoor work that they were accustomed to, and he even came into the kitchen and helped Jessie wash up while Catherine put away. He did it so simply and naturally that it seemed right and natural to them.

One day he began digging in the garden, and, from taking up the potatoes they wanted, went on to other things. 'You oughtn't to be doing this,' Jessie said. 'It's your holiday.'

'You don't know how I enjoy it,' he answered, and his eyes, travelling over the upturned loamy earth to the blazing persimmon trees and the bush beyond, had in them a look of love and longing. She knew that he spoke the truth.

He went out fishing and brought back strings of fish for their supper with pride and gusto, and then had to watch Catherine cook them. There seemed to be something special about Catherine cooking the fish he caught.

He helped Catherine pick fruit for jam and she was aware that for all he was thin and stooped he was much stronger than she, and it gave her a curious, pleased feeling. Jessie, alone in the house, could hear their voices in the orchard, a little rarefied and idealised, in the still warm air.

Angus Campbell told them about himself. He was a clerk in a secure job and for years he had looked after his invalid mother, coming home from the office to sit with her, getting up in the night to tend her, his money going in doctor's bills. She had often been querulous and exacting. 'The pain and the tedium were so hard for her to bear, and there was so little I could do for her. Of course I remember her very different. No one could have had a better mother. She was very ambitious for me, and made great sacrifices when I was a boy, so that I should have a good education and get on. But I never did — not very far.' It was evident that he thought he owed her something for that disappointment. Two months ago she had died and he missed her bitterly. 'She had become my child,' he said. He felt, too, the cruelty of her life that had been hard and unsatisfied, and had ended in pain. Now there was no hope of ever retrieving it.

One day it rained, great gusts of thick fine rain that blotted out the lagoon, and Angus, kept in, took his book on to the verandah. Passing to and fro doing the work, Catherine saw that he was not reading, but looking out into the rain. Then he went and stood by the verandah rail for a long time. She came and stood beside him.

He said, 'If you listen you can just hear the rain on the grass and among the leaves — the smell of earth. It's good, isn't it?

The trees are more beautiful looming through the mist — the shape of them.' Marvelling, she saw that he was half in love with the beauty that she had lived with all her life.

A magpie flew through the rain, calling. He laid his hand on her shoulder and she was a little shaken by that warm and friendly touch. The eyes he turned on her still held the reflection of a mystery she had not seen.

'He is very good,' said Jessie to her sister when they were alone that night.

'And kind,' said Catherine. 'The kindest man I've ever known.' Neither of them thought how few men they'd known.

Jessie raised herself on her elbow to look at Catherine as she slept in the faint moonlight, and thought how comely she was, sweet and wholesome.

When Angus had, at last, to go, he said he would be back for the weekend. They kissed him. He was to arrive on the Friday by the last train again, and Catherine prepared supper for him before the fire, for it was getting cold now. She took the silver coffee pot, the sacred silver coffee pot that had been their mother's, and put it to warm above the kitchen stove. She cast a half defiant glance at Jessie as she did so, but Jessie went and took the silver sugar bowl too, and the cream jug, filled them, and set them on the table.

Angus asked Catherine to go out in the boat with him or to go walking, and then he paid Jessie some little attention. But they both knew. One Sunday, perhaps it was the fourth weekend he had come, the autumn was now far advanced, he and Catherine went for a long walk and he asked her to marry him. He took her in his arms and kissed her. She felt very strange, for she had never been kissed before, not by a man who was in love with her. They walked home hand in hand as if they were still very young, and when Catherine saw Jessie waving to them from the verandah she stood still and the unaccountable tears began to flow down her cheeks.

They said, everybody said, that there was no reason why they should wait, meaning they had better hurry up. The wedding was fixed for three months ahead.

It was a curious three months for Catherine. When Angus came for the weekend they would not let him pay his board, and that made a little awkwardness. Even calling him Angus seemed a trifle strange. He did not come every weekend now. Once he said, 'It seems wrong to take you away from all this beauty and freedom and shut you up in a little suburban house among a lot of other little houses just the same. Do you think you'll fret, my darling?'

Catherine had never thought very much about the beauties of nature. So she just shook her head where it rested against his shoulder. Still, her heart sank a little when she saw his house with its small windows, dark stuff hangings and many souvenirs of the late Mrs Campbell. It seemed as if sickness and death had not yet been exorcised from it.

Catherine and Jessie sewed the trousseau. 'We must be sensible,' they said to one another, and bought good stout cambric and flannelettes, though each secretly hankered after the pretty and the foolish. Catherine could not quite forget that she was going to be a middle-aged bride, and that that was just a little ridiculous. Neighbours, meaning to be kind, teased her about her wedding and were coy, sly and romantic in a heavy way, so that she felt abashed.

A subtle difference had taken place in the relationship of the sisters. Jessie felt a new tenderness for Catherine. She was the younger sister who was going to be married. Jessie's heart burned with love and protectiveness. She longed, she didn't know why, to protect Catherine, to do things for her. 'Leave that to me,' she would say when she saw Catherine go to clean the stove or perform some other dirty job. 'You must take care of your hands now.'

But Catherine always insisted on doing the roughest work. 'He's not marrying me for my beauty,' she laughed.

Catherine too thought more of her sister and of how good and unselfish she was, and her little peculiarities that once rather irritated her, now almost brought the tears to her eyes. One night she broached what was always on her mind.

'What will you do when I've gone?' she asked in a low voice.

'I'll get Ivy Thomas to help me in the busy times,' Jessie answered in a matter-of-fact voice, 'and in between, I'll manage.'

'But it will be lonely,' said Catherine weakly.

Jessie cast a reproachful glance at her. 'I'll manage,' she said.

Catherine was no longer discontented and weighed down with a sense of futility. Another emotion had taken its place, something very like homesickness.

As she did her jobs about the place she thought now, 'It is for the last time,' and there was a little pain about her heart. She looked at her world with new eyes. Angus's eyes perhaps. Going down to the fowlyard in the early morning with the bucket of steaming bran and pollard mash, she would look at the misty trees and the water like blue silk under the milk-pale sky; at the burning autumn colours of the persimmon trees, and the delicate frosty grass, and her heart would tremble with its loveliness.

One evening, coming in with the last basket of plums — ripe damsons with a thick blue bloom upon them — she stopped to rest, her back to the stormy sunset, and she saw thin, blue smoke like tulle winding among the quiet trees where a neighbour was burning leaves. She thought that she would remember this all her life. Picking nasturtiums under the old apple tree she laid her cheek for a moment against the rough silvery bark, and closed her eyes. 'My beloved old friend,' she thought but without words, 'I am leaving you for a man I scarcely know.'

It would seem as if the exaltation of being loved, of that one ripe and golden Sunday when she thought she could love too, had become detached from its object and centred now about her home. She even became aware of a rhythm in her daily work. Objects were dear because her hands were accustomed to them from childhood. And now life had to be imagined without them.

'Wherever I am, I shall have to grow old,' she thought, 'and it would be better to grow old here where everything is kind and open, than in a strange place.' It was as it the bogey she had feared, meaningless old age, had revealed itself a friend at the last moment, too late.

Jessie lit the porcelain lamp with the green shade and set it in the middle of the table among the litter of the sewing. She stood adjusting the wick, her face in shadow, and said:

'We'll have to have a serious talk about the silver and things, Cathy. We'd better settle it to-night before we get too busy.'

'What about them?' Catherine asked, biting off a thread.

'You must have your share. We'll have to divide them between us.' Jessie's voice was quite steady and her tone matter-of-fact.

'Oh, no,' cried Catherine, with a sharp note of passion in her voice. 'I don't want to take anything away.'

'They are as much yours as mine.'

'They belong here.'

'They belong to both of us, and I'm not going to have you go away empty handed.'

'But, Jessie, I'll come back often. The house wouldn't seem the same without mother's things. Don't talk as if I were going away for ever.'

'Of course you'll come back, but it won't be the same. You'll have a house of your own.'

'It won't be the same,' echoed Catherine very low.

'I specially want you to have mother's rings. I've always wanted you to wear them. You've got such pretty hands and now you won't have to work so hard . . . and the pendant. Father gave that to mother for a wedding present so as you're the one getting married it is only fit you should wear it on your wedding day too. I'll have the cameos. I'm sort of used to them. And the cat's eye brooch that I always thought we ought to have given Cousin Ella when mother died.' Jessie drew a rather difficult breath.

'You're robbing yourself,' said Catherine, 'giving me all the best. You're the eldest daughter.'

'That has nothing to do with it. We must think of what is suitable. I think you ought to have the silver coffee things. They've seemed specially yours since that night — you remember — when Angus came. Perhaps they helped . . . '

Catherine made a funny little noise.

'I don't want the silver coffee set.'

'Yes, you do. They're heaps too fine for guests. They're good. What fair puzzles me is the work table. You ought to have it because after all I suppose I'll be keeping all the big furniture, but this room wouldn't be the same without it.'

'No,' cried Catherine. 'Oh, Jessie, no. Not the work table. I couldn't bear it.' And she put her head down among the white madapolam and began to cry, a wild, desperate weeping.

'Cathy, darling, what is it? Hush, Petie, hush. We'll do everything just as you want.'

'I won't strip our home. I won't.'

'No, darling, no, but you'll want some of your own friendly things with you.'

Jessie was crying a little too, but not wildly. 'You're overwrought and tired. I've let you do too much.' Her heart was painfully full of tenderness for her sister.

Catherine's sobs grew less at last, and she said in a little gasping, exhausted voice. 'I can't do it.'

'I won't make you. It can stay here in its old place and you can see it when you come on a visit.'

'I mean I can't get married and go away. It's harder than anything is worth.'

Jessie was aghast. They argued long and confusedly. Once Catherine said: 'I wish it had been you, Jessie.'

Jessie drew away. 'You don't think that I . . . '

'No, dear, only on general grounds. You'd have made such a good wife and,' with a painful little smile, 'you were always the romantic one.'

'Not now,' said Jessie staunchly.

'I'll write to Angus now, to-night,' Catherine declared.

She wanted to be rid of this intolerable burden at once, although Jessie begged her to sleep on it. Neither of them had considered Angus, nor did they now. She got out the bottle of ink, and the pen with the cherry wood handle, which they shared, and began the letter. She was stiff and inarticulate on paper, and couldn't hope to make him understand. It was a miserable, hopeless task but she had to go through with it.

While she bent over the letter, Jessie went out into the kitchen and relit the fire. She took the silver coffee pot, the sugar basin and the cream jug, and set them out on the tray with the best worked traycloth. From the cake tin she selected the fairest of the little cakes that had been made for the afternoon tea of guests arriving tomorrow. Stinting nothing, she prepared their supper. When she heard Catherine sealing the letter, thumping the flap down with her fist to make the cheap gum stick, she carried in the tray.

Although she felt sick with crying, Catherine drank her coffee and ate a cake. The sisters smiled at one another with shaking lips and stiff reddened eyelids.

'He won't come again now,' said Jessie regretfully, but each added in her heart, 'He was a stranger, after all.'

Donalblain McCree and the Sin of Anger

Ethel Anderson

It was some few months after Aminta's wedding that Donalblain McCree, five yesterday, woke up in his room in Mallow's Marsh Vicarage. He was not, even yet, used to waking up and finding that miracle, the earth, precisely where he had left it when, on the preceding night, most reluctantly, he had closed his eyes.

For this reason he had pulled his cot alongside the window, the better to survey his inheritance, his chin on the sill.

He liked to make certain nothing was missing.

The sun? Ah, there it was! With a sunrise in full swing.

It was an elaborate effort which entailed much flinging about of amber and gold, a particularly happy effect having been achieved by piling cumulus shapes right to the zenith of the sky, then topping these with three cirrus clouds of a bright coral pink which floated like gondolas in a sea coloured a pale pistachio nut green.

Even Donalblain recognised this as a successful experiment. He turned his chin up the easier to observe it and the sun, caprice itself, hereupon set out a ray that dropped down through steep stairways of cloud to touch the eager face as if to caress it, as if to say (misquoting Baudelaire), 'This child pleases me'; while the warm sunshine vibrated like far-off chiming bells to articulate in dancing motes the promise of the sun: 'Child, you shall live under the influence of my kiss. You shall be beautiful in my way. You shall love all that I love, the earth, the trees, the sands, all sights, all sounds, all life, rivers, hills, valleys. You shall love through my influence places you have never visited, the memory of scents you have never known shall stir your heart to ecstasy, and my light shall bleach your blond hair and bronze your white neck, and dye your blue eyes to an eternal blue that will never fade.'

Yes, on that radiant spring morning the sun (in his own tongue) said something like this — something of this he said — as Donalblain leaned far out of the window to make sure that the whole of the empyrean was there. Yes, it was. But were such scudding clouds really necessary? Oh, surely not another wet day?

Was the swallow's nest still under the eaves?

Yes, it was.

There was the butcher-bird impaling a lizard on a thorn.

There were the ring-doves who always had the air of falling off a branch before settling on it, pegged, a row of eight on the orchard wall — an erection of grey stones innocent of cement.

Donalblain heard little 'Guinea-a-Week' twittering unseen, but piercingly near, and his chirping soul responded.

The child liked everything in the world except Hasty Pudding, but he found the horses too hoofy, the cattle too horny, the dogs too bouncy and barky for perfect companionship; it was the birds he loved. He had even steeled himself to listen without fear to the curlews calling 'kerloo, kerloo' as they swept in flocks over the roof on windy nights, or danced on moonlight nights in the boggy paddocks; bald, with patches soaked through with the white gold reflection of water; thatched, with shivery grasses and tussocks of Kumbungi, and extending, chequered by grey three-rail fences right from Mallow's Marsh Vicarage to the Razorbacks.

It is hardly to be credited that the sound made by two eyes opening could be heard all over the Vicarage, yet, directly Donalblain peeped himself awake, every woman in the house was aware of it. His mother, meandering like a long 'M' in the middle of a double bed, and, since her husband's death, sleeping with the sheet over her face, would lift a corner of it, smile, and replace it. His sister Juliet in the next room to his would throw her pretty legs over the side of her truckle-bed and feel for her slippers. His grandmama, majestic in a four-poster fringed and curtained in maroon, who, like most old ladies, never slept, would pause in her calculations, her difficult sum in mental arithmetic — 'If four new milch cows would bring so many more pounds of butter to be sold in Parramatta market, how long would it take to save the money necessary to send Donalblain to Trinity College, Cambridge, where his grandfather had been before him?' His grandmama was determined he should go there!

The Vicar's wife was convinced that though St Paul might possible be an inspiration to saints and martyrs, who need not, of course, be people of much social standing, only the classics, only Horace, could create a gentleman. Mrs McCree had no use for 'Nature's gentlemen'. Indeed, she was really desolate that there had not been, that there never could have been, an Epistle from Horace to St Paul.

On this particular spring morning, all these family manifes-tations having happened as usual, the three maids who were engaged in turning out the drawing-room were also immediately aware that Master Donalblain was awake. Cook Teresa, smiling, handed her millet broom to Min, the new housemaid, and hurried to the dairy to pour out from the bubbling bucket the glass of new milk, warm, which Juliet, who had found her slippers, was to carry upstairs to her brother. In the interval Tib, the housemaid-emeritus, getting up from her knees, in which posture she had been 'lifting the nap' — where there was any — from the Turkey Carpet (already twice swept) with a besom no bigger than a shaving brush, poking a head enveloped in a duster out of a side-window to engage Donalblain in that light badinage for which she had a talent; her undoing. Cook Teresa would allow no such pleasantries as those Tib had engaged in with the new boy, Dan O'Leary; this Tib felt to be unreasonable in a woman who addressed Donalblain as 'Young Tinker', 'Young Turk', or even 'You Limb' (of Satan, being understood).

On the day after his grandson's fifth birthday Mr McCree, who had long noticed that the women spoilt Donalblain, also woke the moment the child stirred, to feel an impression, which had for some time been teasing the back of his mind, harden into a resolution; it was in obedience to this impulse that the old man bent his trembling steps uncertainly to the kitchen, just after eleven o'clock.

At this hour, much like a seagull scrap-fishing in the wake of a tea-clipper, Donalblain was to be found hovering in Cook Teresa's rear. Yes! There he was! Already he had not done too badly! He had accepted with red, moist, pursed-lips a mouthful of cream, robbed a basin of rich gleanings of yellow batter, cajoled a generous munching of lemon-peel, and, yes, been given, ever so kindly, a whole delicious cumquat in syrup!

There was sunlight in the kitchen.

The room was gay with the rustle of work in progress.

Three maids all in Delft-blue cotton, worn summer and winter alike (for who could feel the cold when active?), and demure in starched white caps and aprons, in which they took pride, were red of face and arm, for the immense stove, roaring up the flues, was in the act of roasting a sucking-pig.

Like salmon in a Scottish fishing-lodge, or bloaters in a Yarmouth cottage, sucking-pig was no dish *de luxe* at Mallow's Marsh Vicarage. There were always so many male pigs, porkers that must not be kept, and, being a glut in the market, could not be sold, born in the six sties in which, this season, six shameless sows had each produced a litter of thirteen piglets — all of the wrong sex, that it was indeed an economic necessity that they should be eaten.

Mrs McCree was well aware that Mrs Noah and Mrs Job must have known a great deal about life that has not come down to us; she was in their class; but — *seventy-eight young hogs*! Oh, even Mrs Noah, even Mrs Job, would have considered this too much! Just the last straw!

In the face of this misfortune the Vicar's wife, quite losing her nerve, had talked with such severity to the man who kept her pigs that he, usually so meek, had rebelled, and, scratching a straw-coloured mop of hair, kept repeating querulously 'Phut, Mum, phut had Oi to do with ut? How could Oi help ut?'

Today the grateful smell of cooking pork grew every moment more perfect in bouquet, the sizzling of the crackling, the bubbling of beans in a pot grew every minute more full of promise, as, sitting at the freshly scrubbed and sanded table, Lulu, the between-maid, cut white kitchen-paper into picot-edged flounces, meant to hide the nakedness of the dresser shelves and the high mantelpiece above the stove. Her big curved scissors with the vandyked blades snapped and clipped as the spirals of paper lace increased and the roll of paper diminished. Min, sitting beside Lulu, being instructed by Cook Teresa in the more finicky art of fashioning frills for cruets, cutlets and hambones, plied her small scissors on an accompanying *pizzicato*.

Both maids would have been cooler in the housemaid's pantry, but, no! they preferred the hot kitchen with its constant coming and going of male visitors.

On Mr McCree's entrance all four menservants had sheepishly withdrawn from the open doorway; Cook Teresa was in the habit of giving them all a sup at eleven — nothing much — nothing that would startle the household bills; a pewter tankard of small ale, a penny ale, perhaps, or a glass of sparkling cider — both home-brewed.

In this feminine air of comfort, plenty and security, Mr McCree recognised the enemy of his sex. In this cloying, this enervating atmosphere, this 'monstrous regiment of women' the Vicar saw his grandson's undoing; he would become 'soft'. His manly character would be ruined.

Since the poor child had now no father, his grandfather was determined to warn him, to point out to him the dangers lurking in the society of females, and he took him by the hand and led him out through the orchard to the fallen pear-tree, their usual trysting-place, Donalblain's ducklings following.

Every woman looked out of a window to watch them. Eight faces appearing at the toy-like, white-curtained casements in the old-fashioned Vicarage walls, which were like those of a doll's house, painted to look like red-brick or a cardboard building in a harlequinade, registered the same fear, the same knowledge: 'He is going to set the child against us.' Intuitively the women realised this — rightly.

Sitting on the lichened trunk of the fallen pear-tree, which had a living branch or two because the tree had not completely pulled its roots out of the soil when it fell, and some remained to nourish it, Mr McCree nipped his grandson between his knees, and firmly held his restless hands, to keep them from fiddling with the ducklings, and he looked intently at the child with his kind, wise eyes, which were yet as blue as those which looked blandly back at him.

'Donalblain, you are five years old,' Mr McCree began in his quavering, hesitant voice; he had been made speechless by a stroke a year back, and was only just regaining his power of clear articulation. 'I am your grandfather, eighty-four years old. Soon you will be alone, with no father, no brother, and only three women to look after you.'

'It is too sad,' Donalblain said, tears filling his eyes.

'No, it is not a bit sad,' Mr McCree said, testily, 'it is merely inconvenient. Well, now, listen well! If a man has land or a house he can leave his land or his house to his sons, or his grandsons. But I have no land, and no house.'

'Can't I have this land? And this house?' Donalblain asked, looking round him with a wondering air.

'No. These belong to the Church. They are not mine. When I die they will go to the new Vicar of Mallow's Marsh. Well, now, if a man has tools he can leave them to his children, or his grandchildren. But I have no tools to give you. The only tools I had with which to earn a living have been an old book, and a quill pen and a halting tongue. And it cost my father a lot of money to teach me to read the old book, and write with the scratchy quill, and speak with the halting tongue.'

'Mr Noakes, the gardener, has got a pick, a shovel, a pruning hook, a scythe and a wheelbarrow,' Donalblain volunteered, as he looked across the neat, gently swaying branches of the trees planted in narrow arcades in the orchard, to where the four men were digging a drain.

'Yes, so he has. And he can teach his sons to use them, but I can't teach you to use my tools because I am too old and you are too young. However, there is one thing I can tell you, and that is this. You are too big a boy to hang round the house with the women all day long.'

Donalblain was only half-attending. Working one hand free from his grandfather's weak grasp, he swooped on the duckling which was sipping at his boots, and turned it upside-down. A scientist, satisfied with a deduction, he dropped the boat-shaped morsel of yellow fluff and, slipping his hand into his grandfather's again, prompted, dutifully, 'Yes, Grandpapa?'

But his thoughts were with his ducklings. Would they soon lay eggs?

The sun, now quite a fiery affair, was negotiating the bend between the Church tower and the henhouse, and it threw a few diffident shadows across the blossoming fruit trees; across the pears, each bearing a hint of fruit in the last remaining fuzz of varnished petals; the cherries with their dancing and triumphing clusters in full blaze, the red threads left in the peach-branches each shielding a swelling bead that intended to be one of the immense Yellow Mondays for which the Vicarage was famous.

'I have no land, I have no house, I have no tools, I have no money, but I have my integrity,' Mr McCree said, and as he watched his grandson's rosy face which blossomed no less radiantly than the blossoming trees, the old man thought, 'How can I explain the meaning of "integrity" to so immature an intelligence?'

'Mr Noakes says I am to avoid women as I would the Devil,' said Donalblain.

Hearing this, Mr McCree felt a slight lessening of the burden on his conscience; his burden, it appeared, was to be shared; his grandson was, apparently, to be accepted into the garnered wealth of the experience of the world of men; he was to be Everyman's son. Every bit of wisdom each man had gathered for himself he would, in all kindness, be ready to hand on to those who followed him. Of course, so it had always been; so it would always be.

The old man smiled, the sweet smile of age, of one helpless yet unaware of his helplessness, and his whole face brightened with that same look of doting fondness which he had so reprobated in the women of his household.

'Yes,' the boy continued, 'Mr Noakes says, if you meet a girl and a death-adder, kill the girl and cuddle the adder. He says it's safer.'

Sitting in his threadbare black cassock on the grey bole of the fallen tree, Mr McCree, who had served his God devotedly for over sixty years, felt that none of his own experiences had brought him any knowledge so salty. He considered, half astonished, the implications of such an attitude. He was, himself, warning his grandson against the deleterious effects of a woman's love; of a woman's affections. But, need one go so far?

'Little dears,' he murmured to himself, forgetting Donalblain, and sipping as a bee sips at the memory of some flowering hours. And there was his wife, of course, what a good woman she had been — Still —

'You must beware of women.'

'Yes, Grandpapa.'

'You must never allow a woman to get the whip hand of you. They are weak creatures.' Delving again into the depths of his memories, he added, 'Sometimes you must protect them from themselves.'

'Yes, Grandpapa.' Donalblain was mystified, but he was a polite child.

'You must look after your poor grandmama, your mother, and your sister, and make enough money to keep them.'

The Vicar of Mallow's Marsh looked at the small church in which thirty years of his life had been spent, mostly on his knees, where, in all happiness, he had learnt the beauty of holiness and the delight of serving his God. But his had not been a profitable life as regards material things, no, not at all! And when he had passed to his rest, and joined the Communion of Saints (as he was assured he would, meeting, he hoped, several other men from Trinity), the ninety pounds a year with which his labours had been rewarded would cease to support his family — and then? What would happen to them? He had saved nothing.

Sighing, he collected further scraps of experience to dole out, hopefully, to his grandson.

'You must have faith.'

'Yes, Grandpapa.'

'You must be a man.'

'Yes. May I begin now?' Donalblain looked eagerly up. 'May I have a catapult? May I shoot at the birds, and keep them from eating the seed?' He had often asked this before, but he saw that his grandfather was in a yielding mood. 'I would not hurt the birds! Only frighten them. That boggart Mr Noakes put up is no use at all.'

There is nothing that so becomes an orchard as ecclesiastical black, however faded it may be, and Mr McCree's cassock, swishing across the green springing orchard grasses was a telling contrast to that amazing medley of cumulus clouds, the exulting cherry trees.

His rosy face, bright with the animation of coming manhood, hopping along to avoid the persistent, nibbling beaks of his ducklings, Donalblain McCree, in his blue smock, chattered away to the old man in the easy confidence of an equal. 'I see your point,' he said, 'Sir' — this was his first claim to the status of an adult. 'I will stand on my own feet (as you tell me) and hang by my own tail (as Mr Noakes advises). I will be careful about women, too, Grandpapa!

'*More wheat*
More to eat!'

the child chanted, in sheer joy of being alive, as they joined the four men, working at the drain. 'That's a poem,' he cried out to them gaily.

Everyone there, Mr Noakes, Boy Bob, Man Jonathan, and Dan O'Leary, the new hand, all agreed that it was a good poem, and putting their picks and shovels and mattocks aside, they combined in the manufacture of a catapult, contrived from the fork of a cherry-tree, a piece of garter elastic and the thumb of an old glove. Everyone there tried the sling out and gave Donalblain good advice, and each man had his own theory about the art of flinging a stone.

Standing beside Mr McCree, who looked on, smiling, Dan O'Leary, the new man, said in a humble, ingratiating voice, 'Indeed, Surr, it's a privilege for us poor folks to spake to the Quality. It does us poor folks good, Surr, just to see the faces of the High Folks.'

He gave a sort of scrape with one foot, and his bold, handsome face took on an expression of gentle humility.

'Why did you wink at Mr Noakes, Dan?' Donalblain, who stood on the far side of the boy, asked, interested.

'Wink, is ut? It was a tear, Master Donalblain. I've had a sad life an' all, and it's new to me to be stepping alongside the gentry, that it is!' And he slid a fierce, angry look sideways at the child.

The other men kept wooden faces and no more was said.

Donalblain, then, with his new catapult, went off to the wheat-field, to drive the birds from the newly-sown seed. He was proud and happy. He could see all the other men at work, and he, too, was at work, and he, too, was becoming a man, and, what was more, his grandfather had promised him a fourpenny-piece, a Joey, as a reward for his labours.

So he sent stones as high as he could, standing under the larks that hovered, pouring out their full hearts, near a heaven that was entirely blue from one horizon to the other. Resplendent, two Wampoo Pigeons, birds of passage, bound for the scrub, rested a moment on the arms of the scarecrow, the boggart, that had been there so long that inkweed was growing out of his hat. A family of 'grey jumpers', called 'The Twelve Apostles', next came hopping over the ground, and when Donalblain, taking careful aim, flung a pebble their way (but not too near) they flew to the branches of a tree on the edge of the wheat-field, ascending from branch to branch in a series of leaps, all the time calling out indignantly and harshly at the disturber of their meal. These birds gave Donalblain lots of fun, and he would break off work sometimes to tell his ducklings how silly they were. And he would refresh his love for his ducklings by rubbing their soft yellow down against his cheeks.

'Do not think, darling, that little scissors-grinder does any harm, because he eats only spiders, my pet,' Donalblain told his eldest duckling, and he did not shoot at these birds when they came chasing their tails over the ploughed clods of earth. But when a whole flock of lorikeets came sailing and swooping in their scalloped flights to assail the cherry-trees, the child had moments of great activity; he thought of nothing else, rushing to the borders of the wheat patch for pebbles, making his ammunition of the smallest he could find, so that they could not hurt even the tiniest bird, and slinging stones widely about.

'Jerrygang! Jerrygang!' he shouted in the exuberance of his joy, and he rolled about in the grass, and the sun shone, and the faintest of zephyrs disturbed the tranquillity of the older blossoms, and wafted their discarded petals about like snow in the warm, soft air that smelt more of honey than of anything else. The Vicarage wall-flowers were out in the Vicarage garden, and their scent came puffing over the field in fragrant gusts of heavier air.

Far off the Razorback hills were a deeper blue than the sky. Nothing stirred in all the waving miles beyond the Churchyard, for the larks had all left the earth, preferring heaven, and the cattle, since it was noon, were out of sight, preferring the consolation of the river and the lower ground, where the cool water ran thinly over the flattened rushes. The men had gone to their noonday meal. There was not a soul about and the sunlight purred like a cat.

It was then that Donalblain noticed Dan O'Leary standing on the far side of the field, watching him. There was something threatening about his still figure, in its three-flounced cape coat and tall hat, and he looked very big. In that flat country even lambs looked like Leviathans. In that beautiful hour the child felt some misgiving in his heart. He hoped that Dan would go away. He pretended that he was looking for stones close to the orchard wall, and that he did not see him.

Donalblain had hoped all along that a big bird, a bird so large that he would not hurt it if he hit it, would come along, and now his wish was fulfilled, for a wild tribe of currawongs, whistling and wailing and behaving in their usual noisy abandon, came rioting down from the hills. They walked and strutted about, picking up sticks and looking coy, and setting their black heads on one side, in their indecorous courtship. 'Let us build nests' was what they were saying to one another, and the cachinnations of the older birds at some shy first-nester were amusing to hear.

Donalblain forgot Dan O'Leary.

He had a handful of stones in his pockets of his Nankin breeches — new yesterday — (and with straps that went under his jemimas, his elastic-sided boots — new, too), and he was fitting a stone into his sling when he saw that Dan, unseen, had come round the orchard wall and was standing not two feet behind him.

'Oh, Hello, Dan,' he said, to disguise his trepidation.

'Hello, young master,' Dan said, amiably. 'You are learning very fast to use your catapult, aren't you? But you don't seem to hit much, I notices.'

'I don't aim to hit the birds, only to frighten them away.'

'You don't seem to have frightened them carrawongs.'

'I've only just begun to frighten them. I scared away the Twelve Apostles, and the lorikeets.'

'They never stay long. They were going in any case.'

Dan was a very handsome lad with curly black hair and dark brown eyes that were apparently black, for their pupils had no light in them; they looked flat, and had no depth in them, and reflected nothing back; and his nose was tip-tilted, and his ears pointed, and his arms, Donalblain noticed, were so long that his fingers, as he stood there holding his bundle, reached his knees. Though he smiled with his big, curled, hungry mouth, there was a wind of fear that seemed to blow about him; he was a figure alien to the calm and peace of that happy hour.

Donalblain felt nervous. He fitted the stone which had fallen out of its place back into his sling, and let fly, to miss a sitting currawong not ten feet away.

Dan laughed heartily with a show of good-fellowship.

'Come, young master! I'll teach you how to hit a bird! he said, and stretching out a large, hairy hand, he took the catapult, and, stooping, picked up a stone, and said to Donalblain, 'You watch me hit that currawong! I'm a dead-sure shot, I am!' He drew the elastic well back, twanged off his missile, and the eldest duckling, quite in a different direction to the big piebald bird at which he was aiming, fell dead, and its head hanging almost off its neck.

Dan clicked his tongue.

'Dear me, now! Isn't that misfortunit? To hurt your duckling! That was the last thing I wanted for to do!' Dan said, watching the child's face fade from red to white.

He would have run over to the bird but Dan put his foot on the child's foot, and said, smiling, 'Wait a bit, little master! I must aim better next time!'

'You are hurting my foot, Dan,' Donalblain said, trying to pull it from under the big, heavy boot.

'Am I, indade? Oh, no, master, I wouldn't for the world hurt the likes of you, indade an' I wouldn't! Why should I?' He pressed his boot harder down on the small resisting foot under his heel. 'It's mistaken entirely you are!'

'Just you watch me,' Dan continued, fitting another stone into the catapult. 'I'll hit that currawong over there — beyond the scarecrow! It's a long shot, that — just you wait.'

The second duckling flopped about, with the soft embryo of a wing trailing on the wheat blades.

'Tut an' tut! Sure an' isn't that the Divvle an' all? Where my cunning gone to, ava? I'm ashamed of meself — to shoot that wide!'

Dan stooped, to look directly into Donalblain's smarting eyes.
'I'd best put the poor thing out of its misery, now.'
Dan knocked the third duckling out with his next stone.
Then the fourth, the fifth, the sixth.
'I hope I am not discommoding you with my foot, Master
Donalblain?' he asked in a gentle, polite tone. 'It's the difficulty
I find in aiming straight, that's what it is, that makes me lean
so heavy on your toes; shall I lift me foot?'
'Yes, please, Dan,' Donalblain said, setting his lips.
Dan lifted his boot and then stamped it hard down on the
child's small foot.
He made an exclamation of annoyance.
'Now, aren't I the fool of a man? I thought I was stamping
on that snail there, Master Donalblain. I don't know what's
come over me this noon, that I don't first kill all your ducklings
then I aims at them blasted currawongs, and then I hurts your
foot — stampin' on it — like that!' He ground his heel on
the child's instep.
'Does that hurt, little Master?'
'Yes, Dan.'
'With its new boots an' all!' Dan murmured softly into
Donalblain's ear. 'Would the other foot be feeling it less?'
He brought his foot down.
Donalblain stood, his lips set, looking at his ducklings.
The one with the broken wing still struggled, bleeding, to
get out of the trough of earth into which it had fallen.
'Don't you think it would be kinder to put that duckling
out of its pain?'
'Yes, Dan.'
'Come over here, then, just stamp on it with your boot, that
will give it comfort, like. You'd like to be kind, wouldn't you,
young Master?'
'I don't want to hurt my duckling.'
'Oh, it's been cruel to be kind, that's what it is, just like me!
I'm teaching you something, that's what I'm doing, but I'm just
a clumsy oaf, just a poor man, Master Donalblain, and I don't
rightly seem to have the gift of it, like my betters. They can
thrash my back with a cat-o'-nine tails, and do me good, see?
Because they're the Quality, and can't go wrong. But I'm no
hand at it.'
Dan walked across and stamped on the duckling.
It was said, in medieval times, that a man in the paroxysms
of an overpowering rage had white eyes.

When, for instance, King Arthur ran 'wood-mad', Mallory tells us he had white eyes, and Langland gives 'Ira', anger, white eyes.

What was so dreadful to see in Donalblain, a child transported with rage, was just the same alarming manifestation. When he saw Dan stamp on the wounded duckling, in his fury his eyes became white; the pupils turned inwards, as it seemed, and slewed round out of sight like a Medium's eyes in a trance. His vibrating feet stamped up and down on the grass, and a swift staccato tattoo, a rapid churning! Up and down! Up and down! Donalblain's legs moved so quickly that they were difficult to see, like flails on a windmill, or like a man trying to keep his place on a treadmill. They whirred up and down. And he thought not at all of his bruised feet which were next day to show black and blue.

The child's hands beat wildly in front of him, sawing the air in a demented fashion, threshing it, hitting out with all his might when, running over, he got close enough to batter Dan O'Leary's knees — he could reach no higher. And the tears fell in immense bright drops, a clear, incredible torrent, pouring down his now flushed, now scarlet face, round which his yellow hair stood out almost on end, and a sort of high keening noise, a most curious whinnying sound came whistling out of his wide-open mouth, moist and dripping with saliva.

It was a noise so piercing that it seemed impossible that he could be making so strange, so clamorous a shrieking; an animal braying, a primitive echo from the first abortive transports of man.

Dan O'Leary was amused and gratified.

At that moment he almost liked Donalblain.

He stuck the catapult back in the little boy's breeches pocket and started tickling him.

At this last outrage the inverted eyes came back into focus.

Donalblain turned and ran back over the ploughed field, over the once-hopeful arena of his first initiation into the service of his fellows, racing back through the shadowy orchard, where so lately he had stood, a happy child between his grandfather's knees; he ran pelting back, still screaming at the top of his voice, past the laundry, the kitchen door, along the narrow strawberry-beds, screaming, screaming in that high ass-like bray of sheer terror.

Every woman's face again appeared at the Vicarage windows.

Eight alarmed, compassionate women, leaving their points of vantage, rushed out to meet the child, and even his mother, throwing aside her novel, jumping up from her rocking-chair, after one wild look from her bedroom window, rushed downstairs so quickly, her white spotted wrapper streaming out behind her in the wind of her swift passage, that she was the first to reach him, and Donalblain flung himself into her open arms, that maternal refuge, and cried till he slept.

Like that first Dove sent out from the arc, Donalblain had come home. Of the death of his ducklings, of the knowledge of evil, of cruelty, which he had gained in that moment of his initial experience of the world outside the nursery, he spoke never a word. He answered no questions. Instinctively he conformed to the masculine code.

There is nothing so mysterious as the way that the seeds of the future germinate in the character of a child.

It is a miracle like that of a bud, which has, folded in it, the uncurled petals of the rose.

It is time's triumph, like the fashioning of the cone, the brass cone, which is to be the trumpet, silence until breath animates it, till breath blows the fanfare for which, from the first casting of the instrument, preparations had been made.

On that spring day the child Donalblain's destiny was made manifest; it was made coherent on that spring day when, on waking, he approved of the sunlight, when his teeming heart was united with the singing bird's, when he and little 'Guinea-a-Week' sang their psalm together; when he was happy among the women of his grandfather's household, when (with the eyes of a scientist) he studied his duckling, and with the eyes of a dutiful child he looked up at his grandfather to learn, without speech, the meaning of the word *'integrity'*.

On that spring noonday when, without rancour and being for the first time conscious of a sense of duty to others, of the pleasure of service, of a male desire to protect the weak, when he drove the birds from the patch of wheat; his family's bread; and then, seeing the death of his birds, felt in his young, untried heart the anger of the Saviour unable to save, of the pitiful soul unable to exercise the virtue of pity, or to save the helpless, the suffering, or to master (with his puny strength) the evildoer; in that moment, when Donalblain realised that he was helpless in the presence of cruelty, or wickedness, his fierce emotion operated like a dye, like woad, like murex, to colour his whole nature. Like a piece of cloth, dipped in a vat, to come out purple, he was metamorphosed, by that moment of his childhood, his youth, his manhood, his age.

Yes, Donalblain's character was stabilised by all that he suffered then. His experience on that bright noonday made him the child, the youth, the man he was always to be; the crisis of that encounter, the agony of that defeat, which taught him he was not omnipotent, that he was powerless in the presence of sin (it is a lesson we must learn), stood like a peak in the accumulated sensations of his whole life.

Like a child he cried himself to sleep. Like a child he accepted the comfort of his mother's embrace, but deep in his heart he had learnt all he was ever to know of man's capacity for grief beyond the reach of consolation.

He had exhausted himself in this knowledge.

That night the moon, caprice itself, looked down on Donalblain, sleeping by the uncurtained window, sleeping with his cot drawn as close as he could get to the wide-open window, and the moon said (misquoting Baudelaire), 'This child pleases me.'

And the moonbeams dropped down through gigantic stairways of parting cloud, and streamed, unimpeded, through the panes of glass, the doubled panes of the pushed-up window, high above his head, and touched his face as if to bless it, as if to caress it, to print on it the splendour of the human knowledge of good and evil, of sorrow, or joy, and this radiant light became articulate with the moon's promise:

'You shall live under the influence of my kiss. You shall be beautiful in my manner. You shall love all that I love, water, clouds, silence, darkness and the illimitable sea.'

And from that day and that night, the sun was Donalblain's brother, and the moon was his sister, and in his long, useful and distinguished life, though love informed him, he cared to make no nearer relationships.

But Tib, the housemaid-emeritus, the girl of sixteen, knew nothing of such depths when, after the moon rose, she slipped out from her attic to join Dan, who was waiting for her behind the orchard wall in this three-tiered driving coat and rakish hat; clothes which Mr Noakes had called 'a nob's togs', and had asked him how he came by them?

Tib had her neat carpet bag, bright with roses as big as cabbages, which had enclosed in it the wardrobe which the Duke of Wellington himself had chosen for female emigrants; a mixed bag of eight calico garments (in the selection of which the Duke had betrayed a singular innocence) and two pocket-handkerchiefs, and one Huckaback towel, she wore a dress of grey linsey-woolsey, and a coal-scuttle bonnet, into which, with great daring, she had stuck a rose.

The child had a month's wages — the twelfth part of two pounds — tied in a corner of her handkerchief, and she was not afraid of anything that might happen to her.

Though man's inhumanity to man may make angels weep, Nature shows a singular and impartial beneficence, bestowing on king and tinker alike the best earth has to offer; Dan, walking in that soft moonlight night through the orchard with Tib, was simulacra of last year's apples, the dust of last autumn's toad's-meat crumbling and dispersing under his footprints, was triumphant.

While the lovers trudged the long miles into Parramatta his voice murmured untiringly, as he told Tib all he had suffered and all he meant to achieve.

And they delighted in each other, the strong, handsome young man in the pride of his manhood, and the innocent girl in the beauty of her budding womanhood; and they had no fear of each other, or of the future.

And peering out through the white muslin curtains of her bedroom window Donalblain's mother, the young widow, watched them go, and her tears fell faster than Widow Dido's, indeed they did.

Proem

Henry Handel Richardson

In a shaft on the Gravel Pits, a man had been buried alive.
At work in a deep wet hole, he had recklessly omitted to slab
the walls of a drive; uprights and tailors yielded under the lateral
pressure, and the rotten earth collapsed, bringing down the
roof in its train. The digger fell forward on his face, his ribs
jammed across his pick, his arms pinned to his sides, nose and
mouth pressed into the sticky mud as into a mask; and over
his defenceless body, with a roar that burst his ear-drums, broke
stupendous masses of earth.

His mates at the windlass went staggering back from the belch
of violently discharged air: it tore the wind-sail to strips, sent
stones and gravel flying, loosened planks and props. Their shouts
drawing no response, the younger and nimbler of the two — he
was a mere boy, for all his amazing growth of beard — put his
foot in the bucket and went down on the rope, kicking off the
sides of the shaft with his free foot. A group of diggers, gathering
round the pit-head, waited for the tug at the rope. It was quick
in coming; and the lad was hauled to the surface. No hope: both
drives had fallen in; the bottom of the shaft was blocked. The
crowd melted with a 'Poor Bill — God rest his soul!' or with a
silent shrug. Such accidents were not infrequent; each man might
thank his stars it was not he who lay cooling down below. And
so, since no more washdirt would be raised from this hole, the
party that worked it made off for the nearest grog-shop, to wet
their throats to the memory of the dead, and to discuss future
plans.

All but one: a lean and haggard-looking man of some five
and forty, who was known to his comrades as Long Jim. On

hearing his mate's report he had sunk heavily down on a log, and there he sat, a pannikin of raw spirit in his hand, the tears coursing ruts down cheeks scabby with yellow mud, his eyes glassy as marbles with those that had still to fall.

He wept, not for the dead man, but for himself. This accident was the last link in a chain of ill-luck that had been forging ever since he first followed the diggings. He only needed to put his hand to a thing, and luck deserted it. In all the sinkings he had been connected with, he had not once caught his pick in a nugget or got the run of the gutter; the 'bottoms' had always proved barren, drives been exhausted without his raising the colour. At the present claim he and his mates had toiled for months, overcoming one difficulty after another. The slabbing, for instance, had cost them infinite trouble; it was roughly done, too, and, even after the pins were in, great flakes of earth would come tumbling down from between the joints, on one occasion nearly knocking silly the man who was below. Then, before they had slabbed a depth of three times nine, they had got into water, and in this they worked for the next sixty feet. They were barely rid of it, when the two adjoining claims were abandoned, and in came the flood again — this time they had to fly for their lives before it, so rapid was its rise. Not the strongest man could stand in this ice-cold water for more than three days on end — the bark slabs stank in it, too, like the skins in a tanner's yard — and they had been forced to quit work till it subsided. He and another man had gone to the hills, to hew trees for more slabs; the rest to the grog-shop. From there, when it was feasible to make a fresh start, they had to be dragged, some blind drunk, the rest blind stupid from their booze. That had been the hardest job of any: keeping the party together. They had only been eight in all — a hand-to-mouth number for a deep wet hole. Then, one had died of dysentery, contracted from working constantly in water up to his middle; another had been nabbed in a man-hunt and clapped into the 'logs'. And finally, but a day or two back, the three men who completed the night-shift had deserted for a new 'rush' to the Avoca. Now, his pal had gone, too. There was nothing left for him, Long Jim, to do, but to take his dish and turn fossicker; or even to aim no higher than washing over the tailings rejected by the fossicker.

At the thought his tears flowed anew. He cursed the day on which he had first set foot on Ballarat.

'It's 'ell for white men — 'ell, that's what it is!'

"'Ere, 'ave another drink, matey, and fergit yer bloody troubles.'

His re-filled pannikin drained, he grew warmer round the heart; and sang the praises of his former life. He had been a lamplighter in the old country, and for many years had known no more arduous task than that of tramping round certain streets three times daily, ladder on shoulder, bitch at heel, to attend the little flames that helped to dispel the London dark. And he might have jogged on at this up to three score years and ten, had he never lent an ear to the tales that were being told of a wonderful country, where, for the mere act of stooping, and with your naked hand, you could pick up a fortune from the ground. Might the rogues who had spread these lies be damned to all eternity! Then, he had swallowed them only too willingly; and, leaving the old woman wringing her hands, had taken every farthing of his savings and set sail for Australia. That was close on three years ago. For all he knew, his wife might be dead and buried by this time; or sitting in the almshouse. She could not write, and only in the early days had an occasional newspaper reached him, on which, alongside the Queen's head, she had put the mark they had agreed on, to show that she was still alive. He would probably never see her again, but would end his days where he was. Well, they wouldn't be many; this was not a place that made old bones. And, as he sat, worked on by grief and liquor, he was seized by a desperate homesickness for the old country. Why had he ever been fool enough to leave it? He shut his eyes, and all the well-known sights and sounds of the familiar streets came back to him. He saw himself on his rounds of a winter's afternoon, when each lamp had a halo in the foggy air; heard the pit-pat of his four-footer behind him, the bump of the ladder against the prong of the lamp-post. His friend the policeman's glazed stove-pipe shone out at the corner; from the distance came the tinkle of the muffin-man's bell, the cries of the buy-a-brooms. He remembered the glowing charcoal in the stoves of the chestnut and potato sellers; the appetizing smell of the cooked-fish shops; the fragrant steam of the hot, dark coffee at the twopenny stall, when he had turned shivering out of bed; he sighed for the lights and jollity of the 'Hare and Hounds' on a Saturday night. He would never see anything of the kind again. No; here, under bare blue skies, out of which the sun frizzled you alive; here, where it couldn't rain without at once being a flood; where the very winds blew contrarily, hot from the north and bitter-chill from the south; where, no matter how great the heat by day, the night would be likely as not be nipping cold: here he was doomed to end his life, and to end it, for all the yellow sunshine, more hopelessly knotted and gnarled with rheumatism than if, dawn after dawn, he had gone out in a cutting north-easter, or groped his way through the grey fog-mists sent up by grey Thames.

Thus he sat and brooded, all the hatred of the unwilling exile for the land that gives him house-room burning in his breast.

Who the man was, who now lay deep in a grave that fitted him as a glove fits the hand, careless of the pass to which he had brought his mate; who this really was, Long Jim knew no more than the rest. Young Bill had never spoken out. They had chummed together on the seventy-odd-mile tramp from Melbourne; had boiled a common billy and slept side by side in rain-soaked blankets, under the scanty hair of a she-oak. That was in the days of the first great stampede to the gold-fields, when the embryo seaports were as empty as though they were plague-ridden, and every man who had the use of his legs was on the wide bush-track, bound for the north. It was better to be two than one in this medley of bullock-teams, lorries, carts and pack-horses, of dog-teams, wheelbarrows and swagmen, where the air rang with oaths, shouts and hammering hoofs, with whip-cracking and bullock-prodding; in this hurly-burly of thieves, bushrangers and foreigners, of drunken convicts and deserting sailors, of slit-eyed Chinese and apt-handed Lascars, of expirees and ticket-of-leave men, of Jews, Turks and other infidels. Long Jim, himself stunned by it all: by the pother of landing and of finding a roof to cover him; by the ruinous price of bare necessaries; by the length of this unheard-of walk that lay before his town-bred feet: Long Jim had gladly accepted the young man's company on the road. Originally, for no more than this; at heart he distrusted Young Bill, because of his fine-gentleman airs, and intended shaking the lad off as soon as they reached the diggings. There, a man must, for safety's sake, be alone, when he stooped to pick up his fortune. But at first sight of the strange, wild scene that met his eyes he hastily changed his mind. And so the two of them had stuck together; and he had never had cause to regret it. For all his lily-white hands and finical speech Young Bill had worked like a nigger, standing by his mate through the latter's disasters; had worked till the ladyish hands were horny with warts and corns, and this, though he was doubled up with dysentery in the hot season, and racked by winter cramps. But the life had proved too hard for him, all the same. During the previous summer he had begun to drink — steadily, with the dogged persistence that was in him — and since then his work had gone downhill. His sudden death had only been a hastening-on of the inevitable. Staggering home to the tent after nightfall he would have been sure, sooner or later, to fall into a dry shicer and break his neck, or into a wet one and be drowned.

On the surface of the Gravel Pits his fate was already forgotten. The rude activity of the gold-diggings in full swing had closed over the incident, swallowed it up.

Under a sky so pure and luminous that it seemed like a thinly drawn veil of blueness, which ought to have been transparent, stretched what, from a short way off, resembled a desert of pale clay. No patch of green offered rest to the eye; not a tree, hardly a stunted bush had been left standing, either on the bottom of the vast shallow basin itself, or on the several hillocks that dotted it and formed its sides. Even the most prominent of these, the Black Hill, which jutted out on the Flat like a gigantic tumulus, had been stripped of its dense timber, feverishly dis-embowelled, and was now become a bald protuberance strewn with gravel and clay. The whole scene had that strange, repellent ugliness that goes with breaking up and throwing into disorder what has been sanctified as final, and belongs, in particular, to the wanton disturbing of earth's gracious, green-spread crust. In the pre-golden era this wide valley, lying open to sun and wind, had been a lovely grassland, ringed by a circlet of wooded hills; beyond these, by a belt of virgin forest. A limpid river and more than one creek had meandered across its face; water was to be found there even in the driest summer. She-oaks and peppermints had given shade to the flocks of the early settlers; wattles had bloomed their brief delirious yellow passion against the grey-green foliage of the gums. Now, all that was left of the original 'pleasant resting-place' and its pristine beauty were the ancient volcanic cones of Warrenheip and Buninyong. These, too far off to supply wood for firing or slabbing, still stood green and timbered, and looked down upon the havoc that had been made of the fair, pastoral lands.

Seen nearer at hand, the dun-coloured desert resolved itself into uncountable pimpling clay and mud-heaps, of divers shade and varying sizes: some consisted of but a few bucketfuls of mullock, others were taller than the tallest man. There were also hundreds of rain-soaked, mud-bespattered tents, sheds and awnings; wind-sails, which fell, funnel-like, from a kind of gallows into the shafts they ventilated; flags fluttering on high posts in front of stores. The many human figures that went to and fro were hardly to be distinguished from the ground they trod. They were coated with earth, clay-clad in ochre and gamboge. Their faces were daubed with clauber; it matted great beards, and entangled the coarse hairs on chests and brawny arms. Where, here and there, a blue jumper had kept a tinge of blueness, it was so besmeared with yellow that it might have been expected to turn green. The gauze neck-veils that hung from the brims of wide-awakes or cabbage-trees were become stiff little lattices of caked clay.

There was water everywhere. From the spurs and gullies round about, the autumn rains had poured freely down on the Flat; river and creeks had been over their banks; and such narrow ground-space as remained between the thick-sown tents, the myriads of holes that abutted one on another, jealous of every inch of space, had become a trough of mud. Water meandered over this mud, or carved its soft way in channels; it lay about in puddles, thick and dark as coffee-grounds; it filled abandoned shallow holes to the brim.

From this scene rose a blurred hum of sound; rose and as it were remained stationary above it — like a smoke-cloud, which no wind comes to drive away. Gradually, though, the ears made out, in the conglomerate of noise, a host of separate noises infinitely multiplied: the sharp tick-tick of surface-picks, the dull thud of shovels, their muffled echoes from the depths below. There was also the continuous squeak and groan of windlasses; the bump of the mullock emptied from the bucket; the trundle of wheelbarrows, pushed along a plank from the shaft's mouth to the nearest pool; the dump of the dart on the heap for washing. Along the banks of a creek, hundreds of cradles rattled and grated; the noise of the spades, chopping the gravel into the puddling-tubs or the Long Toms, was like the scrunch of shingle under waves. The fierce yelping of the dogs chained to the flagposts of stores, mongrels which yapped at friend and foe alike, supplied a note of earsplitting discord.

But except for this it was a wholly mechanical din. Human brains directed operations, human hands carried them out, but the sound of the human voice was, for the most part, lacking. The diggers were a sombre, preoccupied race, little given to lip-work. Even the 'shepherds', who, in waiting to see if their neighbours struck the lead, beguiled the time with euchre and 'lamb-skinnet', played moodily, their mouths glued to their pipe-stems; they were tail-on-end to fling down the cards for pick and shovel. The great majority, ant-like in their indefatigable busyness, neither turned a head nor looked up: backs were bent, eyes fixed, in a hard scrutiny of cradle or tin-dish: it was the earth that held them, the familiar, homely earth, whose common fate it is to be trodden heedlessly underfoot. Here, it was the load-stone that drew all men's thoughts. And it took toll of their bodies in odd, exhausting forms of labour, which were swift to weed out the unfit.

The men at the windlasses spat into their horny palms and bent to the crank: they paused only to pass the back of a hand over a sweaty forehead, or to drain a nose between two fingers. The barrow-drivers shoved their loads, the bones of their forearms standing out like ribs. Beside the pools, the puddlers chopped with their shovels; some even stood in the tubs, and worked the earth with their feet, as wine-pressers trample grapes. The cradlers, eternally rocking with one hand, held a long stick in the other with which to break up any clods a careless puddler might have deposited in the hopper. Behind these came the great army of fossickers, washers of surface-dirt, equipped with knives and tin-dishes, and content if they could wash out half-a-penny-weight to the dish. At their heels still others, who treated the tailings they threw away. And among these last was a sprinkling of women, more than one with an infant sucking at her breast. Withdrawn into a group for themselves worked a body of Chinese, in loose blue blouses, flappy blue leg-bags and huge conical straw hats. They, too, fossicked and re-washed, using extravagant quantities of water.

Thus the pale-eyed multitude worried the surface, and, at the risk and cost of their lives, probed the depths. Now that deep sinking was in vogue, gold-digging no longer served as a play-game for the gentleman and the amateur; the greater number of those who toiled at it were work-tried, seasoned men. And yet, although it had now sunk to the level of any other arduous and uncertain occupation, and the magic prizes of the early days were seldom found, something of the old, romantic glamour still clung to this most famous gold-field, dazzling the eyes and confounding the judgement. Elsewhere, the horse was in use at the puddling-trough, and machines for crushing quartz were under discussion. But the Ballarat digger resisted the introduction of machinery, fearing the capitalist machinery would bring in its train. He remained the dreamer, the jealous individualist; he hovered for ever on the brink of a stupendous discovery.

This dream it was, of vast wealth got without exertion, which had decoyed the strange, motley crowd, in which peers and churchmen rubbed shoulders with the scum of Norfolk Island, to exile in this outlandish region. And the intention of all alike had been: to snatch a golden fortune from the earth and then, hey, presto! for the old world again. But they were reckoning without their host: only too many of those who entered the country went out no more. They became prisoners to the soil. The fabulous riches of which they had heard tell amounted, at best, to a few thousands of pounds: what folly to depart with so little, when mother earth still teemed! Those who drew blanks nursed an unquenchable hope, and laboured all their days like navvies, for a navvy's wage. Others again, broken in health or disheartened, could only turn to an easier handiwork. There were also men who, as soon as fortune smiled on them, dropped their tools and ran to squander the work of months in a wild debauch; and they invariably returned, tail down, to prove their luck anew. And, yet again, there were those who, having once seen the metal in the raw: in dust, fine as that brushed from a butterfly's wings; in heavy, chubby nuggets; or, more exquisite still, as the daffodil-yellow veining the bluish-white quartz: these were gripped in the subtlest way of all. A passion for the gold itself awoke in them an almost sensual craving to touch and possess; and the glitter of a few specks at the bottom of pan or cradle came, in time, to mean more to them than 'home', or wife, or child.

Such were the fates of those who succumbed to the 'unholy hunger'. It was like a form of revenge taken on them, for their loveless schemes of robbing and fleeing; a revenge contrived by the ancient, barbaric country they had so lightly invaded. Now, she held them captive — without chains; ensorcelled — without witchcraft; and, lying stretched like some primeval monster in the sun, her breasts freely bared, she watched, with a malignant eye, the efforts made by these puny mortals to tear their lips away.

THE DROVER'S WIFE

Henry Lawson

The two-roomed house is built of round timber, slabs, and stringy-bark, and floored with split slabs. A big bark kitchen standing at one end is larger than the house itself, verandah included.

Bush all round — bush with no horizon, for the country is flat. No ranges in the distance. The bush consists of stunted, rotten native apple-trees. No undergrowth. Nothing to relieve the eye save the darker green of a few she-oaks which are sighing above the narrow, almost waterless creek. Nineteen miles to the nearest sign of civilization — a shanty on the main road.

The drover, an ex-squatter, is away with sheep. His wife and children are left here alone.

Four ragged, dried-up-looking children are playing about the house. Suddenly one of them yells: 'Snake! Mother, here's a snake!'

The gaunt, sun-browned bushwoman dashes from the kitchen, snatches her baby from the ground, holds it on her left hip, and reaches for a stick.

'Where is it?'

'Here! gone into the wood-heap!' yells the eldest boy — a sharp-faced urchin of eleven. 'Stop there, mother! I'll have him. Stand back! I'll have the beggar!'

'Tommy, come here, or you'll be bit. Come here at once when I tell you, you little wretch!'

The youngster comes reluctantly, carrying a stick bigger than himself. Then he yells, triumphantly:

'There it goes — under the house!' and darts away with club uplifted. At the same time the big, black, yellow-eyed dog-of-all-breeds, who has shown the wildest interest in the proceedings, breaks his chain and rushes after that snake. He is a moment late, however, and his nose reaches the crack in the slabs just as the end of its tail disappears. Almost at the same moment the boy's club comes down and skins the aforesaid nose. Alligator takes small notice of this, and proceeds to undermine the building; but he is subdued after a struggle and chained up. They cannot afford to lose him.

The drover's wife makes the children stand together near the dog-house while she watches for the snake. She gets two small dishes of milk and sets them down near the wall to tempt it to come out; but an hour goes by and it does not show itself.

It is near sunset, and a thunderstorm is coming. The children must be brought inside. She will not take them into the house, for she knows the snake is there, and may at any moment come up through a crack in the rough slab floor; so she carries several armfuls of firewood into the kitchen, and then takes the children there. The kitchen has no floor — or, rather, an earthen one — called a 'ground floor' in this part of the bush. There is a large, roughly-made table in the centre of the place. She brings the children in, and makes them get on this table. They are two boys and two girls — mere babies. She gives them some supper, and then, before it gets dark, she goes into the house, and snatches up some pillows and bedclothes — expecting to see or lay her hand on the snake any minute. She makes a bed on the kitchen table for the children, and sits down beside it to watch all night.

She has an eye on the corner, and a green sapling club laid in readiness on the dresser by her side; also her sewing basket and a copy of the *Young Ladies' Journal*. She has brought the dog into the room.

Tommy turns in, under protest, but says he'll lie awake all night and smash that blinded snake.

His mother asks him how many times she has told him not to swear.

He has his club with him under the bedclothes, and Jacky protests:

'Mummy! Tommy's skinnin' me alive wif his club. Make him take it out.'

Tommy: 'Shet up, you little —— ! D'yer want to be bit with the snake?'

Jacky shuts up.

'If yer bit,' says Tommy, after a pause, 'you'll swell up, an' smell, an' turn red an' green an' blue all over till yer bust. Won't he, mother?'

'Now then, don't frighten the child. Go to sleep,' she says.

The two younger children go to sleep, and now and then Jacky complains of being 'skeezed'. More room is made for him. Presently Tommy says: 'Mother! listen to them (adjective) little possums. I'd like to screw their blanky necks.'

And Jacky protests drowsily.

'But they don't hurt us, the little blanks!'

Mother: 'There, I told you you'd teach Jacky to swear.' But the remark makes her smile. Jacky goes to sleep.

Presently Tommy asks:

'Mother! Do you think they'll ever extricate the (adjective) kangaroo?'

'Lord! How am I to know, child? Go to sleep.'

'Will you wake me if the snake comes out?'

'Yes. Go to sleep.'

Near midnight. The children are all asleep and she sits there still, sewing and reading by turns. From time to time she glances round the floor and wall-plate, and, whenever she hears a noise, she reaches for the stick. The thunderstorm comes on, and the wind, rushing through the cracks in the slab wall, threatens to blow out her candle. She places it on a sheltered part of the dresser and fixes up a newspaper to protect it. At every flash of lightning, the cracks between the slabs gleam like polished silver. The thunder rolls, and the rain comes down in torrents.

Alligator lies at full length on the floor, with his eyes turned towards the partition. She knows by this that the snake is there. There are large cracks in that wall opening under the floor of the dwelling-house.

She is not a coward, but recent events have shaken her nerves. A little son of her brother-in-law was lately bitten by a snake, and died. Besides, she has not heard from her husband for six months, and is anxious about him.

He was a drover, and started squatting here when they were married. The drought of 18— ruined him. He had to sacrifice the remnant of his flock and go droving again. He intends to move his family into the nearest town when he comes back, and, in the meantime, his brother, who keeps a shanty on the main road, comes over about once a month with provisions. The wife has still a couple of cows, one horse, and a few sheep. The brother-in-law kills one of the latter occasionally, gives her what she needs of it, and takes the rest in return for other provisions.

She is used to being left alone. She once lived like this for eighteen months. As a girl she built the usual castles in the air; but all her girlish hopes and aspirations have long been dead. She finds all the excitement and recreation she needs in the *Young Ladies' Journal*, and Heaven help her! takes a pleasure in the fashion-plates.

Her husband is an Australian, and so is she. He is careless, but a good enough husband. If he had the means he would take her to the city and keep her there like a princess. They are used to being apart, or at least she is. 'No use fretting,' she says. He may forget sometimes that he is married; but if he has a good cheque when he comes back he will give most of it to her. When he had money he took her to the city several times — hired a railway sleeping compartment, and put up at the best hotels. He also bought her a buggy, but they had to sacrifice that along with the rest.

The last two children were born in the bush — one while her husband was bringing a drunken doctor, by force, to attend to her. She was alone on this occasion, and very weak. She had been ill with a fever. She prayed to God to send her assistance. God sent Black Mary — the 'whitest' gin in all the land. Or, at least, God sent King Jimmy first, and he sent Black Mary. He put his black face round the door post, took in the situation at a glance, and said cheerfully: 'All right, missus — I bring my old woman, she down alonga creek.'

One of the children died while she was here alone. She rode nineteen miles for assistance, carrying the dead child.

It must be near one or two o'clock. The fire is burning low. Alligator lies with his head resting on his paws, and watches the wall. He is not a very beautiful dog, and the light shows numerous old wounds where the hair will not grow. He is afraid of nothing on the face of the earth or under it. He will tackle a bullock as readily as he will tackle a flea. He hates all other dogs — except kangaroo-dogs — and has a marked dislike to friends or relations of the family. They seldom call, however. He sometimes makes friends with strangers. He hates snakes and has killed many, but he will be bitten some day and die; most snake-dogs end that way.

Now and then the bushwoman lays down her work and watches, and listens, and thinks. She thinks of things in her own life, for there is little else to think about.

The rain will make the grass grow, and this reminds her how she fought a bush-fire once while her husband was away. The grass was long, and very dry, and the fire threatened to burn her out. She put on an old pair of her husband's trousers and beat out the flames with a green bough, till great drops of sooty perspiration stood out on her forehead and ran in streaks down her blackened arms. The sight of his mother in trousers greatly amused Tommy, who worked like a little hero by her side, but the terrified baby howled lustily for his 'mummy'. The fire would have mastered her but for four excited bushmen who arrived in the nick of time. It was a mixed-up affair all round; when she went to take up the baby he screamed and struggled convulsively, thinking it was a 'blackman'; and Alligator, trusting more to the child's sense than his own instinct, charged furiously, and (being old and slightly deaf) did not in his excitement at first recognize his mistress's voice, but continued to hang on to the moleskins until choked off by Tommy with a saddle-strap. The dog's sorrow for his blunder, and his anxiety to let it be known that it was all a mistake, was as evident as his ragged tail and a twelve-inch grin could make it. It was a glorious time for the boys; a day to look back to, and talk about, and laugh over for many years.

She thinks how she fought a flood during her husband's absence. She stood for hours in the drenching downpour, and dug an overflow gutter to save the dam across the creek. But she could not save it. There are things that a bushwoman cannot do. Next morning the dam was broken, and her heart was nearly broken too, for she thought how her husband would feel when he came home and saw the result of years of labour swept away. She cried then.

She also fought the pleuro-pneumonia — dosed and bled the few remaining cattle, and wept again when her two best cows died.

Again, she fought a mad bullock that besieged the house for a day. She made bullets and fired at him through cracks in the slabs with an old shot-gun. He was dead in the morning. She skinned him and got seventeen-and-sixpence for the hide.

She also fights the crows and eagles that have designs on her chickens. Her plan of campaign is very original. The children cry 'Crows, mother!' and she rushes out and aims a broomstick at the birds as though it were a gun, and says 'Bung!'. The crows leave in a hurry; they are cunning, but a woman's cunning is greater.

Occasionally a bushman in the horrors, or a villainous-looking sundowner, comes and nearly scares the life out of her. She generally tells the suspicious-looking stranger that her husband and two sons are at work below the dam, or over at the yard, for he always cunningly inquires for the boss.

Only last week a gallows-faced swagman — having satisfied himself that there were no men on the place — threw his swag down on the verandah, and demanded tucker. She gave him something to eat; then he expressed his intention of staying for the night. It was sundown then. She got a batten from the sofa, loosened the dog, and confronted the stranger, holding the batten in one hand and the dog's collar with the other. 'Now you go!' she said. He looked at her and at the dog, said 'All right, mum,' in a cringing tone, and left. She was a determined-looking woman, and Alligator's yellow eyes glared unpleasantly — besides, the dog's chawing-up apparatus greatly resembled that of the reptile he was named after.

She has few pleasures to think of as she sits here alone by the fire, on guard against a snake. All days are much the same to her; but on Sunday afternoon she dresses herself, tidies the children, smartens up baby, and goes for a lonely walk along the bush-track, pushing an old perambulator in front of her. She does this every Sunday. She takes as much care to make herself and the children look smart as she would if she were going to do the block in the city. There is nothing to see, however, and not a soul to meet. You might walk for twenty miles along this track without being able to fix a point in your mind, unless you are a bushman. This is because of the everlasting, maddening sameness of the stunted trees — that monotony which makes a man long to break away and travel as far as trains can go, and sail as far as ship can sail — and further.

But this bushwoman is used to the loneliness of it. As a girl-wife she hated it, but now she would feel strange away from it.

She is glad when her husband returns, but she does not gush or make a fuss about it. She gets him something good to eat, and tidies up the children.

She seems contented with her lot. She loves her children, but has no time to show it. She seems harsh to them. Her surroundings are not favourable to the development of the 'womanly' or sentimental side of nature.

It must be near morning now; but the clock is in the dwelling-house. Her candle is nearly done; she forgot that she was out of candles. Some more wood must be got to keep the fire up, and so she shuts the dog inside and hurries round to the wood-heap. The rain has cleared off. She seizes a stick, pulls it out, and — crash! the whole pile collapses.

Yesterday she bargained with a stray blackfellow to bring her some wood, and while he was at work she went in search of a missing cow. She was absent an hour or so, and the native black made good use of his time. On her return she was so astonished to see a good heap of wood by the chimney, that she gave him an extra fig of tobacco, and praised him for not being lazy. He thanked her, and left with head erect and chest well out. He was the last of his tribe and a King; but he had built that wood-heap hollow.

She is hurt now, and tears spring to her eyes as she sits down again by the table. She takes up a handkerchief to wipe the tears away, but pokes her eyes with her bare fingers instead. The handkerchief is full of holes, and she finds that she has put her thumb through one, and her forefinger through another.

This makes her laugh, to the surprise of the dog. She has a keen, very keen, sense of the ridiculous; and some time or other she will amuse bushmen with the story.

She had been amused before like that. One day she sat down 'to have a good cry', as she said — and the old cat rubbed against her dress and 'cried too.' Then she had to laugh.

It must be near daylight now. The room is very close and hot because of the fire. Alligator still watches the wall from time to time. Suddenly he becomes greatly interested; he draws himself a few inches nearer the partition, and a thrill runs through his body. The hair on the back of his neck begins to bristle, and the battle-light is in his yellow eyes. She knows what this means, and lays her hand on the stick. The lower end of one of the partition slabs has a large crack on both sides. An evil pair of small, bright bead-like eyes glisten at one of these holes. The snake — a black one — comes slowly out, about a foot, and moves its head up and down. The dog lies still, and the woman sits as one fascinated. The snake comes out a foot farther. She lifts her stick, and the reptile, as though suddenly aware of danger, sticks his head in through the crack on the other side of the slab, and hurries to get his tail round after him. Alligator springs, and his jaws come together with a snap. He misses, for his nose is large, and the snake's body close down in the angle formed by the slabs and the floor. He snaps again as the tail comes round. He has the snake now, and tugs it out eighteen inches. Thud, thud comes the woman's club on the ground. Alligator pulls again. Thud, thud. Alligator gives another pull and he has the snake out — a black brute, five feet long. The head rises to dart about, but the dog has the enemy close to the neck. He is a big, heavy dog, but quick as a terrier. He shakes the snake as though he felt the original curse in common with mankind. The eldest boy wakes up, seizes his stick, and tries to get out of bed, but his mother forces him back with a grip of iron. Thud, thud — the snake's back is broken in several places. Thud, thud — its head is crushed, and Alligator's nose skinned again.

She lifts the mangled reptile on the point of her stick, carries it to the fire, and throws it in; then piles on the wood and watches the snake burn. The boy and dog watch too. She lays her hand on the dog's head, and all the fierce, angry light dies out of his yellow eyes. The younger children are quieted, and presently go to sleep. The dirty-legged boy stands for a moment in his shirt, watching the fire. Presently he looks up at her, sees the tears in her eyes, and, throwing his arms round her neck exclaims:

'Mother, I won't never go drovin'; blarst me if I do!'

And she hugs him to her worn-out breast and kisses him; and they sit thus together while the sickly daylight breaks over the bush.

BILLY SKYWONKIE

Barbara Baynton

The line was unfenced, so with due regard to the possibility
of the drought-dulled sheep attempting to chew it, the train
crept cautiously along, stopping occasionally, without warning,
to clear it from the listless starving brutes. In the carriage nearest
the cattle-vans, some drovers and scrub-cutters were playing
euchre, and spasmodically chorusing the shrill music from an
uncertain concertina. When the train stopped, the player thrust
his head from the carriage window. From one nearer the engine,
a commercial traveller remonstrated with the guard, concerning
the snail's pace and the many unnecessary halts.

'Take yer time, ole die-'ard,' yelled the drover to the guard.
'Whips er time — don't bust yerself for no one. Wot's orl the
worl' to a man w'en his wife's a widder.' He laughed noisily
and waved his hat at the seething bagman. 'Go an' 'ave a snooze.
I'll wake yer up ther day after termorrer.'

He craned his neck to see into the nearest cattle-van. Four
were down, he told his mates, who remarked, with blasphemous
emphasis, that they would probably lose half before getting them
to the scrub country.

The listening woman passenger, in a carriage between the
drover and the bagman, heard a thud soon after in the cattle-
truck, and added another to the list of the fallen. Before dawn
that day the train had stopped at a siding to truck them, and
she had watched with painful interest these drought-tamed brutes
being driven into the crowded vans. The tireless, greedy sun
had swiftly followed the grey dawn, and in the light that even
now seemed old and worn, the desolation of the barren shelterless
plains, that the night had hidden, appalled her. She realized the

sufferings of the emaciated cattle. It was barely noon, yet she had twice emptied the water bottle 'shogging' in the iron bracket.

The train dragged its weary length again, and she closed her eyes from the monotony of the dead plain. Suddenly the engine cleared its throat in shrill welcome to two iron tanks, hoisted twenty feet and blazing like evil eyes from a vanished face.

Beside them it squatted on its hunkers, placed a blackened thumb on its pipe, and hissed through its closed teeth like a snared wild-cat, while gulping yards of water. The green slimy odour penetrated to the cattle. The lustiest of these stamped feebly, clashing their horns and bellowing a hollow request.

A long-bearded bushman was standing on a few slabs that formed a siding, with a stockwhip coiled like a snake on his arm. The woman passenger asked him the name of the place.

'This is the Never-Never — ther lars' place Gord made,' answered one of the drovers who were crowding the windows.

'Better'n ther 'ell 'ole yous come from, any'ow,' defended the bushman. 'Breakin' ther 'earts, an' dyin' from suerside, cos they lef' it,' he added derisively, pointing to the cattle.

In patriotic anger he passed to the guard-van without answering her question, though she looked anxiously after him. At various intervals during the many halts of the train, she had heard some of the obscene jokes, and with it in motion, snatches of lewd songs from the drovers' carriage. But the language used by this bushman to the guard, as he helped to remove a ton of fencing-wire topping his new saddle, made her draw back her head. Near the siding was a spring cart, and she presently saw him throw his flattened saddle into it and drive off. There was no one else in sight, and in nervous fear she asked the bagman if this was Gooriabba siding. It was nine miles further, he told her.

The engine lifted its thumb from its pipe. 'Well — well — to — be — sure; well — well — to — be — sure,' it puffed, as if in shocked remembrance of its being hours late for its appointment there.

She saw no one on the next siding, but a buggy waited near the sliprails. It must be for her. According to Sydney arrangements she was to be met here, and driven out twelve miles. A drover inquired as the train left her standing by her portmanteau, 'Are yer travellin' on yer lonesome, or on'y goin' somew'ere!' and another flung a twist of paper towards her, brawling unmusically, that it was 'A flowwer from me angel mother's ger-rave.'

She went towards the buggy, but as she neared it the driver got in and made to drive off. She ran and called, for when he went she would be alone with the bush all round her, and only the sound of the hoarse croaking of the frogs from the swamp near, and the raucous 'I'll — 'ave — 'is — eye — out', of the crows.

Yes, he was from Gooriabba Station, and had come to meet a young 'piece' from Sydney, who had not come.

She was ghastly with bilious sickness — the result of an over-fed brain and an under-fed liver. Her face flushed muddily. 'Was it a housekeeper?'

He was the rouseabout, wearing his best clothes with awful unusualness. The coat was too long in the sleeve, and wrinkled across the back with his bush slouch. There was that wonderful margin of loose shirt between waistcoat and trousers, which all swagger bushies affect. Subordinate to nothing decorative was the flaring silk handkerchief, drawn into a sailor's knot round his neck.

He got out and fixed the winkers, then put his hands as far as he could reach into his pockets — from the position of his trousers he could not possibly reach bottom. It was apparently some unknown law that suspended them. He thrust forward his lower jaw, elevated his pipe, and squirted a little tobacco juice towards his foot that was tracing semicircles in the dust. 'Damned if I know,' he said with a snort, 'but there'll be a 'ell of a row somew'ere.'

She noticed that the discoloured teeth his bush grin showed so plainly, were worn in the centre, and met at both sides with the pipe between the front. Worn stepping-stones, her mind insisted.

She looked away towards the horizon where the smoke of the hidden train showed faintly against a clear sky, and as he was silent, she seemed to herself to be intently listening to the croak of the frogs and the threat of the crows. She knew that, from under the brim of the hat he wore over his eyes, he was looking at her sideways.

Suddenly he withdrew his hands and said again, 'Damned if I know. S'pose it's all right! Got any traps? Get up then an' 'ole the Neddy while I get it.' They drove a mile or so in silence; his pipe was still in his mouth though not alight.

She spoke once only. 'What a lot of frogs seem to be in that lake!'

He laughed. 'That's ther Nine Mile Dam!' He laughed again after a little — an intelligent, complacent laugh.

'It used ter be swarmin' with teal in a good season, but Gord A'mighty knows w'en it's ever goin' ter rain any more! I dunno!' This was an important admission, for he was a great weather prophet. 'Lake!' he sniggered and looked sideways at his companion. 'Thet's wot thet there bloke, the painter doodle, called it. An' 'e goes ter dror it, an' 'e sez wot 'e'll give me five bob if I'll run up ther horses, an' keep 'em so's 'e ken put 'em in ther picshure. An' 'e drors ther Dam an' ther trees, puts in thet there ole dead un, an' 'e puts in ther 'orses right clost against ther water w'ere the frogs is. 'E puts them in too, an' damed if 'e don't dror ther 'orses drinkin' ther water with ther frogs, an' ther frogs' spit on it! Likely yarn ther 'orses ud drink ther water with ther blanky frogs' spit on it! Fat lot they know about ther bush! Blarsted nannies!'

Presently he inquired as to the place where they kept pictures in Sydney, and she told him, the Art Gallery.

'Well some of these days I'm goin' down ter Sydney,' he continued, 'an' I'll collar thet one 'cos it's a good likerness of ther 'orses — you'd know their 'ide on a gum-tree — an' that mean mongrel never paid me ther five bob.'

Between his closed teeth he hissed a bush tune for some miles, but ceased to look at the sky, and remarked, 'No sign er rain! No lambin' this season; soon as they're dropt we'll 'ave ter knock 'em all on ther 'ead!' He shouted an oath of hatred at the crows following after the tottering sheep that made in a straggling line for the water. 'Look at 'em!' he said. 'Scoffin' out ther eyes!' He pointed to where the crows hovered over the bogged sheep. 'They putty well lives on eyes! "Blanky bush Chinkies!" I call 'em. No one carn't tell 'em apart!'

There was silence again, except for a remark that he could spit all the blanky rain they had had in the last nine months.

Away to the left along a side track his eyes travelled searchingly, as they came to a gate. He stood in the buggy and looked again. 'Promised ther "Konk" t' leave 'im 'ave furst squint at yer,' he muttered, 'if 'e was 'ere t' open ther gate! But I'm not goin' t' blanky well wait orl day!' He reluctantly got out and opened the gate, and he had just taken his seat when a 'Coo-ee' sounded from his right, heralded by a dusty pillar. He snorted resentfully. ''Ere 'e is; jes' as I got out an' done it!'

The Konk cantered to them, his horse's hoofs padded by the dust-cushioned earth. The driver drew back, so as not to impede the newcomer's view. After a moment or two, the Konk, preferring closer quarters, brought his horse round to the left.

Unsophisticated bush wonder in the man's face met the sophisticated in the girl's.

Never had she seen anything so grotesquely monkeyish. And the nose of this little hairy horror, as he slewed his neck to look into her face, blotted the landscape and dwarfed all perspective. She experienced a strange desire to extend her hand. When surprise lessened, her mettle saved her from the impulse to cover her face with both hands, to baffle him.

At last the silence was broken by the driver drawing a match along his leg, and lighting his pipe. The hairy creature safely arranged a pair of emu eggs, slung with bush skill round his neck.

'Ain't yer goin' to part?' enquired the driver, indicating his companion as the recipient.

'Wat are yer givin' us; wot do you take me fur?' said the Konk indignantly, drawing down his knotted veil.

'Well, give 'em ter me fer Lizer.'

'Will you 'ave 'em now, or wait till yer get 'em?'

'Goin' ter sit on 'em yerself?' sneered the driver.

'Yes, an' I'll give yer ther first egg ther cock lays,' laughed the Konk.

He turned his horse's head back to the gate. 'I say, Billy Skywonkie! Wot price Sally Ah Too, eh?' he asked, his gorilla mouth agape.

Billy Skywonkie uncrossed his legs, took out the whip. He tilted his pipe and shook his head as he prepared to drive, to show that he understood to a fraction the price of Sally Ah Too. The aptness of the question took the sting out of his having had to open the gate. He gave a farewell jerk.

'Goin' ter wash yer neck?' shouted the man with the nose, from the gate.

'Not if I know it.'

The Konk received the intimation incredulously. 'Stinkin' Roger!' he yelled. In bush parlance this was equal to emphatic disbelief.

This was a seemingly final parting, and both started, but suddenly the Konk wheeled round.

'Oh, Billy!' he shouted.

Billy stayed his horse and turned expectantly.

'W'en's it goin' ter rain?'

The driver's face darkened. 'Your blanky jealersey 'll get yer down, an' worry yer yet,' he snarled, and slashed his horse and drove rapidly away.

'Mickey ther Konk,' he presently remarked to his companion, as he stroked his nose.

This explained her earlier desire to extend her hand. If the Konk had been a horse she would have stroked his nose.

'Mob er sheep can camp in the shadder of it,' he said.

Boundless scope for shadows on that sun-smitten treeless plain!

'Make a good plough-shere,' he continued, 'easy plough a cultivation paddock with it!'

At the next gate he seemed in a mind and body conflict. There were two tracks; he drove along one for a few hundred yards. Then stopped, he turned, and finding the Konk out of sight, abruptly drove across to the other. He continually drew his whip along the horse's back, and haste seemed the object of the movement, though he did not flog the beast.

After a few miles on the new track, a blob glittered dazzlingly through the glare, like a fallen star. It was the iron roof of the wine shanty — the Saturday night and Sunday resort of shearers and rouseabouts for twenty miles around. Most of its spirit was made on the premises from bush recipes, of which bluestone and tobacco were the chief ingredients. Every drop had the reputation of 'bitin' orl ther way down'.

A sapling studded with broken horse-shoes seemed to connect two lonely crow stone trees. Under their scanty shade groups of dejected fowls stood with beaks agape. Though the buggy wheels almost reached them, they were motionless but for quivering gills. The ground both sides of the shanty was decorated with tightly-pegged kangaroo skins. A dog, apathetically blind and dumb, lay on the verandah, lifeless save for eyelids blinking in antagonism to the besieging flies.

'Jerry can't be far off,' said Billy Skywonkie, recognizing the dog. He stood up in the buggy. 'By cripes, there 'e is — goosed already, an' 'e on'y got 'is cheque lars' night.'

On the chimney side of the shanty a man lay in agitated sleep beside his rifle and swag. There had been a little shade on that side in the morning, and he had been sober enough to select it, and lay his head on his swag. He had emptied the bottle lying at his feet since then. His swag had been thoroughly 'gone through', and also his singlet and trouser-pockets. The fumes from the shanty grog baffled the flies. But the scorching sun was conquering; the man groaned, and his hands began to search for his burning head.

Billy Skywonkie explained to his companion that it was 'thet fool, Jerry ther kangaroo-shooter, bluein' 'is cheque fer skins'.

He took the water bag under the buggy, and poured the contents into the open mouth and over the face of the 'dosed' man, and raised him into a sitting position. Jerry fought this friendliness vigorously, and, staggering to his feet, picked up his rifle, and took drunken aim at his rescuer, then at the terrified woman in the buggy.

The rouseabout laughed unconcernedly. ''E thinks we're blanky kangaroos,' he said to her. 'Jerry, ole cock, yer couldn't 'it a woolshed! Yer been taking ther sun!'

He took the rifle and pushed the subdued Jerry into the chimney corner.

He tilted his hat, till, bush fashion, it ''ung on one 'air', and went inside the shanty. 'Mag!' he shouted, thumping the bar (a plank supported by two casks).

The woman in the buggy saw a slatternly girl with doughy hands come from the back, wiping the flour from her face with a kitchen towel. They made some reference to her she knew, as the girl came to the door and gave her close scrutiny. Then, shaking her head till her long brass earrings swung like pendulums, she laughed loudly.

'Eh?' enquired the rouseabout.

'My oath! Square dinkum!' she answered, going behind the bar.

He took the silk handkerchief from his neck, and playfully tried to flick the corner into her eye. Mag was used to such delicate attentions and well able to defend herself. With the dirty kitchen towel she succeeded in knocking off his hat, and round and round the house she ran with it dexterously dodging the skin-pegs. He could neither overtake nor outwit her with any dodge. He gave in, and ransomed his hat with the 'shouts' she demanded.

From the back of the shanty, a bent old woman, almost on all fours, crept towards the man, again prostrate in the corner. She paused, with her ear turned to where the girl and the rouseabout were still at horse-play. With cat-like movements she stole on till within reach of Jerry's empty pockets. She turned her terrible face to the woman in the buggy, as if in expectation of sympathy. Keeping wide of the front door, she came to the further side of the buggy. With the fascination of horror the woman looked at this creature, whose mouth and eyes seemed to dishonour her draggled grey hair. She was importuning for something, but the woman in the buggy could not understand till she pointed to her toothless mouth (the mission of which seemed to be, to fill its cavernous depths with the age-loosened skin above and below). A blue bag under each eye aggressively ticked like the gills of the fowls, and the sinews of the neck strained into *basso-rilievo*. Alternately she pointed to her mouth, or laid her knotted fingers on the blue bags in pretence of wiping tears. Entrenched behind the absorbed skin-terraces, a stump of purple tongue made efforts at speech. When she held out her claw, the woman understood and felt for her purse. Wolfishly the old hag snatched and put into her mouth the coin, and as the now merry driver, followed by Mag, came, she shook a warning claw at the giver, and flopped whining in the dust, her hands ostentatiously open and wiping dry eyes.

''Ello Biddy, on ther booze again!'

The bottle bulging from his coat pocket made speech with him intelligible, despite the impeding coin.

He placed the bottle in the boot of the buggy, and turning to Mag, said 'Give ther poor ole cow a dose!'

'Yes, one in a billy; anything else might make her sick!' said Mag. 'I caught 'er jus' now swiggin' away with ther tap in 'er mug!'

He asked his companion would she like a wet. She asked for water, and so great was her need that, making a barricade of closed lips and teeth to the multitude of apparently wingless mosquitoes thriving in its green tepidity, she moistened her mouth and throat.

'Oh, I say, Billy!' called Mag as he drove off. Her tones suggested her having forgotten an important matter, and he turned eagerly. 'W'en's it goin' ter rain?' she shrieked, convulsed with merriment.

'Go an' crawl inter a 'oller log!' he shouted angrily.

'No, but truly, Billy?'

Billy turned again. 'Give my love to yaller Lizer; thet slues yer!'

They had not gone far before he looked round again. 'Gord!' he cried excitedly. 'Look at Mag goin' through 'er ole woman!'

Mag had the old woman's head between her knees, dentist-fashion, and seemed to concentrate upon her victim's mouth, whose feeble impotence was soon demonstrated by the operator releasing her, and triumphantly raising her hand.

What the finger and thumb held the woman knew and the other guessed.

'By Gord. Eh! thet's prime; ain't it? No flies on Mag; not a fly!' he said, admiringly.

'See me an' 'er?' he asked, as he drove on.

His tone suggested no need to reply, and his listener did not. A giddy unreality took the sting from everything, even from her desire to beseech him to turn back to the siding, and leave her there to wait for the train to take her back to civilization. She felt she had lost her mental balance. Little matters become distorted, and the greater shrivelled.

He was now more communicative, and the oaths and adjectives so freely used were surely coined for such circumstances. 'Damned' the wretched, starving, and starved sheep looked and were; 'bloody' the beaks of the glutted crows; 'blarsted' the whole of the plain they drove through!

Gaping cracks suggested yawning graves, and the skeleton fingers of the drooping myalls seemingly pointed to them.

'See me an' Mag?' he asked again. 'No flies on Mag; not a wink 'bout 'er!' He chuckled in tribute. 'Ther wus thet damned flash fool, Jimmy Fernatty,' he continued ' — ther blanky fool; 'e never 'ad no show with Mag. An' yet 'e'd go down there! It was two mile furder this way, yet damned if ther blanky fool wouldn't come this way every time, 'less ther boss 'e was with 'im, 'stead er goin' ther short cut — ther way I come this mornin'. An' every time Mag ud make 'im part 'arf a quid! I was on'y there jus' 'bout five minits meself, an' I stuck up nea'ly 'arf a quid! An' there's four gates' (he flogged the horse and painted them crimson when he remembered them) 'this way, more'n on ther way I come this mornin'.'

Presently he gave her the reins with instructions to drive through one. It seemed to take a long time to close it, and he had to fix the back of the buggy before he opened it, and after it was closed.

After getting out several times in quick succession to fix the back of the buggy when there was no gate, he seemed to forget the extra distance. He kept his hand on hers when she gave him the reins, and bade her 'keep up 'er pecker'. 'Someone would soon buck up ter 'er if their boss wusn't on.' But the boss it seemed was a 'terrer for young uns. Jimmy Fernatty 'as took up with a yaller piece 'an is livin' with 'er. But not me; thet's not me! I'm like ther boss, thet's me! No yeller satin for me!'

He watched for the effect of this degree of taste on her.

Though she had withdrawn her hand, he kept winking at her, and she had to move her feet to the edge of the buggy to prevent his pressing against them. He told her with sudden anger that any red black-gin was as good as a half chow any day, and it was no use gammoning for he knew what she was.

'If Billy Skywonkie 'ad ter string onter yaller Lizer, more 'air on 'is chest for doin' so' (striking his own). 'I ken get as many w'ite gins as I wanter, an' I'd as soon tackle a gin as a chow anyways!'

On his next visit to the back of the buggy she heard the crash of glass breaking against a tree. After a few snatches of song he lighted his pipe, and grew sorrowfully reminiscent.

'Yes s'elp me, nea'ly 'arf a quid! An' thet coloured ole 'og of a cow of a mother, soon's she's off ther booze, 'll see thet she gets it!' The he missed his silk handkerchief. 'Ghost!' he said, breathing heavily, 'Mag's snavelled it! Lizer 'll spot thet's gone soon's we get 'ithin coo-ee of 'er!'

Against hope he turned and looked along the road; felt every pocket, lifted his feet, and looked under the mat. His companion, in reply, said she had not seen it since his visit to the shanty.

'My Gord!' he said, 'Mag's a fair terror!' He was greatly troubled till the braggart in him gave an assertive flicker. 'Know wat I'll do ter Lizer soon's she begins ter start naggin' at me?' He intended this question as an insoluble conundrum, and waited for no surmises. 'Fill 'er mug with this!' The shut fist he shook was more than a mugful. ''Twouldn' be ther first time I done it, nor ther lars'.' But the anticipation seemed little comfort to him.

The rest of the journey was done in silence, and without even a peep at the sky. When they came to the homestead gate he said his throat felt as though a 'goanner' had crawled into it and died. He asked her for a pin and clumsily dropped it in his efforts to draw the collar up to his ears, but had better luck with a hair-pin.

He appeared suddenly subdued and sober, and as he took his seat after closing the gate, he offered her his hand, and said, hurriedly, 'No 'arm done, an' no 'arm meant; an' don't let on ter my missus — thet's 'er on the verander — thet we come be ther shanty.'

It was dusk, but through it she saw that the woman was dusky too.

'Boss in, Lizer?' There was contrition and propitiation in his voice.

'You've bin a nice blanky time,' said his missuss, 'an' lucky for you, Billy Skywonkie, e' ain't.'

With bowed head, his shoulders making kindly efforts to hide his ears, he sat silent and listening respectfully. The woman in the buggy thought that the volubility of the angry half-caste's tongue was the nearest thing to perpetual motion. Under her orders both got down, and from a seat under the open window in the little room to which Lizer had motioned, she gave respectful attention to the still rapidly flowing tirade. The offence had been some terrible injustice to a respectable married woman, 'slavin' an' graftin' an' sweatin' from mornin' ter night, for a slungin' idlin' lazy blaggard'. In an indefinable way the woman felt that both of them were guilty, and to hide from her part of the reproof was mean and cowardly. The half-caste from time to time included her, and by degrees she understood that the wasted time of which Lizer complained was supposed to have been dissipated in flirtation. Neither the shanty nor Mag had mention.

From a kitchen facing the yard a Chinaman came at intervals, and with that assumption of having mastered the situation in all its bearings through his thorough knowledge of the English tongue, he shook his head in calm, shocked surprise. His sympathies were unmistakably with Lizer, and he many times demonstrated his grip of the grievance by saying, 'By Cli' Billy, it's a bloo'y shame!'

Maybe it was a sense of what was in his mind that made the quivering woman hide her face when virtuous Ching Too came to look at her. She was trying to eat when a dog ran into the dining-room, and despite the violent beating of her heart, she heard the rouseabout tell the boss as he unsaddled his horse, 'The on'y woman I see was a 'alf chow, an' she ses she's the one, an' she's in ther dinin'-room 'avin' a tuck-in.'

She was too giddy to stand when the boss entered, but she turned her mournful eyes on him, and, supporting herself by the table, stood and faced him.

He kept on his hat, and she, watching, saw curiosity and surprise change into anger as he looked at her.

'What an infernal cheek *you* had to come! Who sent you?' he asked stormily.

She told him, and added that she had no intention of remaining.

'How old?' She made no reply. His last thrust, as in disgust he strode out, had the effect of a galvanic battery on her dying body.

Her bedroom was reeking with a green heavy scent. Empty powder-boxes and rouge-pots littered the dressing-table, and various other aids to nature evidenced her predecessor's frailty. From a coign in its fastness a black spider eyed her malignantly, and as long as the light lasted she watched it.

The ringing of a bell slung outside in the fork of a tree awoke her before dawn. It was mustering — bush stocktaking — and all the stationhands were astir. There was a noise of galloping horses being driven into the stockyard, and the clamour of the men as they caught and saddled them. Above the clatter of plates in the kitchen she could hear the affected drawl of the Chinaman talking to Lizer. She trod heavily along the passage, preparing the boss's breakfast. This early meal was soon over, and with the dogs snapping playfully at the horses' heels, all rode off.

Spasmodic bars of 'A Bicycle Built for Two' came from the kitchen, 'Mayly, Mayly, give me answer do!' There was neither haste nor anxiety in the singer's tones. Before the kitchen fire, oblivious to the heat, stood the Chinaman cook, inert from his morning's opium. It was only nine, but this was well on in the day for Ching, whose morning began at four.

He ceased his song as she entered. 'You come Sydiney? Ah! You mally? Ah! Sydiney welly ni' place. This placee welly dly — too muchee no lain — welly dly.'

She was watching his dog. On a block lay a flitch of bacon, and across the freshly cut side the dog drew its tongue, then snapped at the flies. 'That dog will eat the bacon,' she said.

'No!' answered the cook. ''E no eat 'em — too saw.'

It *was* salt; she had tried it for breakfast.

He began energetically something about, 'by an' by me getty mally. By Cli' no 'alf cas — too muchee longa jlaw.' He laughed and shook his head, reminiscent of 'las' a night', and waited for applause. But, fascinated, she still watched the dog, who from time to time continued to take 'saw' with his flies.

'Go ou' si', Sir,' said the cook in a spirit of rivalry. The dog stood and snapped. 'Go ou' si', I say!' No notice from the dog. 'Go ou' si', I tella you!' stamping his slippered feet and taking a fire-stick. The dog leisurely sat down and looked at his master with mild reproof. 'Go insi' then, any bloo'y si' you li'!' but pointing to their joint bedroom with the lighted stick. The dog went to the greasy door, saw that the hens sitting on the bed were quietly laying eggs to go with the bacon, and came back.

She asked him where was the rouseabout who had driven her in yesterday.

'Oh, Billy Skywonkie, 'e mally alri'! Lizer 'im missie!' He went on to hint that affection there was misplaced, but that he himself was unattached.

She saw the rouseabout rattle into the yard in a spring cart. He let down the backboard and dumped three sheep under a light gallows. Their two front feet were strapped to one behind.

He seemed breathless with haste. 'Oh, I say!' he called out to her 'Ther boss 'e tole me this mornin' thet I wus ter tell you, you wus ter sling yer 'ook. To do a get,' he explained. 'So bundle yer duds tergether quick an' lively!! Lizer's down at ther tank, washin'. Le'ss get away afore she sees us, or she'll make yer swaller yer chewers.' Lowering his voice, he continued: 'I wanter go ter ther shanty — on'y ter get me 'ankerchief.'

He bent and strained back a sheep's neck, drew the knife and steel from his belt, and skilfully dressed an edge on the knife.

She noticed that the sheep lay passive, with its head back till its neck curved into a bow, and that the glitter of the knife was reflected in its eye.

THE DEAD MAN IN THE SCRUB

Mary Fortune

Some years ago, at the close of what had been a hot summer, two men, who had worked unsuccessfully for some months on a diggings in the Loddon District, determined to go and 'prospect' in a scrub some four or five miles off. It was a lonely and out of the way place; far from any road or settlement whatever; and, as far as the mates knew, had never been penetrated by a human foot. In his opinion, however, a few miles tramp convinced them they had been mistaken; for, after succeeding in making their way through the tangled vegetation for about two miles, they came upon a small spot of partially cleared ground, where there were evident traces of man's labour. Two or three shallow holes had been sunk, and at a small waterhole, not far off, the stuff had been evidently cradled. Looking around for some appearance of a home or pathway near this spot — for of course the man or men who had been working here must have had some place to live in; it was not likely workers would tramp that weary scrub twice in the day — they fancied that in one particular place the vegetation seemed to be less dense. But seeing no way toward that place, they made one slowly with the tomahawk; and after cutting and untangling hundreds of feet of the mallee vine, they came upon a little white tent, almost hidden in the very heart of the bushes. Here an awful scene awaited them; and if you have not heard something of the same sort yourself, I need not attempt to give you any idea of the sound made by millions of those horrible flies that collect around and revel in the decomposition of any animal life in Australia. Inside the tent, which was quite closed up, a continuous buzz, suggestive of innumerable myriads of flies, met the ears of the horrified mates, who were now quite certain that death, in some shape, inhabited this little white calico home in the mallee; indeed another of the senses already assured them that their fortitude would most likely be severely tried by the sight in store for them. What to do was the question; the tent, as I have already said, was fastened, the door being apparently secured closely inside while the slight movement one of the men made in ascertaining this fact, seemed to disturb the feasters upon the dead; they rose in such terrible clouds that through the thin calico one could see them, as they came buzzing in millions against its sides.

'What are we to do?' asked one.

'Go back to Leggat's and tell the police,' replied his mate.

'Tell the police *what*, man?' inquired the first speaker, 'for all we know it may be a dog's carcase that's inside.'

His mate shook his head, 'a dog wouldn't stay in a closed tent to die, Bill, but at any rate I wouldn't like to open the place without a policeman.'

'You know the dog might have been chained up; a digger might leave his dog to watch inside, and maybe something prevented his coming back,' observed Bill.

'Maybe,' replied the mate dubiously, 'but at any rate we can't stop here much longer, I can't stand it.'

Bill walked around the tent, and at the back observed a small hole near the wall-plate, which he slightly enlarged with his fingers, and so enabled himself to peep into the interior. He gave but one glance, and then drawing back with horror ejaculated, 'Oh God, that's awful!'

'What is it?' eagerly enquired the other.

'Oh, it's a man lying there dead — rotten! Look for yourself, and come away for God's sake! I feel like fainting!'

Well these men tramped back these miles, and told me at the camp, and we returned, in a spring cart, to the lonely place. To avoid meddling with the door, I tore up a width of the calico, and entered to witness the most piteous and horrible sight I had seen for a long time. A man, or the remains of what had been a man, lay extended upon the floor, but in such an advanced state of decomposition as to be almost unrecognisable. He was fully dressed, and in good sound digger's clothes: his boots were nearly new, his trousers quite respectable. He had on a blue Guernsey shirt, over a good flannel one, but of course, in consequence of the fearful state of the body, even these articles were not to be identified. The poor fellow lay as if he had fallen out of his bunk, which was close by, one arm under his forehead, but the head, detached by decomposition, had fallen partially away, and not a feature was recognisable; the abundant black hair alone being remarkable. Upon his bunk were good blankets, and in the tent was a billy, and one or two other little cooking utensils; but there was not the slightest appearance of anything to eat, or anything whatever which might have held provisions; not a scrap of paper, not a crumb of bread. Having observed this, I turned my attention to the fastening of the opening, which, in every original tent, forms the entrance, and I was astonished to find that it had really been nailed up from the inside; a stone and a few broken tacks still lay upon the ground near it, and I could readily perceive that the former had been used as a hammer. The first idea that suggested itself to my professional mind was, that of suicide; and suicide most likely induced by want, remembering the absence of anything like food in the place; or, that the poor fellow had really died of starvation, and had fastened the door with the hope of preventing his body from being devoured by dingoes, before it was discovered.

I had not time to speculate about it just at that moment, however, as my duty obliged me to remove the remains and give information to the coroner of the district as early as possible; and so, with great difficulty, we succeeded in enveloping the remains of the poor miner, in one of his own blankets, and, after carrying them some distance, depositing them in the cart. A jury was empanelled, an inquest was held, which resulted in an open verdict of 'Found dead', for the condition of the body rendered it impossible for a *post mortem* to be of the slightest service, and the poor fellow was buried. No one knew anything about him — no person had been aware of a digger being in the scrub, and the general impression was my first one, that he had perished of want.

I say my first one, for I soon altered my opinion, although it was not likely to be of the slightest service to the interests of justice that I did so. Almost as a matter of form, I suppose, I went to remove the tent, which had become the property of Government; it was of so little value as to be scarcely worth the trouble; but I was glad of an opportunity to examine the place at my leisure. Well, there was nothing, absolutely nothing, in the tent, but what I have already mentioned, and a matchbox under the blankets on the bunk, which contained half-a-dozen matches, and at the bottom, pushed into the smallest space, a small piece, about a square inch, of some woollen material, apparently new. I did not believe at all that this unfortunate man had died a natural death, I was firmly convinced in my own mind that there had been foul play; and yet, had I been asked to give a reason for that conviction, I must have been silent, I had none to give. Yet, with all that, I looked for traces of murder, just as if I was absolutely certain it had been committed. The door was nailed *inside*: well, supposing the poor fellow himself had *not* nailed it, where did the person who *had*, find egress? Might he not have ripped a seam of the calico, and sewed it again outside? I set to work and examined the seams carefully. The tent had apparently been made by a woman, no man or tentmaker was likely to have taken the trouble to stitch so neatly; and besides the seams were *all* on the inside, except in one corner, where, for about two feet in length, a much rougher seam had been made upon the *outside*.

'Here, then,' I convinced myself, 'the murderer has got out; fastening the door inside, to leave it to be supposed that the man himself must have accomplished it.'

I pulled down the tent, and removed every little article in it, and, as they were few, I had soon done, and took a last look around before I left. As I have before stated, the scrub was growing almost closely around the tent; and, from the length of time that had elapsed since the owner lay dead inside, the little space was untrodden; and the creeping mallee vine had enwrapped itself over and over, and under and around every near stick. Examining closely the circumscribed space of the tenting spot, I perceived a portion of a dirty rag of some sort, peeping out from the vegetation, and drawing it forth, I was possessor of a pair of old trousers, which, from the size of the dead man, might have belonged to him; they were of a large size, and he had been a tall man. There was nothing particular about them; a pair of old cast-offs evidently, nothing in the pockets, and no difference in them whatever from any other pair of old trousers in the world, only that from the portion least worn, at the back of the leg, a square piece had been taken for some purpose or other. It was no accidental tear, for the piece had been cut out, and the cut extended across the side seam, where it was quite certain it would not have *torn*. So, interested in these old rags, I carefully folded them up with the rest of the dead man's property, and proceeded campwards. Months passed on; indeed, I may say years; it must have been nearly three years before I fell over the clue to the death-tenanted home in the untrodden mallee. I had meanwhile been removed, and was, at the time I resume my story, stationed at Walhalla, a prosperous reefing township, and a great improvement upon the old alluvial 'rush': the tent was the great exception, the slab and bark erection most common, while there were many of weatherboard, and zinc roofing. In short, Walhalla was such a mining township as we may see anywhere to-day. In passing backwards and forwards I had often noticed a snug hut that lay upon my way, or rather I had remarked the clean, bright, good-looking woman who lived there, and as it is our business to know as much as possible about everything and everybody, I was aware that she was the wife of a man named Jerry Round, who worked as wages-man in one of the Companies. There were no children about this hut; but the woman, who might have been some twenty-five years old, was always busy; I think she took in washing.

One day, then, about this time, I was passing this hut early in the forenoon of a Saturday. Mrs Round was apparently having a grand clean out, and the dust was flying in all directions. I was going straight on as usual, when out of the door came flying a pair of dirty old trousers, which, after passing within an inch of my nose, fell directly upon the pathway before me; and there, as they lay sprawling out, covered with the dirt of a week's underground work, I saw upon the knee of one of the legs the identical patch missing from the old pair which I had still safely stowed at home in the camp! I could have almost sworn to it the first moment my eyes lighted upon it; the pattern and colour were peculiar, and I had been too much interested not to have closely marked both; but when I came to perceive that in the patch was the very side-seam of *my* trousers, I had no doubt in the world about it. I stooped down, in a puzzled, bewildered sort of way, wondering to myself how that patch came upon these trousers, and what connection it had with the dead man in the mallee, and how it would all end; when, just as I was carefully, and with as little detriment to myself as I could, picking up the pants at arm's length, Mrs Round herself rushed out in a state of great excitement.

'Good gracious me, sir, I hope you don't think I threw the old things at you a'purpose! I didn't know anyone was passing, and they were in my way when I was sweeping, and so I "chucked" them out! I hope you will excuse it, sir!'

'Oh, you need not bother your head about that, Mrs Round,' I replied, still holding the articles in my hand, 'I guessed how it was when I saw the dust flying out of the door; but I was just taking a fancy to this patch here; if you've done with the old trousers, I am sadly in need of a bit of woollen rag to clean up my traps, and this would be the very thing.'

'Lord, to be sure, sir; Jerry wore them down in the shaft until they would hardly hang together, but anything most is good enough for working on them drives. But wouldn't a bit of old flannel be better, sir? I could give you lots of flannel.'

'No, Mrs Round,' I replied, handing her the trousers, 'these bright buckles of ours want such a lot of rubbing you see, flannel lasts no time, while a piece of that good woollen trousering would be worth twice as much to me; so if you'll just be good enough to rip it off for me, I'll owe you a heap of thanks!'

'And welcome, sir,' she replied, going towards the hut to procure a pair of scissors, and I followed her to the door, holding, when she returned, the trousers while she ripped the piece off.

'It's been a good piece of stuff, Mrs Round,' I remarked, as she clipped and cut, 'you could not buy such a good bit of trousering on the diggings now.'

'No, sir,' replied the woman, a shade coming over her face, 'it's a bit of a pair that came from England long ago; my first husband bought them before we left home, and many a happy gathering of friends they were at!'

'Your first husband? is it possible you've been married twice? you're very young for that.'

'Jerry and I have only been married a matter of two years,' she said, adding, with an effort to change the conversation, 'anyone can tell it was a man that sewed this; I expect Jerry put it on while he and poor Jim were working together; it's as hard to take off as if it was nailed on.'

'And where were you then, while Round and Jim were working together?' I asked, guessing at once that 'poor Jim' meant the dead first husband.

'I was in New Zealand, sir; they came back to a rush at Carngham, and I never saw him again, he died at Sailor's Gully.'

'And you married his mate?'

'Yes, sir.'

There was the shadow of old memories in the poor woman's face, as she simply gave me this information, and I had not the heart to grieve her by questions that might perhaps excite her curiosity, as well as put Round on his guard; and so, for the present, I said no more. The patch I carried home safely, and found, as I had expected, that it was indeed the very piece which had been cut out of the dead man's trousers, and I was, of course, quite certain that the dead man of the mallee was none other than the 'poor Jim' of Mrs Round.

What story did Round tell about his death, I could not but wonder; and I thought long about the best means of finding this out; and the conclusion I came to was to ask Mrs Round herself, and make some reasonable excuse for so doing. So the very first time I went that way, I made it my business to time my walk down the road, so that I met her coming from a hole with a bucket of water, and as she set it down to rest herself, I stopped before her for a moment.

'Do you know, Mrs Round,' I said, affecting an air of great interest, 'I have been puzzling my head ever since I saw you last about your first husband; I believe I knew him; and your mentioning his name as "Jim", made me almost sure of it. I believe I have seen these very same trousers on him a dozen times! You said he worked at Carngham, but he didn't die there, did he?'

'No, sir, the poor fellow died at some little out of the way gully back of Bendigo, him and Jerry were prospecting, and when Jim was taken bad, Jerry had to bring a doctor six miles through the scrub to him. But it was no use, and after he died Jerry brought the news over to me, and bad news it was, I tell you.'

'Well, well! it is strange how things come about!' I ejaculated, 'when I saw poor Jim last, I had no idea that I should make your acquaintance through a patch of a pair of his old pantaloons!'

'It was a sore grief to me, sir,' said Mrs Round, with a sigh, as she again lifted her pail, 'to hear that he was dead, and without my hand to smooth his blankets, or give him a drink! we were very fond of each other, and — and — to tell the truth,' she added, lifting her eyes to mine for one moment, 'I don't know how ever I came to marry Jerry at all, for poor Jim never liked him, though he was his mate!'

''Twas instinct,' I repeated to myself, as I proceeded on my way, 'little cause the poor fellow had to like him! I dare say if Mrs Round liked she could give me a good reason for this wretch murdering the poor unsuspicious husband, so that he might go and inherit his place in the affections of the betrayed wife.'

And so I was going on, thinking moodily over the affair, when my attention was attracted by a great commotion among the deep workings: people were running and shouting to one another, and all were tending toward one place, so, hastening my steps,

I went in that direction too, and soon found that a frightful mining calamity had taken place, one of the drives had fallen in! From the men who had escaped I learned that the drive had fallen in only at the further end, and that, warned by the cracking of the timber, all had escaped in time, save one — it was Jerry Round.

I went down into the drive, where every exertion was being made to extricate the unfortunate man from the most terrible position that can be conceived: he was not buried, that would have been a merciful fate in comparison with what he endured, and my heart sickened as I looked at him. The drive had partially collapsed, and two steps more towards the shaft would have saved him; but those two steps he did not get time to make; one of the cap-pieces of the timbering had fallen right across his body, the fallen earth partially supporting it, and partially also covering his body. His head, however, was quite exposed, his eyes protruding in his great agony; and for a few minutes he was even able to speak, urging the workers for God's sake to hasten. But there was no need for that, every man worked as if his own existence depended upon speed; and, indeed, they could not be certain that at any moment farther breaks would not take place in the shaken timbering, and place themselves in the same position from which they were endeavouring to rescue their wretched mate. A very few moments and he was extricated. But the torture he was enduring had become unbearable before that; he was insensible when they carried him upon a stretcher to his own hut, which was not far away, and where his wife met him, quite unprepared for the sight so horrible; yet, she met it with far greater composure than one might have anticipated. The medical men who were immediately summoned, declared the case of Round to be hopeless; his internal injuries precluded any expectation of a change, save the last great one; and so Mrs Round, the doctor, and I, watched the bruised and broken remnant of humanity stretched out upon his own comfortable bed, comfortable, alas, to him no longer; but we only watched to see the last faint breathing cease, to return no more. He was a dark, stoutly built man, his hair and whiskers were black as night; one of his arms, broken in two places, lay in a twisted, unnatural position beside him, and his nerveless head, rolled over helplessly to one side, was covered with blood from a wound upon his temple; from which the crimson drops still oozing, fell down over his white face, making the whole picture more horrible. Poor Mrs Round wept silently, wiping, meanwhile, the blood gently from his face, and the death damp from his forehead.

The time was not far off now. By his side sat the doctor, holding his fingers upon the wrist of the dying man; and at that moment he gave me a slight nod, unnoticed by the wife; he felt in the fluttering pulse indications of the last struggle. I was about to try and send Mrs Round upon some excuse or an errand, for the purpose of saving her the last scene, when Round opened his eyes, and with a gaze full of consciousness, rested them upon the face of his wife.

'Oh Ellen, I am dying!' he gasped, faintly, and with horror, 'I am dying, and I murdered poor Jim!' And with this last confession the last breath went away too. He was dead!

Mrs Round turned round from her dead husband, and stared at me; some instinctive certainty, I have no doubt, she felt, that I had something to do with the truth of these last words, some recollection, no doubt, of our late conversation, and a multitude of old ones, with which I had nothing whatever to do, would be sure to lend their aid in overcoming the poor woman, for the light of life faded out of her white face. She had fainted.

There was nothing that touches so mutually the feelings of a whole mining community as a sudden death from one of those fearful and frequent underground accidents, to which their calling is so liable, and which, indeed, the carelessness of the miner himself makes so much more frequent; and therefore Jerry Round was followed to the grave by every man in the place who could manage to leave his employment. Little guessed the mourners how guilty was the poor broken mortal, whose shattered remains they followed; and as I watched the sad procession winding away among the rocks and trees, true to the instincts of my profession, I quietly speculated how many of these very mourners would be likely to come within my jurisdiction, if the secrets of all hearts were known.

As I was making these heartless speculations, as you may think them, I was smoking a cigar, and leaning upon the fence which surrounded our Police camp; and the black coffin had scarcely disappeared away on the bush track, when Mrs Round herself stood before me. Poor little woman, she looked very ill; and was, at the moment I speak of, as calm-looking and nearly as white as if she had already lain down in the narrow peaceful resting-place to which they were bearing her husband. She impressed me with the idea of *rigidity*. It seemed as if she had hard work to keep herself calm, and, in the effort, over-produced the appearance.

'Mr Mark, I am going away to Melbourne, to-morrow,' she said, laying her hand emphatically upon my arm. 'I am going, with the few pounds we had saved, home to my friends in England. Before I go it is your duty, before God, to tell me all you know of my husband, Jim!'

'Perhaps it is,' I replied, gently, 'but of what use can it be to harrow your feelings by retailing the crimes of the past? death has covered them all up now!'

'But death hasn't covered *me* up!' she replied, 'and death hasn't as yet covered up all the thoughts that have no guide unless you tell me the truth.'

I felt that she was right, and I led her into the barrack-room, where my traps were, and where I unfolded the pair of old pants which I had got near the dead man in the mallee, and with the piece she had so lately given me herself, I handed them to her. She recognised them at once, said she would have known them among a hundred, from some mending of her own upon them: and then she listened, weepingly, while I told her all about the little tent in the scrub, and its death-tenant.

'And was there no more?' she asked, 'was there nothing else you could have brought? oh, poor Jim! poor murdered Jim!'

'There was this,' I said, giving her the match-box, with the little bit of stuff in it, 'and this,' I added, handing her a lock of the poor fellow's dark hair, which I had cut off, and folded in a bit of paper.

Poor Mrs Round opened it, and looked at the hair; and then, after all the horrors she had heard, she pressed it to her lips. Alas! it was more than I could have done, had it belonged to the dearest and nearest I had in the world! for it had far more than usual of the smell of death which the hair of the dead always has. How could it be otherwise, considering the state of the head from which I had taken it? The piece of stuff in the match-box, too, how well she knew it!

'I sent it to him in a letter from New Zealand,' she said, 'to show him the sort of dress I had bought with the first money he sent me from Victoria!'

And so ends the story of poor Jim; his wife left the next day, as she had said, taking with her all she had left of the young husband she had followed from her home in old England; and that all was an old matchbox, a pair of worn and dilapidated trousers, and a lock of black death-tainted hair!

Biographical Notes

ETHEL ANDERSON (1883–1958) was born in England and educated in Australia. She lived in India, Australia and England. She published three collections of short stories: *Indian Tales*; *At Parramatta*; and *The Little Ghosts*, as well as volumes of poetry and essays.

JESSICA ANDERSON was born in Queensland in 1916 and now lives in Sydney. She has published seven books of fiction: *An Ordinary Lunacy*; *The Last Man's Head*; *The Commandant*; *Tirra Lirra by the River*; *The Impersonators*; *Taking Shelter* and *Stories From the Warm Zone and Sydney Stories*.

THEA ASTLEY was born in Brisbane in 1925. She now lives in New South Wales and has published ten novels: *Girl with a Monkey*; *A Descant for Gossips*; *The Well Dressed Explorer*; *The Slow Natives*; *A Boat Load of Home Folk*; *The Acolyte*; *A Kindness Cup*; *An Item From the Late News*; *Beachmasters* and *Reaching Tin River*. She has published two collections of short stories: *Hunting the Wild Pineapple* and *It's Raining in Mango*.

MURRAY BAIL was born in Adelaide in 1941, has lived in London and Bombay, and now lives in Sydney. He has published three books of fiction: *The Drover's Wife*; *Homesickness* and *Holden's Performance*.

MARJORIE BARNARD (1897–1987) was born in Sydney. She wrote five novels in collaboration with Flora Eldershaw under the name of 'M. Barnard Eldershaw'. Under her own name she published works of Australian history, and a collection of short stories, *The Persimmon Tree and Other Stories*.

BARBARA BAYNTON (1857–1929) was born in Scone in New South Wales. Her first story was published in the *Bulletin* in 1896. Her fiction was collected in *Bush Studies*, and she published one novel, *Human Toll*.

DAVID BROOKS was born in Canberra in 1953 and has lived in Greece, Yugoslavia, Canada and the United States. He has published two collections of short fiction: *The Book of Sei* and *Sheep and the Diva*, as well as poetry and essays.

PETER CAREY was born in 1943 in Bacchus Marsh, Victoria. He has published five books of fiction: *The Fat Man in History; War Crimes; Bliss; Illywhacker* and *Oscar and Lucinda*.

BEVERLEY FARMER was born in Melbourne in 1941 and has lived in Greece. She now lives in the Victorian coastal town of Queenscliffe. She has published four books of fiction: *Alone; Milk; Home Time* and *A Body of Water*.

MARY FORTUNE (*c*1833–after 1909) was born in Belfast and spent her early life in Canada, coming to the Australian goldfields in 1855. She wrote essays and articles and crime fiction under the name of Waif Wander or W.W. Some of her work is collected in her only book, *The Detective's Album*. In 1989 her memoirs and journalism were edited by Lucy Sussex in *The Fortunes of Mary Fortune*.

HELEN GARNER was born in Geelong in 1942 and lives in Melbourne and Sydney. She has published four books of fiction: *Monkey Grip; Honour; The Children's Bach* and *Postcards From Surfers*.

PETER GOLDSWORTHY was born in 1951 in Minlaton, South Australia, grew up in the country, and now lives in Adelaide. He has published three collections of short fiction: *Archipelagoes; Zooing* and *Bleak Rooms*, as well as a novel, *Maestro*. He has also published three volumes of poetry.

ELIZABETH JOLLEY was born in England in 1923. She has lived in Strasburg, Paris and Hamburg, and now lives in Western Australia. She has published eight books of fiction: *Five Acre Virgin; The Travelling Entertainer; Palomino; Mr Scobie's Riddle; Milk and Honey; Woman in a Lampshade; The Well* and *Cabin Fever*. She was awarded the Order of Australia for services to Australian Literature.

HENRY LAWSON (1867–1922) was born on the New South Wales goldfields at Grenfell. He is one of Australia's best-known writers of fiction, having published 136 short stories in periodicals and collections. His finest work is generally considered to be in *While the Billy Boils* and *Joe Wilson and His Mates*. He also wrote a great deal of poetry.

JOAN LONDON was born in Perth, Western Australia, where she still lives, in 1948. She has published one collection of short fiction, *Sister Ships*.

DAVID MALOUF was born in Brisbane in 1934, and now lives in Tuscany and Australia. He has published eight books of fiction: *Johnno; An Imaginary Life; Child's Play, with Eustace and the Prowler; Fly Away Peter; Harland's Half Acre; Antipodes; 12 Edmondstone Street* and *The Great World*. He has also published several books of poetry, and has written plays and librettos.

OLGA MASTERS (1919–1986) was born in Pambula, New South Wales. She published four books of fiction: *The Home Girls; Loving Daughters; A Long Time Dying* and *Amy's Children*. A posthumous collection *Rose Fancier and Other Stories* was published in 1988.

BRIAN MATTHEWS was born in Melbourne in 1936, and has lived in Adelaide since 1976. He has published one collection of short fiction, *Quickening and Other Stories*, as well as essays and articles. He is the author of *Louisa*, a biography of Louisa Lawson, and of a book on Henry Lawson, *The Receding Wave*.

FRANK MOORHOUSE was born in Nowra, New South Wales, in 1938 and now lives in Sydney. He has published nine books of fiction: *Futility and Other Animals; The Americans, Baby; The Electrical Experience; Conference-Ville; Tales of Mystery and Romance; The Everlasting Secret Family and Other Secrets; Room*

Service; Forty-Seventeen and *Lateshows*. He has worked as a journalist and has written a number of film and television scripts.

JOHN MORRISON was born in England in 1904. He came to Australia in 1923 and has lived in Melbourne since then. He has published two novels: *The Creeping City* and *Port of Call*, and a collection of essays, *The Happy Warrior*. He has published eight books of short fiction: *Sailors Belong Ships; Black Cargo; Twenty-Three; Selected Stories; Australian By Choice; North Wind; Stories of the Waterfront* and *This Freedom*.

GEORGE PAPAELLINAS was born in Sydney in 1954 and now lives in Melbourne. He has published one book of fiction, *Ikons*.

'HENRY HANDEL RICHARDSON' (Ethel Richardson) (1870–1946) was born in Melbourne, lived most of her life outside Australia and died in London. She is best known for her novels: *Maurice Guest; The Getting of Wisdom*; and *The Fortunes of Richard Mahony*.

CHRISTINA STEAD (1902–1983) was born in Sydney. She lived in England, France, Switzerland, the Netherlands and the United States, returning to live in Australia in 1974. She published ten books of fiction: *Seven Poor Men of Sydney; The Salzburg Tales; The Man Who Loved Children; For Love Alone; Letty Fox; A Little Tea a Little Chat; The People With the Dogs; Cotters' England; The Puzzleheaded Girl* and *Ocean of Story*.

KYLIE TENNANT (1912–1988) was born in Sydney. She published plays, children's books and biography, as well as a collection of short stories, *Ma Jones and the Little White Cannibals*; and ten novels: *Tiburon; Foveaux; The Battlers; Ride on Stranger; Time Enough Later; Lost Haven; The Joyful Condemned; Tell Morning This; The Honey Flow* and *Tantavallon*. She was awarded the Order of Australia.

JUDAH WATEN (1911–1985) was born in Odessa in Russia and came to Australia with his family in 1914. He spent the rest of his life in Melbourne. He published seven novels: *The Unbending; Shares in Murder; Time of Conflict; Distant Land; Season of Youth: So Far No Further* and *Scenes From*

Revolutionary Life, and two volumes of autobiography: *Alien Son* and *Love and Rebellion.*

PATRICK WHITE (1912–1990) was born in London, spent his childhood in Australia, studied in England, and spent the greater part of his adult life in Australia. He published three collections of short stories: *The Burnt Ones, The Cockatoos, Three Uneasy Pieces,* and twelve novels: *Happy Valley; The Living and the Dead; The Aunt's Story; The Tree of Man; Voss; Riders in the Chariot; The Solid Mandala; The Vivisector; The Eye of the Storm; A Fringe of Leaves; The Twyborn Affair* and *Memoirs of Many in One.* He also wrote plays and essays, and published a self-portrait, *Flaws in the Glass.* In 1973 he received the Nobel Prize, and with it established the Patrick White Literary Award.

Acknowledgements

The editor and publisher would like to acknowledge and thank those people and organizations that granted permission to reprint copyright material in this volume.

Ethel Anderson, 'Donalblain McCree and the Sin of Anger' from *Tales of Parramatta and India,* © Bethia Ogden, 1973; reprinted by permission of Collins/Angus & Robertson Publishers; first published in *At Parramatta,* Cheshire, Melbourne, 1956

Jessica Anderson, 'The Late Sunlight' from *Stories from the Warm Zone,* © Jessica Anderson 1987, reprinted by permission of Penguin Books Australia Ltd, Penguin USA and Penguin Books Ltd

Thea Astley, 'Write Me, Son, Write Me' from *Hunting the Wild Pineapple,* Thomas Nelson, © Thea Astley 1979, reprinted by permission of the author

Murray Bail, 'The Drover's Wife' from *Contemporary Portraits,* © Murray Bail 1975, reprinted by permission of University of Queensland Press; first published *Tabloid* no. 15, 1975

Marjorie Barnard, 'Habit', reprinted by permission of the copyright holder © Alan Alford, care of Curtis Brown (Aust.) Pty Ltd, Sydney; first published in *The Persimmon Tree and Other Stories,* Clarendon Publishing Co., Sydney, 1943

David Brooks, 'The Lost Wedding' from *The Book of Sei,* © David Brooks 1985, reprinted by permission of Hale & Iremonger; first published *LiNQ* vol. 13, no. 2

Peter Carey, 'The Last Days of a Famous Mime', © Peter Carey 1979, from *War Crimes,* reprinted by permission of University of Queensland Press; and Rogers, Coleridge & White Ltd Literary Agency; and from *The Fat Man in History,* reprinted by permission of Faber and Faber Ltd

Beverley Farmer, 'Vase with Red Fishes' from *A Body of Water,* © Beverley Farmer 1990, reprinted by permission of University of Queensland Press and the author; first published under the title of 'Interior with Goldfish' in *Island*, no. 36, Spring 1988

Helen Garner, 'Little Helen's Sunday Afternoon' from *Postcards from Surfers*, © Helen Garner 1985, reprinted by permission of McPhee Gribble Publishers

Peter Goldsworthy, 'Frock, Wireless, Gorgeous, Slacks' from *Bleak Rooms*, © Peter Goldsworthy 1987, reprinted by permission of the author

Elizabeth Jolley, 'Woman in a Lampshade' from *Woman in a Lampshade*, © Elizabeth Jolley 1979, reprinted by permission of Penguin Books Australia Ltd; first published in *Westerly* 25, no. 2, 1980

Joan London, 'Angels', © Joan London 1990, reprinted by permission of the author; first published in *Grand Street* (NY), 1990

David Malouf, 'The Empty Lunch Tin' from *Antipodes*, © David Malouf 1985, reprinted by permission of Chatto & Windus — Random Century Group, and Curtis Brown (Aust.) Pty Ltd

Olga Masters, 'On the Train' from *The Home Girls*, © Olga Masters 1982, reprinted by permission of University of Queensland Press and W.W. Norton & Company, Inc.; Norton edition published 1990

Brian Matthews, 'At the Picasso Exhibition' from *Quickening*, © Brian Matthews 1988, reprinted by permission of McPhee Gribble Publishers and Australian Literary Management

Frank Moorhouse, 'The Drover's Wife' from *Room Service*, © Frank Moorhouse 1985, reprinted by permission of Rosemary Creswell Literary Agency and the author

John Morrison, 'The Hold Up' from *Australian Short Stories* no. 25, 1989, © John Morrison 1989, reprinted by permission of the author

George Papaellinas, 'Christos Mavromatis is a Welder' from *Ikons*, © George Papaellinas 1984, 1986, reprinted by permission of Penguin Books Australia Ltd

Henry Handel Richardson, 'Proem', prologue to *The Fortunes of Richard Mahony*, 1917, reprinted by permission of William Heinemann Ltd

Christina Stead, 'My Friend, Lafe Tilley' from *Ocean of Story*, © The estate of Christina Stead 1984, reprinted by permission of Penguin Books Australia Ltd

Kylie Tennant, 'Auction Sale in Stanley Street', first published in *Southerly*, 1941, © Benison Rodd, reprinted by permission of Curtis Brown (Aust.) Pty Ltd

Judah Waten, 'Mother' from *Alien Son*, 1952, reprinted by permission of Collins/Angus & Robertson Publishers; first published in *Meanjin* 9, no. 2, 1950

Patrick White, 'Willy-Wagtails by Moonlight' from *The Burnt Ones*, first published by Eyre & Spottiswoode, 1964, © Patrick White 1964, reprinted with permission of Barbara Mobbs, agent for Patrick White; first published in *Australian Letters* 4, no. 3, 1963

Permission to use the black and white picture of *The Drover's Wife* on page 49, at the beginning of the short story 'The Drover's Wife' by Murray Bail, is gratefully acknowledged.

Russel Drysdale
Australia 1912–1981

The drover's wife. 1945
oil on canvas
51.3 × 61.3 cm

A gift to the people of Australia by Mr and Mrs Benno Schmidt of New York City and Esperance, Western Australia, 1986
Collection: Australian National Gallery, Canberra
Reproduced by permission of the Australian National Gallery, Canberra, and Lady Drysdale